Women of Sand and Myrrh

Women of Sand and Myrrh

Hanan al-Shaykh

Translated by Catherine Cobham

ANCHOR BOOKS
DOUBLEDAY
NEW YORK   LONDON   TORONTO   SYDNEY   AUCKLAND

AN ANCHOR BOOK

PUBLISHED BY DOUBLEDAY

a division of Bantam Doubleday Dell Publishing Group, Inc.
666 Fifth Avenue, New York, New York 10103

ANCHOR BOOKS, DOUBLEDAY, and the portrayal of an anchor
are trademarks of Doubleday, a division of Bantam Doubleday
Dell Publishing Group, Inc.

Women of Sand and Myrrh was originally published in hardcover by
Quartet Books Limited in 1989. The Anchor Books edition is
published by arrangement with Harold Ober Associates.

Library of Congress Cataloging-in-Publication Data

Shaykh, Hanān.
Women of sand and myrrh / Hanan al-Shaykh ; translated by
Catherine Cobham.
p.   cm.
I. Title.
PJ7862.H356W66   1992
892'.736—dc20   92-9305
                                                               CIP

ISBN 0-385-42358-6
Copyright © 1988 by Hanan al-Shaykh
© 1989 by Hanan al-Shaykh for English translation
ALL RIGHTS RESERVED
PRINTED IN THE UNITED STATES OF AMERICA
FIRST ANCHOR BOOKS EDITION: AUGUST 1992
5 7 9 10 8 6 4

Women of Sand and Myrrh

Suha

1

I dropped on to the couch and the canary landed on my shoulder, chirping. I pushed him off: 'Leave me alone . . . not now!'

I looked at the pale curtains the colour of apricots, and at the glass tops of the little tables, and at the water-colours on the walls, and wished I could stay in this house all the time, just me and the canary. Everything in my house was soothing to look at, not like the furniture in the Institute or any of the other houses I went into, and such a change from the dusty streets, the colourless buildings, and the sand strewn with ruins.

When the men had come in I had been sitting in the restroom, drinking the lemonade that I'd brought from home in a little thermos flask. I froze, then began to tremble. One of them said to me, 'Cover yourself up, woman.'

I saw a towel flying through the air towards me. I don't know who threw it, but I put it around my shoulders, looking down and seeing only the men's sandals and mules and long tobacco-stained nails. I didn't breathe again until I heard the sound of their receding footsteps as they vanished in response to the principal's protests from the next room; her voice raised in anger, she accused them of trespassing in an area reserved for women: 'Can't you read? This is an Institute of Learning and the notice on the door says "Entry forbidden to men".'

I had hoped that going to the Institute would be an escape for me, and perhaps a way of avoiding the anguish and fear which I'd suffered in the past year when I was working in the department store.

Every day there I used to hide in a big brown cardboard box, wondering whether the security man would suspect anything. I pictured to myself how the box looked from the outside, inscribed with the words 'FRAGILE – WITH CARE' and a picture of a glass tumbler. If ever I caught a faint whiff of my perfume I used to feel scared in case the man was blessed with an extraordinarily powerful sense of smell.

The fear that he would catch me was so intense that all other sensations – the sweat pouring from me like a sudden cold shower, the box's distinctive strong smell – were meaningless in comparison. When I had been concealed in the box for some time and could no longer hear the sound of footsteps I calmed down a little and found myself laughing in disbelief. I was hiding because I was a woman and I was working, and yet out in the world there were big cities and space stations; in a clean white room the product of a man's solitary ejaculation could be discharged into an infertile woman and you could see the foetus inside the mother's womb on television; there were concert-halls, applauding audiences, laughter, weeping, crowds of people moving around, hurricanes, schools, nightclubs, hermits in caves . . . I tried to stop working, but I couldn't: to go into the vast store with its white walls, and to see the coloured candles, the batteries, the greetings cards, the blue writing-paper, the aprons and towels with flowers and mushrooms on them, the children's toys, and the ballpoint pens with their sharp new smell, was to be reminded of the comforting trivia of a normal existence. Even the freezers on the far side of the store – white and clean and big, packed with soft drinks and ice-cream in cartons decorated with pictures of mangoes and strawberries, and the portions of frozen meat with veins running through them – looked beautiful to me, and I preferred it all to staying at home or going to visit the other women I knew. When the store's owner, Amer, began to entrust me with correspondence and making out orders, my feeling of importance knew no bounds; before that my work had been confined to arranging toys and displays of household goods on the second floor.

My job divided the day in two. It was as if I began again at four in the afternoon when I'd had lunch with my husband and my son Umar, who came home from school at two o'clock. I had ten minutes' sleep and then got up to help Umar with his Arabic before he went to Sitt Wafa for a private lesson.

In the beginning I was amazed that Amer's foreign wife should offer me this job, and then that I could be satisfied with it. I had a degree in Management Studies from the American University of Beirut, but nobody else had wanted to employ me. They were all scared of the law, the raids and reprisals. Even my husband had wriggled out of his promise to find me a job once he realized what things were like in this country. I kept on hiding in the box until the day I heard the sound of footsteps and then something which I took to be a hand or foot knocking against it. I held my breath, and found that I was praying for help and shaking all over, and I swore to myself there and then that if I got out of that box without being caught and made a fool of I'd give up the job.

On my first day at home after leaving the store I decided not to hang around the house for long. I didn't want to give myself the chance to be discontented and miserable like the time before. Even then I'd desperately resisted the torpor that enveloped this place, resisted being sucked down by the swamp whose waters never grew deeper but never completely dried up. Like the other women, I'd thrown myself into the life here so that I wouldn't feel sorry for myself. I'd given up following the news, local or international, and occupied myself with cake recipes, and with finding friends for Umar, and taking him to see a little ape although I knew it had bitten its owner ... I'd congratulated myself when I'd prepared dinner for five businessmen in an hour, or entertained Umar's friends with a puppet theatre I'd made myself, hammering in the nails and sewing and hanging the curtains. I'd sent for the puppets from Lebanon, and when they'd arrived I'd been more delighted with them than my son and his friends. But when the children's mothers had come and sat around unenthusiastically and not even applauded my attempts, I'd felt a great resentment towards them and kept back the sweetmeats that I'd made for them.

Should I go and see Suzanne, Maryam, Umm Kairouz? Suzanne, Hind, Reem, Stephanie, Laila? Suzanne, Umm Kairouz, Tahani? Suzanne, Amal or Maryam? Suzanne? Shahnaz? Khulud, Raja, Dalal, or Sabah? Suzanne? When I'd put Suzanne out of my mind, I pictured the other women's houses and imagined the sounds of their voices, and knew exactly what lay in wait for me.

Sabah: an analysis of marital relationships, her self-respect, the children. Shahnaz: the house and the furniture, the house and the furniture, her very, very successful son and her daughter who was only moderately successful, which of course was the teacher's fault. Raja: the best method of self-defence was black pepper which she put on a plate near the bed each time her husband went away. Then if somebody tried to rape her she'd throw the plate at him. Stephanie: it was the chance of a lifetime being here in the desert and there was no time to get depressed. She imported everything from her home country, Sweden, and sold it here. She pricked out seedlings and planted them in pots and when they grew into blossoming branches she sold them. She cut hair and coloured it, made clothes, baked pastries, all for a price. She'd roll up the banknotes in an aluminium container and put them in her fridge. Maryam: elegance, regardless of the surroundings. Leather boots in the heat of the desert. What annoyed her was the censors who spilt their black ink all over the pages of the magazines she read, and actually tore some of them out. Exercises to keep slim. The best way of exercising the stomach is to hold in your pee for as long as you can. Umm Kairouz: 'O Lord, may the ones who drove us out be driven out themselves one day. God damn the lot of them! Lebanon, Lebanon! Poor, poor Lebanon! Yesterday they were fighting again, but it's quiet today. I'm ready to go back, bombs and all. It's better than this hole.' Reem in the daytime: 'The housework doesn't leave me a minute to relax. That's what it's like with children to look after.' Reem at night, laughing: 'I can't change the way I laugh – my husband tells me off about it. When I asked a friend of his if his moustache was false he said, "See for yourself". I pulled it and it was real. He said, "So, don't I get a kiss? " and I said, "Why not? " and laughed.'

Tahani: 'I don't know! The telephone rings every second. And there's invitations to tea and coffee, starting from the early morning. Nothing but drinking, eating, telling silly stories, seeing who's got the nicest clothes. Even when we're playing ladies' bridge they come wearing rings with diamonds as big as eggs. For God's sake, aren't we meant to be modern women? We're educated, university graduates, but what can we do here? We're not allowed to work, not allowed to drive cars. There are no places to go on outings. Tell me what you want to drink. Tea, coffee, mint tea? Try these Umm Alis . . . You've never tasted them? God, is there really someone who doesn't know Umm Alis . . . See, you have the sheets of filo pastry ready, and the fruit and . . . Did you know the sheikha had a big dinner party and invited Ibtisam and Manal and they were sitting there and some woman said to them that the sheikha was having the party because her son the sheikh wanted to get married and it was a way of having a look at the likely candidates? And another woman said there's probably a camera hidden behind the curtains. Ibtisam and Manal kept on looking at the curtains until their eyes almost popped out. And afterwards the sheikha said to them that the curtains were made by Valentino. Can you imagine, Valentino makes their curtains for them!'

I got to know them the first year I arrived. Like every woman coming here I felt that this was time lost out of my life. I began to make friends with anyone just for something to do. I was living in a compound. The rooms were small and dark. The bathroom was like a bathroom in a cheap hotel. But the house was passable, compared to the grubby houses and twisting alleys and few primitive shops in the street where I'd lived before. I tried to make it look prettier. I changed the heavy gloomy curtains for lighter ones and threw the family's coloured sheets, which I'd packed with my clothes, over the couches. On the walls I stuck pictures of Swiss chalets and lakes. Umar was staying with my mother in Beirut until I'd finished getting the house ready.

I knew that life here was odd when I found that I had no garlic for my cooking and I couldn't go out to the shops and buy some. So I opened the door and stood on the step, looking about me at the other wooden houses painted white, the sparse trees, the water storage tanks, the sun burning down on the asphalt, and it made me imagine that I was somewhere in space. The houses stood at a distance from each other, the doors were closed, the air-conditioners hummed. Only when I could go in the car with my husband did I feel happy to leave the house. However hard I tried to buy everything I needed, I always forgot many things and the display on the shelves didn't help me. All the goods were mixed together: egg whisks, rolls of material, vegetables side by side with bars of soap, Arabic grammar books, bread, pocket knives and silver Maria Theresa dollars.

I found out that the inhabitants of the compound were Arabs and foreigners mixed. But I hadn't the courage to knock at their doors, perhaps because I had heard the adults swearing and the children shouting. I knew their quarrels by heart, even though their television sets were turned up so loud, and I knew the children's names, the mothers' feeble protests and the fathers' furious oaths.

It was only a matter of a few days before the women thronged to my house, reproaching me for not knocking on their doors. The one called Umm Kairouz said, 'Are you an angel or something? Is that why we didn't even know you were here?' And another, downcast at her own lack of intelligence, commented, 'It's funny. I heard the toilet flushing and thought it was working by itself, and I heard wood creaking and said to my husband, "Stop eating. Every time you move there's a creaking noise." '

I felt disillusioned: this wasn't the desert that I'd seen from the aircraft, nor the one I'd read about or imagined to myself; there was sand and wind but no old houses. I didn't want to pass judgement on it from the few short weeks that I'd spent in my wooden house and my neighbours' wooden houses. But the first impression is the most important, because your eye grows accustomed to its surroundings and no longer connects with the mind and the heart in its responses. Everyday-life existed in the desert, but it was the daily routine of housewives and didn't go beyond the smell of coriander, the neighbour who only half-opened her door because she had wax on her thighs, fortune-telling in coffee grounds, food on the stove, and gossip and knitting and babies' nappies. I always felt that I was different from my neighbours, but still I took comfort from their presence around me.

My husband, meanwhile, had gone further afield and begun to discover what lay beyond our street and on the other side of the shops and buildings we could see from our house: he'd seen houses with good big rooms, and even gardens, although these were made of gravel and sand. He asked to be transferred to another house, and to my astonishment his request was granted. I rushed to tell my neighbours, wanting to bring some joy to their hearts with the news that there was to be a house they could visit outside the compound, for they talked at length about the difficulty of travelling outside the neighbourhood, and discussed the possibility of all the families sharing in the cost of a car and hiring a driver so that they could visit the devils, as Umm Ghassan put it. But instead of being glad at the news of my move they showed signs of resentment. They all began to complain about the companies that their husbands worked for and the directors' wives with their houses and servants and drivers and strings of pearls. Their voices rose and they reminded me of women in a bathhouse when the water supply is cut off, and they sit around still covered in lather, noisily gossiping and arguing. One of them said antagonistically to me, 'You've been here two months and we've all been here for three years,' and added that there must be scorpions and snakes and big rats living in their hundreds underneath all these wooden houses raised up off the ground, and that every day she heard tapping and hissing. They began to vie with one another in telling stories about rats: one said a rat had dragged a chicken right out of the oven, and as they were all gasping in horror, Umm Ghassan interrupted, 'A kilo of meat disappeared from off my table when I went to open to door. They must have been watching me.'

At this Muna seized hold of her son and turned him upside down, inspecting his plump white foot. Then she said, as if reporting back to us, 'There *are* scorpions here. Perhaps it was a scorpion sting he had. I don't know which day it was he screamed and I lifted him out of his bed and he began to swell up. He was blue in the face, then his whole body turned as red as a pomegranate seed.'

They got up to go, and I looked at their empty coffee cups on the table. For a moment I felt a faint sadness, then I started to put all that had accumulated around me during these two months into boxes. When I finally sat down the house looked just as it had done when I entered it for the first time – the thick curtains, the line of dust shimmering in the bright air, the couches coarse to the touch. I couldn't help feeling sorry for my neighbours because they were staying on in these houses. I supposed that I would invite them to visit me in the new house, but as it turned out I never saw them again from that morning onwards, or even caught sight of them at a distance. I used to turn and look the other way every time I passed the compound. The sight of the yellow wooden roofs and walls and the dusty oleander plants reminded me of myself when I lived in there among those god–forsaken helpless women.

On the other hand, the thought that living in this country was only a temporary phase prevented me from feeling the same firmness of purpose as Sitt Wafa did towards her home: she planted basil and radishes and kept hens and a rooster in a coop that she built for them; the rooster had developed a nasty nature and when Sitt Wafa ran after him with a broom he turned round and chased her in turn. An odour of permanence emanated from her home and I saw jars of jam, dried yoghurt, thyme and cracked wheat stacked in the kitchen. I used to love going into her house and drinking mulberry juice, and made the excuse that I was coming with Umar to ask her about him so that I could see the children gathered around her while she instructed them one by one, or gave them dictation while shelling peas and shredding beans. The children loved her, although she shouted and pulled the ears of those who made mistakes, and called them 'Sir' and 'Madam' and continually threatened to take them off to the sheikh's school under the trees. They laughed at this because they'd seen the open-air school and the old man with his stick.

My life seemed to change after I moved to the new house. I no longer felt time stagnating as I had in the compound. I began to amuse myself making curtains and cushions, hanging pictures, tidying cupboards. I borrowed books about gardens and dug the garden and planted seeds, waiting from one day to the next for the green shoots to appear. I invited women to visit me, proud of my beautiful house, and offered them cake and tea in cups that matched the curtains. I decided to make my stay here useful, and joined an exercise class at Maryam's house, three times a week for an hour, another class for baking and decorating cakes, and a literary discussion group. I even became a pupil of Stephanie's learning embroidery and patchwork, and would have taken classes to learn how to arrange artificial flowers if the time had allowed. However I knew deep inside me that the way I was handling my life was doomed to failure; I was scared of the enormous disgust that I felt because I was leading such a sterile, unnatural existence, and to counter this I began to defend the way of life here, as a means of instilling into my mind what it ought to be thinking. In my discussions with women who hated it here, both Arabs and foreigners, I used to struggle to find objections to their arguments and take the discussions to absurd and trivial limits: I told them that the situation here was ideal in a way, and that they were lucky because they were seeing how cities were built, and witnessing the transformation of man from a bedouin into a city-dweller. This was a great opportunity for them, I added: nothing was laid on for them as it was in other countries, and they would have to fight for what they really wanted. Despite what I said, I myself thought that time was wasted in searching for and constructing what existed and was recognized as normal or obvious anywhere else in the world.

Things didn't progress as I'd convinced myself they would when I was forcing myself to attend classes. When the women at the exercise classes with me began to look like birds and animals, and when at the cake-decorating class I became involved in a vengeful struggle with the lid of the confectioner's cream instead of directing my energies to creating a rose on a cake, or when I began to drink coffee and eat biscuits instead of discussing books, and spent an age trying to make the thread go into the eye of the needle, or even just searching for the needle, I gave it all up and stayed at home. At this point, like most of the women here, I began to think in earnest about how fed up I was, how miserable I was, and how much I'd like to go away somewhere. The only solution was to get out of the house again, this time to work in the store.

I handled the paperwork, writing letters and demands and putting prices on everything. I used to flick through the shiny

illustrated catalogues of goods and foodstuffs choosing whatever took my fancy. When the things arrived I rushed to the
crates, excitedly comparing the real thing with the picture I
had of it and feeling that I had a link with the outside world
as I turned a glass or a packet over in my hands. In spite of
my knowledge and my zeal for my work, I made mistakes
and these mistakes led to Amer's goods being censored by the
port officials. They set fire to his crates to get rid of the pâté
de foie gras which I'd ordered without noticing that pork fat
was listed among its ingredients; I ordered games without
realizing that they contained playing cards, and bay leaves
and dried radishes and rosemary not knowing that they'd
arrived saying on their packets that they added a delicious
aroma and flavour to beef and chicken and pork. Amer had
to make his employees cross out the word 'pork' on a thousand packets with their black pens. Although I grew more
accurate with my orders there were still some boxes that had
to be burnt.

The psychological tension that began to hang over the
place became a bigger problem than hiding in the cardboard
box. Amer and his wife were both extremely edgy, and the
day he handed me the notification from the customs authorities to read, he was smoking like a doomed man having his
last cigarette. He'd lost thousands: the boxes from the United
States had been confiscated and their contents destroyed; I
asked excitedly if someone had smuggled whisky or obscene
videos in them. The soft toys and dolls had all been destroyed, every one that was meant to be a human being or
animal or bird, since it was not permissible to produce distor-
tions of God's creatures. Although I was sorry, I laughed, and
imagined those men turning over Barbie dolls and Snoopies
and Woodstocks in their big hands and picking up china
birds and crystal ashtrays in the shape of cats and thinking
hostile thoughts about them, while they stared silently back.

I remembered how keen I used to be to watch the 'Muppet
Show', how I'd laughed at Kermit the Frog and Miss Piggy: it

had never occurred to me that these creatures singing and bobbing about giving amusement and pleasure to their audience were no more than dumb puppets. That was why when Umar asked me one day if they got new ones when the old ones wore out I felt sad, because I'd pictured them being real in spite of the strings attached to their arms and legs. I thought of them piled on top of one another in a box or cupboard in the studio when they weren't being used, their eyes dead, mouths closed and bodies lifeless.

I didn't actually leave my job until one morning I came face to face with the security man in the doorway of the store-room, whereupon I rushed in past him, up the stairs and made for the offices to hand in my resignation.

This time I knew that I wasn't going to visit anyone. My desert experience had to be related to the place, not just the people: I determined to try and communicate with my surroundings.

Claiming that I wanted to help my husband Basem with a study he had to do for the bank, I asked the driver Said to take me around the town, street by street, starting with the airport. He puffed out his chest proudly, although he had no idea what I meant, and touching his headcloth deferentially he answered, 'At your service.' As soon as we'd left the airport I began to take things in, making believe that I'd just arrived from a faraway country, and had never seen the desert before except in pictures. But it wasn't the desert that I saw, and I found myself in the middle of what amounted to a vast building site.

Trucks were unloading or loading up. Huge drums stood with electricity cables and telephone cables coiled around them. A crane that looked big enough to move mountains and cities grumbled and creaked as it lifted its load. A cement mixer turned constantly. There was a string of lorries and a petrol tanker, the sort that people stop and stare at in the street because of its size. It was like a giant that had eaten a lot of people; each of its four compartments was bigger than a car, and its driver hovered in the sky as if he was about to make a parachute drop somewhere in the desert.

I watched the men putting up a hoarding in the sand advertising the opening of a new supermarket that would sell tens of thousands of different brands, and I marvelled at the way that, while old hoardings look as if they've been built along with the city surroundings, these new ones here looked as if they had appeared by magic.

Some of the streets had no names, but there were buildings in them where a few weeks before there had only been steel girders, and they had filled up rapidly with occupants coming to work on other building sites. Interspersed between the real palms were plastic ones and green-painted metal ones planted in tubs down the middle of the streets in an attempt to beautify the place, and ornamental paving stones laid edge to edge around them as if conducting a dialogue with one another. Tools and pieces of machinery lay abandoned where they had been for the past three years, and a black-and-white goat was jumping around on them. After only a few moments she bounded off on to the dusty ground to escape the burning metal.

Then Said took me to the seashore where there were huge water-purifying plants, some already completed and some still being built. A white bird poised on a wire and fluttered its wings. There was a man wearing a white headcloth, his white robe flying out in the breeze as he supervised work at one of the plants. In the distance on top of that enormous steel building he looked like Superman.

The markets were a hive of building activity: they were knocking down the old buildings whose walls were riddled with the effects of heat and damp, buildings with little ornamental stonework or wooden latticework considered lacking in artistic value. In their place rose buildings full of air-conditioners, neon lighting and garish, over-ornate tiles. Everything was unattractive except the calligraphic design of the expression 'What God wills' which was adorning one wall in a contrasting colour.

A strange smell wafted into the car and small murky black clouds swirled around me at street level. A vehicle drove slowly along spraying the people and the empty air with germicide.

Asian workmen swarmed everywhere, on foot, in cars, and up the high ladders, the Yemenis in their skirts and loose jackets and platform shoes, stumbling at every step. Periodically the sand was sprayed with oil to immobilize it but it renewed its attack with fresh vigour over the cultivated parts of the desert and the asphalted roads, against windows, and against the few trees trying to bloom and the luxurious cars jostling for place with the lorries and trucks.

I was a little disconcerted: the feeling I'd started out with of losing my sensitivity to the life going on around me was growing stronger, as was my awareness of the complete absence of women, at least from the world outside. Most of the houses seemed to be devoted to men and their affairs with the signs announcing offices and companies for this and that, and the one house built of red brick with Spanish windows had a sign stuck in the middle of it saying, 'Adli. Attorney at Law'. None of the houses had balconies, and everything was enclosed by high walls.

I found myself asking Said to take me to see Ingrid. Although I felt tired and nauseous from driving round and round in the car, I wanted to be with other people and get warmth and energy from hearing them talk and watching them move, so that I could breathe freely again and get back into the rhythm of life here.

I chose Ingrid because of her garden. The plants in it reminded me of Beirut: the blanket of lilac, the sunflowers, and a third flower, orange with a strong perfume. And apart from that, I had a weakness for her delicious cakes.

'The American? ' asked Said, and he pointed to his head making a circle with his finger.

I answered, half-laughing, 'No. Ingrid's the German, the

one with the garden.'

'Ah, the skinny one! Poor thing.'

Said remembered the women I visited even if he didn't remember their names, and he assessed their characters through their ways of talking and behaving since he didn't know any foreign languages. He could say 'good morning' to all the women I visited, smiling delightedly at his achievement so that his gold teeth, and the gaps in between them, were plainly visible. The first time he asked how to say 'good morning' in English and American and found they were the same, he exclaimed in surprise, 'Praise the Lord! They're the same as each other inside and out!'

Said had been sitting in the Adeni restaurant where he worked, when one of the customers read out in his hearing an advertisement for an accountant in the bank where Basem was manager. Said asked him what an accountant had to do and the man answered him sarcastically, 'Count money.' Said went off to the bank and asked to see the manager. Despite his persistence they wouldn't let him go in. He waited at the door and when Basem came out he reached for the notes in his pocket and counted them in front of him in a flash as if he were a professional gambler, not just an ordinary Yemeni in his skirt and sandals. Then he returned the cash to his belt and adjusted his coloured headcloth. Basem asked him where he worked and he answered in an Adeni restaurant, spiking the meat on skewers and roasting it. Could he read? Could he write? Said contented himself with a smile. He was employed in the bank as a cleaner and teaboy. After a while he asked Basem to teach him how to drive, and Basem explained the principles to him three times. In a few weeks Said begged Basem to let him drive his car and surprised Basem with his proficiency. When Basem questioned him, Said told him that he'd begun to practise every day, making use of every car that stopped at the bank after convincing its driver that he'd take it off and park it in a shady spot. Those who weren't willing had changed their minds when Said pretended to cry in front of them, muttering something about not being fit to be trusted.

When I arrived at Ingrid's I was sorry I'd come. The note of lethargy was still there in Ingrid's conversation. By the end of every sentence she spoke you were ready to fall asleep. I sat drowsily in front of her, angry at myself for coming and wishing I could sleep with my eyes open.

She was telling me about the man she'd found creeping into her house while I thought about the pastries on the table whose delicious aroma wafted across to me, and about the sunflowers as big as moons. Then she recounted news of her parents: how her mother had to lean on her father to walk, how her father had slipped and brought the old lady down with him and how they'd both stayed on the floor till the next day.

I immediately regretted the strong urge I had to laugh as I pictured the scene. I tried to be serious and concentrate on what Ingrid was saying, but failed and rose to my feet, making excuses. When Ingrid said, 'That was a short visit. You didn't even taste my pastries,' I hesitated, but the expression on Ingrid's face and the vision of renewed boredom made me hurry to the door and not even pause to look at the garden. It was very hot, and when I was in the car I saw the sunflowers peeping over the wall.

I sat in the car looking about me, uncertain where to go. The fierce glare penetrated the windows and the car body in spite of the air-conditioner, and the humidity in the outside air came through to me. Depressed by the concrete gardens I saw, I looked back inside the car.

On an impulse I asked Said to take me to Suzanne's house. To confirm what I'd said he raised his hand once more to his head making a circle with his forefinger: 'The American, Auntie?' I forced a laugh and nodded yes. Said appeared not to notice my curt response as he said, 'It's been a long time since you visited her, Auntie.'

As the car approached the Pepsi Cola works and I saw the

bottles moving along automatically and stopping to be filled behind the factory windows, I remembered how enthusiastic I'd been about my first visit to Suzanne's, mainly because of the Pepsi factory.

When Suzanne's servant, Ringo, opened the door I knew that I'd made the right choice this time. All at once I was in a world that had not the slightest connection with the desert, except for the brass tray hanging on the wall and the little brass coffee jugs arranged on the table. I loved the gloom created by the thickness of the curtains, and I loved the romantic music, the smell of coffee and the smiling photographs of Suzanne positioned carefully here and there.

Suzanne rushed from the kitchen shrieking excitedly, clasped me to her and kissed me, reproaching me for not coming to see her sooner and making me turn round in a circle so that she could look at what I was wearing: 'It's beautiful. Oh, how beautiful you look!'

She began to tell me her news, so full of enthusiasm that she didn't finish one topic before launching into the next, and repeated old news that I already knew. Each time I asked her about something she said, 'Okay . . . ' beginning to answer, then switched to another subject. She reminded me of the letter to her lover, and I found myself smiling as I recalled the day I'd met her in the store. She'd been talking in Arabic, murdering the letter *tha*, sticking out her tongue and swallowing the words like a fish swallowing her young in the face of danger. Now, just as I had been the very first time, I was astonished to go into her house and see the servant Ringo doing her platinum blond hair like a professional hairdresser. When Ringo went to the kitchen to make tea he moved like a girl who knows she's got a beautiful body. He poured the tea into cups in front of me, raising his little finger delicately like a hostess at a tea party and stirring it till the sugar was melted.

On my first visit Suzanne had asked me to write a letter in her name to her lover, a local man named Maaz. The words she told me to put were naïve, sentimental, cheap. Reading between the lines I could guess the sort of relationship they had. When she asked me if I liked her style, I nodded hypocritically. Then she asked Ringo to bring the box of tape cassettes, and from among the cassettes of *The Adventures of Dimbo*, Sri Lankan singers and even one of Muhammad Abdo, she pulled out one with her name on it and asked me to listen to it. For a moment I thought she was joking, but the expression on her face and Ringo's told me I was wrong, and I felt more and more embarrassed as Suzanne's voice sighed and whispered and called out that her Arab lover's face was as beautiful as the moon.

I'd stopped caring about the Pepsi bottles in the factory window and found myself looking forward to my visits to her just to hear her passionate stories about Maaz. Whenever I'd felt my interest in her flagging, her outlandish reports of violent scenes and fake suicide attempts had drawn me back. I only broke off my visits when Amer banned her temporarily from the store because she'd been joking with a salesman. The noise she was making had attracted attention, she was wearing bright red lipstick, and although her dress was long it showed the curve of her belly and buttocks as she moved. However, I continued to defend her and told them that her only fault was that she was too good-hearted. I watched her now as she talked for maybe an hour, and felt sorry for her when she started to cry. She'd got fatter, and the roots of her hair showed darker than the rest. As usual she showed me the traces on her forehead left by the bottle that Maaz had thrown at her, and she didn't stop begging me to go and see Maaz and talk to him and ask him to come back. I was noncommittal, and when pushed refused even to consider it. For a moment I regretted coming back, because I was getting involved once again in her tortuous entanglements. I reminded myself that I was an Arab and should be careful, but I found myself promising to get Maaz back for her another way. Although she begged me to tell her how, I wasn't going to: I was scared of her runaway tongue and her excitability, and I just said I'd see her the next day.

2

Suzanne and I went into Sita's house; Sita cured sickness and healed wounds with herbs and cauterization, and made amulets and ground lead to ward off the evil eye. It didn't seem like two years since my first visit. Sita was just as she had been then in her beautiful dress, whose rich colours had long faded. Her skin was coarse and wrinkled from the desert sun, and from her constant grimacing as she held the irons in the fire's glow. Her small yellow teeth looked like a child's milk teeth. Her room was just the same too, the stuffed peacock on the table and on the wall the inscription which I'd never been able to remember: 'Sita the famous, whose fame has spread near and far, makes jinn lie down, kindles the fires of love, and trust in God comes first of all.' Even the rooster sketched above these words hadn't stuck in my mind.

I'd wanted to go back to Sita's house once more and amuse myself by reading what was written on the wall. Said was always talking about her and would praise her highly whenever I took Umar to the doctor. If he heard that someone Basem knew was ill he'd try to persuade me to take him to Sita, and he swore to me that she'd cured a madman by making him bury his head in the sand for an hour every day, used a vulture's stomach to heal a festering wound, and strange plants for diabetes. When he noticed the surprise on my face he added, 'Even if she's no use she doesn't do any harm. Some people swear by the Almighty that she's cured them and brought back their loved onces from the gates of death, and others say only God can cure disease.'

Her house was half an hour's drive out of town. I remembered the first time, when Ingrid was with me, I'd become convinced that the herb doctor was a figment of Said's imagination. For the desert couldn't suddenly stop short, gather itself in and produce houses and palm trees. But his manner of driving and his continuous talk about her seemed to confirm that he knew the road already. 'We'll be at Sita's house in the twinkling of an eye,' he said. I thought that if it hadn't been for Ingrid's curiosity I wouldn't have come, and then in the distance houses and telegraph poles appeared, though as the car drew near it became clear that the houses were just huts with tin roofs and mud-brick walls, leaning against each other and sprouting television aerials. A couple of boys in vests and underpants were standing in a plastic washing-up bowl, scooping up water from it in an empty dried milk tin and a juice carton, and spraying it over themselves.

Said asked them where the doctor's house was and one of them said 'Sita?' pointing to a hut that was bigger than the ones around it. Said stayed outside, while Ingrid and I had to bend our heads to get through the open door into an unroofed yard. It was empty. I called, 'Sitt Sita,' and a voice answered. 'I'm in here.' We took a couple of steps forward and looked about us. There was another room, or enclosed area of some kind, because you couldn't really call it a room. We were astounded to see a man clad only in underpants stretched out there, his eyes fixed on the ceiling, while Sita bent over him massaging his body. We automatically turned our faces away and retreated a few steps. Before we'd had time to think what to do next we heard Sita's voice: 'Hallo. Just a minute until I've finished with this poor creature.' We laughed to start with, then Ingrid asked me in amazement how this could be happening here, and I answered her seriously, 'Why not? Sita's a doctor.'

We heard a series of shrieks that even seemed to startle the goat who'd been lying there chewing and twisting her head around from time to time to keep the flies off. A few minutes passed. Then the man came out with his clothes on, not looking in our direction. We went in to Sita. She was rubbing her hands in the ashes and explained, looking up at us, 'It sterilises the hands.' When I asked what was wrong with the man, she said, 'A cough and asthma.'

There was an odd smell. Sita put out the little stove, picked up the iron, and then dropped it because it was so hot; if she hadn't said, 'It's the old man's flesh burning,' we wouldn't have believed that she'd actually put the hot iron on his skin. She took hold of it again with the edge of her dress then picked up a rag from the ground and wiped it, repeating, 'It's the old man's flesh burning. Like when someone's burning the hair off sheep's trotters.' She added, elucidating, 'The man's chest is weak. It gurgles and rattles like the beads of a rosary. Creams and herbs don't work. I said to him I've worked on both your shoulder joints and I've cauterized you. I felt for all the joints in his body. There are people whose hip joints are hard to get hold of, and the joints in their calves. No two fingers are alike.' The strange smell persisted and Sita, still rubbing at the iron, remarked, 'The flesh is still sticking to it. It doesn't want to come off. The old fellow's skin must be like cured meat.'

Then it seemed to strike her that we hadn't yet mentioned why we'd come, although she didn't look at us. She threw the iron on to a brass tray covered in verdigris, smoothed down her black head shawl and adjusted the veil that she wore on the lower half of her face. Then she pulled it down slightly and wiped her nose and upper lip on the edge of her sleeve. She was wearing a dress so remarkable that I thought if the most famous designer in the world could have seen it he would have gasped in admiration and wished that he'd thought of it first: it was patterned with purple flowers the colour of indigo plants, and with the sun and grass on a white background; its shoulders and sleeves were embroidered in purple and fuschia-coloured thread, and the sleeves and the hem were trimmed with silver rings. Medicaments and dried herbs were all about the room and oils and creams in bottles and jars were arranged under sheets of old newspaper on the table, watched over by the stuffed peacock with gold-sequined feathers, who looked ready to weep.

Sita was manifestily irritated at our silence and she fidgeted and patted her dress, straightening it. When I said, 'Your dress is nice,' she gave a grudging smile and asked briskly, 'Which one of you is ill? '

'Neither of us, but my friend would like to write about you for a German magazine.'

Sita put her hand over her face: 'God forbid. No television.' I realized I ought not to have broached the subject directly, so quickly as if to cancel out the previous sentence, I said 'My head hurts.' And I wasn't really lying. I got a headache every afternoon. Sita reached out her two hands and grabbed hold of my head forcefully, asking, 'Where's the pain, daughter?' She scared me and I moved my head away abruptly: 'Not my head, I mean it could be anyone's head.' Frowning she replied, 'Have you come here to find out my secrets?' and she sat down, fiddling with the things that lay round about her and pretending to ignore us. In the end we withdrew silently.

This time, once we were sitting on Sita's cushions and she was sitting facing us, I relaxed because she hadn't recognized me and had welcomed us effusively and asked us, 'Tea or coffee?' But Suzanne's repeated urgings made me tell Sita straightaway the reason why we'd come. Sita seemed not to mind, for she rose up before I'd finished talking and lifted a curtain that hung down from one side of the table and took out a basket. Then she sat down again with the basket in her lap, turning over the little bottles in it and examining them, then giving me one uncertainly. I took it, trying to read the label. 'Coconut with jasmine'. Taking it back from me and peering at it she said, 'No, daughter. The writing's not important. They're bottles I get from the women's market and fill myself.'

Suzanne didn't know what was going on between me and Sita but she put her hand in the basket and saw the Indian women's faces, and asked me sarcastically if Sita was going to change her into one of them. I was busy reading the labels while Sita was still rummaging around among the bottles, occasionally picking one out to look at it more closely, then putting it back. In the end she selected a bottle, put the basket down and sat holding one of her toes.

'Perfumed Castor Oil for the Hair.' 'Oil containing forty-two herbs; an ancient remedy invented by the doctor at the Emperor Shah Alam's palace for falling hair.' 'Oil to make the hair grow longer, containing almond oil, lettuce and sandalwood.'

Sita was waiting for me to put the bottles back so that she could move the basket away. She smoothed down her dress and the shawl covering her hair, and looked at the bottle she'd picked out, then rested her hand on mine, saying, 'Here, daughter. Three drops. Only in tea, and best in scented tea. If you can, let him take it on an empty stomach and see what happens.' Then she laughed with gusto, leaning backwards from the force of it: 'See what happens. He'll come after you like a madman on his hands and knees, sniffing you out like a young pup.'

I tried to explain what she'd said to Suzanne and she asked me how she was supposed to give him three drops of the stuff when he'd stopped coming to visit her. I turned back to Sita: 'We might not see him. Perhaps an amulet would be better? ' She placed her hand on my shoulder: 'Daughter, didn't you say he was your husband?' and she didn't wait for me to reply as she knew there was nothing I could say. I tried to translate what had happened to Suzanne but Sita didn't like delay and argument. She was a practical person, and she seemed to be sure of what she was doing. She stood up, cut leather, got the fire going, assembled various preparations. Reciting prayers, she passed a piece of paper back and forth over the fire and took hold of my hand. With an involuntary movement I grasped Suzanne's hand and put it in Sita's, which made me think that I must believe in what Sita was doing.

Sita opened her eyes and wrote something on the piece of paper and laid it on the leather she'd cut. She opened a jar and dipped her finger in it then smeared it around the edges of the piece of leather, stuck them together, and handed it to me. 'The amulet has to be in the room that he's in. That's vital.' And I didn't say to her, 'How can it be when she doesn't see him?' She stood up smacking one palm against the other and saying, 'You're very welcome. Let's hope you don't need me again. Tea or coffee?' Then taking my hand and smiling she added, 'You're doing fine this time. You've made me feel that I can trust you, and you've asked for my advice. Last year you came to cheat me and steal my secrets.' I was amused and said, 'I thought you'd forgotten me.' She struck her chest: 'Forgotten you?' I asked her how much we owed her and she said, 'Whatever you want to pay me. I'm sure that when he comes crawling to you on his hands and knees you'll come back to reward me.' Then almost to herself, 'Lord above! Why are men so spineless? Tired and stale and uninterested in the pleasures of the flesh!' She pointed to the lower part of her stomach: 'A long time ago women used to come to me complaining about the blood and the pain. They'd say to me, "In the name of whoever called you Sita, give us a cure. Something so that our men are repelled by us and don't want to go to bed with us and leave us to sleep in peace." I said, "Shall I make up a charm for them so they'll marry a second time and a third time and spare you the degradation and the pain?" ' Laughing, she finished, 'Their voices reached the sky: "No, Sita. Any degradation rather than the pain of another wife." '

3

I went up to the roof of my house. The rabbits crouched under the motor of the air-conditioner and the pigeons' cage was empty. Grains of corn were scattered on the ground and on the roof tiles. The black-and-white pair had flown away after the female had laid one egg. Umar had asked me, 'Did the mother fly away because she didn't want her babies?' and I'd answered, 'Pigeons' minds don't work like that.'

I looked again over the parapet of the roof-terrace to the roofs of the other houses. Smoke was rising from distant factories. There was an oil blaze in one spot, and a layer of grey hung over it like dirty muslin. A smell of sewers and chemical waste rose up in the air. I thought to myself, 'Perhaps Umar was right.'

I wouldn't go to the Institute the next day: the atmosphere there now was like my last few weeks in the store before I left. And besides, what had happened to me the previous day had upset me a lot.

I'd been walking along the narrow street thinking that I was wrong to feel weighed down like this; I wanted to wipe away the imprint of misconceptions from my mind so that I could go back to being as I'd been when I first went to teach at the Institute, untroubled by reports and rumours of the men who came to inspect what was going on inside. This street was like another country. Little girls' dresses, mostly of cheap lace, hung on display together with more brightly-coloured dresses from mainland China. Veiled women spread themselves on the ground between the shops selling clothes made of nylon. I said to my student Tamr, 'If it hadn't been for you, I wouldn't have believed that there really were oases or springs in the desert like the ones in books.' Tamr laughed proudly; that morning she'd taken me from her father's house, which was in a different region from the one where I lived, to visit springs where mauve garlic flowers bloomed on the banks, and little girls stood enviously watching the boys plunging in and out of the water among the turtles and young frogs. When we were at her father's house she'd shown me the carvings on the walls and ceilings, and the roof still made of palm leaves. My attention had been attracted by the mud-brick dwellings among the new houses built of concrete and stainless steel. Tamr pointed to some glass-plated buildings and said, 'The camel market used to be here and the gold market still exists. In a month's time they're going to demolish it. There are still women selling henna and silver in it.'

I stopped when I saw some local embroidered material, and picked it up and felt it and decided to buy it in spite of Tamr's surprised reaction. Not long before, she'd bought some material imported from Europe. I counted out my money, thinking to myself that life was normal here in this district, perhaps because it hadn't yet lost the old ways. I heard a boy's voice saying, 'She's American,' and turned to him to correct him, afraid that they'd put up the prices. He winked at me and whispered, 'The old man.' Tamr explained, 'That old religious man. If he knew you were an Arab he'd be furious.' I glanced quickly behind me and saw an old man with a white beard and spectacles and a stick. 'Come on, let's go,' I said to Tamr in a low voice, and in English. I imagined that by talking English I'd become miraculously invisible but the man stood in our path and addressed himself to Tamr: 'Tell her to cover herself up. Our women don't walk about unveiled.' Tamr snapped, 'She's foreign, isn't she? They have their religion, we have ours.' I pretended to have no idea what was going on and said, 'Let's go to the car,' in English, as if I was talking to myself. I seemed to have provided an outlet for the old man's pent-up anger and he thrust out his stick, blocking my way, and screamed at me, 'Get out of here. You can't shop while you're unveiled.'

I felt besieged from every direction, as men and boys pushed forward from all over the market and stood in a circle round me and Tamr. Anger welled up in me, starting in my heart and rushing up into my head. When I confronted the man who was blocking my path, and was unable to push the stick out of the way or budge an inch, I knew that I didn't have control over my own life and was a prisoner of this stick and this group of people. I seethed with frustration and was sure I was going to cry. Although I could hear Tamr's voice raised in protest I felt completely isolated and she seemed just like all the other black-shrouded women.

Again a woman at a stall shouted at Tamr, 'Buy the lady an abaya and go to your homes. May Heaven's door be barred to her. And you're to blame too.'

Tamr rebuffed her: 'I didn't know you had the key to Heaven.' Then she turned to me quickly, pulling the bag out of my hand and unfolding the embroidered material. I took it and covered my head with it. And as I walked off, my shame and annoyance blocked out everything except a feeling of hatred towards Basem.

I didn't tell Said what had happened when we got back to the car, although Tamr burst out laughing and clapped her hands together crying, 'That old man! God help him!'

I rested my head in my hands and when I raised it the desert and the oasis of date palms were tinged orange by the evening sky. I was aware only of my helplessness. I had nothing, not even my eyes to stare and marvel. What had happened, I realized very well now, had been for the benefit of Tamr and others like her, to shackle the women's freedom of movement so that it wouldn't seem as easy and relaxed as we'd made it appear when we'd set out on our excursion. I took my head in my hands again.

I noticed that night had fallen while Umar and I had been up on the roof: the apartment blocks were silent; everywhere there were the concrete supports of buildings in the early stages of construction; stillness hung in the air above the hidden layer of noise, disturbed only by a hateful smell of food. The stars and the moon appeared meaningless. Did anything really exist? I tried to stretch up to see over the roof parapet and stared out as I always did, even though all I saw, day or night, summer or winter, were the houses and the oil fields.

Tomorrow Said would go to the Institute and hand in my resignation. The reason I would give: painful backaches that hindered my movement and took away my energy. From that day on I wouldn't see its door which every day had stood there like a portent, warning of tensions and unpleasant surprises to come, or the veiled women rushing through it, always waiting at the mercy of their husbands or brothers or drivers who might or might not remember the right time to come and take them back home.

On my first day at home I didn't rush out as I used to before to visit other women. I decided to live my life here in a different fashion and moreover to think precisely as I'd thought when looking from the aircraft window and seeing the desert for the first time. The stillness of the sands had drawn me to them; I wanted them to divulge their mystery to me so that I could become close to them and the history and geography books would come alive. The camel hair tents, the wide moon, the stars so near to earth, the oases, the mirages, the thirst and the pervasive fragrance of cardamon would all be a part of my life. But the huge airport had all the latest equipment and would have been like any other international airport but for the preponderance of Middle and Far Eastern faces. We drove along a broad motorway on our way to the hotel and I could see the town lit up, plenty of cars and even a few trees; and as we came closer, restaurants, hotels and stridently modern feats of architectural design.

Our hotel was luxurious although whoever designed it had been unsuccessful, obviously seeing things through foreign eyes and wanting to create his own idea of Arab architecture and furnishings, with the result that wealth superseded taste in every room. The picture windows looked out on to distant lights, and in the daytime I saw a big harbour and a sturdy bridge. Who'd said that we were in the desert here, when all the trappings and institutions of city life were to be found in abundance?

Not much time passed before I realized I'd been mistaken: I was neither in the desert nor in a city. The desert was only a place to be explored; even getting to know its natives was an experience like something out of a tourist brochure and they themselves were ill at ease with anything but hair tents and camels and sand. Those in the city, meanwhile, were in conflict with whatever came to them from beyond the desert. Every aircraft that landed on their sands brought something that frightened them and that they didn't want to know about because it didn't spring out of their own arid land. But these aircraft carried people and their different civilizations and they couldn't afford to reject them because the incomers were the ones who knew the secrets of the desert, almost as if they had been created in its belly and knew where the black liquid was and how to turn it into door handles and bathtaps made of gold.

That first day I went around the house, cleaned the canary's cage, sat down on the sofa, and thought to myself, 'Where are all the things that I wanted to do if I didn't go to teach?' I opened a drawer. There were coloured shells, silver rings, material. I closed it. The phone rang. I hurried to answer it. The canary flew from his open cage and perched on my shoulder as he always did when I picked up the receiver. My husband was telling me that he'd come and have coffee with me after lunch: 'I've got a few people from Beirut with me.' I found myself asking him, 'And when are we going to leave this country?' There was a silence, then he said laughing, 'You want to know this minute?' 'Yes. I have to know. I can't go on like this,' then I started to cry. I heard him hesitating on the other end of the line: 'We'll talk about it later. Come on. Bye bye.' Still crying, I shouted at him, 'I want to know how much longer we're staying in this bloody country.'

'What's all this about? Calm down, take it easy. What's happened? I don't understand. What's different since I left you this morning?' I repeated tearfully, 'Nothing's happened. I'm going to explode, that's all. I just want to know.'

And I knew that he didn't know. We were like all the Lebanese who'd transferred their businesses abroad and had been luckier than they expected. I tried to make myself get up but I couldn't and stayed where I was, my head in my hands, the canary on my shoulder, thinking about my family and Basem's family and my friends. None of them were happy in Beirut now, all wavering between staying and leaving. My sister wrote to me from Brazil, the sad letters of an exile. The phone again. Maryam on the line. I found myself gradually growing calmer as if I was getting back into daily life here once more. I took the material from the drawer and began to make a bedouin puppet. I drew in the eyes, the eyebrows, the lips and remained absorbed, unaware of the time until my son Umar came home from school, calling out and shouting at me to take him down to see the baby camel near our house. I was still thinking about the colour of the puppet's lips as he pulled me along with him, the camera in his other hand. Down in the street I saw to my surprise that there was a dog nosing around the camel and it was responding playfully to the dog's interest. I clicked the shutter and we approached the two of them with Said shouting to us, 'Go gently. The camel's afraid and he's a cunning beast.'

Basem and his three friends arrived. I gave them coffee while the canary flew about the house and approached the glass-topped table, and landed on the plate of biscuits. He pecked desultorily at a piece of biscuit but perhaps he found it too dry. He flew off again then landed on my shoulder and moved up close to my face, trying to take some biscuit out of my mouth. 'See that son of a bitch!' remarked one of the guests in surprise. When I stood up with the canary on my shoulder another of them asked, 'How's life? You look as if you're enjoying it here.' I thought it's the canary on my shoulder that's given him that idea, and not only the canary, perhaps the furniture and the nice house as well. I returned, 'I'm all right. But if only I could walk about the place.' Basem chipped in, 'By the way, I've brought you a walking-machine. Don't exaggerate, Suha, you can walk about any compound.' I busied myself putting the canary back into his cage. If this conversation had taken place in our first year here I would have answered him that walking wasn't just an activity of the feet: eyes needed a change of scenery too and in the compound you went along on a green carpet which resembled grass, or on real grass threatened every instant by sand. I always used to discuss the place with him and ask him if the smell of damp bothered him and if he noticed how time stagnated, and he would answer, 'I don't have time to scratch my head.' Fighting off my despair, I would ask curtly, 'Don't you have the feeling that life here isn't normal?'

When the conversation between Basem and the other men turned as usual to money and business, I thought even people who aren't living here have been caught up in this obsession with money and can no longer talk about anything unconnected with money, chances for good deals, petrol. Slyly I interrupted them: 'Do you know, a committee of doctors did ECGs on a large sample of the men around here and thought the machinery had broken down. They all came out blank.' My smart remark was lost on the three men and when one of them asked what I meant Basem replied, 'Suha always likes to philosophize about things. She means we don't feel anything and we're always chasing after money. An instructive summing-up!'

That night I broached the subject of our staying here again. I tried to be realistic, positive, decisive. I told Basem that I wanted the truth, wanted to know how long we were going to spend here so that I could prepare myself psychologically, and impressed upon him that I wouldn't by angry whatever the answer might be. When he answered hesitantly, 'A year. Two years. Maybe three,' I screamed at him. I thumped my hand against the door as I went to open it and echoed Umm Kairouz's words: 'I'll go mad. I could accept life in the fighting, but not this.' I went out but as I reached the door of the overgrown garden I turned back and found Basem standing on the doorstep. I went in with him and said, 'It's good that I found out.'

The next day I decided to do what I'd done the day after I arrived when I was acclimatizing myself to the place: go down to the hotel swimming-pool and jump in off the boards, put oil on my legs, smile at the waiter who brought me orange juice and stretch out contentedly. But the spirit of that day was never recaptured. Then I'd looked at the mosaic in the swimming-pool and thought to myself that it was like the green of the sea, admired the sturdy blue sunshades and the clean comfortable chaises-longues and marvelled at the coolness of the juice in the stifling atmosphere. But the veneer of newness had worn off and I'd stopped going to the swimming-pool after a man had come in and banged on the tables, separating the male swimmers from the females. Most of the women took refuge in the changing-rooms trembling, and the few foreigners among them didn't understand what was going on. In his attempts not to look at the semi-naked bodies in the pool the man had begun to thump his stick looking in the opposite direction, and had slipped and fallen in the water. His head rose to the surface and went under again a number of times, and he swallowed large amounts of water and almost drowned.

Today as I paid the entry fee I made up my mind to speak English. Despite the burning sun I lay back in a chaise-longue by the pool, lifted my hair off my neck and wiped away the sweat: 'God, do I have to stay? I can't take another hour in this country.' Nobody heard me but the flies and the clammy air. I took my face cream and had barely opened the lid before it poured out like a stream of hot water. 'Even cosmetics melt.' I threw it down, opened a magazine, laid it aside. I looked around me. Foreign women. Arab women. Children.

Two days a week for women and the rest of the time for men. No music. Only the racket of motors and a bulldozer working nearby. I closed my eyes, opened them and closed them again when I saw a woman approaching. I didn't want to talk to any woman. I'd stopped visiting and receiving visitors and hadn't even opened the door to Suzanne in spite of being curious to know what had happened to Maaz since our visit to Sita.

I'd been years in this desert and a quarter of an hour stretched out on the chaise-longue. There was no music playing. Music's the work of the devil: it infiltrates the mind and whispers seductively to it. I looked at my magazine for a few moments but saw the signs of normal life in it and felt depressed and threw it down. I thought nostalgically of the first year here and closed my eyes again recalling the shapes and colours of the goats that were new to me then; I'd gone into the shops, few in those days, examining all the Indian merchandise, turning over the daggers and bracelets, the real coral and the fake, and passing my hand over the smooth aged wood of the doors which had been ripped out of the mud brick houses. I even got to know about the foodstuffs in the freezers and the prices of everything. I was enthusiastic about the local people: I'd come here to find out what there was in the women's wooden chests and imagined green and blue and red and white cashmere shawls and rubies and diamonds, one for every finger, but I'd been wrong. The people of the desert had changed and were still changing: they were throwing out their carved sofas, and stainless steel and jewels from Bangkok had become important in their lives.

I no longer felt inspired by the puppets' costumes that I used to enjoy making. Books began to frustrate me because they took me off into surroundings so remote from where I was. In spite of my boredom I wasn't interested in witnessing the building of cities stone by stone, or their expansion, and I could no longer stand the sound of the loudspeakers on the cars that roved around the narrow sandy or asphalted streets enumerating the different kinds of tree they were planting. I did not want to be somewhere that was just starting up. Even the first landings on the moon seemed like ancient history to me now. The newspapers arrived late and the news was already out of date and that was why what went on in the world no longer touched me. Everything seemed as if it was happening on another planet.

The Indian waiter was coming towards me now devouring me with his eyes. I put the towel around me before I asked him if one of the men had come to stop the women swimming. No, they all had to go into the restaurant because the swimming pool had been reserved for a family who were of some importance by the look of them. I just nodded for by now I could see the other women getting into arguments with their children about leaving the pool.

The place emptied although waves still ruffled the blue water where people had been jumping and swimming. I didn't want to rise from my seat for two reasons: I'd have had to get fully dressed to go into the restaurant, and I was curious to see the important family. I expected a woman in a veil and abaya who'd sit on the edge of the pool, like the ones I'd seen at the seaside sitting with children in over-large bathing costumes while their father enjoyed himself in the water. I saw a young girl followed by a pretty woman in a long dress whose hair reached below her waist. Before she took off her dress at the side of the pool she looked around her and saw me, or perhaps she didn't, because she didn't protest, but gathered up her hair, lifted if off her back and went down into the pool. She stood holding on to the steps, then after a while she floated still holding the steps. Her daughter, who was an excellent swimmer, threw water at her and she turned her face away with her free hand on her hair, saying 'Stop it,' in a coquettish voice.

I stood up and jumped into the water, thinking that I now knew why people built private swimming pools for themselves. The water without lots of bodies in it looked much more refreshing. The woman was still holding on to the steps when I got there. We exchanged smiles and before I moved away I heard her asking me in English if I'd teach her to swim. When I answered yes in Arabic she said, 'I told myself that's an Arab face. Are you from Lebanon?'

I stood with her in the water and told her to blow into the water as a first step, but she didn't know how to. I told her to breathe in and hold her breath, then plunge her head into the water and stop holding on and take her feet off the bottom. She did as I said but she couldn't stop herself clinging on to the steps. She tried once again and still couldn't . When she asked me if I'd come to her house and give her swimming lessons I laughed awkwardly. Seeing the reluctance on my face she pressed me with good-natured charm: 'Please. The car will come for you and take you back afterwards. And the pool at our house is big.' I couldn't conceal my surprise and wondered how to reply to the woman whose name was Nur, who clearly realized what I was thinking. 'I was fed up,' she explained. 'and I said to my daughter Ghada that we should have a change and go the the hotel pool.' Then she sat down beside me and began telling me about her time at school in Cairo and how much she liked Lebanon, and every time I stood up to go she insisted that I stayed and I realized that she was bored.

I regretted my capitulation the next day when Nur's driver appeared at the door. I was sleepy. The car drew to a halt with me outside a house that I'd often seen before. It wasn't far from where we lived and Umar called it the spaceship while I had privately named it the moon house. Its walls were built of beautiful stone. 'They must be mad,' I thought, 'spending all that cash as if they were in Switzerland.' Inside the house it was hard to believe in the existence of the dust from the desert and the ugly dilapidated houses, all alike, and the pot-holed narrow streets with piles of rubbish at every corner. I could see trees and green grass in Nur's garden although some of the foliage had withered. How quickly the plants died even in the gardens of the rich houses because of sand storms, or goats that got in and ate everything that was green.

Nur was waiting for me in the swimming-pool. As I dived into the clean water I thought no one looking from outside would be able to guess what lay behind those walls. At first I was annoyed, then increasingly indifferent, in the face of Nur's fear and her failure to listen to what she ought to do in order to stay afloat. But I continued to encourage her, while she apologized and played the part of the embarrassed pupil.

My visits to her became more frequent although I gave up hope of ever teaching her to swim, especially when she confessed to me that this was the fourth time she'd tried to learn. Before me she'd joined a swimming club somewhere in Europe, and her husband Saleh had tried to teach her too. But Nur's personality and the atmosphere of her house, so different from the other houses I knew, attracted me back there.

4

It was difficult for us to become friends, for I had effectively sealed off the channels of communication to every living creature and every inanimate object in this country. I left my house rarely and didn't give myself the chance to get to know people who would transport me to other worlds. I wasn't suffering from the depression of the desert which attacked every woman from time to time, even the ones who were content with this restricted way of life: for a woman never knows why she suddenly withdraws from everyday life for a time any more than she knows why the cloud of depression suddenly lifts from her.

But I wanted peace once I began to grasp the contradictions which existed between my house and the outside world. Every time I walked into my house I felt that I was entering a different world far removed from the other: all the variations and details of life inside appeared reasonable and sensible; the international news on the radio and television appeared important; listening to it, you felt that it was talking about people and events that you understood. While if you heard the same news on the car radio, driving along the sand or the newly-improved roads, it seemed remote from reality, transmitted in an indolent tongue understood by no one, because it didn't consist of endless talk about money and business. Even the news which concerned everyday economic life gave the impression that it didn't change from one day to the next as it did in the rest of the world. After all, the gold market here was a few little shops around an unroofed courtyard with the goldsmiths sitting on the ground in front of low tables covered with gold articles and substances for melting them down and polishing them. Black beetles ran over its sandy floor and women stood around, the gold on their arms jingling as they fingered necklaces and gold belts, or bought gilded Qur'ans and ear-rings and bracelets for their children, while their husbands reluctantly counted out vast amounts of money and gave it to the goldsmith who sorted the notes into neat bundles of a hundred and snapped elastic bands round them.

Nur reawakened my curiosity, but only for a short time. Her house was like a peep-show where servants and nannies of different races milled around with children, gazelles and saluki dogs. A delicate perfume floated to meet me whenever I went through the door, and Arab and foreign music reverberated through the spacious rooms. Beautiful clothes, high fashion, the latest of everything - including the furniture and the chocolates she offered me, like Godiva from Belgium and

Chantilly from Lebanon - mangoes and pineapples from the Philippines. It was a large house with white marble everywhere and the trees in the garden visible through the windows, acting as a buffer between the house and the desert. The noise that filled it reminded me of Sitt Wafa's house, and in both of them I found some semblance of normality.

In Nur's house I used to sit and wonder where to look next. There were two video machines in the huge sitting-room. The furniture was used to divide the room into three sections. Her daughter and Umar and some other children were shouting and screaming as they fought satellites on the video screen. Female friends and relations of Nur watched stars like Dalida and the Egyptian Nellie on television, and the Filipino menservants sang and called to each other with loud whistles. Dogs wandered in, wrestled with the children, and wandered out. Budgerigars and canaries and green and white parrots hopped around their aviaries talking to one another. There was a big aquarium alive with different sea creatures. When the friends and relations got bored they would come over to Nur and me and then I wondered which of them to talk to or look at. Some of them were enveloped in abayas and veils and had henna patterns on their hands, while others wore clothes in the latest styles and colours; their jewellery was either embossed bedouin gold or modern international designer style. Which magazine should I flick through? It seemed as if all the world's magazines, and the magazines produced by all the big international stores, were there on the table. When Said came to take me home I was always surprised how quickly the time had passed.

But Nur's house was no longer so exciting after I'd seen the show over and over again, and swimming in the pool was no longer a novelty, and I didn't pay proper attention to what Nur was saying. The times I did listen to her complaints which were always on the same theme – how bored she was and how much she wanted to go abroad – I used to soothe her in exactly the same way that Basem soothed me: 'Never mind. Be patient,' without meaning what I said. Because I was turned in on myself to such an extent, I couldn't establish a real friendship with any woman here. 'My friends are in Beirut and I don't feel in tune with anyone else.' But I also used to say to Basem that I couldn't break off relations with Nur as I'd done with the rest because she found an answer to every excuse I gave; whether I said Said wasn't around, Umar was ill, I wasn't feeling well or I was busy. When I didn't answer the telephone Nur came in person and knocked on my door asking if the telephone was out of order. I began to feel annoyed by her and her persistence, and complained about it to Basem. He suggested that I should benefit from her and get to know the desert region here. Despite my lack of enthusiasm, I welcomed the idea and thought it sounded better than sitting on my sofa or Nur's hour after hour. So one day we went together right into the desert to an oasis community and visited some of Nur's relations in brand-new tents with sitting-rooms, dining-rooms, showers and toilets and a water pump outside. We sat on Persian and Pakistani rugs. The women seemed more real in these huge tents, although they'd only come to spend a few days in the desert. One of them asked Nur about her husband Saleh; 'May God guide him,' she remarked as she started to speak about him, which I presumed was because he was always travelling: whenever I asked Nur about her husband he was away on business. She took me to watch a bride-to-be being bathed and beautified and decorated with henna, and I saw how different the women looked without their veils and black abayas. They were laughing and shouting to one another and exchanging frank comments and gestures as they watched the bride. At night we went to the wedding ceremony and I was happy just to watch, while Nur danced, chewing gum. I didn't eat anything. Nur ate, while I looked at the women and at the stars that seemed almost within reach.

When the phone rang early one morning I picked up the receiver although I was sure that it would be Nur, and I agreed to visit her because I wanted to get out of the house that day, particularly as I hadn't left if for days. When I entered the house I found the opposite of what I had expected. Nur looked as if she'd spent the night in a cold bath, immersed in icy loneliness. At her side was her bottle of tranquillizers. When Nur took one of these she slept peacefully for hours but when she woke up she moved slowly as if the ground wasn't to be trodden on but just brushed with the soles of her feet. There was a mound of cigarette butts in the ashtray. The pallor of her face made her a part of the sugar-coloured sofa, except for the two points of blackness that flickered there from time to time. Her hands too blended in with the sofa and she held the ashtray listlessly. In front of her on the table was a bowl with pomegranate grains in it, and another of peeled cucumber and carrot. The Filipino maid picked up the two bowls and glanced at Nur before disappearing with them. I was about to ask her what had happened when the maid came back with a bowl of peeled oranges and apples and grapes.

Nur was beside herself. She bent her head and said, 'I want to die. Every day I can feel myself beginning to explode. I want to travel and I can't. Saleh's got my passport. I can't live another moment in this house, I'm going to run away.' I sat beside her and said, feigning concern, 'Calm down, Nur. It's not so bad. Send a telegram asking him to send you the passport. Saleh'll be back soon. It's not such a disaster.' I thought to myself how spoilt she was. Then I looked around me. For the first time I thought about the cost of everything: the ceiling, the floor tiles, sofas, tables, chandeliers, display cabinets; it was as if every piece had been chosen to give an aura of rock-solidness and life as it should be lived. And yet the house was steeped in loneliness, perhaps because of the absence of visitors and their children at this hour. The doors and windows were hidden by curtains as if they didn't exist, as if there were no aperture in this house for the plants to breathe through and everything was crouching under a solid glass cover. Again I pretended to be concerned: 'What's wrong, Nur? Calm down. Don't worry. You'll be able to go abroad soon.'

Nur wept, and the tears brought the spirit back into her face: 'I can't stand any more. I've had enough. He's got to divorce me, or come back to me. I can't live like a date hanging off a branch, neither firmly attached to the branch nor lying comfortably on the ground.' Half interested now, I found myself saying, 'All right. Why haven't you either got divorced or come back together before now?' The only reply I could hear was her bitter weeping. Her long black hair was in a mess from the fury of her fit of crying and she lifted her head and twisted up her hair and threw it to the side: 'I just don't know what to do. I want to die. I've had enough. I want to die.'

I didn't know what to say to her, but I acknowledged to myself that I was hard and self-centred because I wasn't moved by her tears now, and because I was thinking about Umar coming home and wondering whether Said had under-stood that he was supposed to come for me in an hour. Then I justified this by imagining that my reaction would have been different if I'd seen one of my friends in Lebanon crying.

Nur was sobbing hysterically now. I got up and found a box of tissues and brought it over and stood awkwardly before her, not knowing how to make her take one. I tried again in a low voice: 'Nur. Calm down a bit.' I hated myself because these were the only words I could think of to say but for the first time I found myself taking Nur's situation ser-iously. I had assumed that Saleh, like all the husbands here, was just away a lot or had another wife somewhere. The feeling that the house was without a man was clear although Nur was always threatening her daughter: 'I'm telling you, your father's going to beat you. He'll be back soon and then you'll see.'

I thought, 'Nur must trust me and my feelings for her, otherwise she wouldn't choose to seek help from me in preference to all her other friends and relations. Perhaps it's because I'm a stranger? But she's got lots of friends like me, who aren't from the desert.'

I rested my hand on Nur's hair, then patted her shoulder and said to her, 'There's a solution to everything, Nur.' Nur mumbled some words that I didn't understand. She looked up and reached for some tissues and wiped her eyes, then said, 'It's a huge catastrophe.'

I was surprised and pleased that my words had evoked some response in her, and for the first time she appeared ready to look at her situation without crying. I said, 'Ask him for a divorce. It'd be better than living like this.'

It was as if I'd reminded her of something worse. She bowed her head again and repeated, 'It's a huge catastrophe. If I get divorced, who do I marry?' I was taken aback by Nur's question but instead of saying jokingly to her, 'How can you think about marriage when you haven't thought about divorce yet?' I asked reasonably, 'Did you quarrel? What about? Let somebody try and bring you back together.' Dabbing at the tears and sweat on her face, Nur answered, 'He won't budge. He's got a heart of stone, and his head's not much different.' Then leading me back to the main issue she repeated, 'I want to go away. I can't bear living here. If only I could go on a trip for a week or two . . .'

I let Nur cry and I couldn't help looking at my face in the tissue packet holder as I took a tissue from it, to see how I looked; Nur had even thought of getting a metal cover for the tissue box. I thought I looked beautiful. What was the use? I handed some more tissues to Nur who sat up and said, 'How lucky you are, how fortunate to be Lebanese.' I was about to answer, 'But I'm stuck here, like you' but no – the perfume that I smelt whenever I came into Nur's house now coursed suddenly and powerfully through the corridors of my blood, into the blue veins in my head, massaging them. I relaxed as if I was floating on a surface that was like water but without the wetness or the tension. I was suddenly conscious that I wasn't from here, that I could travel, and go where I pleased, by myself, for a year, two years, three, or leave for good. But Nur would return however often she went away and however long she stayed away. I felt invigorated by these sensations and I returned to the box of tissues, pretending to take one while I was really stealing glances at my reflection, assuring it again of the reality which I'd grown oblivious to and which had confronted me in the midst of Nur's passionate outburst. Only now did I appreciate that this outburst was less violent than it might have been, given the situation she was in. So I tried to return to Saleh, to the root of the problem, but Nur was only interested in retrieving her passport and going abroad and a disquisition on the subject of her husband bored her. She was already trying to think of alternative ways of getting out and urged me to help with practical suggestions. I offered: 'You're ill and need a specialist?' 'No. They wouldn't believe it.' 'Your mother's very ill and you have to travel to look for a cure?' 'Possible. But who'd persuade my mother to go?' I was running out of patience: 'Get another passport.' 'No. These days you have to have a photograph. Before it was easy. No photos for women. Just the name.' At this I said with relief, 'If only I looked like you. I could have given you my passport.' Nur answered, 'Thank you, my sweet. And thank you for helping me.' What help could she mean? I'd only handed her some tissues, and in exchange she'd given me a crystal ball where I'd seen my face and my life.

Nur began coming to my house and going to my room, closely followed by a man who slipped in after her like a thief while I sat in the sitting-room or in the kitchen waiting for the outer door to open and close and for the sound of Nur's footsteps, her kiss on my cheek and her words, always the same, 'I don't know how I'd live without you, my sweet.' An hour and she was gone, leaving me to go into my room looking for traces of Nur's meeting with the man so that I could get rid of them, and thinking why does she get in between the sheets? Why isn't she more sensitive to such things? I would open the window and change the sheets, to chase away the smell of Nur, then go over to the table to see if she'd forgotten a ring or a necklace or a bracelet. It was plain that these clandestine meetings were dispelling all the grief and confusion that she'd been suffering from, leaving her calm and in control of the rest of her day. They were like food and drink to her, so that when Basem had the painters in to the house for several days and when even after it was painted she couldn't resume her meetings for several more days, she pleaded with me to come instead to her house at eleven in the morning and let in a man who would be carrying a black briefcase. I received him pretending to the world that he was the doctor and let him into her room after asking the servant girl nicely to shut the door behind her. I went into the bathroom and turned on the tap as hard as it would go looking at myself in the mirror, asking my reflection how long I would be in Nur's life. I opened the cupboards and saw rusty razors and razor blades and bottles with remnants of men's cologne in them in among the face creams and bags of henna. The water was still running and the sound of it drowned out any movement in the bedroom. I opened the curtain at the window and a cloud of dust flew up. I could see a little bit of the swimming-pool and some patches of green grass and trees with pale, sickly leaves. Over the wall came the noise of the water pumps, and I could see the colourless houses with their metallic doors and window frames glinting in the sun. Would anyone passing by this house believe that in one of its rooms there was a woman in bed with a man who wasn't her husband? This man she'd met in a store, and there had been many others like him; one she'd met at a street crossing, another on a visit to the hospital; she'd slept with the man who'd come selling jewels and material to her in her house and the landscape gardener who advised her on the design of her garden when she was considering planting it with Japanese trees. I thought to myself how human beings continually manage to overcome their circumstances, thinking up the strangest ways to give substance to their desires. Before I'd always doubted if sex existed in houses like these and here I was listening to Nur laughing behind the locked door. I turned off the tap to hear better and then turned it on again.

These meetings weren't Nur's lifesavers for long. She began to dream about going abroad again saying that she didn't like daytime encounters, although she didn't stop doing it until I asked her to; one of the men whom she'd seen in my house came to the door one day to ask me if he could bring his foreign girlfriend there. He handed me a bottle of whisky and a big piece of pork. Trembling, I gave them back to him and didn't answer. I wanted to shut the door in his face or to scream at him to make him understand me and Nur and the risks we had taken. But it seemed complicated to explain, and I couldn't look him in the eye and say to him straight out that Nur and I were playing with fire.

5

I didn't hesitate for a moment when Nur asked me to come to her house early one morning, and it wasn't because her voice sounded weak on the line. She was in bed enveloped in a light cloud of steam rising from a vaporiser. It seemed to have opened up her features so that she looked like a fruit that had ripened prematurely in a greenhouse. I said jollily to her, 'Well? What's the fairy princess doing today?' and she wept silently. I didn't take any notice. I wasn't in the mood to listen to her complaining. This was the first time I'd been out after three days cooped up in the house because of the rain. The dark clouds, the pools of water on the road and in the garden had filled me with happiness.

Rain had come to the desert this year. The sun and the moon had disappeared and the voices praying from the mosque sounded dry and echoless, competing with each other in volume and number. I found myself taking Umar in my arms in the night, calming him because he couldn't sleep. He said to me, 'You're a liar. That's not a prayer.' He was used to hearing the prayer regularly at dawn and this was eight in the evening. I answered him gently, 'They're praying for rain. It has to rain for the dates and the crops to ripen, and to wash away the germs.'

During the night he woke up screaming and came to my bed several times. Lightning and thunder chased each other around the sky and the rain poured down. I went back to bed hoping that I'd reassured him and listened to the rain hammering on the bathroom roof. I smiled contentedly. When Basem opened the door in the morning he gave a shout of wonder and I rushed to see the flooded garden. The water in the street was several inches deep and had begun to come in under the garden door.

Even the rain here was different: it didn't stay on the buildings, and they didn't soak it up. They remained pale, the colour of the dust, like the trees, while the rushing waters swept the building materials out into the street, the wood floating along on the surface. In some places the sand turned to mud. Most of the traffic came to a halt and the drivers got out hitching up their robes to just below their knees and wading through the water showing their skinny legs. Jeeps were the only vehicles that could get through despite the muddy spray that stuck to their windscreens. The shops closed and some women went in cars laughing across the street to visit their neighbours but most of them stayed indoors. When the rain stopped and the sun came out, instead of a rainbow hundreds of mosquitoes hovered in the air like ballet dancers with their long legs.

I didn't ask Nur what was wrong but said enthusiastically, 'I meant to tell you, I saw Saleh on television the other day. You so-and-so. I didn't know he was so attractive and so young. He spoke well. I liked him. He's intelligent, and you know, he looks like Ghada.' Nur shouted back, 'He's not worth an onion skin. I didn't even want to see him face to face this time. I just sent Ghada off without making any trouble.' Then she asked what I wanted to drink, to change the subject.

Before I answered she suddenly began to beat her head and her face with the palms of her hands so violently that I jumped up from my seat and took hold of her arms. Her paroxysm showed no signs of abating and she screamed, 'I'm fed up. I've tried and I can't go on any longer. When I'm depressed I say, "Never mind, Nur", but then I get desperate and I feel ready to explode again. Sometimes I hope he doesn't come to take Ghada or that I don't know he's in the country. Then I pray that when he comes I'll be away somewhere. If only I could be!' And she started striking her head and sobbing again, while I grabbed her arms and tried to soothe her. I hadn't realized that Nur was so strong up till now.

I'd grown used to her gentle voice with its soft desert accent and the affectionate words she spoke to her salukis as she patted them on the head; I'd watched her often cuddling the little gazelle, and sticking her finger in the cream and licking it to make sure it was fresh, and lifting her face to be kissed by her veiled visitors. When she put her head in her hands again and I tried to pull them away she pressed my hand with one of her hot hands then cast her head on to my shoulder like a sad child. She hadn't stopped crying all the time but I couldn't bring myself to pat her shoulder or hold her to comfort her. I felt embarrassed and wished Nur would control herself, while she stayed where she was like a child safe in her mother's arms at last. I didn't move but I said,

'Nur. Let's think of a way,' trying to get her off me. Nur's face was no longer on my shoulder but against my neck. I ignored the butterfly fluttering and stayed quite still. I felt a moist warmth, then a light-headedness that made me tremble and still I didn't move. Nur's face was still pressed against me. Suddenly the warmth of her breathing made my heart pound and a feeling surged through me that scared me. I trembled again but I didn't want to pull away. I sat forcing myself to remain immobile, staring at the upholstery. Nur realized what was happening to me and as if she was taking me by the hand and advancing step by step, she paused for a little while before nuzzling her face against my neck, then encircling me with her arms and drawing me to her. The warmth spread over my neck, dropping down into my body at the same time. Shutting out everything else, I said to myself, 'Nur's kissing me,' and I didn't think as I did in real life 'A kiss is between a man and a woman', but just wanted more. Every point in my body that Nur reached she aroused and left in a state of agitation.

My muscles didn't stay tensed up and as they relaxed I found myself lying back on the bed then a rhythmic movement started up which made me dizzy from the different sensation of pleasure it produced in me. It was a beautiful purely instinctual rhythm, which seemed to take off and fly like the wisps of steam still floating about the room.

Reality returned to me as soon as I became aware of Nur's weight smothering me. I pulled my eyes away and fixed them on the ceiling. Then I felt a sudden nausea, then disgust, and wished I could disappear through the cracks in the ceiling. I didn't want to stay lying there and give Nur the impression that I was happy at what had happened, and at the same time I wanted to be separate from my body and give it orders: tell it to stand up and go away just as I wanted to do, open the door and chase it out. But as it was I got up and stood there, not daring to look at Nur, or around the room, or down at my skirt. I'd pulled my skirt over my legs while I was still lying on the bed, knowing that I would never feel quite the same liking for them as I had done before, or look after them so carefully or bother so much about what tights I wore.

My skirt looked as if one of Nur's dogs had chewed it and spat it out. I wanted to turn to her and tell her that I had no connection with the woman who'd been panting with her a little while before. But I just went on standing there, quivering slightly, not daring to move, while Nur sat at her dressing table and reached for her hairbrush, loosened her plaits, brushed her hair, replaited it and pulled down her nightdress. She didn't look at me but smiled in the mirror as she saw me leaving, and said goodbye. I couldn't distance myself from what had happened. I went to the car and sat in it, my face almost touching the window, and saw nothing until I reached my own front door. I heard Basem and Umar talking together and longed to be sitting between them feeling bored, or lying in my bed ill, instead of having to go in to them now. I had a terrible desire to throw myself into their arms and cry. I wished I could rush into my room without seeing them. But I stood rooted to the spot when I heard Umar saying, 'She's here.' I got as far as the dining-room when Basem intercepted me: 'What's happened?' Trying to sound casual I replied, 'Nur's ill and I got the doctor to her.' Jokingly he remarked, 'If she's ill why's your face so pale? ' and I said quickly, 'Her driver hit another car and I had a fright.'

I swallowed. It was as if I had a big stone in my gullet which hurt me every time I breathed. I didn't wait for Umar in the bathroom while he cleaned his teeth, as he asked me to. 'I'll come and see you in a little while, darling,' I said apologetically.

I went into my room and I knew how risky it would be to cry now but I couldn't help it. I looked at the photo of me with Umar and Basem on my dressing table and turned it face down in case their eyes bored through me and saw the recent scene with Nur. Then I turned it back again and stared at Basem with his spectacles and pale eyes and smooth hair, and his big nose that was out of proportion to the rest of his features. The sight of his striped shirt whose collar I always sprayed with some special cleaner for collars and cuffs made him appear familiar, like a brother or friend or someone who had sat next to me at school.

I went about the house like someone immunized against hearing and seeing until Umar's bedtime. Then I went to bed the same as I did every other night, while Basem sat watching a film on the video until late. I closed my eyes and I felt as if I were emerging from a dark cave on to a blue sea glowing with light. I opened a window in my head and looked through it and saw a motor working soundlessly in a room lined with velvety wallpaper just as I'd pictured it before, with red and blue wires around it. I opened a window looking on to my heart and saw a motor boiling and thudding there. I asked my noisy heart, and my mind, which went silently back and forth in its room, what was on the pages which I hadn't yet read. What was passing along those red and blue wires? What were the subjects of the paintings hanging on the velvet walls? What was the significance of a heart being heart-shaped when I didn't even know who was beginning and who was reaching an end, who growing, who diminishing?

I am Suha. I am twenty-five-years old. My mother is Sitt Widad and my father is Dr Adnan. I'm not bent like Sahar, although I've laughed and joked and exchanged comments and gestures about men with other girls like me. I'm normal. I saw myself on a bed in the cold of the mountain with Suhail, Aida's friend, in the middle. All the guests had gone, carrying bags of grapes under their arms. I'd held a party to pick our grapes at the end of the summer. I'd had the idea because my parents were in Europe and I liked having my friends to visit me in my house. The three of us were drunk and I wanted some coffee to sober up. I got it ready but when I took it to the others I found Aida stretched out on my bed facing the wall with Suhail lying beside her, and without thinking I crept on to the bed behind Suhail. It was the smell of him perhaps, or the cold and being drunk, that made me squeeze up against him. He turned and reached his hand out to the back of my neck then moved it down my back and rested it there. I felt confused, comprehending all at once the sort of relationship which Aida and Suhail must have, but I let his hand reach under my skirt. 'How are you feeling, Aida?' 'Fine,' replied Aida, with her eyes closed. His hands were on my flesh, moving up the slope of my body, pulsating. Then he said, 'Chopin,' and Aida asked him, 'Do you like Chopin?' 'I think he's fantastic,' answered Suhail, 'and I like Ravel's *Bolero*.' I knew that Aida wouldn't believe what I was doing now even if she turned over and saw it. She said, 'I tried to make Suha like classical music.' Suhail had begun breathing more heavily. He answered, 'Suha likes rock,' and lifted himself over me so he was at the edge and I was in the middle. I wanted to stay where I was but at the same time I wanted to get up. I wondered whether to let myself go and disregard Aida, but I felt sorry for her whichever I did. She said, 'Suha likes blues as well,' and Suhail said, 'Really?' as he opened his flies. 'My head's heavy,' I said. I began to talk wildly about anything and gathered my hair up off my head while Suhail moved faster and faster then suddenly got up and asked, 'Where's the coffee?'

The heart and the mind opened their two chambers, allowing me to steal a glance into them. I'm indifferent now to Suhail, Maurice, Adnan, Adil, and I understand that time takes a huge eraser and rubs out names and then writes others in and renews feelings and emotions. I'd got to know Basem and fallen in love with him, and my heart had leapt for joy when he asked me to marry him. Now I didn't want to look into either chamber. I chased away all the images and questions and misgivings and convinced myself that I'd forgotten what had happened in Nur's room. But the heart and mind were faithful and searched virtuously through their records, unearthing causes and explanations which might supply them with adequate justification for eradicating the event. They made me see myself a month before, when I'd escaped to my bed and listened to a child crying above the sound of the air-conditioner, and music – Western, Arab and Indian – floating out over the rooftops. I'd put my hand under the pillow to pull it nearer to me and smelt Nur's smell and heard her laughter and seen her thick black hair.

I imagined her with a man, warm and at the same time powerless, pliant and bending like a doll made of dough, wanting what was forbidden. The severity with which it was forbidden reminded people of it at every moment, and it wormed its way into their minds and bodies. Even when you were buying tampons and sanitary towels and perfumes and spray deodorants, the man behind the cash desk changed colour and you knew what he was thinking about as he smiled or assumed an air of indifference. There was a campaign being conducted in the press against the display of women's underwear, and its leader was a girl in her twenties who had already raised the subject of bracelets and other jewellery; according to her they were symbols of slavery reminiscent of the age of harems and slave boys and girls, and make-up and jewellery on a woman was a provocation to adultery and fornication even if it was made from behind veils and black drapes.

Although these thoughts of mine drew things together and had some substance, I couldn't help feeling miserable. I began reminding myself how I'd thought of Nur as having a kind of illness as I stared at the pillows and the cover that day, and said to myself this is where Nur rolled around and breathed fast and slow with a man, separated from him only by their fine body hairs. However, I couldn't see it like that now, much as I wanted to.

A week passed and I drifted in and out of reality, staring out of the window at the dusty desert and the mechanical waste. The telephone rang and I didn't answer. I didn't want to hear Nur's voice. But she came to see me early one morning. She sat down on the sofa, then stood up and seemed to be examining my house for the first time. She grasped hold of the coral and shells, the puppets hanging from the ceiling, the old silver necklaces and bracelets and anklets, and smiled and sat down again in front of me, her limbs loose and relaxed. I was still only half there, trying to make normal conversation and not succeeding. Every question or statement I wanted to utter seemed to have a connection with us, either directly or indirectly, and I only breathed again when Nur left.

When another day or two had gone by I began to feel a yearning. I missed the particular atmosphere that comes into being only if a person is alone, has spare time on her hands and is waiting for something to happen. For recently we had no longer sat chatting like visitors, each telling the other what she'd been doing. We'd begun to live our lives together, going to the department store, visiting Suzanne, entering the hotel in fear and trembling and ordering tea and cake only to rise up together after hastily swallowing the tea, because the looks of the other guests were almost beginning to be directed towards us, almost becoming a reproach. We went deep into the desert and saw a mirage of many colours. Instead of receding into the distance, it had come closer to us as we approached it in the car, and then it wasn't a mirage after all.

I couldn't help exclaiming in wonder at the carpet of yellow and white daisies, other flowers whose names I didn't know, and thick-stemmed ones standing straight as pegs: 'Those are called snake poison,' I said. It wasn't the colours that made my heart beat faster, but the smell, fragrant and powerful and new and strange to my nose. I picked a daisy and brought it close to my mouth and chewed its petals, trying to bring together the taste and the smell. As we went further among the flowers the smell grew and changed, from jasmine, to white iris, to narcissus. We sat down on the grass and sand and Nur pulled the petals off the daisy one by one: 'He loves me, he loves me not.' I stretched out and smiled as a sudden realization dawned on me. My relationship with Basem only existed inside the four walls of the house now; it didn't even extend to the garden or the car or the street. I rarely sat next to him in the front seat of the car. I didn't walk along with him in the street or go to the shops with him. We didn't lie together beside the pool and I didn't sit with him even on the back seat on the way to the airport; he sat in front next to Said. He'd never met Nur yet, or Tamr, and our conversations were brief, restricted to matters connected with everyday life, holidays, the news from Lebanon and family and friends.

Through the rooms of my mind and heart passed images of how I'd gone to bed early, trying to read against the noise of the television and the laughter and talking of Basem's friends. I'd stopped inviting men and women together because I'd become convinced that such gatherings were futile. The women furtively examined each other's clothes, working out the financial situation of each other's husbands so that they could feel either proud or jealous, while the men talked about money and business openly. I was glad that I wasn't obliged to sit with them but it made me realize how lonely I was.

Sometimes I used to refuse Basem when he came unusually early to the bedroom. It would depend on how fed up I'd felt during the day and how resentful that I was still in the desert. Sometimes I convinced myself that he had no alternative but to stay here, and that he was happy in his work. On these occasions I let him take me in his arms and cover me with kisses and I held him to me in memory of the past and the days of normality. However much I tried to relax I felt conscious of every noise outside and every movement in the bed, and the climax of our lovemaking was lost to me like a piece of paper blown near me by the wind, and blown away again every time I caught up with it. Then I felt angry because I'd shown a desire to participate and not come. Throughout the night I tossed and turned unable to sleep, as if I'd commit-ted a sin, and as if I'd found out for the first time that I wasn't in control of my body and that only my feelings could make it move, but they wouldn't forget their dissatisfaction and were rebelling.

Still breaking the petals off the daisy, Nur had said, 'When they brought me back here and I saw the desert from the plane I screamed. In the car I threw up three or four times and when I got to the house I banged my head against the walls. I couldn't sleep or eat and I wouldn't greet my relatives without letting them see how angry I was. I sat for hours and days as dumb as that table. I locked the door of my room and got a mirror and stared at my face; I counted the hairs of my eyebrows and eyelashes, twisted my hair round my fingers, just like mad people do. All my life I never liked seeing the desert. My mother says that before I was old enough to understand, I used to cry and they didn't know the reason. When I became conscious of my surroundings, I closed my eyes in the car. I was the opposite of my sisters and brothers. They loved looking out of the windows. I never did. It's always made me depressed.'

Our relationship wove itself together from day to day. I was like a fisherman who casts his line into water where he knows there are no fish, or even weeds, but feels a sense of calm and a release from the boredom of his routine every time he does it, and prefers it at least to doing nothing, although every day when he comes back to fish again he feels a little restless and disgruntled.

In the days that followed, I plucked up enough courage to kiss Nur, when I'd shut my eyes and opened them fifty times. My limbs went numb before I reached that nameless, other-worldly region with her. I couldn't open my eyes again easily; it was as if I was standing beside a large firework that might go off at any minute, or was dazzled in the presence of Nur the imperious queen bee. This was no longer an experiment; I'd tried a new fruit which I'd thought would be inedible and instead I'd found it intoxicatingly sweet; I couldn't just spit out the stone and go on my way.

Our secret relationship began to complement our relationship outside the house. I sensed a transformation: whatever plant it was I'd tasted had drugged me and made me lose my memory. I no longer noticed how slowly the time crawled by in the desert, or the pervasive smell of chemicals which used to irritate me so much, or the colours of the new buildings which I had once named Instant Ruins, or the wires hanging down from the outside walls, or the lack of trees. Feelings of agitation and rage no longer crept up on me as they had done before: now when I saw the women's tailor poking his head out of his tiny window to receive material and a pattern from one of his customers, I shrugged my shoulders indifferently: and I laughed when I heard one of Nur's mother's visitors forbidding her daughter to go alone in Nur's car. 'If you leave a man alone with a woman, the Devil makes it three,' she pronounced adamantly, despite Nur's protestations that the driver's morals were unimpeachable and he'd been with her for years.

But I felt irritated when one day Nur came to me in my house; only then did our relationship seem a reality. Instead of the smell of incense and furniture and food which filled my senses when I was in her room, and her bed which was like the cockpit of a plane and was studded with buttons on either side and had a chamois leather bedhead to match her wardrobe and mirror and seat, there were Umar's drawings blowing about in the draught from the air-conditioner and my yellow case on top of the wardrobe, and this time I couldn't feel that I was a visitor or an onlooker. Previously I'd gone back home and it seemed as if I'd never left: Basem's freshly-ironed clothes hung on the door knob; his clean shirts were still spread out on the bed to finish drying. I was aware of myself getting Umar's things ready and answering the telephone and acting so normally that I began to question if I'd really only returned from Nur's house a few minutes before, and if me stretching out on her bed and us kissing and clinging to each other and squirming about had really happened.

My room was still as it had always been except for the traces of Nur and her perfume. Bedrooms all over the world are always private and special. I used to love going into my parents' room to see the cut-glass moon mounted into the wood of their bed, although I never once saw it lit up. And I could still remember my European teacher's bedroom when I went to visit her with the rest of the class after she'd had her appendix out. To my surprise I saw toys of every shape and size scattered about the room. My teacher was about fifty years old and she didn't smile easily.

Before I was married I used to love my friends to see my room; I'd leave my tennis racquet lying on the table on purpose and the classical records and thick books on art and literature in obvious places, and foreign dictionaries, and the photograph of me receiving my school certificate. When I was married I chose the colours in the bedroom and took care that my night-dresses and even the tissues all matched each other. Now in the desert I'd come to think of the bedroom simply as somewhere to sleep.

6

I was surprised when I saw the hall packed with women from the desert: I couldn't think where they'd been hiding all the time because the town always seemed forlorn and half-empty. They were like a strange and wondrous kind of bird with their beaks and gay plumage, or female magicians gathered to see the colour of the air that night. They dressed in magnificent colours and styles: Marie Antoinette was there,

Cleopatra, Madame de Pompadour, Scarlett O'Hara and Raqiya Ibrahim.

Their hairstyles too were out of keeping with this hall, which had been built especially for wedding parties after a private house had collapsed because of the great number of guests crammed into it. Even the ceiling of this place had fallen in on some women one night, and with that in mind I sat at the back near the door, although Nur protested angrily. The women looked heartless tonight. Was it because of their clothes, or because their veils hung down to their noses or their hair reached their waists? Nur had gathered up her hair under a white cap fringed with seed pearls on the ends of fine threads, and she wore a long dress by Valentino, who'd designed the same dress in a shorter length for European women.

The concert this evening was being given by a singer named Ghusun. Her fame had spread after she'd met Abd Al-Halim Hafez and he'd heard her bedouin voice and asked her to sing in Cairo. She took along her sisters and female relations to back her on drums and tambourines, but they were terrified by the lights and the audience and refused to sit up on the stage, even with their veils on. So Ghusun was left singing to the microphone alone with her lute.

When Ghusun appeared she looked like a heroic female warrior from an African tribe. Her hair was like a wig she'd found among the bric-à-brac left behind by some Western mission, but her features were African. She wore a dress that was half black, half red, with big gathers at the shoulders that extended down the sleeves. Gold chains and coloured necklaces hung round her neck and rings sparkled on her fingers. She aimed to dazzle the crowd, knowing that her place in society was precarious and her reputation unsavoury, because since she was little she'd sung and played the lute at weddings to earn her living.

Applause rang out but it was harsh and quickly over. The noise level rose. A boy of about four stayed close to the rustle of his mother's dress as she passed between the rows of women. I stared at their dresses and their faces, as they chewed gum with their mouths open, most of them still veiled. Their abayas were bundled up on their laps and it looked as if their dresses had big black stains in the middle. A fat girl, her head still covered, climbed up on the boards where Ghusun was singing and began to dance. She was followed by another, perhaps her sister; a thick gold chain bounced and jingled against her gold belt.

I supposed they were from the singer's band of dancers and musicians but I was wrong, for many more girls and women climbed up on the stage. The rhythms of their dancing, not Arab, and not a rapid European beat, but African, was mostly in the feet, with one hand held up in the air like someone calling out for help. It was as if they forgot themselves on the stage, even the thin girl who'd caught my eye because she was so thin and had such a pretty face. She'd greeted Nur warmly, talking in a low voice which trembled slightly with embarrassment, but there she was now dancing boldly to the beat. Nur chewed her gum and moved in time to the music, almost jumping up and down on the chair. For fun I said, 'You look as if you think you're dancing with them!' She leapt out of her chair and up on to the stage, the seed pearls flying around her head, her dress clinging to her. She stood out from the other dancers like a Hollywood star performing a jazz number.

I felt embarrassed suddenly, and amazed that this music and the naïve words – 'I'm in love, and I've got Indian hair' – could prompt Nur to dance with such spontaneous exuberance.

Ghusun stopped singing to announce jokingly, 'No one who's pregnant should be dancing.' One of them must have asked her, 'What if you're married?' because she went on laughingly, 'Then it's the opposite; it you're married you have to dance so you get pregnant quickly.' She moved her hands and waggled her chest in a gesture of confirmation.

Nur came back to her place and grabbed my hands and pulled me up saying, 'I'll introduce you to Ghusun. She's good fun. And you can see more from up there.' I felt ashamed of my clothes which seemed odd because they were so simple, and my flat sandals. Suddenly I was made uncomfortable by Nur's hand in mine, even though the women here rarely went about without holding hands. As Nur climbed back on the stage I hesitated for a moment despite the dozens of women already there. Nur went up and kissed Ghusun, who didn't get up but proffered a cheek and a hand to me and said with a wink, 'Are you the one from Beirut? I'll sing a song especially for you.' Then she turned to Nur as if she were finishing a story: 'Later on her poor mother shook her to wake her up for school and she was dead.' I interrupted, studying Ghusun's face: 'Who was?' 'Someone Nur knew. She choked to death in her sleep.'

I sat down next to Nur in the middle of all the others sitting there looking at me. Some of them were unveiled and stared at me, chewing gum and sipping tea. I noticed some of their expressions in particular and it seemed as if they were pleading with me. I brushed aside the thought that perhaps they knew about my relationship with Nur. They were passing a narghile round. One of them held it and took a long drag as if it was the elixir of life, and didn't let go of it until she was bending almost double where she sat. Another, older than the rest, drew on it with her eyes closed, not speaking or moving, as if it would give her back her youth. They looked pleadingly still, but as if constrained, into the faces and at the bodies of the dancers dancing to arouse.

' "Do you want to come out?"
"Just try me," I said.
"But don't be jealous," she said,
"You won't be alone."
So I said, "Forget it.
You can leave me at home." '

Ghusun sang this smiling and the women sang along with her through their teeth, resting their gum on their tongues. How could the throat and tongue sing and the ear enjoy hearing words so much at odds with reality? They were like old women trying to darn enormous holes in socks. If they really thought about what the words said they might wish the tea and chewing gum would turn to deadly poison. 'I must be wrong,' I told myself, for they looked happy, clapped enthusiastically, and one of them lifted her veil a little so she could let out a wild trill of joy and appreciation. The henna was black around the fingers of the hands that were clapping. Ghusun stood up; her body was beautiful with her taffeta dress tight across her chest, showing off the slenderness of her waist. Was she leaving? About to dance? With the air of one who has no intention of exerting herself she gave her body a little shake making her breasts quiver, smiled and approached the edge of the stage like a feather fluttering in a current of air. All at once the shouting and laughter rose to a crescendo.

Nur drew my attention to a woman in the first row of the audience. Her hair was tied up in a black kerchief and she was twisting her neck around with enormous strength, as if detaching her head from the rest of her body. The women pushed her towards the stage. I had no idea what was going on. She stood facing Ghusun and both women were trembling slightly. Ghusun couldn't detach her neck from her body in the way that the other woman could. The woman began rocking her stomach and thighs as if she were receiving something with them, then thrusting it away. Ghusun tried to twist and bend in the same way, but she couldn't. The woman facing her bent backwards until she touched the floor and her stomach and thighs began to shudder. The singer didn't try to imitate her this time, but stood there laughing. 'What are they doing?' I asked Nur in embarrassment. 'Dancing,' answered Nur. The woman had got up and stood facing the singer again. She put her right shoulder against the

singer's left, and they moved their thighs and stomachs rhyth-
mically, then paused. One of the women in the audience
rushed up and whispered in Ghusun's ear then went back to
her place. Ghusun's expression changed but she didn't stop
dancing. The woman bowed close to the singer's shoulder
then to her neck and then touched her face. The singer
backed away and the audience laughed and clapped. The
tambourines and drums played louder. The woman moved in
again, a quiet fire burning in her eyes in spite of the lack of air
and oxygen. She was tall and slim and brown-skinned with
gentle features, and her ear-rings were two broad circles of
gold which gave an added sharpness to her large ears. Her
neck was long and slender and carried on it a network of
hundreds of blue, mauve, red and flesh-coloured veins.

I turned to ask Nur who this woman was and she answered, applauding delightedly, 'She's Jaleela, the nanny of
the Sidassi girls. She raised their mother before them and
when the mother died and the father married again she stayed
in the house with the daughters. They take her with them
wherever they go and whoever invites the daughters has to
invite Jaleela first.'

Jaleela was still challenging the singer with brazen movements of her hands, her tongue and every part of her body,
leaving it to transmit its own signals. But the rhythmic nature
of her movement made it into a dance: she didn't sway or
rock her body; she ordered it or shook in response to it,
disregarding the shouting around her; her ear was centred on
the music and her other senses on the full-lipped singer.
Jaleela's eyes were in an agony of passion, her mouth a
stubborn line. She tried to touch the singer's face, to kiss her
on the lips in the midst of the clapping and laughter, the
crashing of tambourines and shouts of encouragement. But
the singer drew back, laughed, put her hand up to her mouth
and seemed to take something from between her teeth which
she held in her fingers, gesticulating to the audience. 'What's
going on? ' I asked Nur, my nerves all on edge. Nur answered

simply, 'They're doing a local dance. One of the dancers grips a ring or a gold sovereign between her teeth and the other has to pull it out with her teeth.'

As if I were Umar I asked, 'Why don't they finish off the dance then? ' 'Ghusun doesn't want to. This woman Jaleela's awful. She must be gay.'

Ghusun's voice rang out singing about beauty, beauty's eye, beauty's form. The women and girls were all dancing although Ghusun cautioned them: 'Just two at a time. Two at a time, please.' But their enthusiasm, the music and the feeling of freedom away from the house and children, and the evening which still promised surprises made them fall over one another to get to the stage and jump around in a primitive dance, more than satisfied with the occasion although it was brief compared to many local weddings and evening parties. I took no pleasure in the songs or the happy dancing atmosphere; indeed I felt angry at the joy which filled the hall, although I tried to imagine how these women felt. A quite different feeling began to creep over me until I could no longer bring my face close to Nur's or turn when she spoke to me. When the singer and the woman danced with the ring between them, one trying to pull it from between the other's teeth, I couldn't bear to meet her eyes, or brush against her sleeve inadvertently, or hear the sound of her voice.

I was weary of the smell of chewing gum and incense, and their shouted conversations to one another from different parts of the hall. Their applause, even their dancing, seemed unacceptable; the music and the songs about love and imaginary love affairs had no connection with these dresses, these perfumes; their emotions that night were out of keeping with their veils. They were six hundred women, their ages ranging from the twenties to the forties, who knew that they were prisoners even in this hall because they couldn't leave it until their drivers or their husbands came to pick them up.

What did the night have to offer beyond the recalling of familiar tunes and the two women's dance? And I knew this was why Nur asked me if I'd go back home with her even just for an hour. My anger, which had died down of its own accord, flared up again at this and I didn't answer her. I was suddenly gripped again by the feeling I'd had when Nur had come into my bedroom and sprawled on my bed, as if the objects around the place which belonged to Umar and Basem had begun to grow sad reproachful eyes. With each day that passed the relationship appeared more furtive and unwholesome because it was inconceivable that it should either go away or be exposed. I began to fight against myself, as if there were two distinct parts of me. Every time Basem made love to me I clung to him trying to drive out Nur's image, angry at my sense of shame in the face of Basem's tenderness. Afterwards I would stand under the shower, and clutch my head in my hands and say out loud that what was happening to me wasn't real, that I wasn't real, my breathing, my head, my voice, my son himself were all illusions.

I found myself getting increasingly impatient as Nur spoke to me like a lover, then moved on to the details of her day, telling me what she was wearing then, what she was doing, who was at her house, what she was going to eat, using pet names and endearments that I wasn't accustomed to hearing even between a man and a woman. Only Nur's desert accent which I loved to hear stopped me making fun of her. I knew that my need to meet her, no longer to exchange conversation or to complain to each other or have fun, was aroused by the thought of one specific aspect, and our muscular spasms increased in intensity whenever circumstances threatened to intervene to impede our activity: a visitor, Nur's mother, Nur's daughter. Every time I stood up, straightening my skirt, I felt a surge of anger and vowed not to see Nur again, and forced my brain to recall the image of a gay bar in Berlin which I'd gone to out of curiosity with Basem and a group of friends.

I sat where I was like a cat watching a mouse, waiting for the right moment to pounce. I thought of the atmosphere in my house; there was a feeling of the past, a sense of order and stability emanating from the furniture, from Basem's talk and from Umar's shouting and laughter; he'd be asleep now between his Superman sheets. Anxiously, Nur asked again, 'Are you coming to my place for an hour?'

I drew back, took a hold on myself, and dared no more than a shake of the head. I decided to get up from my seat, go home and never see Nur again. I understood that it was the dance of the two women and the excitement accompanying each of their movements which lay behind Nur's invitation to me on this occasion. But still I marched off past rows of women to the door of the hall. I turned to look back and saw them dancing under the fluorescent lights as if they were drugged. Outside there was a dust storm, and dozens of men stood at the entrance waiting, appearing to be guarding the women inside.

I saw Basem waiting with Said in the car. He spoke first: 'You're late. I was worried about you. Said told me they might not allow women to go home alone with their chauffeurs at night. Tell me, how did you enjoy yourself? ' I smiled and replied, 'It was great.'

In my mind's eye drifted images of Ghusun, and the lust-crazed old woman urging the girls to dance, pulling them up on to the floor, embracing them and clasping them to her. She sat with desire in her eyes, which descended to her tongue as she complimented the women on their beauty and said other more obscure things in short, jabbing phrases.

7

The canary hadn't sung since a female companion entered his life. She'd bewitched him while he was showing her the secrets of the house. Whenever he smelt the rice and came to the table as usual to peck a grain or two, or flew and landed on my shoulder, she called him to her. She had taken possession of his throat and he no longer sang or made a sound except when she was lost somewhere in the house and called out for help. Then, turning his little head from side to side, he would tell her that he was coming and fly through the rooms searching for her. When they were both in the cage at night he twittered lovingly to her with a sincerity which was plain to see, and touched her beak with his own. I'd realized that he needed a female when he stained his mirror perching and looking in it constantly, bending his head to peck at his reflection and singing loudly. When this female came into his life in flesh and blood he no longer sang of his loneliness and longing.

I stretched my hand inside the cage, trying to get him to hop on to my finger, then on to my shoulder as he usually did. This made the female more scared then ever and her anxious twitterings rose to a shrill cry. When he wouldn't come to me I banged the cage door shut, then smiled bitterly and sang to him:

'I had a little bird
So charming and fine
He woke early, before me
And warbled and sang
And hopped gaily about
And bathed his bright feathers.
But then he got married
And like a balloon

He began to deflate.
O, little bird
O, my canary.'

The garden-door bell rang. I wondered who it was who
didn't know how to open it. It was Kawkab, Nur's mother.
My heart beat fast. I tried to keep my voice normal and asked
how Nur was and why she hadn't come too, as if the mother
knew what was between us. She pulled off her dusty abaya
and rolled it up in her lap, then swivelled her eyes around,
looking piercingly from above her face veil. 'It's nice here.
Did you get the material from Lebanon?' She gestured with
her hand to the curtains then waved towards the sofa.
  She didn't wait for a reply and asked about the bearskin on
the floor: 'What's that?' Then she added, fanning her face
with her hand, 'It's hot. What did you say it was called? A
bear. And you didn't get rid of its head? Look at its mouth
and its tongue hanging out, all ready to eat someone. God
forbid!' I didn't like the bear; Basem had come home with it
one day, and because Umar was so attached to it I'd grown
used to it. I hated Kawkab, hated her face, even though it was
withered with tiredness and the harshness of her life. Suddenly she embarked on the subject which she'd come to
discuss. Putting on a sympathetic voice, she said, 'Nur's not
very well.' I hated the look of her face still more. 'She's like a
stick of incense. She's coughing her lungs up. Yesterday I fed
her a kilo of bananas but her cough's still bothering her and
her chest hurts. You and Nur are sisters, best friends, and yet
you don't come and see her any more.' Her tone changed and
scolding now she said harshly, 'She told me that you're
heartless. You leave the phone off the hook and when she
comes to see you, you don't open the door to her. And your
driver tells lies and says you're not in. You ought to be
ashamed! Ashamed!'
  I looked down at my fingers, trying to stop myself shaking.
I hadn't known that I could be so weak. I excused myself and

went into the kitchen and rested my head against the fridge for a few seconds. I clasped my hands round my neck and pressed. When it started to hurt I stopped and opened the fridge and took out a jug, fetched two glasses and put them on a tray. How I didn't drop them I don't know; my hands were trembling and I walked slowly, my eyes on the tray, pretending that I was concentrating on balancing the glasses: two empty glasses, since I'd left the jug in the kitchen. I smiled at Nur's mother: 'How stupid of me. I've forgotten the lemonade.' I came back with the jug and poured some lemonade nervously into her glass. She raised her veil and swallowed it in one go and put down the empty glass, then said as if rounding off the conversation or replying to a question, 'No, daughter, it won't do. A child's soul is precious to its mother's heart. You're a mother, you should know. Come and see Nur and you can talk to each other and make it up.' As if I didn't want her to hear me, I mumbled, 'I'll try and come this afternoon.'

Nur's mother stood up, laid her hand on mine and baring her yellow teeth attempted a lighter note: 'Come on. Come back with me now for a few minutes. Let me see you telling each other off and making up.' And she pressed my hand and squeezed my fingers tightly.

In spite of her show of affection I could only feel repelled by her. Still, I went with her to the door, opened it and went out with her. I didn't even take my purse and walked with one hand tightly clasping the other. My annoyance had turned into sadness and I wanted to cry. As I entered Nur's sitting-room I realized that we'd made the journey there at high speed; Nur's mother hadn't spoken to me on the way, as if she felt no need to cajole me any longer.

It was ten days or more since I'd been in that house, two days after Ghusun's concert. That day I'd woken up in the early afternoon, morose and discontented. I'd phoned Suzanne, Tamr and Ingrid, but none of them was at home. It was Nur's daughter's birthday party and I'd already decided

not to send Umar. I'd promised myself that I'd read or iron
my blouse, wash a dress, tidy my room, make a puppet, clean
the birdcage, write some letters, repair a broken shell necklace, make a jelly, but I did none of these thngs; I got dressed
and decided to go to Sitt Wafa, the Arabic teacher, but when I
went out Said wasn't around.

I felt irritated with him, then I remembered that I'd finally
given him permission to go to the mosque for the afternoon
prayer. In the past I'd forbidden him because he stayed away
for so long and he'd always given me the same answer: 'It's
the company, Auntie. Every day somebody from home turns
up and the news is fresh, fresh.' He didn't like praying in his
room and for a week he wouldn't speak to me. Then one day
I heard a sharp cry from the garden and when I rushed out I
found him there weeping and he said to me, 'A snake, Auntie;
it was huge. It saw me doing my ablutions and shot out its
tongue to bite me but it knew I was getting ready to pray and
it was afraid.' He realized that this trick hadn't worked so a
bit later he came crying again and said that the sheikh of the
mosque had seen him and threatened him and said, 'You
heathen! You don't come to the mosque any more. Have you
stopped praying?'

I went back into the house and was thinking about taking
off my old nail varnish and putting on some new, when the
phone rang. It was Nur, reminding me about Ghada's party
and saying, 'Everyone's waiting for Umar.' Trying to sound
normal, I said, 'Umar's at Sitt Wafa's and Said's not here,'
but as usual Nur insisted on sending her car. When she'd
hung up I looked around for a present to take and saw the
female canary at the door of the cage, frightened to come out
and fly. I shut the door on her and picked up the cage,
annoyed with myself that I hadn't thought of getting rid of
her before now.

The party was for the mothers as well, and they sat talking
and eating while the children played between the sitting-
room and the garden, chasing the dogs and the gazelles.

When it was over I stood up, reassured and happy because Nur too seemed to have decided that our relationship should become an ordinary friendship; even my initial embarrassment had disappeared within moments of entering. But now Nur clasped my hand and gulped, 'It's still early.' I answered her untruthfully, 'No, really. Basem's coming home early today.' But Umar protested, drumming his feet on the floor, which gave Nur the opportunity to interrupt and say ingratiatingly, 'Would you like to sleep at our house, Umar, and play with the gazelles?' He was silent, gathering himself up to answer, then said, 'Me and mama.' Feeling as if my breathing was being constricted, I said sharply, 'No, darling. Come on. Baba'll be all by himself in the house.'

Umar ran off after one of the gazelles while Nur said beseechingly, 'Me and Umar agree. Please, Suha, stay with me for the night. I'm scared and fed up.' But I walked towards the door, feeling my patience running out. 'That's enough of this rubbish, Nur. I can't possibly stay with you for the night. Grow up! You've got a child and so have I. And I love my husband and you love yours.' I didn't regret bringing our husbands into the conversation but Nur sprang over to the door and stood barring the way with a stubborn expression on her face. I went over and pulled back the curtain and then tried the other door but it was locked. I thought of Umar. What if he wanted to come in and couldn't or if he saw me through the glass door and called to me and I stood there without moving, unable to answer him or open the door?

I looked around me and my eyes rested on the telephone; I pleaded with it to ring. Suddenly I said, 'Now I understand why Saleh left you. You're spoilt and thoughtless.' Nur didn't answer me, but continued to brace herself against the door with all the strength she possessed. Her great house had dwindled to nothing and it was as if her life was all concentrated in that door. She said, 'I don't understand. You're the one I want and yet you behave so coldly. I'm ready to live with you and leave Saleh and my family for you, and you're even worried that the dogs and the gazelles might come in and see us! I really don't understand your nature. If somebody loves you, you run away from them and torture yourself about it . . . '

Things didn't go as I'd planned. Nur fought and protested, but she was like a moth that knows it will get burnt if it comes too close to the lamp. When I reached home after flatly refusing to spend the night with her, I don't know how I got into the house or what I said to Basem or how I looked as I sat waiting. I knew that she would chase me. The phone rang: Nur was crying, saying she was sorry, asking me to forgive her. Afraid that Basem might notice, I said quickly, 'I'll talk to you tomorrow.' A few seconds later she phoned again and I repeated, 'Tomorrow', put the receiver down and unplugged the telephone, to Basem's astonishment. 'Nur's bored, and she's too demanding,' I said carelessly. 'More bored than you?' asked Basem teasingly. 'I don't believe it. And anyway you always have friends who are bored and discontented.'

I stared at my reflection in the mirror and thought, is this really happening to me with a woman? I'd asked myself this question hundreds of times and rediscovered each time that this experience with Nur was deeply shocking to me.

Next day I couldn't see Nur anywhere. Her mother took me by the hand and opened the door of Nur's bedroom, saying, 'Come along, my daughter. Human beings shouldn't abandon one another.' She turned away and then I saw Nur lying full length on the bed. I'd promised myself that I would talk calmly and settle the matter once and for all, and this was what I wanted to do, but instead I shouted, 'So, Nur? You sent your mother, did you?' I knew as soon as I heard myself speak that I'd made a mistake. I'd imagined handling Nur in a completely different way so that we'd be like two friends exchanging confidences and I'd say that Basem had found out about us and threatened to divorce me and take

Umar away from me. But all I could do was say with a sort of malicious delight, 'So, Nur? You sent your mother after me, did you?'

Nur's scream reverberated around the room and made the dust rise from the curtains. Kawkab suddenly reappeared, her eyes transformed into black stones with sparks flying from them; because the rest of her face was covered by a face veil all her anger shot out of her eyes. 'Be patient, my daughter,' she said, lifting Nur's hair off her neck and face to soothe her. 'Be patient. I want to talk to this . . . this woman without a conscience, and find out what's going on in her mind.' What was she talking about? She walked up to me, her eyes ablaze, and shouted, 'Only God Almighty can make my daughter suffer!' Nur shouted at her mother who paid no attention and continued to blaze with anger. She thrust her face right up next to mine and said, 'If anyone harms as much as a fingernail of Nur's, I'll brand her until there's no light left in her eyes.' Then she dragged me out of the room by the arm, although Nur shouted at her and jumped up off the bed and caught hold of her mother's hand. Nur and her mother are vampires, I thought, and I'm their prey. I've got to escape fast. Her mother pushed Nur back inside her room, banged the door shut, and finished, 'Now d'you realize what Nur means to me? So one word from me to Saleh, and you and your husband and family are out. Deported.'

Was it possible? What would happen to Basem? But instead of crying or shouting back at her, I thought she doesn't know what's between me and her daughter. I found courage again and as if they were the only words I knew how to speak I said calmly and slowly, trying to control a trembling in my voice, 'What Nur and I do together is forbidden. We have an illicit relationship.'

The mother cleared her throat and moved her fiery eyes off me for a moment and I thought, quickly now I can get out of the door and forget this house, tear it out of my memory, whatever it takes. I'd actually gone a few steps when I heard a small noise behind me; it was the woman's dress trailing along the floor and when she grabbed my hand I screamed, frightened by the suddenness of the movement. Leaning forward she whispered almost in my ear, 'That's wrong, my daughter. Wrong. But adultery with a man is worse. And you know what things are like between Nur and her husband.' I didn't tell her that I didn't know him, nor did I say, 'Who is this man who can manage to live with your daughter?' I just wanted to get out of the door, and out of the country. The woman reached a hand into her bosom and took out a small cloth bag. Horrified, I thought she was about to try and drug me or poison me but she took out an English gold pound and pressed it into my hand.

The gold between my fingers made my heart race again until it hurt me. The feel of it seemed to bring me to an abrupt decision: I could only resolve the situation by talking to Nur. Going on talking to her mother was like banging my head against a brick wall: she was a creature from another world.

I went back in to Nur and let the gold coin clatter on to the table. She was turned to the wall. 'A gold pound from your mother,' I said, looking into her face, hating it. I let my eyes roam around the room trying not to look at Nur again, trying to ignore her presence and focus my thoughts far away from there for a few moments. I had to get away, to imagine myself in an aeroplane, and ignore Nur's sobs and the smell of food and the bed with studs on either side and the shaded lamps and the curtains drawn to blot out the existence of what lay behind. I remembered the first time I'd come to Nur's house, and the time that Nur had thrown herself on me and held me to her. I saw myself exchanging the impossible with her. It was as if it had happened, but to somebody else, and hadn't left its mark on me. But I cried because what was happening now wasn't what I'd wanted to happen nor what I'd promised myself would happen; because Nur was crying and we ought to have been rushing off together on a wild ride like before; and because it was impossible to get out of this house.

Only this time, like a singer with a beautiful voice who can't help bursting into song, or like a bee compelled to plunge its head into a flower, I stood up and it was as if all the power in the world was spreading along my veins and arriving in my brain. I could do nothing to control it; I just knew how lucky I was because I would never live in this house, and I wasn't lonely and didn't suffer from emotional impoverishment, and because I knew what I wanted and I was about to go through the door and out of the house and garden and I would never see them again even if every hair of my head was pulled out one by one and they tried to drag me back in by force. I saw the mother sitting on the floor; she was leaning back against the sofa, which was covered in material patterned with lemons and strawberries, and she beckoned to me to come over to her. But I walked on like a sleepwalker, a big smile on my lips, past her, out of the door, through the garden and into the fresh air.

I entered my house like a whirlwind. I didn't let Umar watch the end of his TV programme. 'Into the bathroom this minute,' I shouted, rushing ahead of him to wash my face. I piled my hair up under a plastic shower cap, undressed, and finding the hooks on the back of the door empty, I bent and took a shirt of my husband's out of the clothes basket, smelt it, threw it back in the basket, looked around me, then picked it out again and put it on. I turned on the showed and the water came out looking murky. I exclaimed in disgust, 'Ouf! They say the sea water's been desalinated and look at it, it's still sandy!' When the water was warm I called Umar at the top of my voice, and called again. He ambled along and took off his clothes holding on to the door handle, then got into the bath. He approached the spray of water from the shower then backed away again. 'What? Is it too hot or too cold?' I asked irritably. He said, 'From here it seems cold. When I get used to it, it's nice,' and stayed where he was. Again I asked irritably, 'And when are you going to get used to it? Next year?' And again he tried to stand under it, keeping at a distance until I took his hand and pulled him right under. When I started rubbing his hair he wriggled about and said, 'The shampoo's stinging my eyes.'

'This is Johnson's Baby Shampoo. It doesn't sting.' He didn't stop fidgeting and moving away from under my hand, until I slapped his hand hard. Then he realized I wasn't playing, and even when the water got hotter he just said quietly, 'This water's getting really hot,' and squirmed. I dried him quickly and knew that I was rubbing him too hard. Handing him his underwear and pyjamas, I said, 'Put them on in your room, darling. I want to have a bath.' Then I unhooked the shower and washed away the few remaining traces of soap, hung it up again and filled the bath. I threw Basem's shirt back in the dirty clothes basket and stood close to the mirror, examining my face. I was struck by the way it hadn't changed; my turbulent emotions, my confusion, my resolve didn't show on it. I felt happier at the thought that Umar hadn't seen a different face. The water gradually covered me. It was very hot but I withstood the temptation to add some cold to it and lay there sweating. This seemed to strengthen my resolve and I said to myself, 'That's it. I'm leaving this country, whatever happens. I'm no better off than the people still living in Lebanon.'

I would let Basem know of my decision, which I felt was irrevocable. I pictured him coming home from the office, tired and hungry. He'd ask me the reason and I didn't know what I should reply, even though the reasons were flying around in the air, indoors and out, evident and tangible. I was like a prisoner who couldn't give convincing reasons why he should be released.

'I can't tell myself this is just an experience which I have to go through. I'm an Arab. I'm supposed to feel that I have some connection with the culture here, but I feel none at all. I'm completely detached from it. I'm getting older. I'm wasting my time.'

My words were unconvincing. They were words that the

heroine had learnt by heart. I tried again: 'Let me go. I want to live a normal life. I want to walk about, not go in the car all the time, and I want to dress how I like. Yes, I've got a small mind. I don't want to feel afraid when I send a film to be developed if my arms aren't covered in the photos. I don't have any reasons. I can't tell any more lies. I don't want to be afraid. I don't want to tell lies.'

I was overflowing with emotion. I felt as if I was trembling and I lifted my hand up out of the water then let it sink back in. I didn't want him to say, 'It's just one of these fits you have every now and then. It'll pass like it always does then you'll calm down again.' I had to convince him that this time I was serious and there was no room for discussion.

I wavered before Basem, who was sitting with his papers from work spread out in front of him, his pipe cupped in his fingers and traces of sweat on his shirt. Life seemed normal and ordinary and my decision irrelevant. But because of the tone of voice I used and my general coldness I made it sound firm.

Knowing the answer in advance, I said, 'You mean you wouldn't think of leaving and going back with me?'

He interrupted me, stuffing tobacco into his pipe: 'Me? Now? You're mad! Not for at least two years.'

I sat in front of him mentally blocking my ears so that his words wouldn't get through to me. It was as if I'd smeared my body in anaesthetizing fluid to deaden my senses, although I hardly needed anaesthetizing: for months now I'd been getting gradually more impervious to external stimuli. He said, 'You haven't got enough to do, that's the trouble. Go and look for some kind of work again and do it at home.'

'I swear, I've never been properly employed here,' I burst out vehemently. 'I was just killing time.' Suddenly I felt angry and depressed and I shouted, 'Do you think my job in the supermarket was a real job? Or my teaching at the Institute? A woman who'd only been to primary school could have taught there.'

This outburst seemed to give me some comfort. Things appeared to be straightforward. I found myself staring at him as he fiddled with his pipe, and I sensed his uneasiness. All of a sudden I wasn't interested in hearing what he had to say. I began to remember the day he and I had decided to get married.

We were in the terrace café of a Beirut hotel. All the other tables were empty even though the sea was only a few metres away. We'd never thought of coming to this café before but that day we'd met early to apply for British visas so that we could go to Wimbledon, and they'd told us to come back for our passports in two hours.

The ice creams were melting although the heat was pleasant. I looked at the rust on the metal canopy, the potted plants on the tables. 'Maybe this is the first time anybody's sat here,' I said.

Basem replied abstractedly, 'Did you notice the questions in the embassy? What's your relationship to each other? Are you engaged? It must have been to find out if we were fedayeen, or perhaps just because we were a young man and a young woman travelling together. Of course he would have been surprised. He wasn't a European.'

Embarrassed, I remarked, 'Even Mata Hari and Philby wouldn't have been interrogated in so much depth. But it's good we convinced him and he's going to give us visas.'

Basem spoke first: 'Let's get married in London.'

I was taken aback. Although we'd spoken of it before, the sudden mention of marriage now confused me. The beating of my heart seemed to take over my whole body, but I said lightly, 'Why the sudden decision?'

'Because I love you,' he said, taking hold of my hand.

I wanted a house of my own. I would go back to it, open the fridge, take out a bottle of beer, listen to music turned up as loud as I wanted, sit alone or talk with friends in an atmosphere which would be quite different from my parents' house, although that was comfortable enough: people couldn't help relaxing in the atmosphere created by my mother. They all loved visiting our house, eating there and spending the evening with us. The food was always delicious, the drink flowed liberally, and my mother was a talker; she wanted to be the focal point of any gathering and without meaning to, she was always waiting for approval: of the food, the furniture, the pistachio nuts, or of her hairstyle, her lipstick, her outfit, her high heels, the way she'd preserved her youth and had so few wrinkles in spite of her fifty years; then of her liveliness, her original conversation, and the way she kept up with politics and world affairs.

I went on sitting in front of Basem, deliberately blocking off all the ways into my mind and heart. He sat with his head in his hands. I asked him if he was hungry. He raised his head and said, 'Does that mean you care about me?' I didn't answer and decided that I wouldn't enter into any more discussion with him and that it would be better if I left the room. As I stood up he said, 'What about Umar's school? Or doesn't that make any difference to you either?' I answered, 'I'll wait till his term's finished, of course.' When he sensed my stubbornness he played his last card: 'I'm sure you'll change your mind after one week there. Life with your mother isn't easy; you'll probably quarrel with each other the day after you arrive. And I'm not prepared to come back with you to sort out the house or buy a flat at the moment. And renting's impossible . . .' I shrugged my shoulders and said, 'Too bad. I'll have to put up with it for now.'

It seemed the canary sensed my determination to leave. He dropped the piece of biscuit which he was pecking at and flew on to my shoulder.

Tamr

1

I sat in the car alone, queen of all I surveyed, and breathed deeply, inhaling the air through my nose and into my lungs; although my face was swathed in black I looked at the other cars out of the corner of my eye. Riding in a car was no longer a wish or a dream: I was bowling along the streets at great speed and rejoicing; I hadn't reckoned on the distances being so short and all the places so close. I thought, now I can do anything I want.

When I'd first caught sight of the gleam of the car, which was waiting for me at the battered wooden door, my heart beat faster, and I felt the same as when I had a sudden vision of a luscious fruit or cold water on a hot day.

Now I was passing tall buildings with glass fronts and others with façades of marble and gleaming tiles; handsome villas surrounded by trees; foreign restaurants – Filipino, Korean, Sri Lankan, Indian, Pakistani, Yemeni and Lebanese; numerous little plots of green grass and half-finished hotels and apartment buildings.

I shook my head, muttering to myself in admiration, 'It's what God has willed,' although I knew I'd never enter them. Once I'd been on the point of entering the white hotel: I'd bought tickets for a fashion show for me and Batul but it was prohibited. Anyhow all that kind of thing was for men, and for foreigners, who lived a different life. I saw a high wall with patterned tiles. Two marble columns framed the gateway, inlaid with fragments of copper and crowned with copper urns. Said must have heard me gasp. 'That's a new mansion,' he said. The wall stretched away endlessly in front of my eyes. Perhaps this was the place which the Institute had thought of for the Heritage Revival Festival. The woman director had exhorted us to go back to eating local dishes in the open under palm trees, preparing them in big cooking pots over open coal and wood fires in the bedouin manner. The message was clear: we should return to the food of the people, rely on the produce of the area, stop imitating foreigners and be proud of our desert land. I reached out to touch the car's blue upholstery and found myself thinking with faint sadness how it was this which had stood for a long time between me and so many things: shopping, flying visits, celebrating when a relation or friend had a baby, sharing in the sorrow when someone died. The car made me think about the constant apprehensive planning required to gain access to it. It wasn't there for the taking, and was bound up with long waiting, standing firm in the face of despair until either my aunt visited us or my brother Rashid was in the mood to take us on a short excursion. Days here passed like months or years except when there were wedding celebrations and for these I was allowed to stay up till dawn, and they were the only times I felt free.

The car was one of the reasons why at first I hadn't been allowed to go to the Institute to learn how to read and write. The roar Rashid let out when my aunt tried to persuade him to let me go there is still ringing in my ears: 'I didn't like the idea of your going to London in the first place. I know you. You're a rebel. All your life you've played with boys. You ran away from Ibrahim, and you told me that the sheikh got so drunk he divorced you. And now you're asking me to hire a car for you and Batul so that you can go off to weddings unchaperoned with any driver you can find.' My aunt interrupted him: 'I don't know what she's done wrong. The sheikh divorced her after a month of marriage and married someone older, who wasn't as beautiful as Tamr and didn't come from such a good family.' Quickly I replied, 'Really, I'm quite happy. If the sheikh hadn't divorced me, I'd have divorced him. I'm happy now.'

Rashid was silent. Then he spoke again: 'No, Aunt. I have boundless affection for you, and Tamr won't interfere with it. But who gave her a roof over her head and supported her and her son? And who snatched Muhammad away from his father? It was me, no one else. No, Aunt. Tamr's not going to the Institute. I swear that it doesn't bother me having her to live with me. But she must think of her future.'

I went off into my room crying. After a bit I got up off the bed, wiped my eyes and went back to my aunt and Rashid. Struggling to control my voice and slow down my breathing I said: 'What's wrong with me going to study? The Anaiz girls, the Mabruk girls, all of them go, even the old women. And Qumasha and Mawda. Rashid paused on his way out and replied, 'You're not going. I haven't time to take you there anyway. And you're not going in their cars. You'd do better to think about getting married.'

'I'm not marrying for a third time!' I looked first at my aunt, who was sitting with her head bent and her hand resting on her crippled leg, then at my mother who had her hand up to her mouth. I rose and went to bed, but I didn't sleep at all that night. So transport was the problem? He could take me then; he'd occasionally given us lifts when Batul had asked him to. Perhaps Batul would have to enrol at the Institute, but what was to be done about her five children?

The next morning I measured out rice from the sack, picked it over, and cooked it along with the broth, the meat and the vegetables, then had a bath and put on my dress, and my abaya and veil. My throat muscles tightened as they did whenever I rebelled and did what I wanted to do. As I shut the door behind me I called out, 'The food's ready and I'm off to the Institute.' I walked along determinedly in my thick abaya, my throat growing tighter and my palms sweating. Only once I looked back towards the house and saw that its iron door was closed. I didn't notice the heat, or my sweat, or the distance. Instead I concentrated on the obstacles in my path which forced me to cross from one side of the street to the other — heaps of stone and steel beams and mounds of sand left lying about the streets. I couldn't see the Institute building, but it didn't matter. I heard a car horn and stopped myself turning round, drawing my abaya more closely round me and wrapping the black head cover twice round my face. A car horn, and Rashid's voice calling to me. I turned then; he'd opened the back door for me. I stood where I was for a moment but my thoughts were a jumble. I climbed into the back seat and Rashid didn't speak the entire way home. Gradually my throat muscles relaxed, and as I sat in silence I decided to go on hunger strike. When my mother and Batul pleaded with me for the sake of my son Muhammad, I agreed to drink a little tea without sugar, but I ate nothing for three days.

On the fourth day I felt weak and tired. As I lay in bed, I heard my mother saying, 'Are the Institute and books worth getting yourself in this state for?' Batul persuaded Rashid to come in and see me just before the evening prayer and I was confident that my fast must soon be over. In a voice which sounded as if he was making an effort to be kind he said, 'What are you doing to yourself, Tamr?' 'I want to go to the Institute and get educated,' I answered tearfully. His reply was quite unexpected, and I didn't believe it until he repeated it: 'You're not going to the Institute.' 'Then I won't eat,' I said firmly. He went out of the room and I thought I heard him saying, 'As you wish.' I no longer thought about anything. From time to time I opened my eyes. I could hear my mother crying, Batul screaming, and I seemed to see my mother striking her face with the palms of her hands. Batul's children kept asking questions and one of her daughters said, 'Auntie Tamr's going to die!'

Batul appeared annoyed at the strength of my resistance. She came in and made me sit up and tried to force a piece of apple between my teeth without success. I needed all my strength to move my face away and I began turning my head rapidly from one side to the other. My mother eased me back on to the pillow and laid her hand on my forehead reciting prayers. Raised voices echoed off the walls and ceilings.

Batul's voice called out, 'Listen to me, Rashid. I swear to God you won't come near me and you're not my lawful husband unless you personally take Tamr to the Institute. Can you hear me, everybody?' My mother walked around with the incense burner in her hand, wailing and crying. She came towards my bed: 'Batul and your brother are fighting and who knows, they might divorce, all because you won't give up the idea of the Institute. Those English have had an effect on you. They must have put a spell on you and poisoned your mind. Tamr, my daughter, get up and ask God's pardon. Batul and your brother are going to get a divorce.'

My muscles went limp and I no longer seemed to have any interest in what the voices were saying. Batul and my mother came to sit me up, so that I'd be able to face in the right direction and say my prayers, but I couldn't. They stayed with me all night long, pleading with me in the name of the Almighty, kissing me then screaming at me, trying to force my jaws open. They managed to get a spoon in but half the soup dribbled down my chin and on to my neck. I shouted at them but my voice came out strangely weak: 'If anybody makes me eat I'll never forgive them and God won't either.' Batul shouted back, 'My God, you don't love anyone except yourself. I thought you and I were like sisters.'

I opened my eyes and I was frightened. The room was in silence. They must have all wearied of trying to convince me. I don't know how much time had gone by but suddenly Batul rushed in kissing me and crying 'Congratulations,' followed by my mother who was trilling for joy and singing, 'O Tamr, O Tamr, you're going to the Institute by car and you'll come back reading and writing.' I was tired, but even so I struggled into a sitting position, propping myself up with pillows. I opened my mouth to eat without the faintest desire, as if I'd lost my taste for food. Batul reported to me that Rashid had begun to sleep in the sitting-room, took no notice of her, and had stopped speaking to her. Her annoyance had prompted her to march into the sitting-room full of men that afternoon and fling herself at his feet kissing them and weeping. 'Forgive your sister, Rashid; God is forgiving. Knowledge is light. Fatima the Prophet's daughter could express herself eloquently and read and write.'

Rashid had been deeply discomfited. His face became the colour of blood. There and then he found the courage to agree. Everyone in the room knew about his refusal and his sister's fast. In front of them all Batul had knelt at his feet and invoked the Prophet's daughter. He raised her face from his feet and said, 'Be happy, Umm Ashraf. You can tell my sister to stop fasting.'

I said good morning to Said as I climbed confidently into the car, and thank you when I got out. I stood pressing Suha's doorbell with a smile on my face, marvelling at her ideas, as I looked at the ancient door which she'd bought from the herdswoman living nearby; in its place she'd had an iron door installed for the woman. Whenever I went into Suha's house, I felt as if I were boarding a plane and flying away, a similar feeling to the one I'd had the day I went to the Institute and met Suha for the first time.

Inside and out, the Institute building was the same as the other houses round about. High walls surrounded it and its garden was no more than a clearing of sand. The women teaching there made me feel as if I was abroad: they seemed to have no connection with the buildings, or the sign on its door – Gulf Institute for Women and Girls – or the brightly-patterned couches in the sitting-room, and the pictures on the walls torn from books and tourist brochures.

I sat at a table near some old women wearing face veils, and younger women, some of whom had left their headwraps on but bundled their abayas up in their laps.

I was astonished to find that there existed in my country women like the women in London and Lebanon and Egypt, the kind of women I'd seen on videos. Even Mary, my English neighbour, wasn't like that; in fact I'd never seen her in anything but a full length caftan.

I didn't hear a single word of the lesson. I was looking at the teacher Suha so intently that I was staring into her face, at her hair, her clothes, her shoes and her hands. I thought about where she was living and couldn't imagine that a woman like her would be able to go about the streets in her tight-waisted, low-cut dress, wearing that broad gold belt, long purple ear-rings and purple shoes with open toes which revealed her long toenails painted purple. And the hair. I couldn't find words to describe its colour and style: it fell in tousled disarray over her forehead and ears and neck.

During the break I saw the other teachers. They weren't beautiful like Suha. I thought about them too: where do they live? How do they live? Do they walk about the streets? Do they go down to the shops? What are their houses like? Are they like my neighbour Mary's house, ordinary, except for the electric mixer and the tumble dryer? Do they have children? Where do their children play – out among the sand and stones? Even the young girls from the desert were different under their abayas: they'd taken trouble over their hairstyles, their dresses didn't hang down to the floor, and they greeted one another with one kiss on each cheek, not with a third in the customary way.

I went back home and told my mother and Batul what I'd seen at the Institute. My mother clasped her hands together and insisted that I take her with me the next day to see the teacher Suha and the others, especially the American who went around smoking a cigarette in a holder. I laughed and held out my hands: 'No. No, no. I'd be too embarrassed.'

I was scared of the remarks my mother would make and the stories she'd tell. I went into my room and stuck my tongue out in the mirror, examining it closely to see if one of the arteries in it had contracted and that was why it was so difficult for me to speak English; or was it just that English didn't go with a woman who wore an abaya and whose hair reeked of incense?

Every evening I waited for the television to become silent, the children's crying to die down, waited till the door to the garden was shut and the black sheep had stopped bleating, till the women visitors had left and the relations set off back to their homes. Even when I'd excused myself someone would always follow me to my room, jokingly pulling the books away from me, or Batul or my mother would come in with almost the same phrase, the same sigh, on their lips: 'It's not right, Tamr. Really it's not.' When my aunt came to visit us she called to me all the time to come and squat at her side and entertain her.

After some weeks my relations with Suha went beyond those of a teacher and student. She invited me to her house and I made excuses several times before I was frank with her and said that Rashid would lay down the condition that she must visit us first. Suha was delighted and said that she'd rarely been invited into the local people's houses and had always wanted to see them. The first time she came, I was glad to have the chance to ride in the back of the car next to her but I felt embarrassed to see my teacher chatting uninhibitedly with the Yemini driver.

I kissed Suha on both cheeks as usual and asked her if we could sit in the garden. I noticed boxes and cases against the wall but it didn't occur to me to ask who was going away because her house was always changing its appearance and she was always receiving things from abroad. 'In this heat?' she expostulated. 'We can sit on the green grass,' I smiled. 'D'you call that grass, and green?' she asked in a disgruntled way. 'Even though the wind and sand have left nothing, green or otherwise?' But she stood up and handed me a glass of tea and went ahead of me into the garden carrying a glass for herself, and we sat down. Suha's eyes roamed over her garden and she remarked that she could see nothing in it that she wouldn't be able to see on the other side of the garden wall, but I sat benevolently studying the tomato plant with the green fruit hanging from it, the water in the round plastic basin and the mauve and white bougainvillea on the wall. I didn't like the scented tea she served but I sipped it all the same. I preferred it well stewed, and Suha had added a Lipton's tea bag to my glass and left it until the tea became a deep brown colour. I sipped my tea feeling thoroughly happy. I loved foreigners' houses. They were new and spacious. I began as usual to recount my problems with my brother and the bank, not noticing the listless expression on Suha's face nor her distracted manner, until she interrupted me: 'Did you get the paper from the sheikh?' 'Tomorrow,' I replied excitedly. Our eyes met and we both began to laugh, remembering the day not long before when I'd asked to borrow Said and the car and she'd immediately begged to be allowed to come too. 'I'd love you to,' I'd replied, and she'd looked as blissfully happy as if I'd opened the door of Paradise to her. I was amazed because I hadn't come across a person who asked permission like this before. Whenever we had the chance to leave the house we swarmed out like locusts, big and little, young and old. In the car she never stopped asking me if I was upset and if I felt any shame or anxiety. 'Why should I?' I asked. 'Why?' she shouted back in surprise, 'When you're on your way to ask your ex-husband for a divorce certificate after fifteen years?'

I laughed: 'What about it?' I replied. I started to remember the way to the big house; it was the largest one in our area. A sentence escaped from my lips: 'I hope the garden'll be like it was before, Suha. It had an oleander and a prickly pear and yellow roses.'

Suha slapped my hand lightly: 'You're impossible, Tamr. Thinking of the garden at a time like this!'

I began giving directions to Said and we ended up in a dead end street. 'Obviously you've forgotten the way,' Suha remarked laughing.

I looked all around me. 'I don't know what they've done with the road, sister. It's higher, lower, bigger, as far as I can see.' Said asked who was the owner of the house and when I mentioned the name, he said, 'I know him. One of my group of friends is a driver for them.' Not until we drove in through the open gate did I spy it. We got out of the car. Said went forward and hailed the doorman. There were numerous doors in the tall building which was built around an open courtyard. A woman appeared, crying, 'Welcome, welcome,' and kissed us. We followed her up a staircase with a scarlet fitted carpet. As she climbed she talked: 'The sheikha has lots of nice stories to tell. She's just arrived from down south. It was some wedding, there was enough food for a whole valley. Welcome to you. The people who couldn't be there are forgiven.'

Suha asked me what she was talking about. 'They had a wedding,' I replied, then correcting myself I said it again using the Lebanese word for wedding and imitating a Lebanese accent. We followed the woman into the large salon. I went up to the sheikha who wore a dress of gold silk and on her wrist lots of gold bangles set with precious stones which outshone all the gold gleaming around the room. She kissed me on both cheeks and then did the same to Suha. 'Welcome,' she said. 'How are you? Are you well? ' 'Thanks be to God. How are you?' I replied. The sheikha leant forward to move the lump of incense in the burner and Suha looked about her. I too took the opportunity to snatch a glance around while the sheikha wasn't looking. The furniture was new and there was crystal ware and objects made of what looked like silver, a verse from the Qur'an worked in gold, a Ramadan calendar, a stuffed falcon and beside it on a glass table, an arrangement of roses made of semiprecious stones. All this was new to me. Before the room had been no more than a humble sitting-room. Vast sofas stood against the wall. Gesturing towards Suha, the sheikha said, 'Would the lady prefer to sit on the sofa instead?' I smiled. 'It's all right. My friend's Lebanese. She was a teacher at the Institute.' Then I introduced myself: 'I'm Tamr, Tawi's daughter.' The sheikha gasped, her eyes bright. 'I'm sorry, I didn't know who you were. When you got married I was in the south. I was very upset when I heard that you were divorced. I remember, I said to the sheikh, "You divorced Tawi's daughter? The girl whose forefathers' blood is one with the desert sand?" How are you? Are you married again? What's your son's name?' 'Muhammad.' 'Ah – Muhammad. And what is he doing? I see, studying. My son Abd al–Rahman married Nimr's daughter the day before yesterday. You should have seen the bride: she was dressed like they were in the old days and she weighed as much as a camel, God bless her. Couldn't you have been with us?'

'Congratulations,' I said. 'I hope they'll be happy and give you grandsons and granddaughters. But what I came for, sheikha, was a certificate of my divorce from the sheikh. I want to open a workshop and they asked me for it.'

'Fine,' she answered simply, 'Ask for anything you want. There's no problem, Tamr. But tell me, your son Muhammad, was he the one whom Ibrahim's family kidnapped and then your brother chased after them and snatched him back?'

'That's right, sheikha,' I replied smiling. 'So you've remembered.'

The sheikha sipped her coffee and Suha and I did the same. 'I know everything,' she said. 'When I visit here the women in the house tell me all the gossip.' Then she turned to the other women and told them the story of my son's abduction. After some hesitation, because the sheikha wasn't old in spite of her gold teeth and the streaks of white in her black hair, Suha interrupted, 'Is the sheikh your son?'

The sheikha reached out playfully to Suha and gently smacked her hand. 'No, my daughter. I'm his first wife. And then the oil and the money came and the sheikh wanted more wives.' Probably realizing that Suha wouldn't know the Qur'an, she added, 'The Almighty said, "Marry of such women that please you: two, or three, or four. But if you fear that you cannot treat so many justly, then marry one only

. . ." So he married a second wife.' There was silence for a few moments, then the sheikha transferred her attention to the other women. I didn't rise to leave until I'd drunk some cold fruit juice, followed by tea, then coffee, and eaten some cake. I stood up and kissed the sheikha and asked, 'Shall I come tomorrow to get the certificate?' 'Will it be all right when the sheikh comes back?' she said. 'He's gone into the desert for two or three days with a group of his friends to hunt gazelles, but write the year of your marriage and your divorce for me on a piece of paper.' I wrote the two dates on some paper from Suha's handbag. As the sheikha took it from me Suha nudged me, and when we got outside she said, 'What d'you bet that'll never reach the sheikh?' I laughed but answered reassuringly, 'It'll be all right, God willing.' I said goodbye to her and, my cheeks flushed, thanked her for coming with me and lending me Said and the car. Suha couldn't help conveying her misgivings to me once more, and I reassured her again, saying confidently, 'She promised and it's my right.' Then she asked me, 'What do you feel, seeing the house after fifteen years?' 'Nothing,' I answered laughing. 'It wasn't my home. I was like a guest in it.'

I noticed that Suha still looked distracted and had stopped talking. 'You look as if you've got a headache,' I said. 'Perhaps it's the heat. Let's go inside where it's air-conditioned.' I told her what had happened between me and Rashid and how he'd turned down my new plan. Without waiting until I'd finished speaking she burst out, 'Maybe Rashid's right. Maybe you'll lose out, putting everything you've got into a dressmaking business, and sewing machines and hair dryers and Filipino women.'

'What else can I do? The schools don't accept qualifications from the Institute. You have to have a university degree. Besides, everyone complains about the shortage of dressmakers. Women aren't allowed to be measured. There isn't even any consultation between a dressmaker and his customer – the little window that he opens between you and him isn't enough – and nobody buys the ready-made dresses in the shops. How can a woman buy a dress without trying it on? Then there's nobody to do hair and colour it. Honestly, Rashid's not thinking about me making a loss. He just wants me to get married. He thinks I'll bring shame on him. It's Batul's fault. She told him about my quarrel with Ibrahim: Ibrahim said to me on the phone, "I don't want people to say that the mother of my son's like a woman from one of those Far Eastern expatriate families, doing people's sewing, and washing their hair. On top of that there'll be women coming and going. How will my son be able to show his face in public when the authorities come and close the place down?" When I'd heard what he had to say, I lost control of myself completely. The blood rushed into my face and I buried my head in my hands and screamed out loud. Then I took my hands away to see the blood which I thought I could feel pouring from my head and face, and clutched my heart and imagined my hands covered in bruises from its wild beating. I rushed off into my room and tore my nightdress and banged my head against the chest and the wall, and struck my face. Poor Batul couldn't get hold of me. I took off all my clothes, screaming, "Come and look, everyone. See for yourselves if I'm a slut." '

I took a sip from my glass waiting to hear Suha's irritated comments and her expressions of sorrow at my situation. But instead of sympathizing she stood up to pour more tea, then as if the words had been on the tip of her tongue for a long time and came tumbling out all at once, she asked, 'Why don't you go abroad to live and be free of all this?'

'How can I?'

With renewed enthusiasm Suha said, 'Your English friend Mary could put you up for a bit and afterwards something would come along.' I laughed and patted Suha's shoulder. 'Come on, Suha. What are you thinking of? Do you want me to go away and never come back? Leave my country and live in London? What would I do in London? A person away from his country and his nearest and dearest isn't worth a stick of incense. It's true I was happy abroad. But how I missed it here! I even missed the humidity and the dust and the heat, believe me. And what would they say about me? That I'd run away. For what reason?'

Suha said, 'I'm running away. Look, everything's packed.' She pointed towards the wall. I laughed, not bothering to look over at the case and the trunks. 'Impossible. I don't believe you. You must just be going on holiday.' 'I promise you,' she replied, 'I'm leaving in two days and not coming back.'

Still amused by what I thought was her exaggerating, I said confidently, 'That's what you say, but as soon as you find out what it's like to be away from here you'll be back.'

Suha was plainly annoyed at my implying that she had no alternative but to live here, and answered sarcastically, 'God forbid. I hope I never even see it in my dreams.'

'What's the reason?' I asked her. 'You go to restaurants. You've got a car. You go to the pool.' Then looking about me, 'You've got a big house, air-conditioning even in the bathroom, a garden. No, you've nothing to complain about.'

She sighed, and then almost screamed, 'For goodness sake, Tamr! Where do you live? Out by the date palms. Of course. You're well named, aren't you!* I can't breathe. There's no freedom here. You can't play tennis, go to the cinema, go for walks. There's no entertainment — didn't you hear how a crowd of them went to the hotel, dragged the men in the band off the stage, broke their guitars and threw them out? And they told the women to wait in another room.'

'God forbid,' I interrupted her, 'Those are just rumours.'

'What do you mean, Tamr? ' she cried. 'A friend of mine was there. And the trouble was that her husband was away. Imagine if they'd known that she'd come out in the evening

*Tamr means 'dates' in Arabic.

without her husband! Thank God she escaped. All the women got out through the window.'

'Why should they keep their mouths shut?' I retorted sharply. 'Once when Batul and I were settling up with a supplier a quarter of an hour before prayer time, an old man came into the shop and banged on the table. I shouted at him and asked him what he wanted, but you have to excuse them – there are so many foreigners here.'

Suha changed the subject; forcing a weak smile she asked me, 'So what are you going to do?' 'You'll see tomorrow,' I answered with enthusiasm. 'I'm going to get a licence to open my own workshop, in my name, that's if Said can take me and bring me back.' 'Said and I are at your service,' answered Suha. I rose to kiss her on both cheeks. 'I don't know what I would have done without you. Thank you from the bottom of my heart, darling.' Suha thought I meant the car and Said, but what I was really grateful to her for was introducing me to another way of life in the desert which I'd known nothing of, starting with colours and furnishings and ending up with civilization. I thanked God that I'd gone to the Institute, had Suha as my teacher, eaten a slice of cake on that white plate with flowers on it, drunk tea with honey in it instead of sugar, which according to Suha was "white poison", and seen Suha's canary chirping, flying freely about the house, from her shoulder to the telephone receiver to the chair. It was all new and my mind had picked it up and recorded it.

2

'Tamr. Not another word! Listen! Don't turn me into an infidel and make a mockery of my prayers.'

I was silent. I watched a fly swoop down on to my mother's hand. My throat muscles tightened. The fly took off again and I sat facing my mother without speaking, watching it hover over her dry white skin.

'Tamr, Tamr. Don't let me regret the past. Four years . . .'

I didn't want her to finish and I got to my feet irritably. 'I'm not listening. I'm not listening,' I shouted, and went into the kitchen. I put the kettle on the stove and waited for the water to boil. I felt as if I had something sweet like Turkish Delight in my mouth and it passed down over my throat muscles, making them relax. If I'd stayed in the other room I would have seen my mother put a hand up to her face to adjust her veil; she would have disengaged a finger to touch her nose and the sweat under the eyes, before shaking it in my face. 'Four years,' she would have said, 'and not a day went by without me saying my prayers, not a year without me fasting; I missed my period and the doctors said, "There's a child in your stomach," and I swore to God that I wouldn't break a fast or miss a prayer. I know my Lord will take this into account on the Day of Reckoning, although while I was pregnant I could have been exempted from ninety days of fasting and about two hundred prayers.' As usual I would have corrected her: 'A hundred and twenty days of fasting,' and, trying to calculate the number of statutory prayers my mother would have prayed in the course of four years: 'It comes to much more than two hundred.' I used to enjoy my mother's stories about how I'd had needle marks on me and been completely bald when I was born, especially since now my hair hung down my back and my eyebrows and eyelashes were thick, and there was no trace of the needle on my hands and thighs as far as I could make out from my mother's constant intimations; she was for ever grabbing my hand and peering at it, bringing it closer until her face touched my skin, when she would mutter 'Ha!' and let it go. But I no longer liked this story of her four-year pregnancy, nor the one of my aunt's about her daughter Awatef being born with her insides hanging out – imagine her swimming around in the womb with her guts trailing – and the doctors cutting her open and restoring every organ to its proper place. There was another one they told about two cats, sisters, who'd lived in their grandfather's house, which I didn't much like either: when the older cat was pregnant the other was jealous and after a while became pregnant too even though she never came out of her place in the box. The two went into labour together, cut each other's umbilical cords and couldn't tell their off-spring apart.

I used to look at my aunt and my mother as they finished off the tale and mumbled, 'God preserve us from the Devil.' They sat together morning and afternoon whenever my aunt visited the place, which she used to do a lot after she became half-paralysed. Their conversations wouldn't develop and take off in different directions until after lunch between cups of tea and coffee and fruit juice and biscuits. Each of them wanted to tell her own stories and my mother didn't listen to what my aunt said, nor my aunt to my mother. This was obvious from the way they behaved; my mother was absorbed in her fingers, my aunt poking about in her ear, then counting the beads on her necklace; or else my mother would get up for no reason and go off into the bedroom or the kitchen while my aunt continued her tales.

My aunt Nasab captured my attention more than my mother; her powerful voice, which had a huskiness about it, her gold teeth, her deep colouring, her gold heavy-looking neck chain, the henna reddening and blackening her hands and feet, everything about her was exaggerated; she put kohl on her eyes and the line along her lower lid was as broad as a finger; under her head cover she wore her hair in two black plaits which she sometimes untied; then she combed her hair with her fingers and replaited it, and I never once saw a single white hair among the black. She would sigh and say, 'Tamr, God is above and understands everything. Praise be, He is all-knowing. That Awatef's innards were tangled, and why, He knew. But He tries human beings and examines their faith. By God and the Kaaba, when I saw her come out as beautiful as the full moon, with huge eyes, looking at each of us in turn, and her guts hanging out on to her skin, I said, "O Lord, I'm not going to complain or abandon my faith. I want to love and cherish her as long as there's life in her." Darling Awatef. She was all eyes, eyes that took in everything. Sita said to me, "You moved when God was breathing life into Awatef." I realized that this was true: while I was asleep my feet would change places with my head.'

I noticed that the water had almost boiled dry and I was still standing right next to the whistling kettle. I poured what was left of the water over the tea bags and sugar, put the pot on a tray with glasses and took it into the sitting-room. My mother was watching television, although the picture was unsteady. I couldn't imagine that I'd be able to sit there as I had done before, content to drink tea and talk to the visitors who would surely come. The sunset call to prayer was stamped on my memory among the glasses of tea and the conversations, the noise of the television and the children playing, and the women praying wherever they happened to be.

Now I sat down at a distance from my mother and aunt, pretending to read, then pretending to write figures on a piece of paper, deliberately making a noise as I did it: the rent, the running costs of the workshop, the licence, the cost of bringing seamstresses from the Philippines.

My mother addressed my aunt: 'Nasab. When Tamr was in London someone must have put something in her food or drink; or perhaps the Devil appeared in the shape of a nurse or a doctor and whispered evil thoughts to her. They're idolators and evildoers over there, and they want to make the believers turn away from their faith so that they can increase their own numbers. And that foreign girl next door – the Virgin Mary or whatever her name is . . . '

I didn't laugh, because she never remembered the name of our neighbour Mary, and I didn't raise my eyes from the piece of paper.

My aunt replied, defending her, 'I understood that her name was Maryam. And I swear by God and the Qur'an that she came to see me in hospital one day.' She stretched her hand down to her healthy leg and went on. 'May this leg of mine become like the bad one if I'm not speaking the truth. I swear to you, Taj, she talked to me for ages, and she spoke in Arabic. "Sitt Nasab," she said, "My husband's not here. He's in a country a long way off, and I just have my children with me. I'll take Tamr on the bus to see the Queen's palace, Oxford Street, Big Ben, the Zoo." And I was nodding my head, making out that I was sometimes unconscious, not always listening, not talking much.

'Tamr had melted the foreigner's heart, but as my own heart softened towards Tamr, because I saw her crying, I muttered to myself, "Lord deliver me from the devils of the cold and the rain; if anyone sees Tamr or she gets into trouble, Ibrahim's family and the sheikh's family will come buzzing around like bees," so I said aloud, "No. No." '

My mother beat her chest and said in a quarrelsome voice, 'Let me understand this. Let me understand it. What turned her mind upside down, and who put two bagsful of tears in her eyes? When they kidnapped her son, she didn't let out a whimper.' My aunt interrupted: 'Didn't you see her? When they stole Muhammad she was as white as a ghost.' She sighed and drummed on her chest with her hand. 'I'm telling you the truth. For twenty days and twenty nights when I was in hospital Tamr didn't leave me. She was always on the sofa or at the window. When Awatef came they went to Oxford

Street and bought perfumes and material, and I said to her, to Awatef, "You and your husband are free to do as you please but Tamr has to stay with me. I want to see her on that sofa." '

I found myself listening intently but I didn't comment on their conversation as I normally did, or shout when my mother said, 'Rashid was right all along. The Institute has turned her head, and the Lebanese teacher, and the cars. She needs a home of her own and children.' Then she looked in the direction of the door, afraid that Batul, who was in the kitchen, would hear her, and whispered, 'I'd like to live with her and relieve Rashid of the responsibility. It's true that Rashid – God grant him a long life – doesn't ask for a thing from us. He has a sense of duty towards the family, but what concerns him is his sister's future. Nobody believes that Rashid's only my stepson, and in the past I've bitten his mother and she's spat in my face. He acts as if I were his own flesh and blood.'

My aunt listened thoughtfully, then remarked, 'God bless Rashid, and God bless us. English people are born and die strangers to their families. When the English doctor found out how we live, how we don't abandon members of our families, he said to me, "You're more civilized than we are." I asked the English girl Maryam who was there with Tamr – my dear Tamr who stayed by my side and never ever left me – what the doctor meant and she explained the word "civilization" to me in Arabic: it means progress and modern life, aeroplanes and machinery. I said to her, "Tell the doctor I've got faith in aeroplanes because I've travelled in them, and in steamships and cars for the same reason. But I don't believe that a person's landed on the moon and I wouldn't even if I saw a million pictures of it. How could a man stand on it when it's the size of a loaf of bread or a water melon, without it falling down? And tell the doctor that I don't believe the earth rotates and is like an apple. If the earth went round, this bed of mine and that table over there would change places.

Tell him these are fantasies. Or perhaps it's better not to make him angry so tell him my aunt believes in the radio and the television; they're excellent and they help to pass the time – even though when we listened to the radio for the first time we said it was the Devil, and when we watched television we said it was the Devil's grandfather." '

I put up my hand to touch my hair, all that was left to me of London. A stylist there had cut my long straight hair and given me a light perm. London, with its shops, the white bathroom, the clean hospital corridors; the green expanses there reminded me of the gardens they tell us are in Paradise with rivers flowing underground. I loved the rain, the red buses, tea and biscuits in the cafés, and the respect shown me by every man I met: the air steward, the nightporter at the hotel, the doctors at the hospital, the taxi drivers.

In London I decided that when I went back to the desert I'd enrol at the Institute and study. Learning to recite the Qur'an with the teacher of religion wasn't everything. I would take English lessons too so that I could reply when someone spoke to me. I couldn't say a single word as it was, and I couldn't fill up the forms at the customs even in Arabic. I pictured myself sitting in front of the television explaining to Batul and my aunt and my mother what was really going on in the foreign films: the woman whom Mr Rochester kept shut away in *Jane Eyre* was his mad wife, not his mother.

3

The following day I collected the divorce certificate from the sheikh. It was as if a chicken had taken a pen and scratched its name. When I reached the government building I said to Said, 'Ask the official to come to me here. I'll wait in the car.' Said didn't show any surprise. 'One moment, Aunt Tamr,' he said, getting out of the car.

Although I stayed in the car my heart was knocking against my chest just as it had done a few days before when I went into the bank. On that occasion I'd known that what I was doing was wrong; I was probably the first woman to cross its threshold, but women went into shops and stores and bought things. Who was going to stop me? The thick black cover was over my face. Through it I could see all the eyes, all the bodies. Nobody said to me, 'You're not allowed to come in,' and I went forward confidently and handed the man a paper. He went away for a little while, then came back and asked me if I had my identity card with me. I said yes, thinking a few seconds and this tension will be over, but then he told me that my money was in Muhammad's name. I gasped. 'He's my son,' I cried. 'He'll have to come and see us himself,' said the official. I went out of the bank, wondering why Rashid had entered my money in the name of my son who'd been five years old when my father had died and left it to me.

The next day when my son came, I made sure that he had his identity card. Without delay I wrapped my abaya around me and went towards the car. His astonished voice made me halt. 'What are you doing, mother?' Embarrassed, I answered, 'I'll come with you and wait for you in the car.' In even greater surprise, he replied, 'You're coming with me to the bank? And waiting in the car? Have you gone mad?'

I didn't argue with him and went back into the house with my hand on my heart. Twenty-five thousand, to be handed over to my son who wasn't even sixteen years old. I didn't take my hand off my heart until he came back with the money in a paper bag.

The same sensations had returned the first time I came to this building to apply for a permit for a workshop and hairdresser's. Silence hung over the place, and when I approached an official sitting at a table he appeared tongue-tied and waved me over to another table. From there I was passed from one person to another, and I realized that by coming into a government building I had made another big mistake. But it wasn't forbidden, and why should it be? The black cover was on my face, the black wrap around me decorously hiding my charms, and the hem of the dress I wore underneath it trailed behind me on the floor. I knew that Rashid would be furious. He'd kill me. Too bad. I returned to the first table. The dejection which had taken hold of me was transformed into a kind of daredevil courage. 'My name is Tamr daughter of al-Tawi,' I declared, not caring if anyone heard me or not. 'I want to open a dressmaking business and a ladies' hairdresser's.' The man answered in spite of himself, as if he had come under my sway: 'The dressmaking business is possible. Not the hairdresser's. Are you married?' 'Divorced.' 'Get a certificate of your divorce, then let your guardian bring us the lease and we'll examine the premises, and afterwards if everything's all right we'll give you a permit.' Looking down at the ground, he went on, 'But next time, stay in the car and send your driver, and someone will come out to the car with the papers for you to sign.' I thanked him and left. A certificate of my divorce? I hadn't seen such a thing when I divorced my first husband or my second and I didn't remember signing my name on a single official document in my life.

I ran away from my first husband Ibrahim one hot noon-day, with my son Muhammad in my arms. My husband's family were asleep because their stomachs were heavy with food. I was divorced by my second husband early one morning. I woke up at the sound of knocking on my bedroom door which was locked from the inside. As I hurried to open it I remembered the sheikh, my husband, saying to me the day before, 'Lock your door. My friends are sure to get drunk and one of them wants to see if it's true that you look like Nabila Ubaid. You know the wicked notions they get.'

I looked like a film star? I'd examined myself that night. Brown skin, large eyes, small nose, even white teeth, average height; my body wasn't bad except that my bottom was too fat.

I opened the door hastily and found the maid outside, holding Muhammad's hand. I smiled at him and held him. 'Good morning. Good morning, Hammouda.' The maid said shortly, 'Your brother Rashid's downstairs.' This astonished me, and I wondered what could have happened. Batul wasn't due to have her baby for another month. Ibrahim's family must want my son. I flung my dress over my silk nightdress and rushed downstairs.

Rashid greeted me angrily, but with some malicious satisfaction in his voice: 'Congratuations. The sheikh's divorced you.'

I didn't believe what I was hearing. The previous day the sheikh had calmed me down when he saw me crying, terrified by Ibrahim threatening to take Muhammad away from me. He'd said, 'Nobody's going to harm a fingernail of yours while you're my wife.'

Confronted by the news that he was divorcing me, I felt surprise and curiosity, and didn't know whether I was glad or sorry. I learnt from the maid as she helped me to pack that she'd been woken up by the sheikh shouting. He was very drunk but she'd seen him hammering at my bedroom door. When the door remained closed, he'd fetched a revolver and started trying to break in. He'd had to be restrained by the driver and the servants, and even then he wouldn't give in until he'd sworn to divorce me, asked for two witnesses and done it. No one believed me when I swore by God and his prophets that I'd heard nothing but the roaring of the air-conditioner, although it was rare for me to sleep so deeply.

After a few days in Rashid's house I realized that I was pleased to be divorced. The sheikh was a drunkard, with a bottle to hand twenty-four hours a day. He would sit all day long, never rising except to shake hands with a visitor, drinking glass after glass until his head slumped forward and he slept. He would wake up in the afternoon sometime and call until I came to him. He smelt strongly of drink and I would remind myself that I just had to bear it for a little while; soon he would leave me. Sometimes he would fall soundly asleep when he'd barely climbed on top of me. This delighted me and I longed for it to happen every time, for I found the smell of drink hard to take. I knew that my aunt and my brother and all of them were happy that I'd married into a big house that was like a palace and had servants and cars and drivers. The sheikh was an important person, and he was affectionate and generous; presents and money, like drink, were always available and he distributed them lavishly. He treated me like a daughter although he was no more than fifteen years older than me. Every day he asked me, 'Have you had something to eat or drink? Thanks be to God. Has Muhammad eaten? Thanks be to God. Has he had plenty? Thanks be to God.' Muhammad was my son and thanks be to God the sheikh rarely saw him, and even when he did see him he didn't play with him.

When I told Rashid all of this he said, 'What business is it of yours? It's not you doing the drinking, is it?' But coming back to my brother's house, living among them all, me being unmarried, was hard on Muhammad. I began to sell my jewellery and clothes to the neighbours at low prices so that I could buy Muhammad what he wanted. He was always telling me that his cousins were much better off than he was and instead of studying and doing his homework he would deliberately set out to annoy me. I knew that my separation from Ibrahim had changed him into a nervous, unpredictable boy, uncertain which of us to go to. When he was staying with me he rejected me and the life he lived with me, and asked to go back to his father; two days after he'd gone, Ibrahim would contact Rashid and say that Muhammad wanted me. On one such occasion Rashid came with me to fetch Muhammad. The boy looked happily out of the car window until we'd been travelling for a few minutes, then a scowl decended upon his face and he didn't say another word until he asked his uncle to stop the car because he felt sick. He got out and ran off and up on to the dunes where he sat crying forlornly. He refused to come down and began to throw sand at me and Rashid, but he wouldn't go back to his father's house.

4

Rashid agreed with my plan for a workshop once he'd read the permit and saw that it was registered in my name. He agreed to bring in the Filipino seamstresses on condition that Batul came in as a partner but didn't visit the place, and the Filipinos slept in the workshop and didn't cross the threshold except in my company. My aunt trilled, I jumped for joy, Batul cheered, and my mother wept.

I didn't pay any attention to the fact that my mother went on crying and her tears turned into a convulsive fit of sobbing. My thoughts revolved happily, busy with images of the workshop: the reception, the sewing room, mirrors, cupboards, the fashion photographs in Suha's magazines, the Filipino seamstresses – one of whom would have to be a hair stylist. I had an exact idea of the table and chair I would have to work from, just like I'd seen in the shops. And all the big families and the sheikhs' wives would be my customers.

Between her sobs my mother said, 'I swear, I carried you in my womb and gave birth to you but you cling to Nasab. It's as if she's a hyena who's pissed on you and got power over you. Four years I was pregnant with you . . .'

She cradled her head in her arms and I didn't know how to answer her. I knew she wouldn't stop crying for days and nights as usual, and I was scared that she'd revert to her raving and chattering, losing her mind as she always did when she became very angry. I approached her and spoke soothingly as I would have done to a child. 'No, mother. I swear by my son, you're wrong. I listen to you and I do what you want. You know Rashid and his stubbornness, but my aunt has an influence over him and she makes him embarrassed. You know he owes her a lot. She's like his mother.' Tentatively I touched her red plait. I saw the little white hairs at the roots. Her head appeared small. Even the henna didn't colour the original red of her hair or the striking whiteness of the palms of her hands. I stared at the fine blue veins in her neck and caught sight of one of her bare feet, small and slender, looking as if it were made of glass.

I pulled her hand away from her red face. When she lifted her green eyes to me they were swollen. As usual when I noticed her colouring, I thought that she couldn't possibly be my mother. 'God forbid,' I uttered involuntarily, warding off this notion of mine, and my mother cried out, 'Even you, Tamr, say "God forbid". By God, I'm not mad!'

I kissed her on both cheeks, tasting the salty tears, then kissed her hands and embraced her, saying 'You're Taj, Crown of the Bride and Crown of Kings.* You're no more mad than I am!' This last sentence made my mother's weeping rise almost to a lament, and she made a noise like a cat in distress.

*Taj means 'crown' in Arabic, and Taj al-Arus 'the bride's crown'.

She rocked her whole body and covered her face with her hands again.

Gradually her sobs abated and she indicated in the direction of her nose, then reached out a hand to me. I gave her a handkerchief from my pocket, and when she'd cleaned her nose and wiped her eyes she tried to speak without crying. Out came one sentence that I knew by heart: 'I felt you between my shoulders.' I wanted to say to her, 'I know, I know,' but I was afraid of annoying her and I let her go on. 'I felt you between my shoulders, and I never once slept on my back, always on my stomach or my side. Every day I drank camels' milk and sheeps' milk and ate three dates, and the doctors injected me with a needle a span long. When you were born I saw the needle marks in your hands and thighs. God is great! You had no hair, no eyebrows or eyelashes, not even any hair in your nostrils. I began to put henna on you every Friday night. The other wives and their children laughed at me and said, "You're wasting your time putting henna on the Safwan stone." And I made myself deaf and dumb and blind. I hennaed your scalp and bought you combs and hairbands and even medicine for headlice. In the woman's market they all made signs behind my back when they saw that damned Mawda trying to sell me a big bottle and saying to me, giggling and winking, "Perhaps Tamr needs this medicine from India. Everybody swears it's like Solomon's devils. One drop applied to the head does away with lice as if they'd never existed." Just to show them all I said, "It can't do any harm to have some," put my hand in my bosom and paid for it.'

I looked at my mother's breast, which was scarcely visible in the folds of her voluminous dress and answered, bored but sad at the same time, 'I know, Mother. I've caused you anguish in the past and I'm still doing it. I know. I mustn't talk to Aunt Nasab so much. In any case she's just a guest, and in a couple of days she'll be going back home.' Then I added hypocritically, 'From the way she was so hard on me and spoiled Awatef when we were in London, I know where I really stand with her.'

My mother gulped in agreement. 'You don't have to tell me about Nasab and Awatef. When the sheikh divorced you your aunt didn't tear her hair or claw her chest in sorrow. Maybe she was glad. How could Tamr be married to a sheikh and not Awatef?'

'God forgive her,' I replied appeasingly.

Then I took my mother by the hand and pulled her up off the bed. 'Come on, Crown of the Bride and Crown of Kings. Wash your face, put on your dress and do your hair. We've got lots of work to do.'

As I picked over the rice, minced the meat and chopped up the vegetables with enthusiasm, Rashid came in with the permit in his hand, still not able to believe that the ministry had given it to me. I smiled triumphantly and said nothing. I had to cook quickly. Batul had offered to help me with the cooking that day but I'd refused to let her. I wanted to prove that my opening the workshop wouldn't mean I did any less housework.

I had many things to occupy my thoughts — such as purchasing machines, curtains, pins, scissors, a small fridge and two beds for the Filipinos — but still I was concerned about my mother. I thanked the Lord she was continuing to recover. Her anger and her sadness were normal this time and she didn't refuse to leave her bed.

When I was little I lived with my mother in one room of a three-storey house. I used to wait for her to come to bed, watching her as she plaited her red hair and dipped her fingertips in warm oil. She would say to me with a smile, 'You must be sleepy, Tamr. Don't you want to hear about the Little Fish?' I would be smiling too, knowing that she was teasing me. She never changed her way of speaking even when she was ill. She adjusted her veil as she said the story's name, and always began by biting her lips. 'Tamr, O Tamr, the Story of the Little Fish is the story of a poor girl whose mother had died, and whose stepmother was harsh and wicked. She made her stay in the kitchen, polishing the brass, fetching water, sweeping, dusting, stoking the fires and cooking, doing the washing, preparing the incense burner and putting henna on her stepmother's hair.

'O Tamr, O Tamr, one day her father caught one hundred fish, and the poor girl had to stay up all night gutting them. Her stepmother said to her, "You must clean all the fish tonight. If they weren't full of evil, they wouldn't make such a horrible smell." When the girl took hold of the last fish it slipped from her grasp. She thought to herself that her swollen red hands must have grown tired, but the Little Fish cried and said in a loud voice to the girl, "Spare me and I'll make you rich." The girl was astonished that the fish had spoken, and she took fright. "God preserve me from the Devil's curse," she said. She looked hard at the Little Fish and saw that it was beautiful: its eyes were black, its nose small as far as she could see, its mouth a tiny opening; it had little even teeth and a shining silver skin. The Little Fish cried louder and begged the girl again, "Spare me, and I'll make you rich." The poor girl took pity on the fish. She put it under her arm and slowly opened the door. The snores of her stepmother and her father rose to the sky. She ran until she reached the sea. There she took the fish in her hands and said to it, "Little Fish, Little Fish, don't cry and don't wail. Go back to your mother and father and sister and brother, and to your neighbours and your Qur'an teacher. Goodbye." The girl went back to the house, and when she heard the snores of her stepmother and her father still rising to the sky, she heaved a sigh of relief. The next day the Sultan's son was giving a party to end all parties, with meat and rice and sweets in abundance. And every boy and girl and every man and his wife went to the party, all except this poor little girl. Her stepmother left her in the kitchen with a big bag of rice and ordered her to pick the weevils out of it grain by grain. Then she sprinkled salt on the floor and ordered her to gather it up grain by grain, and scared her with stories about the Judgement Day and how God would make her spend eternity sweeping salt off the floor with her eyelashes if she didn't do as she was told now. The poor girl sat on the floor crying, and began trying to pick the weevils out of the rice, but the creatures slipped through her fingers. Suddenly she heard a sweet voice saying, "This is the Little Fish. I've made you a dress of coral from the sea, and jewellery of shells and pearls so that you can go to the Sultan's palace." The poor girl turned in surprise and called out, "Where are you?" Then she looked back at the floor and said, "What about the weevils and the rice and the salt?" The Little Fish replied, "Don't bother about them. I'll make the rice clean and white for you and drown the weevils and put the salt in a jar. Off you go. Goodbye!"

'The girl looked down at herself and found she was wearing a lovely dress, and from the window she saw a coach with a huge shell for a seat, driven by a young giant. So off she went to the palace and the Sultan's son fell in love with her beauty and her sweet disposition, and she married him, Tamr, and lived till the Judgement Day and had both sons and daughters.'

Only when I was stretched out in bed listening to the tale of the Little Fish did I feel happy, for my mother looked peaceful and beautiful, and the smell of food and coffee and laundry soap had faded from the room which was our home.

My mother cooked our food and washed our clothes in this room, and we didn't leave it except to rush down the long staircase and back again, my mother clutching meat and vegetables in her arms as if she were a thief. I grew used to hearing her voice cursing and threatening up the stairs from the first floor. Sometimes the sound of another voice mingled with hers. I was glad whenever I saw that she had the bucket, because then I would run out of the room and lean over to watch her hauling up the rope with a frown on her face.

Because she was in such a hurry, most of the water in the

bucket slopped out on its way between the two floors, and sometimes one of the boys, in spite of the speed at which it was moving, dropped a pebble or a date stone or a bit of paper into it, to see my mother Taj go crazy with anger and curse Jauhar and Najeeya at the top of her voice. I rarely left the room day or night except to go to the lavatory, and then I went with my mother. As we descended the two flights I would try to loiter and she would scold me in annoyance: 'No time ago you were clutching yourself, and now you're prancing about as if you've got all the time in the world.' I wanted to see the other children, and Jauhar and Najeeya, and stare into their faces, for I could see more likeness between me and them than between me and my mother. But without realizing it I lowered my gaze each time I met one of them in the hallway of the house or at the bathroom door.

I felt as if I lived with them because I could hear the sounds of their voices and the noise they made as well as if they were in the room, and when I couldn't hear them I waited expectantly until I could. My mother told me their life histories from the moment she opened her eyes in the morning until she went to bed at night; she recited stories that I didn't understand, but I recognized that at the core of them lay a deep hatred. All the same I was curious about them, and longed to go down to the rooms where they lived and talk to them and play with their children. More than once I'd seen Jauhar and Najeeya pulling my mother's hair and jumping on top of her and hitting her; they would shriek when my mother bit their hands and their thighs, while the children cheered them on delightedly, chanting, 'The Turkish woman's mad! The Turkish woman's mad!'

I even began to long for us just to open our door because they used to leave their rubbish beside it, a dead rat, potato peelings, a gold paper crown, all of which, as far as I was concerned, formed part of a dialogue between me and them.

How I wished I could explain to them how much I longed to know them – even though our mothers fought and I'd once seen goat dung thrown outside our door – and how much I'd loved the gold paper crown which they'd discarded there; I'd tried it on and I wanted to keep it, but my mother pulled it off and tore it with her teeth.

It was when my mother lost my gold bangles, a pendant formed of the words, 'What God has willed', and a Qur'an studded with diamonds and sapphires which had been a present from the Sultan, that my aunt came to take us to live with her, for my mother was frantic. When she discovered the things were missing she'd rushed down the stairs to Jauhar's like a tornado, as if she were certain that Jauhar was the culprit, and overturned the furniture and even ripped the bedding and began feeling around in it. Jauhar and her children couldn't do anything to stop her, and my mother turned her fury on Najeeya and twisted her arm and spat in her children's faces. When she found the door locked in her face, she began to retreat, then returned to the fray, charging the door like a bull. It withstood her assault and she raised her eyes to heaven, beseeching God to destroy them one by one. Nejeeya and Jauhar were afraid of her coloured eyes and the red freckles on her face and her red hair, the like of which they'd never seen before. Each of them hurried to protect her own children, covering their little faces with the hems of their dresses.

Life was different in my aunt's home, and I couldn't help wondering why we hadn't moved there before instead of staying in that room, why indeed we'd never visited her, nor she us. For my aunt had an abundance of love, a broad smile, and a laugh which everyone in the house could hear.

Even my mother sat calm and beautiful at my aunt's side, except sometimes when she remembered episodes with Najeeya and Jauhar. She was the focal point of any gathering. Her appearance was so different from all of theirs that she dazzled and shocked them, but what she said must have fascinated them, for all the women, even my aunt, listened as if they were bewitched. I began to enjoy playing with my cousins, especially Awatef who was the same age as me. The boys went to school and came back with books full of pictures, which opened my mind to things I hadn't known existed: once I asked about the pictures of fishes that caught my eye, and one of my cousins told me all about them. I waited for him at the door in the heat of the sun and afterwards I shook my head sorrowfully and said, 'If only the woman who teaches us about religion gave us books like the ones you're allowed to read.' I took the books in my hands, staring at the pictures. Once I read the word 'God' and was amazed to find that I could read and understand a book that wasn't the Qur'an. When I began to be able to read what he read, and study what he studied and write what he wrote, the tears that I had shed regularly every morning when it was time to go to the Qur'an teacher were replaced by a sense of gratitude. I no longer minded her hard eyes, and I gave up counting the buttons on her veil and lavished all my attention on her mouth, deciphering the symbols for the words and then asking her if I was writing my name correctly.

With my aunt I visited the market, rode in the car, went into the desert and slept in a tent, and with my aunt looking on, I stood while our Indian neighbour fitted material on me for a dress. Running my hands over the gold and silver threads, I asked my mother curiously if a feast day was approaching. It was my aunt who answered: 'No, Tamr, this is for the daughter of one of my relations in Iran.' I didn't ask which one as she had many relatives over there. Not a month went by without her inviting a family from Iran or Bahrain to stay; I used to think that every woman wearing an abaya and a veil was a relation, and I would stop in the street and refuse to go on until my mother had said hallo to the moving abayas.

But the nice clothes were for me: they hennaed my hands and feet one morning and dressed me in one of the dresses that same afternoon. They took me to my father's house where Jauhar and Najeeya and my father's fourth wife were waiting, and for a moment I thought of the bucket and the rope and the servant. My mother and my aunt were there to accompany me, and I suddenly wondered if this could be my own wedding. The neighbour's daughter once told me that she'd known about her father's second marriage because there had been so many baskets and metal containers around, full of cooked rice and meat, and here I was confronted with bags and boxes of provisions, and my mother tasting a bit of rice and saying, 'They're obviously mean. God help us! You can count the cardamon pods and cumin seeds with the naked eye. God help my precious Tamr!' Then I heard drumming and women trilling. 'Mother, mother!' I cried. 'Are you marrying me off? I'm not even a woman yet!' I knew about puberty from the Qur'an, although it was the teacher who had described monthly periods as 'dirty'. 'Are you marrying me off when you know it's wrong?' I asked again. 'It doesn't make any difference whether it's to a boy or a grown man.' 'Hush, Tamr,' replied my aunt. 'Don't be ungrateful. A man is an adornment, a crown for your head, a staff to strengthen your heart.' I wept, without knowing why. 'Mother, mother, will you be staying with me?' I asked her, and when she nodded I felt reassured.

The women beat the drums and trilled and sang. Women I didn't know entered the gathering. The chanting and songs rose higher, and I saw the professional entertainer whom I'd seen singing at other weddings. I'd always wondered why money was showered upon her and watched her hiding it in her breast, as she was doing now. When I saw the neighbours and their daughters kissing my mother and looking at me, I thought, 'Perhaps I'm already married,' but I pushed the thought away. I'd heard that the bride was wrapped up in a carpet or rug. Before my father came in my aunt shouted, 'Anyone who's unveiled should cover herself!' The women gasped and if they saw my father picking me up it was only by sneaking a glance, but when I screamed 'Mother! Mother!' they couldn't resist throwing back the covers from their faces.

He carried me to his room at the centre of the house and I saw a young man sitting on a mountain of mattresses with a white cover draped over them. I screamed. When my father had gone, the young man stood up. I screamed again and took a few steps backwards. He didn't move or speak, and I retreated to the door. I stood there for about an hour and whatever he did, whether he took a step in my direction, climbed up on the bed, or said something, I screamed. I wanted to open the door but I could hear the tambourines and drums and the women's trilling. I kept my face to the door and when the noise died down and the drums fell silent, I opened it and closed it again. I stood for perhaps another hour before I opened it and this time went out and ran from room to room searching for my mother. I found her in her bed and squeezed up next to her, and put my arms around her, sobbing. She put out an arm to hold me and I wished she'd recite the story of the Little Fish to me until I was calmer. I couldn't sleep because of the long gold ear-rings and chain and belt that I was wearing. I took them off and put them down on the floor. When I heard the dawn call to prayer, I started up in fright and found that my mother was no longer beside me in bed. She was doing her ritual ablutions. Kissing me, she said, 'Good morning on this blessed morning, Tamr.' I didn't answer: I wanted to cry, but I didn't.

My father's fourth wife made the breakfast, and my mother arranged the dishes on the mat. I sat by my aunt who hugged me and quoted some expression about the musk from deer. I didn't know what she meant but the phrase stayed with me until I was grown up, and one day I asked her what it meant. She didn't remember saying anything about musk on my wedding morning but told me that it was the most precious of all scents, and they gathered it from sacs under the bellies of certain male deer. She had some which she'd acquired from a woman whom she met on the pilgrimage, in exchange for a sheep. Then I remembered that distinctive smell which had dominated every detail of the wedding and stayed in my sensory memory, so that whenever I smelt it the wedding came back to me.

That morning they put me in another dress and replaced all my gold jewellery and sat me on mats piled high in the heart of the gathering. The tambourines began to play and the dancing and singing started up again and went on till night-fall. Everyone enjoyed themselves enormously. I saw the boys and girls I used to play with, and even the younger ones were peeping round the door, sticking out their tongues and rolling their eyes, making me laugh. Amidst all this excitement I forgot the coming night, although I hadn't thought about what was going to happen and why I was afraid. This time my mother took me to the room, and before my eyes had adjusted she left abruptly, and the confused young man took her place. I screamed and shrank against the wall. He took no notice and said nothing. Now it was his turn to stand for ages with his face to the wall. When I stopped shouting, I stood where I was and only moved my eyes when a sound came from the bed and I looked to see him stretched out there facing the wall.

I undid the bolt and pushed the door but it didn't open, so I lay down on the floor far from the bed with my face touching the wood of the door and my arms hugging my chest. I don't know whether I slept at all: I remember staring into the darkness in the direction of the bed and feeling reassured. The gold chain and belt were in my way but I didn't want to take them off; they were protecting me. When I heard the dawn call to prayer I pushed the door with all my might and found out that I was also pushing a table wedged against the other side of it. Once I was through, I ran off to my mother's room.

After that, a pattern of events developed which repeated itself every night: when the door wouldn't open, I screamed and screamed and bit his hand and my hand and any flesh I could reach with my teeth. At this the youth lost patience and opened the door and let me escape.

When I'd escaped, I ran straight into another trap: all the doors were locked from the inside, including the kitchen and the bathroom, and the only one that opened was the outside door. I opened it and stepped out into the street, then went back in again, closing it behind me.

It was my aunt who made me change my mind; she sprinkled cold water on my face, heated up some milk for me and fed me with sweets and chewing gum while she sat with me in the kitchen. She asked me if I remembered the girl who'd been tied up to the palm tree. I remembered her without hesitation, as I remembered in detail anything which happened to interrupt the daily routine: weddings, funerals, births, swarms of locusts, riding in a car, riding a camel, my gold dress, my mother's quarrel with Najeeya and Jauhar, and the story of the Little Fish. I remembered the girl tied to the palm tree; she was there till she and the tree looked like Siamese twins. My aunt and my mother had taken me and Awatef in the car to visit one of my aunt's relations. There were women and children standing between the houses and on one side of a big open piece of ground, and there were men on the other side of it. My mother didn't like the idea of stopping to watch with the women, in spite of my aunt's entreaties, and she forced the relation to come into her house with us. Inside the house, the women began to take turns at the window, while Awatef and I tried to squeeze our heads between the grown-ups' bodies. My aunt's relation said, 'The girl's been without food and drink for three days.' Then she pointed out the girl's mother; she was with the other women, circling around the girl, shouting and singing, weeping and laughing. The women were touching her and striking her, wiping the sand off her forehead then throwing it at her. Her mother replaited her hair and struck her face with her plait again, held her dress together where it had been torn and then started to tear it again. The women swarmed around the girl like hungry locusts.

'What's the girl done?' I asked excitedly.

'She hasn't bled this month,' replied my aunt, 'and her stomach's grown. Listen to me, Tamr and Awatef. When you become women, you have to bleed every month; if you don't, dig yourself into the sand like cats do. Lie down and stay quiet and never get up again. That girl didn't find any blood and yet she didn't dig herself into the sand and lie low.'

Awatef, who had sometimes seen spots of blood on her mother's dress, said, 'Why didn't the girl bleed?' The women laughed loudly and my aunt answered, 'Someone who was playing with her must have left his stick behind in her.' Before Awatef could ask her what she meant, the relation addressed my aunt and my mother: 'The slut. She swore on the Qur'an that she and another girl were playing around and what had happened was a miracle. Her mother and all the rest of the women told her not to tell lies.' But an old woman called Watfa couldn't stand it and shouted, 'A girl with another girl is like two hands.' And she pressed her palms together with all the fingers touching, and the thumbs, so that the two hands became one, and gasped, 'Is that possible?'

We all moved away from the window to eat. In the morning of the next day when we left the place we saw the girl still tied tightly to the tree. She was dozing with her eyes closed and her black hair was touching the ground. Two days later her cries rent the air. The knife had descended on her lower abdomen. There was a woman called Aleeya Tattoo, because she'd punctured the hands and faces of so many young girls with her needles to draw black tattoos on their flesh. When they screamed she swore that she would stick needles in them and leave them there if she heard another sound. She was the first to meet newborn children, the first to see the dead and bury them or help bury them. This woman was muttering there, almost raving to herself, the knife in her hand along with a small piece of the flesh which had been in direct contact with the other forbidden flesh. She screamed as she tried to force open the mouth of the girl tied to the palm tree: 'Open your mouth and eat this. Chew it up.' She brought the knife down again rapidly as she did when she was slaughtering a young lamb on a feast night. She shouted as she tried to feed the girl with the piece of flesh; and the girl, as if finding relief from her pain, bit Aleeya Tattoo's fingers, which were as dry as a billy goat's horns. Perhaps sinking her teeth into something helped her bear the wound which must have been oozing blood by then. It extended up to her stomach and the pain around there grew, and the girl screamed and screamed. The sand seemed to be joined up to the sky, and it was as if little grains of salt were covering her wound. 'Eat this. Open your mouth. Chew it up.' This time it came forcefully, for Aleeya Tattoo felt the teeth digging into her fingers. The girl moved her head away, to the left, to the right; the palm tree hurt her face. When she tasted the blood and the flesh she closed her eyes and vomited, and was no longer aware of anything.

I was twelve years old and I was jumping around on the roof of my husband's family house with the neighbours' daughters. I rushed down into the house to see the white dust come rumbling from the ceiling, then went back up to the roof. This was the only time when I forgot that I was married and playing in a strange house. I played only for two days, in the time after lunch when my husband's family were sound asleep. The noise I made woke them up and they found out what I was doing. My husband's mother, Reehan, disapproved of my game and frowned into the faces of the little neighbours who had been delighted with the young bride. They no longer came to amuse her because of that, and because their mothers told them the bride had begun to know about other things and might unsettle their minds. The days began to grow interminably long in the new house. The burning heat of the sun made its way inside in spite of the fans constantly revolving. The only things I liked about it were the designs carved on the ceiling and the wooden doors, because they were more beautiful than the carvings in my aunt's house, and their colours were not the same, but after a few days they no longer interested me. Silence hung over this house. There was no laughter and noise in it as there had been in my aunt's house. Reehan and her daughter wore stiff expressions and I didn't once see them laughing. Even seeds and chewing gum were in short supply, and when I asked about this one day, Reehan replied, 'We don't have small children in the house.' I wanted to tell her that even my aunt and my mother like seeds and gum, and I used to stock up with them whenever I visited my family or my mother and my aunt came to see me. I hid them in the bottom of the chest in my jewel box between the nose ring and the other rings, just as I had earlier hidden two photographs, one of me dressed up for a feast day, and the other of me and my mother holding palm leaves. As the days went by I became certain that Reehan didn't like me or my mother or my aunt. She shouted at me when I fidgeted as the dressmaker fitted me for a dress: 'Stand absolutely still or you won't have any dresses to wear.' Stubbornly I replied, 'I've got some other dresses. My mother and my aunt'll bring them for me.' 'Do you mean those rags?' she asked sarcastically.

I started to cry, defending my aunt and my mother. I decided that I would tell them as soon as I saw them. I realized too that I didn't like Reehan and that I was bored: I wanted to play and run and learn about the fish and the animals which I'd seen in my cousins' books, and I longed to be with my mother and my aunt all the time, not just for the one day in the week when I regularly visited them to share in the hustle and bustle of the house and listen to songs all day long. Going back to Reehan's house was always hard. Just before it was time for the servant Khaizuran to collect me I used to pray 'O God, please don't let me see Khaizuran,' but her tall thin shape would always loom into view. I would fly to her inviting her to have a cup of tea, some sweets, to delay her for as long as possible, but Khaizuran would remain –

like her name which means bamboo – as dry and unyielding
as a bamboo cane.

I thought of running away from the new house whose floor
was unwelcoming to my jumping step, and whose walls
rebuffed my laughter. Then one morning I felt blood on the
inside of my thighs and knew that I'd grown up. I remembered what I'd said when I wanted them all to have pity on
me and change their minds about making me get married:
'Are you going to marry me off when I'm not even a woman
yet?' My aunt had answered, 'God willing you won't become
a woman before he's been in you! As well as marrying Tawi's
daughter, he's getting you when you're still a little girl so you
can grow up at his house and he can raise you.' I asked
Khaizuran for a piece of cloth, refusing to tell her what it was
for. Then I began to cry. I wanted to go home for an hour,
but Reehan refused to let me, insisting that there were three
days to go before I was due to visit my family.

Khaizuran discovered that Ibrahim had fewer and fewer
headcloths with every day that passed, and that some of the
family's sheets had had strips torn off them. Then Reehan
found bits of sheet, headcloths and even underclothes with
bloodstains on them, tied up in a dress and hanging in a
bundle on the back of the bathroom door.

Every time I woke to the sound of the dawn call to prayer, I
thought of my mother and my aunt listening to the same call
without me there; all that separated me from them was two
streets and a few houses, and I sat sadly, unable to understand why they didn't love me, and why they'd sent me away,
since I hadn't been greedy or made my clothes dirty. And why
did I have to take Reehan as my new mother and aunt
combined, and listen to her and sit with her relations and her
neighbours instead of with my family?

I cried every time I visited them, refusing to go back to
Reehan's house with Khaizuran, and when my mother and
my aunt visited me and brought Awatef with them I was
overjoyed and my courage came back to me. I walked about

the house with firmer footsteps; even my voice changed: there was a ring to it; and I felt secure and happy as if I knew that Reehan couldn't criticize me or tell me off in front of my own people. I took Awatef into my room. She tried on my eight gold rings and the silver one off my thumb, then my gold dress, and said enviously, 'You are lucky!' She asked about Ibrahim and what we did when we were in bed. I pushed my hair back off my forehead and didn't answer.

When my mother heard that I was pregnant she trilled for joy, kissed me on the cheek and put out a hand to feel my stomach. She closed her eyes and even though Reehan had come in and was standing waiting for my mother, Taj al-Arus, to open her eyes, she said, 'God willing, your child will be in your womb for nine months and not a day longer; God willing your child will come out with thick eyebrows and curtains of hair in his eyes, and with hair on his head and on his stomach and between his legs.' I wished my mother would be quiet: I didn't want Reehan and her daughter, or even Khaizuran, to hear this talk. I didn't know that the details of my birth and the story of my mother's four-year pregnancy were known near and far. To my surprise Reehan adjusted her veil and remarked 'That's just talk, Taj. Fairy tales. The Almighty doesn't make mistakes, and He has power over all things.'

My mother was nonplussed for a moment, not knowing how to answer Reehan who'd just accused her of lying. She was visiting us alone; for the first time she'd come without my aunt, who was unwell. She wanted to speak up for herself but she was afraid that Reehan would be angry and take it out on me. She changed the subject: 'O Tamr, my precious, O Tamr, my love. Perhaps you're tired and you ought to lie down?' 'No, mother,' I replied eagerly, then after a pause I added boldly, 'But I want to go with you and visit my aunt.'

There was a general silence broken by my mother who said, 'And leave your husband Ibrahim at night? You shouldn't do that, my daughter. The day after tomorrow you can visit us and your aunt will be better.'

I began to cry and found that I was shaking. I would have liked to throw myself into my mother's arms and hold on to her and ask her to tell me the story of the Little Fish. I didn't feel married or pregnant, even if Ibrahim had lain on top of me and jiggled up and down and made a sticky liquid come out, and now my stomach had swollen out. I cried louder, picturing myself left alone with Reehan, and my mother Taj al-Arus rebuked me: 'No, Tamr. I don't like the way you're behaving. How can you cry when you're at home with your family?' Later on she told me that she'd been thinking something quite different: 'Their coffee's like hot water and so's their tea; there's no taste to them. And the dates aren't easy on the teeth or sweet to the tongue.' She said that she'd been wishing she could have seen me living like a sheikh's wife, with dresses which shone as bright as stars and my hair smelling of jasmine, henna patterns on my hands and dozens of maids in attendance bearing trays of tea and coffee and dates. Then she'd heard me shouting, 'I want to go home. I don't like this house.'

I didn't come back to life properly until the next time I visited my family. My aunt was bent on taking me and all the women of the house on a trip, once she'd persuaded Rashid. We climbed merrily into the car, which was to take us wherever we wished: into the desert, to the streets where the only shops were, to the hill always known as the mountain, and to the seaside. She made the car stop so that we could look out of the window. We pointed to some beautiful birds and cried out in wonder, 'Glory be to God.' My mother put out a hand to cover my eyes. 'Don't look,' she ordered. 'Don't admire them. If you gasp in wonder and say that those birds are beautiful, the child in your womb might grow feathers.' The return trip to my aunt's house was another excursion in itself, and when we arrived there was drumming and singing and dancing all the afternoon and into the night. 'You're pregnant. Don't dance,' they told me, proud of me.

They swung their long hair about; my mother danced, and Batul danced a dance which was different from the others except for the swinging hair. They all sang to me and smiled at me. I sat with my hands resting on my stomach and counted the days to my next visit.

When my mother left Reehan's house, Reehan ignored my bad mood, perhaps because my mother had entreated her to remember that I was still young and ignorant. But she did remark, 'I've never known your poor mother Taj to hold a conversation before. She's quite normal.' I didn't make any comment, but I felt angry. I couldn't defend my mother; everybody knew the story of Taj al-Arus, and nobody – child, girl or woman – left my mother without having heard her life history.

When I felt the labour pains starting I fled to my aunt's house. I didn't want to be in pain and to push and strain in front of Reehan. To my mind she didn't deserve to be there even at this special event.

They fetched Aleeya Tattoo to me; she forbade me to make a noise then she shouted herself as she pulled and pushed, as if she were the one giving birth. 'It's a boy! It's a boy! ' she cried as she pulled him out. 'Glory be to the Creator! His eyes are dark, he's as beautiful as the moon, and he's got a big prick: he'll only have male children. His chest's powerful. You can see the breeding in him. Naturally, since his mother's descended from sheikhs and his father from merchants.' She was lying: we weren't descended from sheikhs! Then she turned to Nasab and Taj al-Arus, screaming, 'Cover her eyes! She mustn't see the afterbirth. Go and dig deep, deep and bury the afterbirth deep, deep, because the dogs are always hungry.'

Once again I fled from Reehan's house and my son Muhammad was in my arms. It was an ordinary afternoon, the same as all the rest, and as usual Awatef had slipped in to see me when everyone in the house was asleep and the fans and air-conditioners were going full blast. We laughed a lot and chewed gum and cracked seeds between our teeth, tried on rings and imitated Reehan's glowering expressions and Khaizuran's walk, and Awatef snored, imitating the sounds rising up from Reehan's bedroom and the sitting-room where Ibrahim and his father had stretched out directly after the meal. Awatef wanted to scribble in Ibrahim's school books but I stopped her.

We padded cat-like to the kitchen. The smell of onions and garlic and the recent meal pervaded it. We began opening the cupboards, poking around for nothing in particular. Awatef took two sticks of incense and hid them in her pocket and I took a packet of sugar candy. We went on opening more cupboards until we heard someone clearing his or her throat.

Muhammad was still in his bed. I picked him up and he went on sleeping. I said to Awatef, 'He's my child and they don't even let me hold him. I want to take him and leave. Yesterday Reehan boiled a piece of lead to protect him from the evil eye and it shot out of the pot and grazed his forehead.'

Awatef winked at me and said, 'Come on, let's run away.'

I wanted to put the idea out of my head because I knew that this time I wouldn't come back. Ibrahim's family wouldn't even try and fetch me back. The scandal of my running away to have the baby in my aunt's house still occasionally cropped up in conversations and caused a stir. But all the same I took down a small suitcase from on top of the chest and put Muhammad's clean nappies and a packet of dried milk in it. I whispered to Awatef, 'You take this and I'll carry Muhammad.'

Without hesitation Awatef nodded her head, stifling her laughter. We held our breaths and went along on tiptoe. We didn't talk until we were just a few metres away from our house. The first words my aunt spoke when she saw us were, 'O Tamr, O Awatef, you're the colour of turmeric.'

5

Women normally flocked to my place in the afternoon and at sunset with their children and their relatives, bringing lengths of material and cuttings from fashion and hairdressing magazines. But during this month of Ramadan, I opened from nine in the evening and was closed all the afternoon just like the other businesses. I stayed in the shop from the morning onwards, the hair dryers idle around me, the clean towels folded one on top of the other: around the walls were photographs of hairstyles, a nature scene, and in the middle of one wall there was a clock which wasn't working; Filipino music played and a smell of food made its way down into my lungs. I felt hungry; the seamstress and the stylist were in the kitchen cooking, singing along with the cassette tape and writing letters. I wondered anxiously how I was going to get back to my brother's house in the early morning; the place wouldn't close before five and sometime tonight Jameela and her six daughters were coming to have their hair done before they went away the following day. I couldn't sleep in the shop: my brother's orders. 'Sleep by yourself in the same place as the Filipino women?' Perhaps I would ask Jameela to accompany me to the house to keep Rashid quiet.

I forgot what was troubling me as the women came cheerfully pressing on the doorbell, knocking at the door, and sat down, chose fashions, posed in front of the mirror, went into the other room to have their dresses fitted or stuck their heads under the sprays in the basins to have their hair washed. They left their abayas flung down on the chairs, all except the client waiting her turn, who kept hers around her shoulders. I sat at my table content at the throngs of women around me, the heads under the dryers and the money in the till, already more than I'd expected to take that night.

I got up from the table and walked proudly around, at ease

with every step I took now among the women who sat waiting to be called, as if they were in a government clinic. I'd felt that I had to open up a place like this to establish my independence, and I'd become well-known among families here and in other areas. The old women who accompanied their daughters, just to watch, made me pleased because the fact that they came and sat there in my shop meant that they trusted me and gave my venture their blessing.

Gradually I became unafraid of the morning and of Rashid. The door bell rang insistently. Before I opened the door I asked as usual, 'Who is it?' and heard my mother's voice reply. I turned in delight to the women sitting behind me and said excitedly, 'It's my mother and my aunt.' To myself I added, 'My aunt must have convinced Rashid.'

I turned the key in the door and before I opened it, I said to the women, 'Veil yourselves. My cousin will carry his mother in.'

They rushed into the inner room while the women under the dryers threw their abayas over the hairdryers so that their heads and the dryers were hidden from view. When I saw that my son Muhammad had come to help his cousin I was overjoyed: I cried, 'God protect you from the evil eye; stay alive for me, Muhammad,' then I laughed at myself for what I'd said. My aunt didn't want her son and Muhammad to lift her out of the wheelchair on to the ground where I'd spread out a mat in the twinkling of an eye: 'I want to see Tamr's place,' she said to the men, 'So goodbye to you.'

I locked the door behind the two of them and bent eagerly to kiss my aunt who took my face in her hands, saying, 'I said to Rashid, let's go and give our blessing to our darling Tamr's new place.' I wriggled free from my aunt's hands and went up to my mother to kiss her, and joked, 'Crown of the Bride and Crown for my Head, welcome. What do you say? Shall we take my aunt around and you can both give me your blessing for opening this place?'

I didn't let go of my mother's arm until she had wheeled

my aunt's chair into the sewing room. They touched all the dresses hanging up there, the sewing machines, the scissors and the clippings of material. My mother shouted, 'God is great! A headless jinnee!' and pointed to the mannequin which the seamstress had made out of cloth stuffed with paper and rags because she hadn't been allowed to buy a wooden dressmaker's dummy. She began striking it with the flat of her hand until it toppled over. I introduced them to the two Filipinos. My mother smiled at them and said, 'I wouldn't like to see them in my dreams.' Then she added, 'Poor things. They haven't much money and they're far away from home.' We proceeded to the next room where the Filipinos slept. The two women examined everything, even the calendar on the wall; they fingered the two girls' letters and their numerous lipsticks, the little magnifying mirror, the rush fan, and their clothes which were folded on their beds. If the stylist hadn't come into the room pretending to look for something, Taj al-Arus and Nasab wouldn't have agreed to leave the room unti they'd discovered the secret of the large orange candle burning in the centre of the table. Meanwhile I was keen to know the details of Rashid's allowing them to visit the shop; I asked them, 'Where's Batul?' 'She's coming,' replied my mother. 'She's waiting while Rashid takes Ahlam to her friend's house.' Rashid hadn't commented when Batul had said to him, 'I was going to take Ahlam with me to the salon, but she's scared that one of the women'll see her and like the look of her and tell her son or some other male relative about her. I know these young girls go around in wraps as thick as camel hide, and it's certainly not because they're thinking about what's forbidden and what's allowed in religion – they just don't want to get married yet.'

The telephone rang. I hurried to lift the receiver and replied with a smile, 'Yes, we do henna patterns. No massage. We *can* do it. Of course, I've a Filipino who knows how to do it but it's prohibited. We've got facial masques. Egg and milk, yes. The Filipino girl knows how to do it all. She's specially trained.' I replaced the receiver and announced proudly, 'That was the daughter of the Shufan family. Her mother want a massage.'

When one of the Filipino girls brought two cups of coffee, Nasab refused hers. 'I don't want it,' she said. 'I'm hot.' In English I asked the girl to fetch her a carton of juice and my mother exclaimed delightedly, 'You've got a place of your own *and* you speak English? God is great, Tamr of Tamrs.' But my aunt refused to let the Filipino pour out juice for her, and she wouldn't have any tea. She drew me close to her and whispered something to me which made me laugh. 'O Aunt!' I chided her playfully. The Filipino girl went off into the sewing room and so my aunt spoke out: 'Tamr, listen,' she said. 'There's nothing unclean about her sewing. When the other one washes hair, the women should say, "In the Name of God, the Compassionate, the Merciful". That doesn't matter too much, it's a minor uncleanness. But to take food and drink from an infidel like her is a huge uncleanness. It's forbidden. We're in Ramadan.' 'Never mind, Aunt,' I replied, irritated.

She interrupted me: 'I know. Ask any man of religion and he'll confirm what I've said, word for word. When I came into the town from the desert I wouldn't drink coffee or tea, or eat town bread or meat. My husband and his family didn't understand why. They felt sorry for me and thought I was shy. His sister Zaynab said, "Your wife's growing weak. She won't eat." My husband replied, "She's weak, is she? Every time I get into bed with her she throws me out. And when I pick myself up and try and huddle up in the bed with her, I find myself back on the floor." '

The women laughed loudly, while my aunt arranged her plait of hair. She sighed and put a hand down to her leg. 'Where's that strength gone now?' My mother reminded her of another story: 'And when they brought you a nightdress . . .' She seemed to be encouraging my aunt, so as to make it an entertaining evening. Nasab laughed and picked up the story: 'And when they brought me a nightdress I left it where it was. Zaynab said to me, "Put that on." "Why?" I asked. "Put it on and you'll see," she said. So I put it on, and before we went to bed she asked me what had happened to it and I said, "I've got it on." She didn't believe me and began to look for it under the bed. I lifted up my dress and said, "See. I told you I was wearing it." She started to laugh. "Take your dress off," she said, "and just wear the nightdress." When I asked why that time, she just said, "You win," in a weary voice.'

'What did you eat and drink in the end?' asked one of the young girls. My aunt drew herself up haughtily, seeing that she'd become the centre of attention. She struck her thigh with the flat of her hand for emphasis and replied, 'I saw Indians and Ethiopians and I was afraid that the animals hadn't been slaughtered according to religious law and that the bread had been baked by an unbeliever. I got hold of more flour and made dough, and cooked the bread in the frying pan myself, and I didn't trust the coffee unless I'd ground the beans. I knew that they were lying to me when they said that my brother-in-law had slaughtered the sheep. I ate it the first day, but not the second, and I told them that meat wouldn't pass my lips again unless I saw the animal being slaughtered with my own eyes.' An old woman who'd accompanied her daughter and granddaughter was listening to the conversation. She took out her dentures and polished them on her dress and remarked, 'I said to my son to get me a human cat like that one there,' and she waved in the direction of the Filipino girl who was bending to pick up the tray in front of them. 'He said to me, "What use would she be to you when you won't even take a drink from her?" "Turn her loose in the valley," I said, "and she can work the land, use the scythe, and harvest the crops."' 'What did he say?' asked my aunt, annoyed at being interrupted.

The old woman didn't understand; she didn't even hear the question and went back to shifting her gaze around, intently studying everything that was going on in the shop.

My aunt was playing with the coral in her necklace; between every coral bead silver coins were threaded. She continued, 'We came from the desert, your father and I,' and she turned to me. I was busy trying to add and subtract on my fingers. 'We didn't know any sweet things except dates. When we saw grapes and oranges we burst out laughing.' Then she began to laugh and slap one palm against the other. Every time she tried to stop herself she only laughed more and curiosity spread and mounted among the women around her and they begged her to tell them what she was laughing at. 'Next I found out that the drainage holes in kitchens and bathrooms weren't for squatting over and doing your business. I was visiting the sheikh's wife and they showed me the bathroom. There was a white seat in it. I lifted its lid and saw water in the bottom of it. I said to myself, "That's to protect it from flies," and washed my face. Thank God I didn't drink from it. Then I looked around for the lavatory. I got out of the place and went to ask again. They took me back to the bathroom, but this time the Ethiopian maid came in with me and opened the lid of the seat and pointed.'

The women laughed briefly, then were distracted by the hairstyle on Jameela's daughter. But my aunt didn't want to be quiet, so she found herself having to direct her conversation to me. 'Your grandmother wouldn't leave the desert except on my wedding day, and when your father married Najeeya, poor mother, the heat was enough to dry a gazelle's tears and she wouldn't leave the desert. Your father and I looked for her and when we saw that the water had dried up we went from oasis to oasis. She didn't realize this. She sent us messages — desert lavender and camels' milk. She didn't like townspeople; when we were having an argument she would scoff at me for sleeping in a bed, using electricity, letting my voice be carried in and out on a telephone, not knowing the difference between a lizard and a gazelle, nor how to stop a locust sliding around in the cooking fat. "O mother," I would ask her, "who married me to someone from the town? Who said that she wanted Nasab to live in a house built of bricks, with a television, and to buy seeds and chewing gum from the shops?" ' Nasab took a deep breath and continued, 'Even when my father, your grandfather, came into the town complaining about his gut and your father took him to the Sultan's doctor – as he and the Sultan had become like brothers – your grandfather wouldn't leave his camel. Your father agreed to tie the camel up at the door of the house. Your grandfather fled from the house whenever Najeeya turned on the radio. He didn't like sitting at the table to eat: he would put some food on his plate and go and keep the camel company.

'Poor thing. He didn't like Najeeya going into the room where he slept; your father had to give him a clean towel and sheet and do his washing for him and bring him his food. Whenever Najeeya wanted to go and visit relations your father lied to him and told him that Najeeya was ill and was going to the doctor, because as far as your grandfather was concerned women were forbidden to leave the house.'

One of the women opened a bag of ear-rings and bracelets and combs which she'd brought from Beirut. I was glad for her to display them in my place. The women and children fell on them and they were scattered, some on the floor, some picked up by the children, some stuck in hair, or hung on ears. In the twinkling of an eye the women had bought everything in the bag. My aunt was plainly irritated: she wanted to say a lot and found herself with no one to listen to her. So I said to her, 'And what next, Auntie . . . ? ' and she took a deep breath and laughed loudly to attract attention to herself again, then continued: 'We missed the desert, the smell of sand and goats and coffee and roasting meat and fires being kindled. But I liked the easy life in the town and quickly picked up the ways of the people, and my mother-in-law was happy with me because I had an enormous capacity for hard work. Although I must say, at the beginning I thought the people odd: they liked useless things and put them in their houses. It was hard for me to eat three times a day, and as for the amount of meat they ate . . . I refused to take hold of fish without covering their eyes with the edge of my handkerchief. I used to say, "There is no strength and no power save in God," to allay my scruples whenever my mother-in-law took a needle and thread and sewed up the chicken's backside after she'd stuffed it with breadcrumbs and rice; it surprised me to see them cooking tomatoes when they were so precious. I'd never imagined that one day I'd move freely in town dwellers' houses even when my father married me to one; I thought that he'd live in tents with us. But I went back with him, and I could have gone back with one of his friends instead, except that when my father told the two of them that he had a girl of marriageable age it happened to be him who shouted first, "I'll marry her." '

The women were bubbling like a hive of bees. My mother and my aunt laughed secretly at the hairstyles, comparing them to goats' horns, bananas, roosters' crests, especially when the woman covered her head and the cover was raised up high. They signalled comments about the Filipinos to one another, wiggling their eyebrows about every time one of the girls passed in front of them. 'That one's lust incarnate,' remarked my aunt, 'because she hasn't had a taste of her husband for three months; she's got children of her own. Every day she has a fight about something. She wants to go out to the shops and Tamr knows that it's to chat with men of her own type and religion. Tamr said to her, "You're not going out except with me." Anyway the neighbours and the shop owners round about are just waiting for a sign: they don't want a woman to start up in business and they're watching for evidence in any shape or form to use against her. The Filipino girl knows that.'

I shut the ledger and locked it away in the drawer, then moved my chair round until I was facing my mother and aunt. 'Guess who came this morning!' 'The men who close down shops owned by women,' surmised my customers.

Laughing, I replied, 'No. Not this time. They came the day before yesterday and asked if we had any men in here. I said to them, "Can't you read what's written on the door?" but they asked me again if I was quite sure. So I said to them, "If you like I'll open the door for you. Wait a minute while we get veiled." But they didn't come in.' My mother and aunt couldn't guess who'd come to see me and they began to look impatient, so I said enthusiastically, 'Reehan, Ibrahim's mother, with her granddaughters. They were going to a wedding. If you'd seen her clothes: they were all silk and her jewellery was Italian and her handbag was real leather. But she was still mean: she asked the price of henna and when I told her she said, "Hell!", and wanted us to use some that she'd brought with her, but I refused. The Filipino gave her granddaughter a facial – what's the girl's name? I remember, Khulood – and for a whole hour Reehan didn't stop cursing and complaining that the prices were too high while the girl tried to make her be quiet. Anyhow, those are days I'd rather forget.'

It was all quiet in the room except for the sound of my mother's voice as she spoke to the old woman: 'And Mauza said, "You can have contact with this other man, Antan, as long as there's a door between you and he doesn't see you and you don't see him. Nobody'll know and you'll become a Sultana and your son will be a Sultan . . . " '

I rose and went over to my mother, annoyance showing on my face. But the old woman looked confused and I felt reassured; it appeared that she hadn't understood a single word of what my mother was saying. 'Would you like to have a dress made, Taj? ' I asked her, relenting.

6

I became irritated every time I was with my mother in a gathering of women, and could no longer bear sitting like a shepherd, frightened to close his eyes even for a second in case his flock should stray. Taj al-Arus could never resist telling the story of her life, and I'd threatened more than once not to accompany her over the threshold of a house.

While she sat waiting for my aunt and me to come home, she would think in anguish how I was no longer a sheikh's wife, remembering how my aunt Nasab had brought embroidered cloth back from Iran to make a nightdress for my wedding night, and how she herself had insisted that the cloth be cut in the shape of a big heart at the navel and a little heart at each breast, and then that there should be henna patterns in each of these openings.

Taj al-Arus had been certain that this wedding nightdress would ensnare the sheikh's heart for ever, for the Sudanese girl whom the Sultan had taken for his wife and kept as his wife for a long time, asking for her and no other every night, had once told them her secret. In front of them she put on her white wedding nightdress and showed them the hearts on it, some embroidered and some open to show off henna patterns on her skin. She told them that night that the Sultan used to open a jewel box and play with her for hours, trying to fit pieces of jewellery into each heart-shaped hole and, where he succeeded, giving the ring or trinket to her for her own.

Taj al-Arus had heaved a sigh as she listened to this story, and thought that perhaps the man who'd been waiting in the room when Mauza pushed her through the door, and who'd lain on top of her and hurt her while she kept her eyes tightly shut, wasn't the Sultan: he hadn't played with her like that even though his room had been large, his bed gold, the carpet soft, and an air-conditioner had been humming in the room.

She wanted to hear more and she felt envious of the Sudanese girl, although the others talked about what she'd said and called her a liar.

Whenever she was in a gathering of women it always struck Taj that she might have been Sultana over them, and she found herself interrupting them and telling them her story however much she'd promised not to anger me in future, and not to open her mouth except to eat.

She used to sing traditional Turkish songs in a gentle voice, and the kohl round her green eyes was washed away by her tears; these eyes were sometimes cloudy, sometimes clear, and her cheeks turned the colour of roses. Her long neck grew longer as she looked constantly at the ceiling or out to the horizon, never meeting the eyes fixed upon her. It was as if she were pursuing her memories, or as if they had been there with her constantly since the day she went bewildered to the train, and saw her father bending to kiss the Sultan's hand and heard him saying in Turkish, 'Taj al-Arus is your lawful right, as she is your wife, and your sister should you divorce her. She's my youngest daughter and the apple of my eye.' The Sultan pressed his hand, and he walked away gathering in the skirts of his abaya which were flying up in the wind. Her curiosity was directed at the prospect of travelling in a train, and she felt a simple pleasure at the thought of seeing another country, mixed with fear because she couldn't understand the language which these men were speaking. 'You're a Sultana,' her mother had said to her, as she searched her long red hair for lice, massaged it with black mud and poured rosewater over it. Then she rubbed her body all over with a loofah and olive oil soap, poured water over it and dried it, saying, 'The Crown of the Bride has become a Crown of Kings.'

Their house was the largest in the village, and her father was the village mayor. The Sultan had come from the desert with his retinue to take a water cure, and had been her father's guest. In the time it takes to blink, Taj al-Arus, her seven brothers and sisters and their mother had been moved to her uncle's house, the whole of which was transformed into a giant kitchen. The women and girls stuffed ducks, rolled up vine leaves, plucked and roasted sparrows, and impaled meat on skewers for kebabs. Her father, her brothers, her uncle and her cousins carried the trays of food. On the last night her father bowed so low that his head touched the ground, and the Sultan presented him with a gold watch with his picture on it, and a gold ring set with a diamond; her father found himself telling the Sultan that he was ready to give him his soul, and the most precious thing in the world to him was Taj al-Arus.

One of them translated her name for the Sultan – 'Crown of the Bride' – and it pleased him and he said, 'I accept her.'

Before Taj boarded the train she turned to look behind her and saw all the people of her village waving brightly-coloured handkerchiefs; the women were trilling and the children running along beside them. As the train moved away and Taj's heart sank, she stretched her long neck out of the window and saw all the village dogs chasing the train, barking wildly, and she felt a surge of affection for them and laughed out loud. As the train drew away the dogs were still running.

When the train halted after many hours, Taj stuck her head out of the window again, and all she could see was sand. Then the men got down and she was left by herself. She wondered if they'd forgotten her but they came back for her and sat her in the back seat of a car, and the party set off again. After some time they stopped and got out and again she stayed where she was, wondering if they'd forgotten about her, until in the end one of them came back and pushed a black wrap at her, and an abaya, and indicated that she should put them round her: she was wearing a dress with trousers under it, and her head was covered by an embroidered scarf with little silver beads hanging from it.

All she could see was sand and a few houses, and tents;

they went into a courtyard without a single plant growing in it; there was sand here too and small stones and beyond it a large colourless building. She could hear noises of children and women's voices, but saw no one. She didn't move until the driver opened the door and signalled to her to follow him into the big building. When they were inside he shouted 'Mauza!' three times and disappeared. A woman emerged. Only her face was uncovered but Taj could see that she was tall and broad. She kissed Taj on both cheeks and took her by the hand. They passed through a large room with huge brightly-coloured sofas ranged around the walls, and into a corridor with numerous other rooms opening off it. Taj found it extremely hot. The woman opened a door at the end of a passage. The room turned out to be taken up almost entirely by a brass bed. Taj stood with her eyes downcast until the woman vanished, closing the door behind her. Taj had scarcely poised herself on the edge of the bed when the woman came back, handed her a towel and soap, and led her along the corridor to a bathroom; here she pointed to some water in a barrel and to the soap and then reached out a hand to Taj's chest. Taj understood and began to wash, her eyes on the closed door, thinking uneasily that she would lose her way as soon as she went out of the room. But the woman was waiting for her; she took her back to her room and signed to her to undo her bundle of clothes.

When Taj had done this, the woman looked through them and threw them aside. She went out of the room, and Taj al-Arus fingered her clothes and the things which her mother had collected for her from the neighbours and her female relatives, and thought about what the woman was doing. The woman returned with a long dress which she gave to Taj to put on. It was tight across the chest; Taj al-Arus held her breath and climbed into it, then sat back down on the bed. The door opened and the same woman entered with a tray with a glass of very sweet tea on it. Before she'd drunk it the woman handed her some dates, then poured a green fluid from a copper jug into a little cup. Taj ate the dates voraciously, but when she tasted what was in the little cup she moved it abruptly away from her lips.

'That's our coffee,' said the woman. 'You'll have to get to like it. It's nice.' Taj al-Arus smiled at her, not understanding. The woman turned to leave and gestured to Taj to follow her. They passed through silent rooms, then through rooms noisy with shouting and boisterous laughter. Through the black cover which the woman had thrown around her face Taj saw a man's face, and then another.

It was difficult to walk with the black abaya wrapped around her. All of a sudden she was met by a stinging heat like the heat she'd felt when she put her hand on the coals and glowing ashes in the copper stove at home. It didn't leave her until she went inside again, this time into another building in the yard itself, and found out where the noise of children and the women's cries were coming from. The woman took her into a long chamber where there was a table with chairs all round it, laid with a plastic cloth and trays of rice and meat. She thought it must be in her honour, but soon changed her mind, and turned away from the eyes which bored into her with scorn and hostility as their owners talked to the woman who'd brought her; then she heard laughter interspersed with words. When she reached out a hand to eat she found her plate heaped up with rice and pieces of meat. She sat for some time until the woman got to her feet, wiping her mouth on her sleeve, and signalled to Taj to get up and go with her. Again the heat struck her and seared into her until she reached the other building. Taj realized that it was the first building when the woman opened a door and she saw her bundle. The woman went away for a few moments and came back with a bottle of perfume in her hand. She sprinkled it over Taj and asked her, 'Is that nice?'

She went away again briefly and this time she came back with an incense burner which she placed near Taj, gesturing to her to fan the smoke about. When Taj clearly couldn't understand what she had to do, then woman held the incense burner close to Taj's chest, then she bent down to lift up Taj's skirt and Taj felt warm smoke on her thighs. The woman raised her own dress and wafted the burner around her thighs, then set off in front of Taj still carrying the burner. She went up a short flight of stairs and knocked on the door at the top. When she heard the sound of a voice, or a throat being cleared, she pushed Taj al-Arus gently forward.

The following day, the same woman came to her and gave her a Qur'an inlaid with diamonds and sapphires, gold bangles, and a pendant with 'What God has willed' inscribed on it. 'From the Sultan,' she told her. Taj was delighted with the jewellery which shone like nothing she'd ever seen in her life before.

She found herself thinking of her family and her neighbours and friends for the first time since she'd arrived, and she pictured their eyes and their fingers pursuing the sparkling treasures, not believing that it all belonged to her. The woman took Taj down to the ground floor, across the yard, and into the other building which resembled a Turkish army barracks. The woman no longer summoned her to eat with her. Taj felt as if she was in the middle of a market: movement and noise; women, girls, and boys of every race, age and colour. She began imitating the others, sitting down to eat when they did, going out into the yard if they did, then attaching herself to groups of them, sitting as they sat, even beginning to drink the thread of green liquid when it was poured out into the tiny cups.

The day after that Taj al-Arus began to learn how she should behave in the yard, in the gatherings of women and in the bedrooms. The noise no longer bothered her; she grew accustomed to the presence of large numbers of black and white children and their loud voices and their talk and laughter. She was no longer shy at table and she picked up the rice just like all the rest of them, gathering it together in her fingers and throwing it into her mouth. She tore the meat apart, remembering her sisters and brothers and how at home everybody had shared out the food together; now she was on her own.

In the yard a fire was burning with a giant spoon resting on the coals containing green beans – coffee beans; she saw a woman roasting them for several minutes then pounding them until they looked like cracked wheat; then she stood close to the fire and watched the coffee powder and sugar and fat simmering together. She wished that she could take the old woman's place at the fire; she wanted to know how she was going to live, what she was going to do: in Turkey she had been used to starting work at daybreak.

Had she done something wrong when she'd gone into the vast room and the Sultan had approached her and lain on top of her? Even when it hurt her she hadn't started to cry. At the sound of the muezzin she'd thought of her mother and father and brothers and sisters, and of the walnut tree, and how she used to pick a nut and rub its shell on her lips until they were stained red, turning to a deep dark brownish crimson after a few moments.

She forgot about her family when she heard a loud voice echoing all round the building: 'Prayers! Time for prayers!' She had to hurry like the rest of them to do her ritual ablutions and pray with the other women in the large chamber, while the men had their own mosque. She copied the others and prayed humbly to God.

That evening when she met the first woman's eyes and she didn't call her over, Taj wondered if she was expected to sleep in the Sultan's room like the night before. Then she remembered her bundle of clothes and went off to try and find the way to the outside door. It was locked. She tried to ask a woman but she couldn't understand a word she said and didn't know how to get rid of her. She made her way back to where the other women were and smiled at them and searched for Mauza, the one who had looked after her on her arrival, afraid that there was nowhere for her to sleep. Taj slept in her clothes in an empty bed surrounded by four other empty beds, her hand on her brassière where she'd hidden the Sultan's presents.

In the morning she woke early and lay there taking in the room, which was bare except for big ceiling fans: the centralized air-conditioning wasn't enough for all the rooms. She thought of the mirror at home which had pictures pinned all round its wooden frame. The bedrooms here were more or less empty except for beds, chests and cushions propped against the walls. When she bent down to get her shoes she noticed dust under the beds and all over the floor; in some places it had accumulated in little fluffy balls which looked to her like grey mice. How she wished she could swill water over everything and give it a thorough cleaning from top to bottom, but she remembered that she was a Sultana.

She knew for sure that the Sultanas in this place were different from the Queens she'd heard about. Here a Sultana ate, drank, prayed, slept, danced, sang, and didn't work, unlike a Queen in a story who sat on a throne with a crown on her head and a whip in her hand, ordering the sun to set and the moon to shine. And the Sultan didn't sit counting his jewels: indeed, a lot of his time was spent travelling. When she came to think about the small children, of whom there were perhaps more than a hundred, her mind became confused.

The place had a smell, incense and food; even the clamour, the running and movement from room to room, the lying on beds and on the floor had a smell. It was the women's perfume floating out into the air. Strange perfumes; Taj didn't know that they were Indian and desert perfumes, and that only the Sultan's paramour wore European perfume. They rose up from the tinkling of the gold bangles and the belts and jewelled Qur'ans, smells of henna and oil and jasmine.

She grew used to the comfortable noisy life, the mixture of sleeping and staying up late, sometimes till dawn. All the same she didn't open her heart to a single one of them; the only points of similarity between them and the women from her village were their plump bodies and the gold in their teeth.

She no longer thought of the language as the obstacle, as she had done previously. The reason she felt distant from them lay in what she saw at nights, the rustling and whispering which she heard; Fatima's sighs and the creaking of her bed; the uproar around the door as Belkis clung to it. These things kept Taj awake for hours. After some time she found out why Fatima was sighing; one night another of the women who slept in the room crept up and whipped back Fatima's covers while at the same time another switched on the light: her lower half was naked. The more she swore at them, the more they laughed and when she screamed at them they imitated her. Since she could do nothing against them she rolled herself up in a blanket and closed her eyes.

After this episode Taj refused to eat for two days and was moved into another room. It was Mauza who arranged for her to move and she also brought her the bundle of clothes she'd carried from Turkey. The new room only had a few beds in it; the girls were beautiful and they were Taj's age or slightly older, whereas Fatima and the others had been much older, and more than once one of them had tried to be affectionate to her by putting a hand on her chest: at first Taj had thought she was trying to steal her jewellery.

The first night in the new room didn't pass as peacefully as she had expected, and nor did the following nights. It agitated her the way Belkis stood waiting for so long, then leant against the locked door after Mauza had gone round locking all the rooms, turning out the lights and listening to the complaints.

Taj al-Arus didn't dare to ask Belkis what she was doing every night at the locked door, supporting herself against it with her hands held above her head, although she didn't think she was trying to open it for she emitted faint noises as she stood there. By the time Taj al-Arus found out the reason she knew, despite the fact that she was only fourteen years old, a lot about men and women; she also knew the secret shared by all the women there, the young and old, the black and the light-skinned; she knew about the children, the Sultan, the Sultana, and about herself: she knew that she was waiting and they were all waiting with her, even the Sultan, for the end of the month. If she didn't have a period, all the rest of them would envy her, and the Sultan would be told that he was expecting a son or a daughter from his red-haired Turkish bride; she would still be his wife and the contract which had been drawn up in the village between her father and one of the Sultan's aides would remain valid. 'Shall I become a Sultana?' Taj al-Arus asked Mauza, who clearly knew all languages: Ethiopian, Somali, Syrian, Albanian, even a bit of Turkish. Mauza nodded her head: 'A Sultana. He'll give you an allowance, gold jewellery, dresses. You'll have a room of your own, maybe even a palace. And the Sultan will come and see you and his offspring. Everyone will listen to what you say; in social gatherings they'll bring the incense burner to you first and give you a leg of mutton and a cup of coffee before the other guests, and you'll have two personal attendants.' Because all the women wanted this for themselves Taj al-Arus wanted it too. Her eyes were aglow with the heat of her enthusiasm, and she looked upwards, supplicating God. For the first time she understood the secret of the eyes fixed on the ceiling: the young ones must have been praying to be pregnant, the old ones devoutly hoping for the opposite.

Taj seized Mauza's hand beseechingly. 'What if I don't get pregnant?' she asked, pointing to her stomach. Mauza smiled. 'You'll get pregnant, God willing,' she said. 'You follow my advice and your stomach will swell up under your chin, and when the Sultan hears the cry of his newborn son he'll give you his weight in gold, and if it's a girl half her weight in gold. And you remember Mauza and give her whatever you feel you should.' Quickly, Taj al-Arus asked again, 'What if I don't get pregnant?'

'You'll get pregnant if you trust Mauza,' she replied.

Taj al-Arus learnt that she would have to lean against the door after the rest were asleep, and when she heard a rattling, she should lift her nightdress and drop her pants down around her feet and press up against the door just where there was a big wide hole, and there would be a man outside ready.

Taj al-Arus hid her face in her hands, not wanting to hear more, while Mauza, seeing the girl's reaction, hurried to make light of it and said she'd been teasing her. Taj al-Arus discovered that even if she gave birth to a son or a daughter, the Sultan would eventually divorce her and she'd never become a Sultana; she'd been wrong to think that he had over a hundred wives; the fact was that he would even divorce her, his youngest wife, to give himself the chance to marry others.

Three of the women besides her were still the Sultan's wives and the rest were divorced from him but preferred to stay in the big house helping to bring up the little sultans; some of them married again to drivers and servants.

Taj al-Arus didn't get pregnant, but she didn't consider going back to her village because she was still enjoying the light blazing from the lamps, and admiring the water flowing from the tap.

Another month passed and Mauza came asking Taj to gather up her possessions and prepare to leave. She asked her for a keepsake. For the first time for ages Taj al-Arus thought about her family and her heartbeat quickened, but Mauza told her that the Sultan had divorced her and was going to marry her to a friend of his, and somewhere in the building the first chapter of the Qur'an had been recited and the agreement concluded in her absence. She left the big house wrapped in her abaya. She touched her jewellery; when she wore it she felt like a Sultana, because hers hadn't changed colour like the others'. She remembered how she'd heard some of them shriek when they saw their emeralds and sapphires changing colour as they washed their hands or rubbed their clothes in washing powder; after that they'd avoided washing powder like the plague. Through the black cover she saw the yard – sand and small stones without a single plant. She was told to sit in the back seat of the car. The roads were like the yard, only long, and the car didn't stop until nightfall. When the driver and the man who'd been sitting next to him got out of the car, she did the same.

When the Sultan's friend saw her he said, 'So you're Taj al-Arus? ' He took hold of her long red hair and pulled it, not believing that such hair could belong to a human woman and thinking she must be a jinnee. When she gave a cry of pain he was satisfied that she was human. He didn't leave her room for three nights. He'd put her in a high room the night they'd brought her to him. The two of them had climbed a long flight of stairs and he'd taken her into a room which smelt of dates. He told her not to leave this room except to go to the bathroom on the second floor, and not to talk to any woman she might see. She was brought food on a tray by a young girl, and on the third day the door was pushed open: two women stood there without speaking. They took her down the long staircase to the entrance.

One of them pointed to a bucket of water and indicated to Taj that she should pick it up and take it upstairs and empty it into a large barrel there. She followed her and directed her to go back downstairs again where she lifted up a plank of wood, hauled up another bucket on the end of a rope and poured water from it into the first bucket. She gestured to Taj to do as she'd done then looked up, pointing to the long flights of stairs. Taj al-Arus was frightened of the well and said nothing. When her husband came to her she cried. He asked her what was wrong and she told him, but he didn't understand. He left the high room and later when he tried talking to her again she didn't understand a word he said.

In time she found out that the two women were Jauhar and Najeeya, his wives, and that they had taken it upon themselves to order her about; they blamed her for everything that went wrong and even invented mistakes she was supposed to have made: burnt food, water spilt on the stairs; when the children screamed they accused her of hitting them. They even stole from her and her husband. Taj became pregnant twice, and gave birth to two stillborn children, a boy and then a girl. As soon as she'd learnt some Arabic she told Jauhar and Najeeya that she'd been a Sultan's wife, and that if she'd had his child she wouldn't have been there with them then. When she got pregnant again she stayed in bed in the high room and refused to get up because she'd realized that they'd made her carry the bucket as an act of hostility towards her: she'd seen the black servant letting the bucket down to his wife who was standing by the well, and then pulling it back up. She noticed that her husband had changed. He no longer called her 'Crown of Kings'; he shouted at her and inquired of her sarcastically why there had been all that trouble and waiting if she was going to give birth to two dead children. Sometimes he panted with excitement on top of her, but no sooner had his head touched the pillow than he fell asleep and started to snore. He no longer came to her each night. One morning she held the pillow in her arms wondering why her husband slept as soon as he rested his head on it. She felt it and her hand came up against something hard; she began pulling apart the fibres of the pillow and saw embedded in the cotton some charred pieces of paper with writing on them. That night she showed them to her husband. He seized them with eager rage and descended the stairs: she could hear him shouting and threatening as he went. Later on he came back into the room and shouted at her and beat her and told her that he'd found out about her being unfaithful to him with the servant. Then he pulled her by the hair down to the second floor and pointed to a rifle hanging on the wall. He screamed at her that he would wait for the black boy or the stillborn black girl before he fired it. She smiled and went back to bed and slept as she'd never slept before. She gave birth to me after she'd been pregnant for four years.

My father came back to the high room with silver and dates and a box containing English and Turkish gold sovereigns and necklaces of coral, sapphires, gold and emeralds and placed them all around me. I was beautiful and my skin was the same colour as his. From the terrace adjoining the room he made two big rooms, so that I could run about and go down without falling on the stairs. But Najeeya and Jauhar wouldn't keep their mouths shut. Misery and spite made them ever more inclined to accuse Taj al-Arus of everything that went wrong in the house, and she never knew why he came to her after a long trip to India and said he was divorcing her. She didn't leave the house, saying that she would wait until I was married, and she no longer saw him, although she heard him talking to me and playing with me, as he married a young girl he brought back from India with him. She didn't ask him why he divorced her and not Jauhar and Najeeya; she was told that they were related to him and what's more she wasn't from the desert. She asked, 'Why didn't he bring his wife to live in this house as he brought me?' Jauhar answered, 'The man's afraid of you. Glory be to Him who made you different. In the Name of God the Compassionate, the Merciful! Your head's like a piece of cloth unrolled and blown here and there by the wind. Your eyes dance and move around and never focus on a fixed point. And your voice – in the Name of God the compassionate, the Merciful! – one moment it's sensible, the next it's wild, and one moment you're a pious Muslim, the next you're the Devil's creature. Tell me, tell me, are you right in the head or crazy?'

7

The noise lessened with the departure of most of the women. When my cousin and my son Muhammad came I went down with my mother and we sat in the car and waited for my aunt. The two Filipino girls stood in the middle of the street, happiness written all over their faces; this was one of the few times they'd been able to go out into the street, see the night and breathe air which was hot and sticky but at least wasn't manufactured by the air-conditioner. They helped lift my aunt into the car and when they'd gone inside I got out of the car and locked the shop door behind them. I called out good night but didn't hear them reply.

I closed my eyes as the car sped along with us, wondering why they were so annoyed at not going out. How could I let them go out when the men here were like traps set ready for them? I felt happier as I began to think about renting a second flat now that there was no longer room for my clients, in spite of the objections raised daily by my son. My aunt remarked suddenly. 'Congratulations, Tamr, and God willing we'll be able to congratulate you on finding a new husband before long.'

Once in the past she'd given me the names of three highly eligible men and urged me to speak to all three of them on the telephone and choose one of them. I insisted that I should meet them: I would only marry a man whom I'd seen and talked to. The past was no longer clear, or painful. I felt tired and turned to my mother. Her eyes were closed and there was a half-smile on her face: she must have been dreaming of her homeland.

Later that same night everyone in the house was asleep except Taj al-Arus. She was afraid that if she closed her eyes an angel or a devil would whisk her away to Turkey, and the smell of the gaseous springs for which her village was famous would penetrate her mind, used by now to the smell of humidity and sand and the noise of air-conditioners, and make her lose it.

Taj al-Arus opened her eyes in terror and recited, 'In the Name of God the Compassionate, the Merciful.' She stared in front of her for a long time and could see nothing. The darkness had swallowed everything up. 'Tamr. Tamr. Rashid. Batul,' she screamed. She screamed until she saw the three of us bending over her; she didn't know why these faces looked scared and asked them what was wrong. Our hands shook her and our fingers brought water up to her lips and one face was crying: my face. When we were all gathered around her she could see everything she was used to seeing each day in the distorted mirror: heaps of bags and clothes in one corner, the cracks in the walls, a cord hanging from the ceiling with a bulb on the end of it; the room had no window.

'Rashid. Tamr. Batul.' She knew these names, but not the faces. She told us that she'd been with her mother and father and other relations and heard herself calling out to them and laughing with the village girls; she knew each one, remembered the dress each one wore, the colour of her kerchief. She remembered every house in the village, the colour of the earth and the mud, the distance between every corner, every street. She saw herself pushing her kerchief back off her forehead so that the pearls and gold rings didn't go in her eyes while she was plucking a duck and making kebabs, and she saw again the freckles on her firm white hands and on her face. She peered into the faces in front of her and muttered, 'God protect me from the accursed Devil,' and realized that she was dreaming, and that we were the faces that went with the names which she knew. Rashid and Batul went back to their room while I climbed into bed next to my mother; she closed her eyes and turned on her right side as usual. She didn't sleep, and she didn't cry out although her heart was pounding and there was a rattling in her throat which obstructed her breathing. 'What's wrong, mother?' I whispered. 'What's upsetting you?' And she was saying, 'Forgive me, Lord. Forgive me, mother, father.' She sat up in bed and told me that she'd remembered carrying her little brother and sister one on each hip, and running with them for fun, the chains around her neck chinking and rattling, and how they'd wailed and clung to her in fright. She could picture the dress her little sister had been wearing and her brother's bare feet knocking against her as she ran, and even the shape and size of the blisters on them.

Taj al-Arus felt a heat in her chest, and pushing the cover back she got up and paced about the room like a cat search-ing for her little ones, even though she's seen them all dan-gling from the mouth of a wild animal. The heat rose up into her head and she cried out to herself, 'Why so long? What's become of them?'

When the floor began to reverberate to the sound of her feet, even though they were so small and slender, I rose to take her back to bed. My aunt had heard her cry and called from her room, 'What's got into you, Taj? The Sultan's a heap of bones. Tamr isn't going to marry any sultans. For God's sake go to sleep.'

Nevertheless, Taj al-Arus sat describing the roads and pathways to me, telling me the names of the trees, recounting how the whole village thought that the hot springs were the Devil's bath. She described her mother, her father, her brothers and sisters, the earthenware jar of figs the size of stones, the snow, the ducks, the pomegranate juice; how they'd distilled rose water, fattened the sheep, made rag dolls, and cats of clay and water. When I showed interest and prompted her to tell me more, she settled into her stride and plunged ahead impetuously as if she were coming closer and closer to her village. All of a sudden she stopped and asked in Turkish, 'Do you think they remember me?'

In the morning I got up, my aunt grumbled restlessly, and it seemed as if the daily routine of the house had begun: Rashid's children made a noise; Batul shouted at them; the water boiled on the stove and the smell of coffee filled the place. Taj al-Arus gathered her nightdress around her as if she didn't want any person or thing to reach her or come near her feelings, in case they took away what she was bent on preserving. She withdrew, her rosary in her hands, telling its beads. She couldn't see any freckles on her hands and for a long time there hadn't been any on her face either. Jauhar or Najeeya had once said to her mockingly, 'God protect us. You've got eyes all over your face!' When my father stopped coming to see her, Taj never missed an opportunity to ask every woman she met, old or young, how to remove the freckles.

She got up from her corner and announced to us all that she was going to Turkey. My aunt laughed but I was afraid of the turn my mother's thoughts were taking, and replied quickly, 'They might have died a long time ago, then what would happen to you?' Taj al-Arus didn't make any comment but she was determined to go, and began bundling her clothes into my case, and preparing the reply she would give if anybody asked her whether she was really a Sultana. Her clothes were not the clothes of a Sultana, nor were the earrings and necklaces and bangles she wore now the jewellery of a Sultana. She deliberated and went off into corners by herself and wept constantly, until Rashid eventually decided to arrange the trip for her, although she swore that her village wasn't far from Bursa and that she had been to Bursa on foot. Rashid made enquiries about the area she came from, but unexpectedly no one could help him: the countless women who'd been brought to the Sultan were from every country under the sun. Rashid didn't feel at ease about her until he'd entrusted her to some Turkish pilgrims who were on their way home, and who assured him that they would bring her back to the desert whenever she wished to come.

During the time she was away from the house, my Aunt Nasab made predictions: 'Taj al-Arus must be staying at one of her sisters' houses now. Or perhaps her mother is still alive . . . ' while I blamed myself because I hadn't stood up to Rashid when he forbade me to go with her, then took comfort when my aunt laughed and remarked, 'Taj is sure to be lying to them, and pretending she's a Sultana!' I pictured my mother's bewilderment at being alone for the first time in forty years.

When Taj al-Arus came back after a week, she handed out boxes of Turkish Delight to us with an expressionless face, and refused to say anything about her trip.

She had known, as soon as she arrived in Bursa, that she would never reach her village. Even the ornate and plentiful minarets, which she was told were hundreds of years old, looked strange to her. She was taken to a number of villages, and in the village squares the people gathered around her, old and young, men and women, wearing clothes very different from how she'd remembered them. She could no longer see the pathways which she'd seen in her dreams, nor the trees, nor the houses which she'd remembered stone by stone, and she didn't go running up to her own house. When the guide told them her story, in case any of the old people remembered the Sultan's visit and the cars parked in the village field and the dogs which had barked and followed the train for miles, it was passed around from ear to ear. The crowd took several paces forward to see at close quarters the woman whom the Sultan of that far off land beyond the railway line had married. When this happened she gathered herself in and pulled her abaya more closely round her. Her heart beat fiercely and she took refuge in silence, praying fervently. She found an opening for one eye to see through the blackness, and looked at the inquisitive faces. One man introduced himself to her and said that she was his aunt, and took her to his strange house.

As she studied his strange face, she couldn't smell the springs, and when she asked him about them she realized that he'd been lying. All the same she kept waiting for something unexpected to happen. As soon as he found out from the women clustered around her that there was no gold in her bag he handed her back to the guide.

She didn't despair, except once when she was sitting in a village square under a spreading tree surrounded by men and women and children, and she started to think. There were birds twittering right overhead and they didn't stop singing even though small children were pelting them with stones. Like every other time she felt embarrassed; but this time that embarrassment was mixed with disappointment and sorrow, perhaps because the children were unconcerned by her presence as they threw stones at the birds, and the grown-ups said nothing when the stones landed all around her and one of them hit her on the hand; and perhaps because she was starting to get bird droppings on her abaya. She found herself thinking for the first time, 'Why? Why?' She pictured her father bending happily to kiss the Sultan's hand, the whole village lined up to watch Taj al-Arus leaving to become a queen, and only the dogs chasing after her.

Suzanne

1

I moved the packets and jars out of the way and took down the slender bottle. Although I could hear Maaz joking with Ringo, his loud laughter like the chattering of monkeys, I went to the door of the kitchen to make sure, then hurried back and poured Scotch and water into the glass, took the lid off the narrow bottle and brought it close to the glass. How was it going to be possible to add just two drops? I was at a loss, and afraid that Ringo and Maaz would come in while I was holding the bottle. But all the same I began to tilt it slowly towards the glass as if I was squeezing the breath out of it: one drop, two, or twenty? This time I hid the bottle in a cooking pot and picked up the glass, but I didn't leave the kitchen. Had I put in three drops or twenty? Perhaps he'd be poisoned, die even. I went towards the sink to pour it away, but then drew back. This was my last chance and I had to risk it. I encouraged myself with the thought that if anything terrible happened nobody would realize the cause. They'd blame the Scotch and bundle the case out of sight, just as they'd bundle him away if he died. I found I was shaking my head, revolted by my own thoughts. Was I trying to calm myself down because I was scared, or had I really grown that hard?

When Ringo saw me coming with the glass in my hand, he rose to his feet announcing that he would begin by cleaning the rooms on the top floor. I gave the glass to Maaz, hoping that he wouldn't notice my hand shaking. I looked at Ringo and pointed to my mouth and my cheek. He nodded and went upstairs and came down a few moments later with my make-up bag. I sat down facing Maaz, trying to appear indifferent, although my heart had begun to beat violently and my mouth was twisted to one side with the force of my agitation.

Each time his mouth went down to the glass and he drank, I felt a throbbing pulse in my neck; when he'd finished he handed me the empty glass and said, 'More iced tea, Suzie. Why aren't you drinking with me?'

I stood up holding the glass, trying to control my twitching mouth. With a forced coquettishness, I pronounced, 'You can't live without Scotch, and I can't live without you.'

Maaz laughed his loud laugh and put his hand to his heart: 'Our hearts are our witnesses, Suzie.'

I went into the kitchen and put on lipstick and powder, using the glass door of the oven as a mirror. I told myself solemnly that I'd hear his body crashing to the floor any moment now. As I poured more Scotch and water into his glass a voice of guilt whispered inside me, blotting out everything else, 'Sita said I had to mix the drops with tea or coffee, and here I am adding them to Scotch,' But then I pushed away the idea that something would happen to him, offering myself the justification that Sita would never have heard of Scotch and wouldn't know what it was.

I was still shaking and I blamed Suha for ever taking me to Sita. Irritably I thought to myself that in spite of her clothes and her excellent English, she was like Sita and the rest of them whom I saw walking around the streets like sacks of coal. I found myself wishing I'd responded more positively to Ringo's scheme and seen it right through instead of using this potion of Sita's.

I'd woken up that morning, or rather I'd left my bed, still more or less asleep. A whole month had gone by since we'd come back from our trip together and I hadn't seen him. I'd heard his love talk and his voice trembling with emotion on the phone every week or so, and he'd brought me a gazelle that he'd caught out hunting, and then not waited to see me when I came out of the bath. My longing for him was unbearable, and yet I couldn't manage to have him in my grasp although I telephoned him and went to his house and sent Ringo to his office.

That morning I'd shouted at my husband, and then sat crying loudly. This craving was agony; it opened up a chasm in my body which the blood couldn't reach. For the first time I'd thought about playing with myself; I'd controlled the hand hovering over my stomach the night before and put it back by my side, vowing that I would try to get Maaz back and marry him, whatever the cost.

Ringo had patted me on the shoulder soothingly and told me he'd get Maaz to come that same morning. When I shook my head disbelievingly, he insisted that I'd see him sitting on that very chair, pointing to a chair untidy with newspapers and James's clothes; probably he was thinking as I was that he'd begun to neglect the housework because I'd stopped giving him orders and distracted him from what he was supposed to be doing. He bent down to gather up everything that was on the chair, and repeated, 'Maaz will sit on this chair today.' Then he began to explain his plan to me, taking out the pin which he usually kept stuck in his shirt pocket. He lit a match and held it to the point of the pin until it turned red as a glowing coal, then black, and I thought Maaz would rise up out of it. At the same time Sita's bottle gleamed in my head and I began to laugh. Ringo handed me the pin and told me to prick my finger a few times until I had some drops of blood on my hand. I did as he said, and when a few drops of blood were just appearing he mixed coffee with tincture of iodine and sprinkled it on a bandage which he bound around my right wrist. Then he made me sit down on the sofa, and brought a jar with the remains of some cream in it which he rubbed all over my face, and I burst out laughing again. When my pallor still wasn't convincing enough for him he went to fetch the saffron used for colouring the rice and dissolved some in water and began massaging my face with it. All this time, I was holding a mirror and trying to see what was happening to my face. Then he asked me how to say, 'She's killed herself,' in Arabic. I got up to phone Suha, although I didn't think there would be an equivalent expression in Arabic. I couldn't imagine anyone taking their own life in this country: there was no need for it. In her usual fashion, Suha had forgotten our recent rapprochement and our visit to Sita a few days before, and replied tersely that she was busy and hung up. I rang again, cursing her inwardly, and told her that I was about to give Maaz Sita's drops. When I sensed her enthusiasm returning, I asked my question, and she asked me sarcastically if I was planning to kill myself. Then she asked me to let her know what happened to Maaz.

I repeated the expression over and over again until Ringo had mastered it; this was the whole sentence: 'Uncle Maaz, Madame Suzanne has killed herself.' Then he ordered me not to open my eyes and not to answer Maaz except when he swore that he would never split up with me again.

'No,' I added involuntarily. 'He has to marry me. He asked me to, or have you forgotten?'

'How could I forget?' said Ringo, going over to the door. 'He chased you like a wasp shamed by its own buzzing.'

Ringo's words made me feel happier, even though I didn't understand the comparison. I wasn't stretched out on the couch for long, or it could be that I didn't notice the time passing because I was going over and over the same subject: I wanted to get him back, and to marry him even if I had to be the second wife.

If I'd stood and repeated this to myself in the mirror a few months before, I would most likely have thought there's a woman who's gone beyond the nervous breakdown stage and is well and truly mad – Maaz al-Siddiq's second wife?

When I heard the car roaring to a halt, I closed my eyes. I heard Maaz's voice before I heard the door: 'You heathen! You don't believe in God. You'll go to hell.' When he added in English, 'You crazy, you suicide,' I was overcome by a desire to laugh. He shook me and I couldn't stop my eyes opening. I began to cry but instead of being cut by my tears, he told me reproachfully that anyone who tried to take their own life without waiting for God's will to be fulfilled went to hell. The minute he showed signs of pity for me because I'd be going to hell, Ringo came up and took hold of my hand, gesturing to Maaz and shaking his head sorrowfully.

Maaz obediently took my hand from Ringo and I seized the opportunity and flung my arms round him, crying violently and pressing my breast against him with every convulsive sob; I hissed like a snake in his ear that I couldn't live without him, why had he left me, and where had his love for me gone? The strength of my resolve convinced him, and created just the effect I'd imagined, and did it quickly, because he turned to Ringo laughing and said, 'God damn you! Bring me some iced tea!' But as Ringo went towards the door of the kitchen, warning bells rang in my mind. I pictured what was going to happen between us, maybe standing up, maybe for no more than a few moments, then like someone who'd relieved himself of a burden, he'd be off. At this, the picture of the Indian woman on Sita's bottle, holding up her long hair, flashed into my mind and I recalled her words: 'Even if it doesn't do any good, it won't do any harm.'

I couldn't hear a sound; he must have guessed from the taste of it: perhaps Fatima had resorted to Sita and her potions and that was why he didn't want to leave her even though she put oil on her hair and had yellow teeth. But he was strolling around the sitting-room and he stopped by a model aeroplane which David had made. As soon as he saw me he reached out to take the glass from me. 'God, I need this, Suzie,' he said. 'Tell me, where did you buy this plane? It must be the biggest you can get. Has David been into the desert to fly it yet?' 'I've told you a hundred times,' I answered irritably as usual, 'David didn't buy it. He just bought the motor, and you know he goes into the desert to fly it every Friday.'

I forced a laugh, annoyed at myself for answering him in this way, and aware that the days of the proud pleased assurance which his love had brought to me were gone.

He stretched out his hand to my breast and said, 'It's been ages since we ate pomegranates.' When I asked him what they were he began to explain, and I nodded my head without really understanding: a pomegranate was a fruit like a pearl, he said, and if one of its seeds dropped on the ground, God wouldn't let us enter Paradise. He went to put both hands on my breasts and I stopped him, making the excuse that David would be home soon. At this he looked so put out that I asked him why he hadn't been in touch with me if he felt so passionate.

The image of Sita's bottle gleamed brightly, and I remembered her promise that a few hours or a night after a man took these drops 'his body would be ablaze as if he had peppercorns up his backside'.

'Don't lie, Suzanne,' he yelled at me. 'Lying's a sin. David doesn't come back at noon.' I found myself swearing in God's name, just like him, that when Ringo had saved me from cutting my wrists he'd sent for David too and when he hadn't been able to find him, he'd left a message.

Only then did I suddenly remember that my attempted suicide was supposed to have been the main topic of the morning, to the exclusion of all else, and I realized that because I knew it wasn't real I'd forgotten all about it.

'I want more iced tea, Suzanne,' he said. 'Since there are no pomegranates, I'll drink tea.'

Why didn't he try again? Or didn't he love me any longer? I went up to him and embraced him and clung to him and told him how I'd missed him. When he pulled me closer, I knew that he still wanted me, whether Sita's drops got to his brain or not, and that what had happened between us during our trip abroad didn't matter. And because he could squeeze me and pull me to him for a few minutes and feel happy, I pulled away like a fish slipping out of the net and said provocatively, 'I'll go and get the Scotch.' I'd dreamt for so long of being in his arms and of the pleasure he gave me, and yet I didn't feel any longing or desire at this moment; could my passion have been no more than the result of his abandoning me?

He sat drinking. Then he asked, 'Why this long separation, Suzie?' Before I could answer, he stretched out his arm to show me his new wrist-watch.

I wouldn't have believed that he could be so sly as to turn the question round like that. But he jumped to his feet suddenly, and seized hold of me, pulling me up off the couch. 'Suzie, I can't wait. Come on, let's go upstairs. We can go into the bathroom, or do it standing up behind the door.' Pushing him off, I said, 'How did you wait for a whole month?'

He struck one palm against the other, then one palm against his forehead and said, 'Maaz, you bastard! It's been a month since you were blessed by Suzanne's fragrant aroma! Suzie – I went to the bedouin to see my mother. She wasn't well at all, nor was my father. And I went on a trip hunting gazelles with some of my relations.' Perhaps he was telling the truth; perhaps he did go to his mother's for ten days. When I didn't make any comment, he must have imagined that I'd agree after a while and we'd go to the top floor, into the bathroom, or stand up behind the door, because he added, as if exonerating himself further, 'When I got back, we had people from the oasis coming to stay with us.'

My eyes bored into his, trying to find out the truth.

'Where are they? In your house?'

'What do you think? Would they be sleeping in the street? '

I raised a hand to silence him.

He sipped a third glass of Scotch, then turned to me: 'What was your answer, Suzie? Are we going upstairs?' I heard the shrieking of children in the garden and answered, 'No. Why don't we go in the garden?'

He began to laugh: 'God, like the Imam of Yemen's apes. His house has been turned into a museum and when we went to visit it, I saw apes in the garden one on top of the other, just like human beings, not paying the slightest attention to anybody round them.'

I said nastily, 'I saw the guests. One day I went to visit Fatima and I saw them.'

With complete lack of affectation he said, 'I swear Fatima didn't tell me, Suzanne. She must have forgotten. She's got the children and their problems, and the little one worries her to death. He's still eating earth, and it'll kill him.'

I lost faith in Sita's drops. If they'd changed anything in him, they'd made him more balanced. Laughing, he asked me, 'You've seen Aisha, you know how beautiful she is? Three men want to marry her and she refused them all because she wants to marry a man from the town, not a bedouin.'

My heart missed a beat but I nodded my head, while he went on, 'She drives a tractor and a landrover. When the desert guard told her that it was forbidden for women to drive, she said, "Try and stop me. I'd like to see you bringing drums of water in by camel, and winter supplies." She comes in to town every three months.'

I sensed that the way he talked about Aisha was out of the ordinary; I began to understand Maaz. 'Does Aisha want to marry you? ' I asked.

He started to laugh, slapping one palm against the other, until his eyes disappeared into his head, and his teeth showed white like pearls. 'Fatima must have told you?' he said, questioningly. 'I swear she's joking, Sheikha Suzanne. Aisha's father is a nomad and a real bedouin. He lashes people with the cord of his headcloth and they say one of his strokes is enough to take your fingers off. He decided to marry Suad, relying mainly on God to help him, but also on me. He told me that Suad, who's a nurse, had fallen passionately in love with him when he was a patient in the government hospital here. Aisha asked him how he knew that Suad loved him and he regaled us with stories of how she'd washed his face for him, changed his sheets, brought him hot food and even helped him to eat, and not been disgusted by him; when she took his temperature she'd always rubbed the thermometer on an apron tied around her waist so that a trace of him stayed with her. It was while he was still in hospital that he'd told Aisha he wanted to marry the nurse and Aisha, the wicked girl, had said, "There's nothing to stop you." Then she went off and told Suad, who was Lebanese, and the two became close friends and laughed together over the old man. When he was better and they took him back to the oasis, he couldn't get Suad out of his mind, and began saying to his sons and daughters, "It's not right. The girl Suad's waiting for me. I must keep my promise. Take me to the town, or bring her here to the desert." Aisha assured him that Suad was preparing herself for the wedding, and so the father began dictating poems to a bedouin who'd learnt to read and write, then he folded some money inside the poems and gave them to Aisha: "The money's for winter clothes for Suad," he said, "because I can see one cloud chasing another, and the cold winds will start to blow at any moment." '

I realized what was awaiting me, and cried out, 'And you love Aisha, and she loves you?'

Maaz was unconcerned by my accusation and went on, 'Listen! I told Aisha not to play tricks on her father, because one day he might crack up over Suad and it would kill him. Or he might try and go to the town and wander off into the desert and lose his way . . . Every day he says to her, "Take me. Suad's waiting for me." '

Again I asked him, 'Are you and Aisha in love?'

He laughed and said, 'Let's go upstairs, and I'll tell you.'

'I'm tired,' I replied. He didn't look disappointed. He'd begun to know me very well and he came over to me and pulled me up. Although I usually submitted at the first touch, sometimes at a glance, I found myself feeling remote from him, thinking that desire too was just an idea in the head. I felt how strong I was now, and how he needed me.

He whispered, 'Never mind. Let's go up. You know what I want.'

I went in front of him to the door, rejoicing that I still held the key to our relationship, and said, 'Go now. Tomorrow I'll be waiting for you.' He made for the Scotch bottle and began sipping from it. I pulled it away from his mouth and asked him maliciously how his cousin Muhammad was. (The doctor had implanted a small instrument in his body to help him give up drinking.) Maaz replied laughing that Muhammad's body had adapted to the instrument and even to the sensation of nausea which it produced, and continued to swallow a tumbler of Scotch as if it were water.

He asked if he could use the bathroom. I knew he wanted to be by himself, as usual when he was drunk or had been looking at pictures of women in magazines, and I wouldn't let him, claiming that my son was about to come home. I went with him to the door, moved out of reach and his kisses, said goodbye and closed the door behind him.

In spite of my sense of victory, I thought sadly that there must be some way that I could marry him, and yet it appeared that the chance had passed me by. Maaz was no longer that ripe fruit hanging on a tree in the middle of the path. He'd changed and even seemed able to behave tolerably when he was drunk. In the past would he ever have left so meekly when he was in that state?

Alcohol used to make him crazy, and put me in a state of shock at the effect it had on him. Once he'd crumpled up on the sand and fallen asleep. I'd been terrified of the darkness and silence of the open countryside and when I tried to wake him up he opened his eyes and didn't know where he was. It was as if he couldn't see me properly or had forgotten who I was; he threw his empty bottle at me and then ran after me and I crept behind the car to hide. I heard him calling me an Israeli spy and asking me how I'd learnt Arabic so quickly, then he collapsed on to the sand again and I heard him snoring. I looked around me, frightened even of the moon and the stars. I was certain that the moving lights I could make out in the distance were a caravan of camels, but it was only a car because I heard the roar of its engine. I began to

use it and other lights to guide me up on to the main road.
Only then did I discover that blood was dripping from my
forehead and that I'd left my shoes behind on the way. I
stopped a truck by shouting and waving my hands about; the
driver must have thought I was a stray camel from a distance
because when he saw me and heard me saying 'Please, home,
please,' his mouth dropped open, and he mumbled, 'In the
name of God the Compassionate, the Merciful,' and looked
around him. When he made no attempt to open the door, I
said pleadingly, 'You open door?' and when he still didn't
move, I went round and opened it and got in. He went on
looking at me as if I wasn't real. I don't know if he noticed if I
was barefoot or not. I found myself repeating, 'Thanks,
brother,' and this sentence of mine put him in a state of utter
confusion because my blue eyes and blond hair didn't go with
my Arabic and my desert accent. When at last he started up
the truck I relaxed, but only for a moment, because one hand
was on the steering wheel and the other resting on his thigh
and his glances travelled between my face and my body. I'd
felt something hurting me on my forehead ever since Maaz
had thrown the bottle at me but I'd ignored it. As a pre-
caution against what I feared might happen, I put my hand to
my forehead and when I saw a smear of blood on it I gasped,
pretending to be frightened, and then became engrossed in
wiping off the sand which was sticking to my face and hair. It
wasn't long before my fears that he had only one idea in his
mind were confirmed: he stared at me, then, reducing speed,
he moved his hand from his thigh to put it beside me; I cried
out 'God is great! God is great!' looking at the blood on my
hand and then striking myself on the face just as I'd seen Arab
women doing when they were lamenting because someone
had died. I kept saying, 'God is great! God is great! ' then
'Thank you, thank you,' as I directed him to the street where I
lived, using my hand and the word 'left' or 'right', until I
called out, 'Just here, brother,' and opened the door and
climbed down, leaving him stunned. I saw him in our street

again every day for a while, alone or with others, driving slowly around in his truck as if he were looking for me; sometimes he seemed frantic, as if blaming himself for missing his chance.

2

Maaz came back sooner than I expected. I'd spent the whole afternoon in a state of nervous apprehension, thinking that he would surely have hit a tree or a telegraph pole and now be locked up in jail for being drunk. He stood facing me, and every cell, every drop of his blood, all his bones and the pores of his skin, his inhalations and exhalations, had abandoned their proper place and landed here in a mass which hadn't properly gelled. It was as if he hadn't known how to find the way to my house. He was bellowing at me, then kissing my feet, trying to eat the varnish off my toenails and when it wouldn't come off he bit it and said it tasted red, then he pulled my hair and muttered to himself, 'I don't understand her scent. It's not perfume, or incense, or sandalwood.' He called me Suzie, Susu, Sinsin, Suad. This time I wasn't aware of his body in spite of my longing for the pleasure of sex. I was waiting for the right moment to whisper to him that I was his wife and that we must get married. As if I'd actually told him what I wanted to say he began shouting at me, swearing to me that he was going to marry me and that I was his woman, the Suzanne of a lifetime, that without me he was camel dung, he was a toothpick; without me he was a eunuch; he told me that he'd seen me naked passing by his office door, and how as he'd pulled up in his car he'd seen my breasts undulating before him. He wouldn't be quiet, and I left him shouting out his feelings while I went into the bathroom; I did my hair looking in the mirror, unable to believe what was happening; I put on fresh lipstick, powdered my face and neck, and splashed perfume everywhere, even on my thighs. 'Long live Sita and herbal medicine, or magic,' I thought. Then into my head there floated a vision of rows of bottles bearing my name and a picture of me in the main stores in America, and I saw myself talking on television about the time I'd spent going between desert and village and from tribe to tribe to collect prescriptions that could be classified under the heading 'Love'. Then I saw myself in my own private clinic, wearing a white overall, with medicines and lotions all around me like Sita had, but mine would be in containers looking like bottles of French perfume. I'd be just like the foreign women who collected old silver jewellery and bedouin clothes and produced books with their pictures on the cover.

I heard a knocking on the door and went out but I couldn't find him anywhere in the room. He was hiding behind the door and he snatched the towel off me and began looking all over the room: how should he start and where? On the bed, on the floor; he opened the curtains and closed them again; in the clothes cupboard, standing up, sitting down. The black pupils of his eyes darted about like a falcon's eyes, pursuing his thoughts and stopping motionless at the impossibility of what he was thinking. I was flying through space, except I had one eye on my watch to see when it was time for Jimmy to come home from school. I became an instrument in his hands, the willing subject of his fantasy, and he didn't leave me until sleep overcame him. Then I kept watch, not letting any noise infiltrate the room where he was sleeping, while Jimmy, delighted that Maaz had come back to visit us, sat trying to count his snores. I felt like a bedouin woman sitting with her son in her lap, waving the flies away from him, and giving him her breast day and night so that he'd stay young and be satisfied within the bounds of her breast and her lap.

My self-confidence returned and I no longer needed constantly to turn for comfort to the memories of the first few times with Maaz to feel confident and to make myself believe that he'd have to come back to me; this had been a short-lived confidence in any case, rapidly turning to dejection. I'd always begun by remembering the falcon which he left in the office on its wooden perch. Its wary, frightened eyes moved whenever I moved or hit a key on the typewriter. From time to time it spread its great wings, then fixed its eyes on my face again. The office was empty; even my boss Ahmad had gone off with the falcon's owner. I couldn't bear the bird looking at me any longer and I began to swear at it and tried to think of some way I could get out to go home. I gathered my courage and stood up and took one step; the bird moved, fluttering its wings, as if it wanted to fly. The noise of them was shockingly loud, and I clung to the wall again, even though the falcon remained chained to its perch, and stayed where I was until its owner returned. He laughed when I begged him to rescue me. I found his name hard to remember but I couldn't forget his black eyes which were like the eyes of his falcon and watched me all through his visit to our office and began to amuse me after a while: I hadn't known before that a man like that could exist in real life and not just on the cinema screen.

He smiled constantly and sat in front of me like a faithful dog; as soon as my hand reached for the cigarette packet, he lit a match and fetched the ashtray, having first rubbed it with his fingers to make sure it was clean. He brought in a thermos flask of coffee which had cardamom in it. He took my cup in his hands and whenever I put it down on the table he held it against his heart and raised his eyes to the ceiling. When I laughed he presented the cup to me, mumbling something, and when I asked what he was doing he answered in broken English that he was bewitching the cup so that I would exchange feelings with him. Each time I reached the end of a piece of typing and heaved a sigh he came across and bent over me and asked if he should fetch a doctor. It was the way he kept on insisting that he would drive me home which really annoyed me: I was afraid that he'd make it difficult for Ahmad and me to be alone together, and answered him irritably. He pretended to be angry and disappeared, but when I went home I found he'd preceded me to the house.

Three days after I first saw him in the office he began to visit us regularly, never coming without presents. He brought a bottle of monstrously expensive cologne for Jimmy, who was no more than eight, a lamb and a gazelle, then a tortoise, a snakeskin, a basket of dates and leather slippers. We clustered around him and his presents, not believing what we saw. He brought a lizard and as he tried to extricate his hand from between its teeth, he struggled with it and spoke to it as if it was human; he asked us if we'd like to eat it if he slaughtered it and cooked it. He left his sandals at the door and wandered round our house barefoot and happy, touching everything and asking what you did with things, anything from my son's toys to the automatic egg whisk. I would find him standing entranced by the rumble of the dishwasher, asking how it cleaned the plates, scoured the dirt off them and dried them; and how the oven cooked the chicken while I was away and stopped of its own accord.

After a while we began to be aware of the fact that we weren't friendly with him just because of the presents he brought or the magazines, banned for their politics or the amount of bare female flesh in them, which he could get because of the work he did. It was more as if he was the unfamiliar desert land come into our midst. Jimmy grew accustomed to him and considered him a necessity in our life because we were here, just as Ringo was a necessity in the house. Meanwhile he admired our way of life and our possessions, and my knowledge and worldly wisdom: I read out to him the instructions accompanying medications; I sprinkled something from a bottle on a stain on his clothes and it disappeared; I could type a line in a flash without looking at the keys; I knew how to find my way around and what the street names were in Arabic; I loved Arab food and dipped my morsels of bread and rice into the meat juices the way that they did. I knew how to adjust the television, change a light bulb, paint a wall, read books, drive a truck.

For our part, we grew accustomed to eating the rice and meat which he prepared, to the way he ate with his hand, gathering the rice into a little ball and throwing it into his mouth, and the way he drank water straight from the water bottle but never touching it with his lips; the way he drank Scotch at our house, then got drunk and sang songs, the way he circled around me and the numerous questions which his curiosity provoked; his incomprehensible English, the way he kept saying my name; on one occasion this led me to answer exasperatedly, 'Suzanne yourself', and perhaps he hadn't seen my expression because he immediately bent and kissed my hand repeating, 'Suzanne yourself: that means you and I are one person.' Then he said that he loved me very much, with a love that was as vast as the sand and the sky. He was bouncing around me and I extricated myself, laughing despite my embarrassment. He followed me into the kitchen, insisting that I visit his wife, Fatima, and when I refused he said that he wanted my opinion on installing an American kitchen just like mine in his house. I knew he was thinking up excuses, and I said to him, 'I'll give you the name of my kitchen and you can order it from the States.' The sentence was hardly out when an idea flashed into my head: why didn't I order a kitchen for him from the States and benefit financially, be a trading link between the desert and America?

I began to calculate in my imagination how much I'd make, and agreed to go; in any case I was anxious to see his wife: one day he'd telephoned her from my house, and tried to hand me the receiver so that I could talk to her, saying in English, in a tone of voice that was almost an order, 'Speak to

Fatima.' At first I'd refused, uncertain what I should say, then I gave in when I saw the disappointment in Maaz's eyes; Jimmy, disillusioned with me, had already decided to have a go and had snatched the receiver out of Maaz's hand and shrieked down it in Arabic, 'Hallo. Hallo, darling.' When I spoke I said in Arabic, 'Hallo, Fatima, how are you?' and her voice came down the line to me like the speaking clock or the recorded information services, 'Hallo. Hallo. Hallo,' then silence, then laughter, then again, 'Hallo. Hallo. Hallo.'

I think I understood the reasons why Maaz was attached to us from the moment I first entered his house, but I couldn't fathom his wife's attitude to me. She was young with a shy smile. When I held out my hand to shake hers, she embraced me and kissed me three times on alternate cheeks, and kissed my son, then ran into the kitchen. The house had a particular smell, and after a while I came to know that it was the smell of incense and basmati rice and heat all mixed together and that it was in all the Arab houses I visited, except Suha's. I cast my eyes around the house. There was only basic furniture: a rug in deep colours, sombre sofas, dust over everything, and heat, because not every room had an air-conditioner in it. Maaz wandered between the kitchen and the room where we were sitting, just as he did in my house, carrying plates and cups of tea and fruit. I turned to Fatima and said, 'Maaz's doing the housework.' She smiled and covered her teeth with her hand and turned to look at him: 'Just today. For you.' I thought, this house hasn't seen a blond hair before today, and Maaz doesn't trust his wife to do her duty towards the guests. Gradually I began to comprehend that they saw me as an important guest from Nixon's land, the land of the oven that cleaned itself without spilling any water. My sense of my own importance began to increase, as if my yellow hair which hung lifelessly round my face had turned into shining gold, and my speech into pearls, for his children's eyes were fixed on me and my son, and the neighbours' children poured in to greet us and sat asking

Maaz for an explanation of every word I said, then giving me smiles of admiration and encouragement. I thought to myself that at home in my own country I had never been spoken to or even looked at admiringly like this.

Fatima sat facing me, bending forward as if she was sitting on a sofa for the first time, her long dress covering the floor at her feet; she wore a headshawl, a veil over her eyes, and her hands and feet were stained with henna. We conversed with fleeting smiles, and I found that I was laughing and smiling without reason; I felt as if I were years younger than her, and like a spoilt child. Maaz interrupted, urging her to bring me more biscuits, since my son had swooped down on the plates like a flock of pigeons. Maaz's two daughters had withdrawn into a corner and stood looking at me in astonishment. Only his little boy was unaware of my presence and cried continuously because his father had shut the door, and he still had the habit of eating earth in the garden. Maaz dominated the gathering with his movements and way of talking, as he did when he came to visit me; he didn't care who was there when he told me in English that his love for me was vast as the sands and the sky, while Fatima smiled, then held out her hand as if apologizing to me for her husband's behaviour; she didn't understand what he said but perhaps she guessed because I did no more in reply to him than look arch and say, 'Stop it!'

She seemed happy and told Maaz that having me to visit was more fun than watching television or going for a drive in the car. I smiled at her, trying to appear especially grateful because I'd noticed that she was hiding something in the folds of her dress. Perhaps like Maaz she liked to give presents, either as a social obligation or because it made her feel happy. My curiosity grew and I followed the movement of her hand intently to try and see what she was hiding but only succeeded because her little son wanted her to pick him up. I saw a packet which in disbelief I made out to be jelly. Maaz began to sing in Arabic, pointing to his heart, his eyes dancing, till I ordered him to stop, smiling at Fatima who was happy and at ease with the company; the jelly packet must just be a wrapping for something else: in the women's market I'd seen them putting gold in milk tins and silver in empty soap-powder boxes. Maaz's little son threw the jelly packet and Maaz caught it and said to me, 'Fatima wants you to teach her how to make jelly but she's shy of you.' I stood up inpatiently, trying to hide my disappointment, and Maaz took me to the kitchen with Fatima following slowly behind. I strutted proudly along in a new way, indifferent to my surroundings, pulling in the muscles in my bottom to make it look slimmer and more shapely. I tried to explain to her, but she only smiled and didn't look at what I was doing, didn't even seem to be listening to me, but just nodded and covered her mouth with her hand.

In the car Maaz tried to persuade me and Jimmy to go with him to a small village to see a newborn camel on a farm belonging to a friend of his. I didn't raise any objections; his interest in me and his amorous behaviour amused me, and the monotony of these days needed some such novelty, especially since I no longer saw Ahmad.

When Maaz took off his headcloth and cord to try them on me, I saw his head, his hair, his forehead – and I saw a man, and as he reached out his hand to take the headcloth back I felt a fierce heat touching me. He returned his hand to the steering wheel and I longed to feel the heat again, and turned to Jimmy in the back of the car, smiling at him as if to excuse this urge in me, then turned back to look at Maaz's brown hands which were covered in little black hairs. I caught sight of his white underpants through his loose robe and looked away, staring out of the window; his attempts to reach me had eventually succeeded: I'd previously been convinced that the whole idea was absurd, because I'd been sure that he knew all about my relationship with Ahmad from the first day he'd come into the office with the falcon.

So I asked him casually if he could find me a job as Ahmad

no longer sent me anything to type. He answered that the pressure against women working was increasing and he didn't think that I ought to work. It wasn't this pressure which had forced Ahmad to do without me, but the arrival of his family from Egypt. I was about to ask Maaz when Ahmad's family was leaving, but I stopped and asked him instead if he'd seen Ahmad. 'Ahmad's taken up with his wife and children,' he answered, and I understood from this that Maaz only saw him in his office since there was no mixed visiting. Then suddenly Maaz asked me if I'd like to go abroad with him. I stared hard at him but he was asking in all innocence, and when I asked why, he replied, 'I've never seen anything but sand and sea.' He went on, 'Perhaps the best thing would be when you go to America on holiday, I could visit you and you could show me around. You in the daytime and David in the evening.' All I could do was wonder fruitlessly how he could make amorous advances to me and at the same time visit us and talk to David, indeed establish a firm friendship with him, and take me to see his wife, and how she could welcome me royally even though she knew how he frequented our house and spent many long evenings with us. Were the two of them more liberated than me and David? And I didn't answer him, although it struck me that we'd planted in him a germ of curiosity about a world which he'd never previously given a thought to.

I found myself wishing I could be alone with him at that moment; since I'd stopped seeing Ahmad, the rooms in the house had grown cramped, the shouting of the children in the compound louder, and Jimmy's requirements more preposterous. I began to feel the need to go out of the house and talk to anyone I happened to meet, my neighbour opposite for example, or to get into the car and ask the driver to take us for a drive around; we would go to the store to buy what Jimmy wanted, and what my greed prompted me to buy, much of it, especially the American products which I didn't need, without regard to the inflated prices. I felt that money here had no value. I didn't think of visiting the other women here and I didn't find things to complain about like they did, because unlike them I didn't mind the voice of the muezzin in the early hours of the morning or the fact that the shops closed during the daytime prayers.

Nevertheless my life here was different, and had been since my third night in the desert when I'd opened my eyes in alarm at a sound, neither a song nor a sermon, proceeding from a microphone: I found myself naked in a garden surrounded by a high wall. I looked frantically around me for my clothes and when I found them in a heap near me I began to wonder about my husband; I covered my stomach with one hand and pulled on my clothes with the other. What had happened to me? Where was David? When I stood up with some difficulty I remembered that I'd had a lot to drink. I could only move slowly in spite of my anxiety to find out what had happened to David. I went into the house and saw the owner of the firm fast asleep on the sofa, and traces of the previous night's dinner, glasses and the remains of food and cigarette ends, and cassettes scattered here and there. I remembered the blue movie and how I'd refused to watch it at first, then laughed and demanded to see it. I'd been happy, hardly able to believe in the interest that was being shown in me, the dishes covering the table, the respectful behaviour of the two servants bringing us drinks, the firm's owner telling the driver to go and fetch a video of 'Dallas' from a friend's house simply because I'd asked him whether he'd seen the last episode. I couldn't remember if this had happened before or after David had left the party to check on Jimmy. Had he come back and seen me watching the movie and gone angrily away again? I sat down, pushing ashtrays and plates around in the hope of waking up the sleeping man on the couch. Dawn was beginning to break. I looked out of the window but could see only the high wall. The man was still asleep. I went to the front door and unlocked it and saw his car. Leaving the door open, I went down to the outer door and opened it and looked out.

A few houses were all that I could see and the light made my eyes smart; I went back into the room, closing the door noisily behind me. At this the man sat up; he didn't seem surprised to see me, and smiled at me. Feeling embarrassed, I asked about my husband and he replied simply, 'David went home.' I was on the point of asking more questions but felt confused and said nothing. He stood up, searching for the car keys which were hanging on the door latch. Then he bent and took my hand and kissed it, then he kissed my neck and I felt a faint quivering in my thighs. I moved backwards, but in spite of my nervousness I couldn't help being aware of the warmth of his brown skin. I let him kiss me, put his hands on me, and when I surrendered my body to his I felt a great happiness flooding through me in spite of my disordered thoughts. I tried to recall his name and couldn't. He wouldn't agree to write it on a piece of paper for me, but he taught me to remember it: Ahmad. We'd met him for the first time that morning when I'd gone with my husband to stock up with food and buy second-hand furniture from him. When he invited us to dinner we'd wondered whether we were dreaming, and thought how lucky we were to have been posted to a country where people were more concerned about others than they were where we came from.

Jimmy asked me if he could touch the baby camel. Maaz answered for me and told him that the camel's mother was tired and might bite him if he went too close. He bit his own hand to make his words more impressive. I didn't care about the baby camel or its mother, or Maaz's friend or the women who were watching us through cracks in the door in spite of the veils which covered their heads and hung down the sides of their faces. Even eating dates and drinking tea out of a glass was dull. Maaz's agitated longing for me had been obvious from the moment I got into the car with him. It reminded me of the incomparably happy times I'd spent with Ahmad and made me long for them again now. On the return journey he drove at a crazy pace as if with the speed he came closer to me and touched me; when we reached home I invited him in for a cup of tea. I noticed that the veins in his hand were standing out and he was pressing one leg down on the other. When I put the tea down in front of him I deliberately brought my face and breast level with him. He asked me if I had an aspirin and I knew he wanted to follow me into the kitchen even though there was a danger that someone might come in and find us there. He held my breasts and rubbed his face against them and held me close for a second and seemed happy. I felt irritated and wondered what I'd been expecting, seeing that we were in the kitchen.

As I opened my legs for the first time I didn't think about what he made of my relationship with my husband and why he was always winking at me and laughing as he asked me to marry him. Instead, I watched him closing his eyes, letting his body go loose, murmuring that now he would welcome the Angel of Death. I didn't understand and he explained that he wanted nothing more from life after this. At the start I was convinced that he was acting: when he saw me without my clothes on he gasped and struck his head with the palm of his hand, exclaiming bitterly, 'Why did God create foreign women different?' When I asked him what his wife's body was like he didn't answer me, but passed his hand over my flesh saying, 'It's like silk. Pure silk.' When he let out a noise like a bull roaring I nearly laughed. He said I was like one of the houris whom God had prepared for true believers when they entered Paradise. He even grabbed my foot and smelt it, muttering, 'More fragrant than sandalwood or incense.' I started to laugh out loud then. I was relaxed. The curtains were drawn and a gentle gloom enveloped the room. It was eleven in the morning and the house would stay quiet until three o'clock.

I kept on laughing even though he pleaded with me to stop. I couldn't help myself in the face of what he was doing with my body. He was like a man worshipping at a pagan shrine, uttering incantations, most of them incomprehensible to me.

I couldn't understand why he wanted to restrict me: he refused to let me move about or get off the bed or even cover myself up.

Suddenly he was on his feet, shouting at me. Although the veins were visible on his face I went on smiling. As his anger mounted and I watched the expressions following one another across his face and his hands shaking, I thought to myself that he must have seen a lot of silent films: his black eyes almost made holes in the screen, or in my face. I had no idea of the reasons for his outburst of emotion until, nearly in tears, he asked me why I was laughing. I didn't tell him that it was his melodramatic admiration of my body and his manner of loving that I found so funny; I made do with saying that there was no need for him to talk and behave as he had been doing because I was quite happy with him. Later I realized that he wasn't acting and that he really meant it when he called me the Marilyn Monroe of the desert. If I gestured, sat still, walked along, I was exciting; if I spoke, there was someone picking up my words as if they were kisses. He wanted me on the sand, in an empty house, in the open desert, at an oasis, waiting till midnight and keeping a big stick near him in case anyone surprised us. He wanted me in a camel hair tent, even at his mother's after he'd drunk some camel's milk and his mother had fallen asleep; in my house, in the bathroom or in bed. I abandoned myself to glorying in my plumpness, not caring about the blue veins in my legs and thighs; I no longer wore a girdle: Maaz took hold of the folds of flesh as if he were snatching up gold in Ali Baba's cave. Only my stomach worried me still and I devised various schemes to prevent him seeing it in daylight. I always pushed his hand off it or covered it with a sheet until eventually, like an explorer, he began to enjoy what he'd already discovered, whereas before his concern had been to find out where further advances would lead. He began to notice what I was doing and one day he asked me if it was not done in America for him to see my navel. I forced a laugh but kept my hand over my stomach. Then he asked, 'Do you think there might be a baby in there?' Laughing, I shook my head and all at once he pushed my hand away over my thigh, using his two feet. When he only saw bare flesh he seemed surprised, and I too was surprised that he didn't remark on the wrinkled skin or on the broad white lines and the deep brown ones or on the ridge of flesh around the navel. He wasn't interested in listening to me as I told him how embarrassed I was about my stomach since I'd had my second daughter, and bent over to kiss it. Gathering the flesh to one side so that my stomach looked smooth as if I was a young girl, I told him I was going to have surgery for it. Maaz took a renewed interest in the subject of my stomach and with a look of revulsion on his face he gasped, 'God forbid. You should be grateful your stomach's healthy.' Then he kissed it again greedily, in an exaggerated attempt to convince me of its flawless beauty. My mind wandered and the idea that David's lack of interest in me was related to my stomach or to my plumpness in general seemed more remote, as it certainly hadn't the slightest effect on the harmony of my relations with Maaz. Although at the beginning I used to keep control of my body like a Playboy bunny who has to think herself into the part, his way of behaving made me feel that I really was a bunny and I wanted to be intoxicated with passion. I never once envied him when he abandoned himself to his own passion as I used to do sometimes with David or in a fleeting affair I'd had with a distant relation, or with Ahmad; and I never once faked it with him and opened one eye, as I had done with the others, to make sure that they were noticing me shudder. With him I was silent in my ecstasy, confident that he wasn't going to leave me unsatisfied, because he always wanted me again and for a long time.

3

Two days had passed since Maaz had come back to me and Sita's drops had exploded noisily in his head. When he got up he called me Maryam and said from now on my name was Maryam not Suzanne. 'Like the Virgin Mary or Mary Magdalene?' I asked, pretending to be gentle and at ease. 'Maryam. The wife of Maaz al-Siddiq. And if anyone calls you Maryam the American woman I'll break his neck.' I didn't ask him when our wedding was going to be or say what about David, and Fatima, afraid that he might withdraw his offer, and he merely repeated, 'Your name's Maryam, and if anyone calls you Maryam the blonde he'll be my enemy for all time.'

I stood up, full of delight at being the only woman he wanted in the wasteland of the desert. I didn't feel the same as before when he asked me to marry him. In the early weeks of our relationship it was because he wanted to own me, exactly as he wanted an American kitchen; this time it was the result of a relationship between a man and a woman, and it meant, as well, that he must have grown accustomed to the idea that I and his wife belonged to the same sex, even if there was a vast difference between us.

I draped the bed cover over my head and let it hang down around me just like an abaya. I smiled, wishing I could get used to an abaya and cover my face with a black handkerchief and become like the others, wrapped up because I was precious and easily damaged and had to move about from place to place. A second wife. It didn't matter, on condition that I didn't live with Fatima. Of course I would never live with her for one reason – the children – unless there could be some acceptable arrangement like the one I'd seen between the bedouin woman and her husband's new young wife.

I'd gone with Suha to visit her bedouin neighbour because

the bleating of one of the woman's nanny goats had disturbed her son's sleep for several nights. We stood in the doorway with Umar and my son, and Suha asked her why the goats bleated day and night. The woman laughed, showing her gold teeth, and struck one palm against the other and insisted that we come in. She tried to shoo away the nanny goat, addressing it as if it were a child, while Umar stood face to face with the little creature he was so used to hearing, and it continued to bleat. We followed the woman and left our shoes at the door, as she did, and went in to see a young woman with fair skin and long hair sitting on a rush mat painting her toenails. When she saw us, she rose quickly, excusing herself and welcoming Suha with a pleased smile. We were astonished. What was she doing here, this young woman? Her nail varnish, her short dress, her fair hair and her accent were all alien to the surroundings. She insisted that we should go into the sitting-room to sit on sofas, then disappeared and returned in a flash with dishes of fruit and cake and green almonds. 'Fresh from Syria,' she announced. At this, Suha asked her if she came from Syria and the young woman answered, 'Of course I do. Do I look as if I come from this country?' Then she added that she was the second wife and we could only stare in amazement. Looking towards the door as if to indicate the other wife, and as if she had understood our surprise, she said, 'She's like my mother, and I love her. She does the housework. She cooks. She washes my clothes for me. When I get angry with my husband she brings us back together. As long as no one interferes with the goats, everything's fine.' When Suha asked if her husband was old, the Syrian woman smiled, gathering her blond hair to one side, and said, 'Not at all. He just married young. Imagine how much he must have loved me. He would have done anything to make me marry him, but he didn't want to divorce her. He said she was the mother of his children — they're grown up now. He said to me, try it, and I tried it and now I really love her.' Then she winked at us and whispered,

'There are times when I can't believe she's his wife, poor thing.'

I wanted to ask her a lot of questions, but Umar came rushing in excitedly to tell his mother about the goat, while my son stood by looking bewildered because he didn't know what Umar was saying. The first wife was standing in the doorway with the goat close beside her; she stuck her head into the room and said, 'Excuse me. This goat won't let me talk to a soul.' Then she bent down and picked it up and came into the room, looking at her husband's Syrian wife: 'Don't worry. I'll take care that she doesn't make a mess.' She sat down. The leather of her face veil had faded and looked like an extension of the skin on her face. She nursed the goat like a child in her lap, stroking it gently, never taking her hand away from its face. When Suha asked her if the story of the goat was true, looking at Umar, she answered, 'It's quite true. God bless him, he understood perfectly. He asked me one question after another like a bubbling spring. God bless him. I told him about the goat's mother who died, God rest her, while she was giving birth.' She pointed to the lower part of her stomach. 'If I hadn't pulled hard on the little one's legs she would have smothered in the mother's stomach. God decreed that she should live, and I began giving her milk from a bottle. She grew accustomed to me, and because I was always in black she thought I was her mother. She follows me wherever I go. She doesn't like going out in the street with the other goats. She wants me near her, lying beside her. Whenever I go out and bang the door behind me, she begins to cry out like mad; a couple of days ago I went away to see my sister and the poor little thing missed me.' She raised the goat's chin and addressed it: 'You were missing your mother, weren't you? ' Then she stood up, still holding the goat, took some nuts and returned to her place, eating one and giving another to the goat who was waiting expectantly.

I thought of Fatima's smile and her thinness, and banished the thought from my mind: I was older than Fatima, and the second wife was always the younger one. I dropped the cover on the ground and sat at the typewriter, banging out all my thoughts on the subject of arrangements regarding the children and divorcing David. I had this habit of writing everything down in order to arrange my thoughts, and consequently my feelings. Sometimes I had more than ten lists on the go at a time: lists of what food to buy, of people I had to write to, of people I should visit, of what I ought to say to Maaz, of the gold jewellery I owned, and of the gold I thought I should acquire.

I sat there just as I had done before we left Texas to come here, when I was getting ready to let the house, and finding boarding-schools for our three daughters. The difference between me then and me now was a difference in the way I felt. The world beyond the desert seemed far away. I seemed to be a different Suzanne now, and I found myself speaking my name: 'Suzanne. Susan.' Then in a louder voice: 'Suzanne. Suzanne,' until I heard Ringo asking if I was calling him. I was calling myself, asking if I was the same Suzanne or Susan who'd sat in Texas, a woman in a house like any other house, or an ant in a garden like any other garden.

Here, because I sat at a typewriter, people looked at me with surprise and admiration on their faces. I passed through the minds of everybody in the houses round about, just as they passed through mine, and those people who went by my door, if they didn't long to come in, at least they thought about me. This knowledge stole all through me and made me feel calm and secure.

I'd been an ordinary American housewife in the past, washing my children's nappies and enjoying folding them up neatly, switching off the lights in their rooms every evening with a feeling of real happiness because they'd eaten and washed and gone to sleep. I would pick their clothes up off the floor and be delighted when I saw dirt on them because it saved me the trouble of deciding whether to wash them or not; seeing the family eating sandwiches without asking where the cooked food was pleased me too as I calculated to myself that they could eat the roast which I'd prepared for that evening the next night. I sat in front of the television from the early morning following the soaps. I read romances and detective novels and drank Pepsi continually. I couldn't find any real reason why my relationship with David was lukewarm; we never quarrelled and I was sure that it was what happened to married couples, even after a passionate love at the start. Even though I was relatively young, I can't have been in touch with any lively circles of people. I never gave a thought to other countries or even to neighbouring states, until I talked to Barbara. Barbara was the owner of a gallery, which I'd never entered in my life although it was near my home. She caught my attention because she dressed like the magazines and television commercials in cotton and silk, clothes by designers whose names I'd heard of and thought were for a special sort of woman, like Jackie Kennedy and foreign princesses. I don't remember ever seeing her in polyester trousers or with her hair tied up out of the way; her hair was always clean and newly done, the gold bangles jangled on her wrist and the chains and necklaces round her neck. Barbara stopped me, just as she stopped everyone else she saw and asked them to visit her. I knew that her interest in me was instrumental, since it was inconceivable that my mundane personality could have attracted her; I was a potential customer and she wanted me to see her gallery. But I was wrong, for after a short time things which I'd never seen in my life before like engraved wood, copper and brass, paintings on silk, appeared less interesting to me than her conversation. She talked a lot about her life in India where she'd been a teacher, and her two train journeys round the subcontinent, on one of which she'd surprised a gang trying to smuggle stolen jewels in her luggage and got to know her husband who was one of the passengers who'd jumped up to help her. At this, I stared at her necklace, so she took it off and dropped it into my hands, telling me that it was made of precious stones. I felt embarrassed by my red hands and my nails next to her long painted ones. She went on to explain how she'd won over the Indian jewel merchant and begun buying a single stone from him every now and then. At last she asked, 'What about you?' and fell silent. I smiled at her and reached for an ashtray, cheaper than most of the other things, and refrained from telling her that my life had been uneventful except for a burglary at our house some years before.

I remembered the strange feeling that came over me when I took that brass ashtray out of its bag and put it on the table at home. For the first time I was unable to sit indolently, my mind undisturbed by anything but the most obvious domestic duties; I began to think about Barbara and her way of life and her liveliness, and was curious to see her again. This feeling led me to another feeling which I can't describe but it was as if I'd lost something, or as if I was watching an isolated episode from a television series.

I visited Barbara again the moment David told me that he'd been offered a job in an Arab country in the desert. It seemed that at last my chance had come to tell her with pride that our life too was interesting. She gave me great encouragement to go there and said that we'd live like characters in *A Thousand and One Nights*. I smiled in polite acquiescence, although I'd never heard of the book, then she began to tell me about the riches, the palaces, the jewel-studded fabrics, while I looked at the gold she had and thought happily how I would surely be able to buy similar things in the Arab country since David's salary would be double what he earned here. She said that Omar Sharif came from the same country, also the Empress Soraya. I was at a loss to know whom to believe: my father told us to watch out for fleas and lice, and my aunt warned us against scorpion stings and said they loved blondes' blood.

The feeling that had come over me when I was looking at the brass ashtray, an article that had no connection at all with the rest of the furniture in the house, came over me again the night we landed at the desert airport, and I was sure that something which would be quite unfamiliar to me was about to happen. The black eyes stared at me often, and I stared at the white cloths on the men's heads. My son pointed at them and asked if they were the shepherds who'd come to see Jesus in the manger. I laughed. When I laughed, the black eyes smiled. The man who stamped my passport looked at my photo then at my face then back to the photo. He passed a finger over his lips and sighed, and I realized that the bold eyes were admiring and pleading at the same time.

When David came home, I'd organized on paper and in my mind what was to be done. I told him that Maaz and I were going to get married. With great deliberation, and continuing to spread butter on his toast, he asked, 'When?' This reaction should have put me at ease but I burned with anger. He went on crunching his toast and I didn't answer that we'd have to be divorced first. Perhaps he'd forgotten that we were still married. I felt a strong desire to tear the toast out of his hands and rub it into his face. 'You seem pleased,' I said, and then I began to scream at him, accusing him of being without feeling, self-centred, weak. In a loud voice I remarked that I wondered how he'd been able to land this job of his. Then I answered my own question with sarcasm, still talking loudly: 'You must have deceived the evil spirits themselves.' 'I'm pleased,' he answered, 'because it's what you want, a divorce from me, because you're unhappy with me, and naturally I want your happiness.'

'The children stay with me,' I shouted, 'and Maaz will be their father, and you won't see them at all.' 'As you wish,' he replied amid the crackling of toast in his mouth. 'You're mad!' I cried. 'Do you think I'm going to pay for them? You're their father, and you can be responsible for them.'

This time his only response was a sigh, a shake of the head, as if to say, 'Give me strength.' I stood up, pushing the plate and the bread and butter and honey away from him to the other end of the table but trying to make my voice sound normal, as if it were unconnected with my actions: 'Jimmy will stay with me, and the three girls will stay where they are and we can share them in the holdiays.' 'Fine,' he replied, and I went on provocatively, 'Of course I'll convert to Islam and bring up Jimmy as a Muslim.'

'As you wish,' came the answer.

I pictured Jimmy trying to read the Qur'an in a Muslim school, and the teacher scolding him for his ignorance, and I shouted, 'You're the same as you always were and you'll never change: cold and selfish, interested in nobody but yourself; you don't care what happens to your children.'

It was obvious that I'd tried his patience as far as he was prepared to allow me, for he began as he usually did on such occasions to tell me that I was mad, talking in his normal voice as if debating a point with me.

I responded by saying he was the one who'd reduced me to this state, and I meant what I said. I accused him of being cold, of feeling pleasure only when he was flying his model areoplanes, and suggested that he preferred sex with other men, and was having a relationship with Ringo. When he remained with his head bowed over the table, I screamed at him that he must have taken money from Ahmad, otherwise why would he have left me alone that first night with all the men, and here he was now giving his blessing to my relationship with Maaz.

At this point he could no longer control his agitation, perhaps because Ringo was in the kitchen. He got up, but instead of coming towards me he made for the door and went out.

I opened it and shouted after him, 'I'll be in touch with our lawyer.' 'I was in touch with him several weeks back,' he replied. 'He's doing the paper work for the divorce.'

Only then was I forced to confront my fears: two days went by without Maaz contacting me. On the third day I thought I could feel the beads of sweat seeping through the faint hairs on my upper lip. I wiped them away with my hand, and leapt up to dial his number. Fatima answered with a laugh, and said, 'Maaz's at work.' I dialled his office number, and a colleague of his drawled, 'Darling. Honey,' when he heard my voice. I shouted back, 'Can you get Maaz, please,' but he knew that I was Suzanne. The whole town must have known about my affair with Maaz. Then I heard Maaz saying in his usual way, 'Darling. Honey. Ooh darling, I miss you.' I wasn't reassured. These were the words he always used, even in the days when he'd stopped coming to see me. 'When will you come today?' I asked him, talking fast. He asked me if Ringo was at home, which surprised me, because he didn't usually bother. 'That doesn't matter,' I replied tersely. I heard him talking to his colleague and interrupted irritably, 'Hallo, Maaz.' 'Darling,' came the reply, 'I've got some brochures for Sri Lanka.' As if I hadn't heard properly, I repeated, 'Brochures for who?' 'Sri Lanka,' he said quickly. 'Tell that son of a gun Ringo to wait there till I come.' I held my tongue, not wanting to argue with him or question him. I was anxious that no animosity should develop since he'd come back to me.

I hovered about, thinking that I couldn't wait for Maaz without doing something to take my mind off my feelings of hatred for David, which were growing with every breath I took. I thought about taking down the Afghan rug from the wall, and gathering together everything which I'd bought or Maaz had given me. I picked up the stuffed lizard with a snake in its mouth, and put it beside the brass coffee pots, and the skin of some animal I didn't know. I couldn't think where to begin, and what to do with all this stuff, or where we would get married, and where we would live. I threw myself down on the sofa in a state of collapse and instead of thinking about myself and Maaz I began thinking about David, and clenched my teeth as if I were about to enter the ring with him.

Fifteen years I'd been with him. Fifteen years and I didn't

know him, even though I knew the number of hairs on his shoulders. After a few years of marriage his interest in me had begun to grow less bit by bit. If I'd read about this in the problem pages of women's magazines I wouldn't have believed it. It was a feeling that led to madness, and after a while to recklessness and then to frustration. Gradually he cut down on the time he spent talking to me, then on how often he slept with me. I assumed he must have another woman. I tried to catch him out, and I kept an eye on his mail, stood waiting at a discreet distance opposite the building of the company he worked for, and eavesdropped on his telephone conversations. I discovered nothing, except that he was no longer interested in me. If ever I tried to put my arms round him when we were watching television, he pushed me away saying that he'd rather wait till the sports programme had ended; it seemed that he was genuinely fanatical about sport on TV, and that it absorbed all his attention. In bed I would approach him and he would move me off, saying that he didn't like me to be the one to start. When I waited for him to make the first move, he turned on his side away from me, wishing me good night. But I didn't know the full extent of his indifference to me until that morning when I'd found myself naked in Ahmad's garden.

I remember that when Ahmad brought me home in his car and dropped me in front of the house and disappeared, I stood for a few minutes at the door, not daring to knock. When I knew that I couldn't bring myself to knock, I gave the door a push to prove to myself that I was capable of some action, and to my amazement it wasn't locked. I took off my shoes and picked them up, and went into Jimmy's room, then into our room. David was fast asleep. I crept quietly into bed and held my breath, waiting. In spite of my fear I couldn't help thinking about how much I'd seemed to mean to the men I'd spent the evening with, especially Ahmad, and how I didn't mean anything to David. In his looks, his ways of behaving and the amount of respect he showed me, he didn't compare with Ahmad. For the first time I criticized David's heavy body and large stomach to myself.

The next morning David got up and said good morning to me in a normal tone. Then he asked me if I'd got on all right with the Sri Lankan servant. I nodded my head and remained silent for a while, not knowing what to say. In the end I asked him if he'd enjoyed himself last night. 'Nice people,' he replied, tying up his shoelaces. 'Shall I send the car round for you?' I didn't answer. I was astonished at his behaviour, and didn't get out of bed for some hours.

4

Maaz arrived carrying tourist brochures and a number of fashion magazines. I wasn't interested in the magazines or the fashions, although I pretended to take them with some enthusiasm so that he'd feel useful. I begged my ears to let me hear what I wanted to hear from him, but I despaired and my ears grew numb with waiting.

I began to blame myself for not marrying him the day he'd come back to me, when he'd lost his equanimity and shouted that I was his wife. Here I was now listening to details about travel, hotels, cash, the sights to be seen. I found myself gripping the edge of the sofa, afraid to let slip a single word in case I said that the most distant place I wished to go to was well within the confines of the desert; but then instead of just listening as I'd promised myself that I would, I interrupted: 'We don't need to take planes and travel abroad. We can marry at your mother's.' 'Aren't you getting divorced first?' he asked. 'It'll only be a short time before my divorce comes through,' I replied.

He put up his hand as if to wave a fly away from his face. 'It'll work out fine, God willing, Suzanne.' Then he turned back to Ringo, all eager to hear about Sri Lanka.

Every time I began to think that there would be no harm in going abroad with him now, a light flashed in my head, warning me that he was planning to make the trip alone. I sat there, trying to put this notion out of my mind, and actually covered my mouth with my hand to stop myself saying anything: I didn't want to give him even the slightest impression that I had any doubts about whether I was meant to accompany him.

I began to compare the preparation for our previous trip abroad with what was happening now. He hadn't believed that I was really going to go with him. He'd paced around me with his ticket in his hand, wanting to make sure that the date of the flight was written on it, and his name, comparing his ticket with mine to see that we were travelling on the same day. This was because he'd bought his own ticket, but given me the money to buy mine myself since he'd begun to be scared about our relationship. It was Suha who'd made me understand that Maaz was genuinely afraid, when I recounted to her how he sneaked into our house, how he wore a different headcloth every day – white, striped, blue, red, brown – how sometimes he'd hide his eyes behind dark glasses, and sometimes he'd wear spectacles borrowed from a colleague at work even though they made him trip up; how he began to come empty-handed, without his confiscated goods; and how when he started to jump up and hide under the bed, imagining that he'd seen something move or heard a noise, I could no longer restrain myself from laughing uncontrollably. It had always seemed to me that he was putting it on, for I'd never before seen him at all concerned at the prospect of being caught. Around the same period, I grew weary of him accusing me of not loving him each time he asked me to marry him and I refused, ostensibly because of

Fatima and David and my children and his children. So all in all I had welcomed the idea of a trip abroad with him, the more so because the hotel where he'd made reservations was like the luxury hotels I'd seen in advertisements, and this was a unique opportunity to visit Europe. I avoided looking at him when we were at the airport although he wasn't looking in my direction; he was comforting his son who'd been hit in the face by the bag hanging from his shoulder in the crush of people saying goodbye to him, kissing him on the nose and forehead as if he were about to embark on a journey from which there was no return. He looked like a stranger to me, dressed in a suit and shoes which seemed to make it difficult for him to walk.

Although we sat side by side we didn't move close to one another or speak until the aircraft had taken off and the noise of the engines was drowned by the passengers who broke into applause to express their joy at the freedom and the drink. Maaz began to order one glass after another, and to joke with the stewardess, and with the other passengers round about him. Then he stood up and began distributing dollars to them, insisting that they accept them, while some laughed at him and others joined in the game. I was embarrassed and sank down in my seat, pretending to be asleep. He talked and drank and guffawed all the way, and to my surprise when the plane landed, he took the names and addresses of several of his fellow passengers and promised to be in touch with them. I decided to myself that we wouldn't go out much in order to avoid the embarrassing situations which arose all the time with him. But he wasn't content, as I'd thought he would be, to draw the curtains and stay in our hotel room: I didn't know that he and I had other means of communication besides our bodies.

Maaz grew tired of staying in our room. He wanted to walk about, and go into the shops, and watch television. He wanted to remain constantly at the heart of the roar and clamour, just as on our first day he'd stood on the pavement, holding my arm and trying to take in the noise and the cars and the people and the different way of life. He saw women and breathed, 'Praise God.' As well as staring at breasts and bottoms, he began to take in the trees and the water and to lie in the park watching the girls stretched out on the green grass, their dresses raised high, revealing white thighs which changed to a pinkish hue as they lay there. He even stopped and stared at armless mannequins in shop windows waiting to be fitted with new clothes, and said laughing and pointing to their breasts and bottoms, 'Fantastic! My God!' He was thunderstruck at the sight of men in tight trousers. 'Where are you, Ringo?' he asked, 'You should be here. It would blow your mind.' Then he went on, 'I tell you, if that man walked along Nafoura Street, even a newly-married man would jump him.' He wanted to run along behind the pigeons, and he paused for some time before a dog who was wearing a coat, shaking his head in wonder. He wanted to touch everything he saw in the department stores, pick the roses in the gardens, and wash his face in the pond where ducks were swimming. When we went to a striptease show he began to laugh and asked me why they had bits of spangly material the size of lentils covering their nipples. He exclaimed at the shapes and colours of the spectacle, then seemed to forget that the women were naked because they were putting on a show, and asked if they were mad, and began comparing them to the animals we'd seen in the morning. We'd been to the zoo, and he'd watched the apes and monkeys and played games with them, knocked on the glass of the reptile house, swearing at the snakes, and stood for a long time by the falcons, telling them about his own falcon, who'd been poisoned to death. Then he turned to me and asked me why I wasn't smiling, and I replied that I was bored with the animals, and that going in and out of stores fingering the merchandise, or buying a Mickey Mouse telephone and a machine to make popcorn wasn't my idea of fun. I wanted to say that I would have preferred to buy jewellery for me, or a leather coat like the ones I'd seen in the windows, but I kept quiet. Deep down, I knew what was annoying me: I'd begun to notice how fat my legs were, how fat I was all over, and was sure that this was the reason why he didn't say passionate things to me and want me like he did in the desert. The fact that I wasn't enjoying myself showed on my face: round about us adults and children alike were urging one another to buy packets of seeds and so Maaz joined in and bought some himself and began trying to bite on them; I said nothing, but just sat there at the edge of the fountain, aware of a man and a boy laughing at him. When he realized that the seeds were for the pigeons, he laughed back at the two without a trace of embarrassment. I wouldn't agree to take a photograph of him standing next to a beefeater resplendent in his uniform. I found I had not an atom of patience left in me, and that night when we got back to our hotel, I sighed and said I was fed up with the crowds and the noise. I didn't know how much I missed the desert until I talked to David and my son that evening and their voices came to me serene and carefree down the telephone. I stood with my face to the window, seeing the car lights flashing by, and pictured the calm of the house in the desert. When the telephone rang there it seemed to ring slowly, the voice on the other end of the line was always calm, even Maaz's loud voice. I realized that I'd grown used to the routine of my life there, far from the hurly-burly of humanity and its inventions. Even finding a taxi here seemed to be a serious business, and I began to see why I was in a bad mood and felt ill at ease, and it went beyond missing the monotony of the desert. I watched the women here, hurrying along with their bags of shopping, bent over with the weight of them, leaning to one side as they waited at bus stops. I saw a toy bear propped up in a window opposite the hotel and thought of the mother who'd be scrubbing the clothes or doing the ironing, and my mind wandered, comparing myself with her, then comparing my life in the States with my life in the desert. I was a different woman, unrelated to the one who bit her nails every time she remembered something she'd forgotten to buy; I was a woman living in luxury and I could ask the driver to go and fetch me as trivial a thing as a box of matches, and Ringo to wash even my hairbrush. Food stuffs were delivered, clothes from the dry-cleaners, money from the bank. I no longer even had to sit down and write cheques to the newsagent, or cheques to pay for the electricity and the phone. I didn't drive my son to school in the early morning, or wait in the afternoon with the other mothers, our lips turning blue with cold. The sun shone brightly all the time; even the cold weather in the desert was like springtime.

Wanting to bring some joy to Maaz's heart, I said to him that I preferred the desert to this place and to America. He rotated his hand and pointed to his head, indicating his view of my mental state, although he did say afterwards that he missed the desert too.

I stretched out on the bed, happy to hear the chink of the ice in the glass as Maaz poured Scotch over it. We'd come back to our room because I'd succeeded in exciting his interest while we were out shopping. Before that he'd insisted on giving a gold pen to a salesgirl who'd been nice to him and laughed at his jokes, and I hadn't intervened until he'd put his hand to his stomach and said that he was hungry, and began asking if there was a good restaurant with rice on the menu nearby, as if he was about to invite her to eat with us.

The first time we made love, I couldn't get into a rhythm with him because I could hear voices in the corridor and I was distracted by the noise of the lift. It didn't bother me, and I stopped trying because I knew there was always a second time. But suddenly I thought that perhaps there wasn't going to be a second time and as he lay on top of me limp and relaxed, I fidgeted and gripped the small of his back with both hands. Then I moved, not caring that he was stiff and unresponsive, and took his hand and put it on me and raised myself up so that I was clinging to him and he couldn't escape. Although I felt his body resisting me and refusing to submit to me, I kept moving, the sweat pouring off me. To my surprise Maaz jumped up off the bed before I had grown still, in a manner which made me forget my pleasure of a moment before. 'In the Name of God the Compassionate, the Merciful!' he cried out. I closed my eyes. 'Damn your race!' he shouted again. 'You're a devil! God preserve me!' I didn't take any notice. He always behaved in an exaggerated way after he'd made love to me. Sometimes he banged his head against the wall and sometimes he covered my body with kisses, beginning with my painted toe nails, and sighing that I'd always be in his heart, that he wished he could have my name tattooed on him. I wanted to sleep, and I wondered if he'd had a lot to drink that night. When I woke up at noon he was already dressed. I spoke to him and he answered curtly so I asked what was wrong, but he didn't reply. As I got out of bed, I deliberately showed my thighs as usual, and I didn't hitch up the straps of my nightdress which had slipped down over my shoulders. But he lowered his eyes and certain now that something was wrong I asked him what was the matter with him. He seemed to regret me not pressing him and after a bit he asked why it was that God created foreign women out of the same clay as men, or at any rate not out of the same clay as normal women. I didn't understand what he was getting at – much of what he said I didn't comment on. Then I washed my hair and sat drying it with the hair dryer, at which he said he was off to have a haircut at the hotel barber's.

When he didn't come back after an hour I felt uneasy. I went out and bought several nightdresses and some novels. For the first time I felt confident and pleased with myself as I chose what I wanted and paid for it, and even as I walked along the street. After some time I returned to the hotel, but I didn't find him there. I wanted to teach him a lesson. I marched off into the city as if I was on a military exercise, and didn't stop until I came to a bridge. I was experiencing a sensation which was new to me: for the first time I was alone, and there was no place for me in the whole world if I didn't go back to the hotel now. Deliberately I thought about David, and realized that he meant nothing to me, for he didn't act as a safety net and he definitely wasn't a friend. When I'd had an awful tearing pain in my guts one day, he'd carried on sleeping, oblivious to my cries of pain. It hadn't surprised me: he dealt with his illnesses alone. And my children? My children were my children, wherever I was and wherever they were. Nobody could take that away, but all the same I felt lonely. I thought of Maaz and felt less lonely; perhaps there was a place in the world for me after all. He must have lost his way, and I started back to the hotel once more. When he didn't open the door, I told myself that he must have come in really drunk. I went back down to the desk to ask for a key and was handed it along with a telephone message: 'Jimmy says hello.' When I opened the door he wasn't in the room and, perplexed, I tried to think where he might have gone. I couldn't believe that he would be alone because he wasn't confident of his English without me – the only person, it appeared, who could understand him. I went out to look for him in the hotel restaurant and café, in the sauna and the swimming-pool, and then returned to our room. My eye fell on the message again: 'Jimmy says hello.' An hour passed. I was sure he must be lost. I turned on the television and flicked it from one channel to another in case there was any news of him. Then I phoned the desk to ask if they'd heard or seen anything of him. I occupied myself picking his clothes up off the floor, then it was as if I tried to clutch on to him and ease the pull I felt towards him by gripping the clothes in my hands. The shirt was silk, likewise the socks, yet he'd dropped them on the floor just as he used to his white robe. When he was buying them it hadn't occurred to him to convert the price to desert currency. Every time I hesitated over something, he would buy it, although I knew he wasn't as wealthy as all that. Since I'd first visited

Fatima I'd been amazed at their generosity and their lack of greed for material things. Before that, I'd imagined that his presents to my family were because of me. I remembered one day when Ringo had pains in his stomach and Maaz heard David and me deliberating whether we'd be the ones who'd have to pay the doctor's fee: he'd put his hand in the pocket of his robe and given Ringo all the money he had on him, laughing and saying, 'I hope they find a snake inside you.' Then there were the fountain pens he handed out here, even to the waiter in the restaurant, and the tips he insisted on paying, even to the shop assistant in the jeweller's. Maaz went about catching people's attention with his laughing face and the atmosphere of easy familiarity which he transmitted to everyone we met. People weren't attracted to him because of his tips or his presents, but for his simplicity and charm. I'd begun to feel important when I was with him, and to have a sense of security which wasn't only the result of the affection which he lavished on me. I found myself learning from him, and grew accustomed to never hurrying to keep an appointment. If the train had gone, there was sure to be another. If it meant the end of the trip, there was no need to get in a state. It didn't matter, there was plenty to do here; we could even be quite happy strolling around the station. I put his clothes on the chair, and the Mickey Mouse telephone which he'd bought for his family back in its wrapping, and smiled. I began to think of him in a different way, almost jealous of his quick perceptions and secure tradition, his grasp of what was happening round about him as if it was already there in his memory and he just had to dredge it up. I clasped his clothes to me again, to feel close to him. When another hour went by, I felt a heat encircle my head. I opened the door and stood looking up and down the long empty corridor for a few moments, then went back in. I contacted the casualty departments of the local hospitals and when the woman at the desk stopped answering, I called the police, who asked me to wait a few hours and call back. I leaned back on the sofa, my fears for him growing with every sound I heard, although I couldn't hear much beyond my own breathing. I wondered whom I should contact, and dismissed the idea of getting in touch with his embassy. The fear of our relationship being discovered was as great as my fears for him. I went over to his suitcase and took out his passport and turned over the pages. They were all blank, except for the one with the stamps of his country and the country where we were now. Then I opened my handbag and made sure that my passport and the airline tickets with our names on them were still there. I wondered if he'd told anybody that I was going away with him, and I'd just decided to ask to be put through to David, when I heard a movement at the door and the sound of Maaz's voice and someone else's. He must have been lost. But when I opened the door I knew that the woman standing there with him hadn't been showing him the way, and that he hadn't been lost at all. I stood there calmly, despite the sensation of heat enveloping my head once more. But what he said made the volcano inside me erupt. He'd forgotten her name and he pointed to her: 'This is a nice woman who likes Arabs. Susan, honestly, I've been away and come back again like a homing pigeon.' The woman was standing in the face of the volcano moments before it spewed out its lava, and she only increased the ferocity of its explosion as she spoke, bending over towards him. The smell of Scotch filled the place. I screamed at them, pushed them out of the room as if they were two pieces of dough, and slammed the door violently. What had finally made me snap was the woman's tone of voice, which made her sound as if she were talking affectionately to a little boy. He was like a bird whose mother had fed him from her beak constantly, and then when the time had come for him to spread his wings he'd learnt from a stranger and flown off with her. Besides feeling angry, I was depressed as I seemed to see the nice things I'd been thinking before he arrived torn to shreds by millions of hostile fangs; I was frightened that the tenderness and concern which he'd bestowed on me alone were figments of my imagination, and when I heard shuffling and laughter, as if the two on the other side of the door were joined by fate, I flung the door open, pulled Maaz in by his arm and pushed the shouting woman away.

In spite of other doors opening, voices being raised in protest, and the intervention of the man from the desk trying to be civilized, the woman continued to bang on the door and call out threats and demand to be paid. I turned to Maaz, who was lying on the bed fully clothed, and told him to give her some money. As usual his hand went down to his trouser pocket, then to his other pocket, then to his jacket and he gave me everything he had on him. I took some of it and bent down and pushed it under the door. I didn't wait to hear her taking the money and going away, but turned to Maaz, thinking how beautiful the woman was, and wondering about the coat she was wearing. My curiosity grew to the point where I had to ask him why he'd brought her back with him, why I was no longer Suzie, and Sand-and-Sky; but Maaz just laughed, and his laughter caught at my throat. I'd lost my stronghold. In my frenzy I found myself shaking him, and that night I didn't sleep beside him; I sat up on the couch and he only called me once. I prepared myself to hear him calling a second time and to find out why he'd brought the woman and why I was no longer Sand-and-Sky. Before I'd made up my mind to ask him myself, he said to me as if he wasn't saying anything in particular, 'Suzanne, that woman was nice. And she liked Arabs. Honestly, I don't understand why you insulted her like that.' Then, in all seriousness, 'God forgive you.' I realized that he had no idea why I was angry and jealous. He must have thought I was Fatima who didn't feel either emotion, and I heard myself saying scornfully, 'She liked money.' 'Poor thing,' he answered, 'Perhaps she wasn't married and didn't have any family.' Then he asked me confidently, and as if I were a friend, 'Did you think she was pretty, Suzanne? ' I pretended not to be interested, although I knew he hadn't meant to provoke an outburst from me. I'd calmed myself with the thought that in a couple of days we'd be going back to the desert, and what had happened today would fade into memory. I tried to control my irritation and changed the subject. I asked him how he'd known his way around the streets. A mixture of interest and pleasure appeared on his face. He got up and, using his hands and his eyes, he told me how, as he'd left the room, he'd been making himself remember everything he saw: the flowers growing in a pot, the mirror, the room numbers, so that he'd remember where our room was. Then he asked the name and address of the hotel from the man at the desk. When the man gave him a card with everything he'd asked written down on it he knew that his English must have been comprehensible, and his self-confidence returned. But as soon as he'd stepped outside the hotel into the narrow street, he began to feel scared of the main street which ran parallel to it. It was as if he were seeing the crowds, the cars and the lights for the first time. He kept reaching into his pockets for his piece of paper and his money. He felt that he was in a strange, odd country, where the cigarettes with cats on the packets were called Craven A. In the desert the names on the packets corresponded to the pictures: the ones in the packet with a camel on it were called Camel, and the ones in a packet with a gipsy dancer, Gitanes. He didn't know why he felt a sudden sadness. It seemed that he didn't know how to walk along pavements, or how to look at people, or how to decide when to stop walking. He tried to give himself encouragement, reminding himself that he'd always wanted to travel and see the world – the countries which produced everything that came to the desert. He wanted to go back, but he knew in his heart of hearts that he did really know how to go about things (here he mentioned that he'd learnt from me the right way to stroll around the streets). He went along until he came to a news stand where he saw some Arabic magazines and newspapers. When the man at the stand counted out the money and handed him the change Maaz, full of pride, said 'Thank you' in English, and began to walk with a more confident step. Enthusiastically, he went into a restaurant, and as he wasn't hungry he ordered a Scotch. He paid for it and when he heard the 'thank you' coming back at him he relaxed. He went on his way again and didn't stop until he saw the word 'Bar'. Inside, it looked like he'd known for a long time that it would, low lights, high stools, just like on the videos. He was pleased at his discovery and smiled to himself. On his right a woman sat drinking. When he turned in her direction she smiled welcomingly at him. He felt as if he was flying through the air with joy. He couldn't understand what she was saying, but she understood him and asked where he came from, and what he was doing here. When he told her, she asked him if he was a sheikh, and he felt like nodding his head. Then his eyes fell on the bottles in their dozens behind the man pouring the Scotch. Laughing and talking to himself, he said out loud, 'I could take them and smash them like I have to at home.' The Scotch had affected his head. He couldn't help thinking that what he did in the desert was ridiculous, and he seized the magazine he'd bought and went through it, pretending to censor parts of it. The woman didn't understand, and a picture of himself sitting at his table at work went round in his mind: he saw himself swooping down on the magazines, turning the pages and enjoying looking at the women's bodies, with the thick black pen motionless in his fingers; then he would go to the bathroom and play with himself, and return to the woman who was blonde, dark, thin, a foreign star, an Arab star, depending on which magazine she was in. When he visited friends of his who worked in embassies they used to show him the small black and white photographs on visa application forms, which also triggered off their desire, so much so that they went to the lengths of stealing the photographs of all the pretty women and copying them and enlarging them and swapping them with one another; eventually the authorities had introduced a regulation to the effect that a form would be refused if the accompanying photograph showed any part of the woman below her neck or if a seductive expression could be detected in her eyes.

Then, recalling the high point of his adventure, he clapped his hands and turned to face me to be sure of having my full attention: 'Listen, Suzanne, if it hadn't been that woman, when I was in the underground city, I would have – O God, it was all twisting passages as if you were inside an ear – I would have been lost and starving, I could have died down there and nobody would have known. How would I have got up again?' 'An underground city? Like an ear?' I repeated, losing patience.

'Yes. The woman took me in a tram, and she began walking from one underground tunnel to another. It was like being in the land of the jinn. She'd go up a level and down a level, with me clinging to her hand and clutching my heart, terrified that she'd leave me . . .'

When I heard him snoring, I jumped up, but instead of shaking him by the shoulders I switched on the light and went to fetch a glass of water. I sat on the edge of the bed and called his name. When he opened his eyes, he said, 'God bless you. What's wrong?'

I handed him the glass of water, acting cool and calm, and said that I'd decided to accept his offer of marriage. To my surprise he didn't answer, but closed his eyes again and said, 'God willing.' For a moment it was as if I'd gone back to being the Suzanne who sat in front of the television in the suburbs in Texas with my hair tied back and nothing in my life but sentimental soap operas. Miserably, I wondered how he had dared to bring home a woman, and why I was no longer Suzie and Suzanne and Sand-and-Sky. I went to wake him again, and shook him, not realizing how violent I was being until my arms and shoulders began to hurt. I was full of anger because I'd agreed to marry him and he'd refused me. As usual when I wanted the truth from him, I made him swear by his children before he said anything. He sat up in bed, and to my surprise he announced that he'd been afraid of me the previous day and felt disgusted by me. My thoughts strayed back and I couldn't think of any reason. Was it because I'd bought another piece of jewellery, or told him that I preferred life in the desert to life here? 'Why? Why?' I asked him, irritable in my curiosity to find out what sin I'd committed. He answered that I'd done things for my own pleasure like a man. When again I sifted through what had happened the day before and still couldn't guess what he meant, I shook my head questioningly, and he said calmly and gravely, 'God created you to bear children, and to give pleasure to a man, and that's all.' I didn't understand. Perhaps I hadn't understood his English? Naturally I'd had children, and naturally a man enjoyed me just as I enjoyed him. Wide awake by this time, Maaz repeated seriously, 'God created woman to make children, like a factory. That's the exact word, Suzanne. She's a factory, she produces enjoyment for the man, not for herself.' I laughed, and replied quickly, 'If God doesn't want her to enjoy it, then how and why do I enjoy it?' He looked confused and, not finding a ready answer to my question, he shouted, 'Yesterday you were like a she-devil.' Then he mumbled, 'I swear, in God's name, I was disgusted by you, and by your whole race. You seemed like a man to me, when you were crying out. I said, Maaz, this woman's a hermaphrodite. She's both a man and a woman.' Then he added, 'You enjoy it because you're a hermaphrodite.' Although I felt embarrassed when I remembered my unstoppable wave of desire of the day before, I began to laugh. I thought of the grave way he had spoken, the pain he'd expressed, and I laughed. No doubt my laughter confirmed to him that I was indeed a devil, for he began looking at me with distaste. 'And what about Fatima,' I asked, tears of laughter running down my cheeks, 'is she a devil too?' 'Foreign women must be made out of different clay from ordinary women,' he replied. I didn't find it strange about Fatima, and her lack of pleasure and desire; when I was in America, I'd stopped having sex with David or doing it by myself, and I was no longer conscious of my body and sexual enjoyment, except occasionally when I was asleep and I dreamt that I had it with the local policeman, or my children's teacher, or the edge of the table or the bath water, and I'd thought at the time that it was my body fulfilling one of its functions in spite of me.

I moved closer to him and, in an attempt to reawaken his desire, asked him if he'd brought the woman back here to sleep with her. 'Poor woman. You insulted her,' was his only reply. 'I thought that I'd introduce her to you because she was nice.' I tried again, playfully: 'Does this mean no more Suzanne? Ever, ever?'

When he went on staring at the ceiling, I was sure that he'd made up his mind not to give in to me, even though he wanted to, but suddenly he shouted, 'Now I understand why you've never got pregnant by me . . .'

Serious now, and eager to understand his way of reasoning, I exclaimed, 'For God's sake, why?'

Before I'd finished, he interrupted, 'I know you're not a man, but you're not a woman either otherwise I would have made you pregnant.'

Laughing again, I told him that after Jimmy was born I'd had an operation to seal off my tubes. At this he brought his palms sharply together, then rubbed his eyes and said, 'God forbid! You heathen.' Then with spiteful glee: 'I see, God's punished you, so now you're a hermaphrodite.'

My thoughts strayed to the occasion he'd first seen me naked, and how he'd said something which I hadn't understood then, but now I did. I found it strange that he'd been amazed at the sight of my pubic hair, and felt sure at the time that it was because he'd never seen a completely naked woman before me.

I would have liked to reply to him, but I heard his breathing growing louder, and turned over to try and sleep myself. I concluded that I'd been protected all this time by his *naïveté* and ignorance, and wondered why I wasn't annoyed by what he'd said, or hadn't taken him more seriously. I vaguely tried to think what my reaction would be if David thought about me in the same way, and automatically clenched my fist. But I looked at Maaz and smiled, captivated by his sincerity and spontaneity, which put me on a level with Marilyn Monroe. I felt safe at his side and vowed to myself that I would always sleep beside him like this, with his money, his gold watch and his possessions on the floor the other side of him.

Only as I packed my bags, delighted with the clothes I'd bought for my daughters and the gold jewellery Maaz had bought for me, and delighted to be going home, did I think how much this trip had changed Maaz, and our relationship. But I didn't doubt that he would keep coming to see me, until we were back at the desert airport and I saw how he behaved with the friends who'd come to meet him, and how they looked at me, and then how he went off with them, without even bothering to find out if David was waiting for me outside.

I continued to sit there, resting my cheek on my hand, while Maaz and Ringo pored over the dozens of brochures about Sri Lanka, talking in English and Arabic and using their hands. Ringo was encouraging Maaz to go to Sri Lanka as if it were the only place in the world worth visiting, and when he felt that his description might not be conveying a true picture he would purse his lips into a whistle of admiration. I couldn't stand it any longer. I didn't want to shout at Maaz, so I attacked Ringo instead and asked him why he didn't go back to his own country if he liked it so much and thought it was the most beautiful country in the world. Ringo didn't understand the reason for my outburst and said hesitantly, pushing a lock of hair off his face, 'I'm happy here.' Mockingly, Maaz took his hand and pointed to the gold bracelet with his name on it and the gold ring, then stood up to pull the chain with a gold heart on the end of it from around Ringo's neck, and said, 'How could he get all this gold in Sri

Lanka? He'd only be given tin there!'

5

Sita's bottle stayed where it was, and I was still in my house in the desert. I no longer saw Maaz. From time to time it was again as if I were the only woman who existed, almost a rare specimen. I wasn't under a misapprehension about this, and it wasn't difficult to find men. The men in their white robes searched for women among the freezers and foodstuffs in the supermarkets. They tailed foreigners and car passengers who weren't wearing veils. As they walked along the street they stole glances at the gates of houses just in case a woman going in behind the high walls gave them a smile: telephone and electricity workers and private gardeners were the worst offenders. The first time I was hesitant; I pushed my trolley around the supermarket, and concentrated on reading what was written on the packets and tins, not looking at the man who was looking at me and going through a charade of coughing and spitting to attract my attention, nor at another who tried to test whether I was really there to shop by moving his lips and moistening them with his tongue. I pushed the trolley along at speed, paid the man at the cash desk and rushed to the car. But on the second occasion, in the bookshop this time, I found myself making an approach to a man who I'd heard talking in English, whose American accent and good looks gave me encouragement. For some reason I said to him, 'Since you speak English, perhaps we could talk together and you could help me understand the nature of the males in your country.' I began to tell him about

Maaz and how he'd left me, although I knew that these things weren't relevant while I was with this man. He looked at me in astonishment, obviously thinking that I was crazy, and didn't reply, but went on turning the pages of a magazine, then looked around for the foreigner he'd been talking to before. I told him that I wasn't mad and seriously wanted to understand the personality of the Arab male. The man looked to one side then the other, before feeling in his pocket and taking out a card which he left on top of a magazine at the edge of the table. Then he vanished. I snatched up the card, covering it with my hand, and stuffed it into my bag with a sigh of relief. I dialled his number day and night until one day he answered and said that he'd been at his engineering project in the heart of the desert. I had to meet him: his voice gave me a strange feeling of warmth. The boredom I'd felt since returning from my trip abroad evaporated, and I rested my hand on my heart, afraid that he'd try to avoid meeting me. A long time passed before he did arrange to meet me. He asked me to come and visit him at his project, and agreed a time with me and described the car which would be waiting to take me at the entrance to the store.

The other man was the one who had come from the department of health because of a dog which used to come to my neighbour's doorstep at dawn every day with a cat or a large rat in its mouth. The man didn't even want to look at the dog which we'd shut up in my neighbour's garden. Instead his gaze shifted between me and my neighbour, and he told me later that he knew from the way I'd spoken to him on the phone that it was him I was interested in, not the dog.

I didn't think about Maaz again until a tall man knocked on the door of my house one morning. Ringo opened it, smiling, thinking that he'd come to see him. The man ignored Ringo's smile and as I stood behind the kitchen door listening, I heard him asking if this was Mr David's house. Then he asked about me. I hesitated before coming forward. 'I can't say anything until I've consulted my lawyer,' I told him. The man looked startled; he said quickly that he was a friend of Maaz's and had come with a request from him. Maaz had begun to pester me in various ways, hanging around my friends, phoning me and then putting the receiver down or hanging on without speaking; once he'd come to drink Scotch at our place, accompanied by an Indonesian nurse. Why had this man mentioned my husband's name, and how could he permit himself to come in and sit down on the couch and help himself to a cigarette? I thought the time must have finally arrived when they were going to make me leave the desert. Who was behind this tall Arab? Maaz? The engineer I'd met in the bookshop? Someone from the telephone exchange? The owner of the bookshop? The owner of the drugstore? The man lit his cigarette and said that Maaz had told him where my house was and sent me his best wishes. He was lying, but I regained my composure and said nothing. I stood listening and wondering whether I should contact David, chase him away, phone Maaz, or believe what he said. Then I heard him coolly stating that he preferred them between the ages of sixteen and twenty and that he was ready to pay from three hundred to five hundred dollars provided that the meeting took place in my house. He fell silent while he extinguished his cigarette and I stood before him in amazement. 'They must be going to force me to leave,' I thought, 'and they need evidence against me.'

I told him I didn't understand what he was talking about. He laughed and struck his hand against his thigh, and I noticed the clean whiteness of his robe, the gold watch, the expensive ring. With another affected laugh, he said, 'You understand quite well. When will you be in touch?' He stood up, put his hand in his pocket, and took out a card. I hesitated and then fear made me take it. Under his name I read the title of his official post. This time his laughter was genuine and, adjusting his headcloth, he said, 'Government officials are men too . . . and you know the situation here.' 'They've spoken against me,' I thought, confusedly. The neighbours, Maaz, the engineer whom I no longer saw, the owner of the bookshop, the pharmacist. The man went calmly over to the door. He turned to me and reached out his hand to shake mine. 'Don't forget. I'll be waiting.' Although he spoke in a low voice, his tone was commanding. I held out my hand and he immobilized it between his and said, 'Maaz's very lucky.' Then he thanked me for the coffee and my kind hospitality. I almost leapt back into the sitting-room. I didn't see the coffee cups but pictured myself packing my bags and cast my eyes around me, taking in everything at a single glance. Mad with anger, I stamped my foot, vowing that I would never leave this place. My thoughts were in a turmoil and I no longer knew how I should act. I called Ringo and told him what had happened, pacing around the table and not paying attention to him telling me in a soothing voice that he was sure the man had genuinely come in search of a woman. I knew there was nothing for it but to enlist Maaz's help, but he hadn't been to the house since I'd refused to let him in late one night.

When I couldn't find him at his office I made my way to his house. Fatima opened the door and seemed astonished to see me. She looked at the telephone as if she couldn't believe that I'd really phoned her minutes before and here I was now in front of her. Although I begged her not to go away because I could only stay a few minutes, she rushed off into the kitchen. I sat there smelling the same old smell, which I'd never liked. How the house had changed since they'd known me! Everything my eyes fell on was pleasingly familiar: the horn fish, the picture of Mecca worked in white metal, the shaggy mustard-coloured moquette rugs, the artificial flowers which we'd bought together.

Fatima appeared with a big bowl of fruit and a broad smile. She pointed to her stomach and said, 'I'm having a baby.' I smiled back at her, as if it didn't concern me, which it didn't. All I wanted now was to seek help from Maaz so that I could stay in this country. When I asked Fatima where he was she shrugged her shoulders. 'Son of a bitch,' I said in English. 'Thank you, Madame Suzanne,' replied Fatima, smiling delightedly at her English. She pointed at the dish of fruit, then at me, wanting to know why I wasn't having anything. When I started towards the door, she stood in my way seizing me by the hand and dragging me towards the fruit. She held out the bowl to me then took a banana and apple from it herself and pushed them into my hand.

I went back to the car. I must be imagining things. This wasn't the way to drive me away from here. Maaz must come and visit us again like before. He was a lifeline: his regular visits to us had given me a sense of security and I was beginning to miss it on occasions, like today for example. Or the man may have been genuinely after a woman and known Maaz. He must surely have heard about my daughters' visit from the States: perhaps he'd followed us and conducted his own investigations, or perhaps he knew about me from friends of Ringo's. Ringo's desert admirers were on the increase and he accepted every invitation, claiming that in this way he stood the chance of meeting one suitable person and then he would break off his numerous relationships and settle down. It wasn't that easy: the desert was full of people like him; European firms had begun to favour appointing gays to desert posts for both practical and financial reasons. They spared them the expenditure on large houses, family travel, children's schooling, and problems with wives who had too much time on their hands. There was no desperate longing for a woman, no sexual frustration leading to lack of concentration at work and an inability to tolerate the desert, and requests for transfers back home or continual holidays.

It could have been the engineer whom I hadn't wanted to meet again after I'd visited his scheme in the desert. Although he phoned frequently and circled the house in his car, he was the one man I couldn't even bear to remember. The journey had been long, two hours' drive into the heart of the desert with nothing to see except black crows against the changing hues of the great expanses of sand. The Filipino driver had met me at the door of the store as I'd agreed with the engineer, and all the time he looked at me in the driving mirror which he'd trained on me for the purpose. He played one tape after another until we reached an outpost of human existence dotted about with tools and machinery and workers with their heads and faces swathed in cloth as an armour against the stinging sand.

It wasn't easy to recognize the engineer when he was dressed in trousers and a shirt. To my surprise he began to take me on a tour of the place, explaining to me seriously how the machines worked and what the men were doing. The sun grew hotter by the moment as we walked to the furthest point of the scheme and he took me into a trench, talking and explaining non-stop, redoubling his efforts when he saw that the men were watching us. I asked him where he'd got his American accent from, to shift things on to a more personal level. 'New York State University,' he replied, walking a few steps ahead of me. I despaired and caught up with him and we arrived back at his office, a concrete room smelling of cigarettes and wet cement. He sat down at the table and asked me about my Arab friend, but before I opened my mouth he stood up and opened the door for me saying, 'The air-conditioner isn't working in the office,' and took me back into the sun. Disappointed, I felt that I'd been wrong to come, and was angry at myself and sick with exhaustion and the heat. He went up to one of the workers and the man handed him a bundle of photographs. He began giving me one after the other, pictures of steel foundations and trench-digging equipment. I told him irritably that I was thirsty. His features didn't change. Retaining his solemn expression he led me over to the car and opened the door for me. As soon as I got in I wished I was still in the sun. It was boiling inside the car. I swallowed down a scream. My thighs were almost on fire from the plastic of the seat. I wiped sweat off myself with my hand, thinking that I was no longer of an age to be able to handle these tiresome escapades. He stopped the car in front of a small building and I followed him out; I'd begun to understand his behaviour: he was afraid and on edge. The coolness spreading through my body in the little cafeteria, which was fragrant with the smell of curry and rice, made me forget the outside. He spoke constantly to the workers who were seated at tables round about us, then he showed me the photographs again and stood up. I was scared of the burning car and wished I could stay in the restaurant or go back home straightaway. So I said that I had to be getting back. He nodded, as if this request of mine had made him feel easier. He said that he wanted to go in the car to fetch some papers and although I didn't understand my connection with these papers, I nodded and followed him out again. Without waiting for the air-conditioner to take effect, I opened the car window and stuck my head out. We only went a short distance. When he got out, I stayed in the car, but he signalled to me to get out too. I did so hesitantly, telling myself that I'd soon be free of him. There was a secretary typing there. He introduced me to him, then led me into another room. The moment he'd closed the door he took hold of me and we stood there right by the door. He felt my breasts, then opened his flies at speed, as if he was receiving orders from somewhere. He brought me close to him, and I was forced to cling to the wall to keep my balance. Then he turned away, closing his flies and straightening his shirt. He picked up an envelope off the table and began talking to me again about engineering terms. There were signs of annoyance and impatience on his face now. He was hurrying me and didn't wait even while I reached for my bag. Still talking in technical jargon that only another engineer would have understood, he went out ahead of me. Then he gave me the envelope which he'd been holding. 'Say that this is for the firm,' he instructed me, and I was left completely at a loss.

It was inconceivable that any of these men would have

reported me, I told myself confidently. I stood up and, on Ringo's advice, I called the man who'd come to the house the next day but he wasn't there. After I'd tried for several days in a row, I was told that he'd gone away. When I'd had numerous conversations and the voice at the other end had started to get flirtatious, although I wasn't sure whether it was the man himself or another man in his office, I felt reassured. My fear evaporated altogether when I saw him by chance in the street with a veiled woman, and he hid his face in fright.

6

I returned home one day and Ringo rushed to meet me saying that Maaz had called dozens of times. Instead of going to the phone I went to the fridge to look for something to drink, Ringo started to tell me that Maaz had been shouting in a way that wasn't like him, and he'd scarcely finished speaking when the telephone rang. I rushed to pick up the receiver not expecting it to be Maaz again so soon. His voice came weakly and thinly down the line. He asked me to visit him; he was ill, he said. He must have thought I'd refuse because I was angry with him since the day he'd come to ask about Sri Lanka and gone off there without me. He went on urging me to come and I made the excuse that there wasn't a driver around. 'What about Ringo?' he asked. Then I heard him cursing in a loud voice: 'God damn the yellow bastard. He can bring you.' It usually made me laugh when he cursed Ringo, but not this time. 'Tomorrow,' I replied. 'I'm tired.' And I put the receiver down. I'd scarcely flung my head back on the couch when the phone rang again. It was Maaz and he was pleading with me. I got up in spite of myself. I thought I knew exactly why he was so insistent, and it was as if just for a moment I missed our times together. I asked him why he didn't come here; I was tired. Lunch with the owner of the drugstore and his family had been a heavy meal and the drink had flowed in abundance, but he persisted to a degree that was uncharacteristic of him.

When Fatima opened the door to me, I knew that something was wrong in spite of the broad smile and her kisses on my cheek. 'Maaz's ill,' she said, clasping her hands together then pointing to her head and inclining it to one side. I followed her, still beset by feelings of tiredness. The smell of incense seemed extra powerful that day. We passed through the sitting-room and I couldn't help noticing the new things: there was a picture on the wall looking like a television screen, depicting slowly changing images. I remembered the present which he'd been promising me since he returned from Sri Lanka. Maaz was in bed in the room which I'd thought would one day become part of my daily life. There was nothing in it but the bed against the wall, a pile of mattresses against the facing wall and a chest. Smoke from the incense rose into the air.

Maaz was thin, his face was pale, there were mauve circles under his eyes, and his hair was on end. Inclining his head to one side, he accosted me with words that I couldn't understand. He talked about electricity, lights flashing on and off in his face, a dirty house. Then he spread out his hands in front of me, and made them shake. I was struck by how bad his English was and wondered how I'd understood him before. I must have helped him to express himself and here he was now unable to do it, even with the help of Arabic words and sign language.

I found myself turning to address Fatima who stood there looking at him and talking about him as if he were a stranger, not her husband. 'He doesn't eat. Doesn't drink coffee, tea.

The poor thing has a few crumbs at each meal, and a drop of water to get them down.'

He seemed like another person to me, unrelated to the Maaz I'd watched in a storm of emotion as he talked to Ringo about the trip to Sri Lanka, while I sat making plans to marry him; the man whom I'd thought of following to the airport, indifferent to the shame, and then even accompanying against his will, when I'd heard that he was travelling without me. Now he was asking me for help, just as he had done when the washing machine didn't spin the clothes and when the oven didn't work, only to have me discover that they hadn't pushed the right button or the electricity was cut off that day. 'Has Maaz seen the doctor?' I asked Fatima, whose stomach had swollen visibly. She held up two fingers: 'Twice,' she replied. Then she disappeared and I asked Maaz, 'What do you feel, and where does it hurt?' He didn't bother to answer but sat up in bed and moved his head about restlessly. When I repeated the question, he answered, 'Ask Ringo. God damn the yellow bastards. Gog and Magog. They don't fear God. They're devils. God preserve me!' At this point Fatima came back in. All the time she'd been away I'd heard her scolding her youngest child, the boy, in the kitchen. He must have been eating from the dishes she'd got ready for me and wanted to place before me untouched: dishes of pistachio nuts and fruit. I tried to find out what the doctor had said to Maaz, but he was talking again about the light which went off and on, about his face, his head and especially his spine, about the dirty house where there was a big rat, and about the funny-tasting Scotch. Then he stretched out his trembling hands so that I could see the veins protruding on them, put them up to his eyes and began crying like a child. I couldn't bear to see him crying, and it was made worse by his two daughters crying in the hall and Fatima trying to calm the little boy and to finish what she'd started to say: 'I swear to God, I said to him don't go abroad on your own. Take the Qur'an and put it under your pillow. He

didn't listen to me . . . God forgive him.' I noticed that the
small veins in his temples were standing out and I rose to my
feet, saying to Fatima, 'He must have a doctor.' Together,
Fatima and I helped him up. I noticed a large gold ring on his
finger, set with a wine-red stone. To my amazement Maaz
couldn't stand. He leant on my shoulder for a moment, then
sank back on to the bed. I asked the name of his doctor and
turned to Fatima, saying that I'd contact him. Maaz held out
both hands in protest, then bowed his head and kicked out at
me with his feet. I couldn't understand why he was objecting
and said to him reassuringly that the doctor would have to
come if I spoke to him. But Maaz stopped shouting and said
some words which sounded like gibberish to me. Fatima
explained, 'He wants the doctor from your husband's firm.
An American doctor.' Only then did I realize why he'd asked
me to help. I spoke to David, then the doctor, then Ringo,
who promised to bring the doctor here. I sat drinking coffee,
feeling proud of myself. Nothing was hard for me in this
country; it was as if I owned it. To date I'd sold five kitchens;
telephone cables led up to our house in three different spots,
over other houses and across the desert, because storms had
brought them down. The road leading to our house had been
surfaced with asphalt where before there had been sand. I got
what I wanted either by making telephone calls or by con-
fronting people in person, or through friends. Maaz wiped
away his tears with the sleeve of his robe. I noticed his
luxurious leather sandals and the suitcase on top of the chest,
looking out of place in this room. The doctor came and
opened up Maaz's eyes and peered at the whites. The first
thing he asked him was if he was taking any medicaments. I
asked Fatima and she hurried away and came back with a
little bottle. She gave it to me and stayed outside the room
while I went in to give it to the doctor. The bottle contained
tranquillizers and the doctor asked Maaz what dose he was
on. Fatima replied from outside, 'Four or five.' She may have
heard me gasping, for she went on, 'It was him

who said he wanted more, so that he'd get better quicker.'
When I translated for the doctor he laughed and said tht he'd
had a patient who'd refused an injection in his thigh, saying
that the pain and the swelling were in his eye, not his thigh. I
left when the doctor said he wanted to examine him, and
when Fatima and I went back in later, she remarked, 'Thank
God he's repented. No more trips abroad.'

The doctor said he hadn't found anything wrong with
Maaz, except that his nerves were upset; he was to stop
taking the tranquillizers and meanwhile the doctor would
have some tests carried out on the specimens of blood and
urine which he'd taken. Maaz wanted me to stay and I could
only leave by slipping out of the room when his attention
wandered.

At dawn the next day the telephone rang again and it was
Maaz asking me to fetch the doctor. I told him to wait for the
results of the tests and he began to shout at me. He came to
me in the afternoon because I hadn't been to see him, accompanied by one of his neighbours. As I went through the
motions of contacting the doctor, I could see Ringo urging
Maaz to sit down and the neighbour devouring me with his
eyes. Then I heard him telling Maaz that he ought to register
with the nearby clinic: everybody returning from the Far East
had to be examined, and their wives as well. Maaz held out a
hand to silence him: 'What do you know about it? I've got
this burning light in my eyes.' He went on talking, saying
things which I couldn't understand. I couldn't bear his shouting, the movements he made, the sound of his voice: was he
crying, laughing or ranting unintelligibly? I found myself
phoning Suha. Agitatedly I asked her to come round, not
giving her any scope to invent excuses. When she asked me
what was going on, I screamed at her, 'Please. I can't explain.
Please just come.' I went into the kitchen and asked Ringo to
go and sit with the visitors, and I could hear a renewed burst
of shouting from Maaz and the same old cry: 'Yellow bastards. Gog and Magog.'

I stayed in the kitchen until I heard the door bell. I'd refused to go in with Scotch for Maaz or for his friend although both Maaz and Ringo were calling out to me, and Ringo had begun to repeat to Maaz that since he'd stopped visiting us the Scotch supplies had been cut off. He was lying: Scotch, gold chains, Persian rugs were all in greater abundance than ever.

I didn't understand why Suha was annoyed when she saw Maaz and his friend, even though I explained to her that he was ill. She wouldn't agree to sit with them and let him tell her what was wrong. She came into the kitchen looking at her watch and saying that she had to contact her husband so that he could send Said for her. But when we heard Maaz calling, we stopped and listened; his calling turned into shouting and I saw Suha laugh. I laughed too and we collapsed together in helpless floods of laughter. His tone was more one of laughter and weeping mixed than of protest. Was he acting? 'The light shining in my eyes, aah . . . I put up my hands to my eyes. They pulled them away. The light was like a fire and it shot down my spine, burning me. I cried out, and I heard them laughing. I said, "Forgive me, Lord. Cast the devil out of me as you cast him out of Paradise." And her black mole. If the whore's uncle had got rid of the mole, none of this would ever have happened.' I was waiting for just a sign from Suha and then I thought we'd both begin to laugh again, but this time she ignored me and rose quickly and went into the sitting-room. I heard her asking boldly, 'Who was she, Maaz? Who was this woman?' Maaz tried to stand up to greet her but he sank back down again. 'Madame Suha. There's a light shining in my eyes. A burning light. It never goes away, even for a second. Aaah. The rat was as big as a chicken. It strutted around and stared me straight in the eyes. I should have guessed from the story of the black mole and escaped with my manhood. But I bought her a diamond like the one in the picture; she talked a lot, pointing to the diamonds and then to her mole. Every time I met her she talked about diamonds and the mole, and she cried, and I didn't understand. Bit by bit the group she was with made me understand that she wasn't married yet because of the big mole on her cheek. They said that the family who'd come to betroth her to their son had seen the mole and changed their minds. It was near her eyes and so the tears would flow over it when she cried; they took this as an omen and said that if she married, her husband might die. Her uncle bored into the mole with the thorn and blood came in its place, then a scab which healed up and fell off, leaving the mole where it had always been. And they told me that she wanted to cover it up with a diamond stud so that she could get married. I said I'd marry her and I wasn't afraid of the mole. On the contrary, I told them, where I came from it was considered a sign of beauty.'

It was many days before Maaz began to show signs of recovering. I didn't go back to see him, being content to ask after him on the phone from time to time, until one day Fatima invited me and Suha to lunch: she'd slaughtered a sheep to celebrate Maaz's return to health. Suha agreed to come and arrived with her son, carrying a box of chocolates. I couldn't stop myself asking her in a challenging manner how she'd found the time to have lunch with Maaz and Fatima when she'd completely given up visiting her friends because she was getting ready to leave the country. She laughed and said, 'I was bored with everybody. But hearing Maaz tell the story of his illness is quite amusing.' We went with Said who came into the building with us at Maaz's request. He took him off into another room, and Suha looked at me and smiled. For the first time Fatima took off her face veil, after Suha had told her that one of her daughters was like Maaz. Fatima looked young, with an innocent expression in her eyes and a beautiful smile, yellow teeth notwithstanding. Her thick black hair hung loose but was sticky with all the oil she put on it. She wore a gold chain around her neck with King George gold sovereigns hanging from it.

I noticed Suha's eyes roving over the house. She picked up

a red plastic mug, then put it back on the plastic table, which was the colour of a pomegranate. 'The same colour,' she commented. Then she asked Fatima about the bunches of grapes made of interlocking metal rings, which were hanging on the partition. Fatima smiled and brought some bunches of plastic grapes and insisted that Suha should take them. I thought she liked them even though she refused them. But when Umar grabbed them and ran off with them, I heard her telling him in English to put the horrible things down. He didn't stop pestering Suha until she let him ride the huge stuffed camel which had hair like a hedgehog's spikes and eyes that were two green pearls, and a brown tongue and brown lips. Umar fell off repeatedly, so Fatima brought the two boys a damp wooden stool from the bathroom. They climbed up on it and hurled themselves on the bunches of grapes on the partition, fighting to pull them down; Fatima hung them up somewhere else, and seemed delighted at the uproar, even though Suha and I were scolding our sons vigorously.

When Maaz came into the room where we were after the meal, it was as if he banished the spectre of drowsy boredom which had begun to steal in on the three of us and especially Suha, who at once asked him where Said was. 'He's on an errand. He'll be back in half an hour,' answered Maaz. Then he said, 'Come and see what I brought from Sri Lanka.' At his bidding, Fatima bent down and pulled out a wooden box from under the bed and opened it. It was lined with red velvety material, and contained prayer beads and rings set with semi-precious stones – mauve, dark blue, pink – and with pink and red coral. I picked out a ring which appeared to have more gold in it than the others. 'This is beautiful,' I remarked, hoping fervently that he'd say to me as usual, 'Please have it,' and he did, quite happily: 'Please have it, Suzie.' He took out a necklace and put it in my hand, then proffered the case to Suha who'd remained standing. 'Please, Madame Suha. You're my sister, I swear to God.' Suha refused, as I thought she would. Although Maaz pleaded and insisted that she should take anything she wanted, she wouldn't and eventually she asked Fatima for a glass of water and followed her into the kitchen.

My eyes became riveted to the box again and I said playfully, 'So you went away without me?' 'It was a mistake, I swear, Suzanne,' he replied, laughing. 'See how it's drained my strength and health and left me with hallucinations. After the land of God and Magog, God's decreed a new life for me.'

I wanted to bring him back to the main issue: I reached for a ring set with a pearl and a red stone and slipped it on my finger. 'Fatima's lucky,' I sighed. 'Fatima doesn't like Sri Lankan work,' he answered, 'nor Italian. She says the gold's poor quality. I promised her a chain from Bahrain.' I pretended that the ring wouldn't come off my finger and he said, getting to his feet, 'Leave it there, Suzanne.' Suha came back in, asking when we were going to leave. I smiled at her. I'd put everything that Maaz had given me in my handbag, afraid of what she would think. She turned to Maaz challengingly. 'You didn't finish the story,' she said. 'What happened to the woman with the mole?' I didn't feel like hearing the story again. I was pleased with the jewellery and I wanted to take it home and look at it properly. I stood up: 'We must go.' But Maaz gestured to me to sit down again and turned to Suha, appearing happy at her interest in him. I'd sensed for a while that he was anxious to talk to her. 'In the hotel they told me to make the trip home and be with my family when I died. They looked for my papers and then contacted the embassy. A man came to show me how to get to the airport and he stayed with me right up till I boarded the plane, God bless him. I told him everything that had happened to me, and he said, 'You're very lucky.' And it's true, I am. If I'd died in Sri Lanka I would have died unclean, without the prayer or the creed.'

I had no idea what he was talking about, but Suha asked him, 'What caused it? You haven't told us what caused it.'

Maaz paid no attention to Fatima who came in carrying a stainless steel coffee pot, and answered, 'The woman with the mole cried and said nobody would marry her, and she wanted to hide the mole with a diamond. I told her that I'd help her escape from them and take her to my country and marry her. The following day I went to the casino. She didn't turn up. Some of her group were there, and they took me away and tortured me with fire and with lights that hurt my eyes and made me confused. Maybe they put sleeping pills and pills to make me crazy in the drinks they gave me. I didn't know why they were doing it, and every time I asked about her they tortured me some more. When I understood what was wrong, I told them that I was married already, and I'd said the things I'd said for a joke.'

I smiled at Fatima, and so did Suha. Fatima returned our smiles, raised her hand as if she was throwing something over her shoulder, and repeated, 'God guide you, Maaz.' Without sitting down, she began pouring coffee into the cups. She stood up nearly all the time we were eating. Whenever Suha invited her to sit with us, she poised for a few moments, pretended to eat something, then stood up again, listening out for Maaz to call to her. She sat down again to fill my plate and Suha's with rice and meat which she broke up with her fingers, although we tried to stop her. When Suha stood up, I did the same, and with difficulty we prised Umar and James off the camel. We shook hands with Maaz, then with Fatima; she held out a bottle of cologne and shook a few drops from it over our hands and on the ground. Meanwhile Maaz went to fetch an aerosol; 'Haven't you sprayed any incense over them?' he asked, spraying it at Suha's face, while I moved out of reach. A smell of incense spilled into the room, sickly sweet like sugar, mixing instantly with the smell of the cologne. Fatima said in embarrassment, 'Really, I only like to burn sticks of incense. They cheat us by selling us these aerosols instead of proper incense, and you can't see smoke coming from it or anything.'

In the car Suha told me that Fatima didn't believe that Maaz and I were having an affair, then she began to laugh. She wouldn't tell me the reason until she'd made me promise that I wouldn't be angry whatever she said; but she couldn't stop laughing. Fast losing my patience I said that if she didn't tell me I really would be angry. So she told me and I didn't understand why she'd laughed such a lot: Fatima had said that the blue of my eyes was like glass, my skin was the colour of a red fish, and my bottom was like a sheep's buttocks.

Eventually she told me the rest of the conversation: Fatima didn't believe what the neighbours said about my relationship with Maaz because I was married and had children; I taught him English in exchange for Arabic lessons as I and my husband wanted to start a business; Maaz took us to visit villages so that we could get to know the country, and he'd become a real friend to us. Then Suha laughed again, and told me at last after more hesitation all of what Fatima had said, that she presumed I left my pubic hair unshaven like a forest, and since this was unclean, and Maaz was a good Muslim, he wouldn't have risked invalidating his prayers. I found myself sharing Suha's laughter, and I recounted what Maaz had discovered when we went away together, and how he'd moved away from me as if I were a leper.

7

I knocked on Maaz's door again – it wasn't passion, or the memory, or boredom – but his door remained silent. I saw an eye looking through its newly installed spy-hole and began to bang with the flat of my hand, as I thought of the return to the States coming closer all the time. I paused, then started up again when I heard his daughter's voice, and then his son crying. I couldn't make myself move away from the door: it was as if I had to see it opening now or it would turn into an aircraft door. At the thought of this I kicked it. There was a rattling noise from inside but the door remained closed.

I leaned my head against my hand which still rested on the door, and wondered who I could turn to for help. Maaz was the only one lodged in my mind and I returned to him instinctively as the sole person I felt I had any power over. It was as if I was still contining to exact payment from him for his relationship with me which had shown him another life beyond it and allowed him to escape out into the world. I'd contacted all the men I knew; they were the ones with young frustrated bodies always wanting me. Through them I found out that Maaz's frenzied infatuation and jealousy were both quite normal: most of them, especially those who'd never been abroad, pursued me day and night. More than Maaz, they made the fantasy of A Thousand and One Nights come true for me. They held parties for my benefit and had caviare and salmon flown in. They procured the latest videos straight from the studios, and I probably used to find out what happened to Sue Ellen before the television companies. When I'd begun to get in touch with them one by one about my problem, and asked them if they could think of a solution, I felt that I was becoming more aware of their delicate situation for the first time. The man who replied seriously to my requests was not the same man whom I'd seen dancing, drinking glass after glass to forget some woman or other. All of them avoided the issue of my wanting to stay here and tried to talk about something else. The company David worked for had been declared bankrupt, closed its offices, and named the day on which its employees were to leave the country, but I was desperately anxious to prolong our stay so that perhaps David would find another job and we wouldn't lose our residence permits for ever. As I knocked on the door these ideas were on the tip of my tongue and I only needed to come face to face with Maaz to put them into words.

Suddenly I heard his voice. 'What's wrong with you, Suzanne? We were asleep.'

Quickly I replied, 'Open the door. You must.'

He was silent, then he said, 'I'm not well. Perhaps we can talk on the phone . . .'

Without letting him finish his sentence, I replied like a stubborn child, 'You must open the door. Just for a minute.'

When he didn't, I thought about what was going on, and could hardly believe how crazy relationships were which came about as a result of a desperate need. In the past he'd knelt humbly at my feet. Now he wouldn't open the door to me. I let my mind wander, remembering the time I'd gone away with David to another part of the country to spend the day with his boss. When we opened the door on our return we were met by a horrible smell. Ringo wasn't at home and there were glasses all over the place, empty Scotch bottles, vomit, cushions strewn about. I realized that Maaz hadn't left the house since saying goodbye to us that morning; he'd turned up with a bottle of Scotch, asking if we minded him drinking a glass there because Fatima would tell the neighbours if he drunk it at their house. I found him lying on the floor with the curtains drawn. I took hold of his face and shook him awake. Then I went into the kitchen to get him a glass of water. When he'd drunk it, David left me with him and went pointedly upstairs. Maaz wept and said that he'd missed me and hadn't wanted to leave my house; he'd lain on my bed and smelt my clothes and kissed them, even kissed my shoes. I helped him to his feet, afraid of the burden of his attachment to me. And David who'd made me run away with him so that we could be married and who'd cried to see my suffering at the birth of our first child stopped taking me in his arms. As I remembered, my sadness changed to anger. I swallowed it back with my spittle as I drew breath, then drummed on the door in a subdued manner and said, 'David hasn't got a job any more. We have to leave and I want to stay here.' His reply came back fast: 'Never mind. You go, and I'll come and visit you in the States soon I hope.' 'No. I'm not going,' I shouted. 'You have to fix my passport and David's, or mine anyway.' 'I can't. I'm not well, Suzanne. You go back home with your husband. He's a good man: at least he didn't kill either of us.'

With all my strength I pounded on the door. 'You've got to let me in,' I cried, my feet planted resolutely on the ground like an animal about to be led to the slaughter.

When the only response was a movement behind the door, which remained firmly closed, I felt as if a power secret as the wind had stripped me of everything which I'd put my trust in as I moved about the rooms of my house deep in the desert. I was like a deposed beauty queen: the jury had turned on me and replaced me with a new queen, dragging off the crown, robe and shoes, wiping away the make-up and taking the sceptre from my hand, tearing the smile off my lips and even the memory of the past happiness out of my heart. I felt like a fortune-teller who'd seen her own future in her crystal ball and then made it go wrong. Nobody would ever understand that I was scared of going back because the roar of cities destroyed people and I was scared of being destroyed. Going back to America was going back to being a speck among the millions, while here I felt aware of my importance every minute of the day; if I just said good morning in Arabic everybody praised me. What does a woman in her forties do in a country swarming with others like her when she's been used to being the one and only? Who'd look at a fat woman in her forties with a lisp which made her hard to understand? Who'd call her on the phone except someone who'd dialled a wrong number? In my mind was an image of my telephone ringing all the time irrespective of the hour, transmitting their crazy longing to me. I was an oasis, green and sparkling in this great drought. I'd become like Barbara, jangling with gold bracelets and confidence and security, even spiritual and material security for years still to come. I could picture exactly what was going to become of me: in the car on the way to the airport I would revert to being a woman with rather a round face, hair hanging on a podgy neck, two fat arms, slack breasts and a stomach protruding over two short fat legs.

In a final desperate attempt I knocked so ferociously that my gold bracelets hurt me. I touched them one by one and although this comforted me the thought of Barbara pained me. Was I going to go home with only these bracelets and a few pieces of jewellery? What had happened to my dreams of doing business and growing rich, my dreams of the man with whom I was going to spend the rest of my life? This time I shouted, 'Fatima! Fatima!' I heard a commotion, followed by another burst of noise, then the key was turned in the lock and the door opened. I didn't recognize the person standing there for a moment, although he bore a resemblance to Maaz. I gasped. It was Maaz, his legs weak and emaciated, his face yellow, with white sores on the lips. When he came to offer his hand to me, I saw red sores on the fingers. Behind him was Fatima looking thin, with a beautiful smile on her face. I noticed that her stomach had disappeared. I was still in a state of shock at the sight of Maaz but I asked her straight out, as if everything was normal, 'Was it a boy or a girl?' She answered me hesitantly, looking at Maaz, 'A boy. But he's not very well.' I found myself wondering if I ought to take the gold chain, with 'Allah' in ornamental calligraphy hanging from it, from around my neck and give it to the new baby like the women did here. 'Where is he?' I asked. Maaz tried to mumble something but it was Fatima who led me into the bedroom. 'Poor thing. He's not well,' she said. The baby was lying in the middle of the bed with some white powder on his face. When I went closer I saw white sores on his hands and face, even on his eyes. I said nothing. I put my hand up to the chain around my neck then let it drop, feeling sick. I tried not to, but I couldn't help looking back at his eyes, where the syphilis showed so clearly. I noticed that the baby was wearing the clothes which I'd ordered for Fatima from the States, and then I don't know why, but when I saw the brightly-coloured cover which Maaz's mother must have woven in her tent, the thought came to me that it was I and the oven which cleaned itself and the aeroplanes which had caused the syphilis in Maaz and his newborn child. Why hadn't Fatima been treated? Why hadn't the doctor given her an abortion, knowing that her baby would be born with syphilis? Then my thoughts trailed away: Maaz must have hidden it from her, ashamed to tell. I considered asking what his name was and a lot of other things, but I just smiled as if I hadn't seen anything or thought anything. A vision of the doorway of the private clinic, jammed with people newly returned from the Far East, flashed into my mind. Only then did I know for sure that Maaz couldn't help me.

I went back to the car, trying to chase away my thoughts, the pangs of conscience, the self-reproach, but they moved back in again little by little, chasing after one another, weaving the syphilis into the story of Maaz's trip to Sri Lanka: this was the first time I'd encountered the disease in real life and not just at second hand in books and pictures. I thought how lucky I was that I hadn't caught it, and moreover I wasn't living with him as I'd so often pictured I would be. This realization made me more cheerful. As I rode through the streets, protected from the burning sun outside, Maaz's house began to seem a continent away. I sensed the slow regular pulse of life, which was apparent even from the men and goats resting in the shade, and found that I loved this reality. I forgot the baby bit by bit and vowed not to leave here whatever happened. This resolve made ideas come tumbling into my head, including fantastic ones. I could say I'd converted to Islam and ask to stay on as a children's nanny, or sign my divorce papers and go through a formal marriage with Ringo, whose residence permit didn't expire for a least a month. I found myself counting on my fingers: I had five days left.

Nur

1

Everything was tranquil, the water in the swimming-pool, the gazelles' house. If Saleh's robe and his white headcloth hadn't been lying on the floor, I wouldn't have believed that I'd really been wearing them. I was lucky to be safely back in bed, although I could still see myself panting along the street. I hadn't taken account of the moon and it had been full, shining down on me and lighting the way so that Suha's house looked as if it was lit up.

Standing before the outside door of the house, I had noticed that my uncharacteristic feelings of agitation were growing, and that the excuse I'd thought of using to her and her husband had suddenly evaporated. But when I looked back along the street I couldn't imagine going home, and I felt a renewed burst of courage at the thought of Suha being inside these walls. The wooden garden door opened easily. I pushed her son's toys out of the way and stood up on the table to open the small window of the bathroom. I'd meant to sneak quickly through it like her son did, but Saleh's clothes held me up and I had to lower myself in gradually until my foot touched the edge of the bath. When the whole of me was inside the bathroom I stood listening: the house was still and the air-conditioners roared noisily. I confronted myself in the mirror in men's clothes and tiptoed out of the bathroom past the canary's cage, which was covered up for the night, wondering whether to scream for help and wake up everyone in the house; I could say one of the servants had tried to come into my room, or a driver had abducted me, so that I'd had to fling open the car door, roll out on to the ground and rush to their house; or should I say my heart was pounding, my breathing constricted, and I needed their Lebanese doctor friend to examine me?

I dismissed all these ideas as I pictured how Suha would

look at me, and slipped quietly out of the door leaving it open behind me. I went back along the empty street, cursing her at first then feeling annoyed with myself for not waking the driver up to bring me; he must have noticed my relationship with Suha, and with the Italian woman who'd come to the desert at my mother's request to design a garden of artificial trees and flowers. I quickened my pace along a street that I'd never been in before on foot even in the daytime, and pulled the headcloth tight around my face, ready to talk in a deep rough voice if I met anyone. With every hurried step I took my dislike of Suha grew. What if I was discovered now? I'd be in disgrace and people would think I was meeting a man.

For the first time I was glad to see the wall of my house in the distance, to take refuge in my room, but as soon as I'd forgotten about the fear which had taken hold of me out in the street, Suha started to dominate my thoughts again. Plenty of people had occupied that place before her, men and women, but only for a short time, and before I got to know them well. Suha was the exception: I'd been crazy about her all the time, perhaps because she'd lost interest in me moments after we met in the swimming-pool. Her thoughts were always somewhere else, and when they weren't, she complained and grew irritable. Even when she began to come round to my house it was because I insisted and phoned her continually and persistently. Only once did I feel that she envied me, and that wasn't for my clothes or jewellery but just for the swimming-pool, when she said that she wished it was in her garden, then took it back and said she'd prefer the merest drop of water away from the desert to this swimming-pool of mine.

At first I thought she was putting on her indifferent attitude, because I'd never met anyone who wasn't attracted by my personality and my way of life, or just my hair, or my house and all the entertaining things in it. She even began to criticize the number of servants that I had and the noise of the video and the general anarchy; she said the gazelles had no life in their eyes, no beauty, none of the magic that gazelles were famous for. Looking at my clothes one day she asked where I was going, and laughed scathingly at me when I said, 'I'm staying at home.' I only realized the full extent of her pride when she refused a present I'd tried to give her, even when I sent it back to her with the driver. When I spoke for too long on the telephone in her presence she left and at that I decided to have no more to do with her, reminding myself of all the people who were only too anxious for my company; but I discovered that I preferred to spend my whole time desperately trying to reach her and dominate her. Being turned down by her had a magic similar to the feeling I had when I was chasing my cat to pick her up and cuddle her: when I finally succeeded in catching hold of her I was always overwhelmed by a desire to give her a lesson she wouldn't forget.

I wished Suha would come to me at that moment, or to be honest, I longed for any human being who would hold me until the first ray of sunlight stretched down through the darkness, but the silence deepened.

I dialled her number and let it ring and didn't put the receiver down even when I heard her husband repeating, 'Hallo. Hallo.' I wanted to hear a human voice; dawn was still a long way off, I was scared of being alone, and the voice repeating, 'Hallo. Hallo,' restored life to me in spite of its dry tone. I got out of bed and took a tablet from a packet in the drawer among my lipsticks and eye make-up. I noticed it was grubby and began looking for a clean one but they were all the same. Without giving it time to work I swung back the mirror near my bed and pulled out a white phone; the existence of this phone was known only to me and a telephone engineer who'd demanded a large sum of money to install it secretly. I dialled a number and heard the voice that I remembered so clearly. He sounded drowsy this time but as soon as he heard my voice, he answered excitedly, 'It can't be . . .' I hadn't contacted him for days because the line had been out of order and I hadn't dared risk using either of the other two. His excitement was obvious, because subconsciously he'd promised himself that he was going to get something out of this call. Every time I spoke to him I wanted more, and as I'd expected I heard the heat in his voice down the receiver and I began to talk to him. I'd learnt his habits, which video films he liked best, and from my knowledge of the details of his life I'd built up a picture of him in my imagination.

'Where have you been all this time? I've melted down my fingertips trying to hit on the right number for you. You must give me your number for emergencies.'

'I was away,' I answered, and thought to myself that the poor man really had no idea who I was. All he knew was that I liked Warda al-Jazairiyya because he'd heard her singing in the background when I was talking to him; since I didn't like being alone I used to beg him not to say goodnight to me even after an hour, but just to carry on talking, even though my eyes were closing and he'd stopped answering. As usual our conversation got on to passion and love and I began to pretend that his voice was penetrating my senses and spoke more caressingly, letting him hear my moans of pleasure. I didn't stop until I heard his voice shaking, as if it was being squeezed out of him. At this point I wished him good night and returned the phone to its place like someone under a spell. Even though I enjoyed myself and wanted this relationship, I never failed to be amazed when I thought about where my voice was going to, and how his voice held my interest and left me waiting for the next day.

My daughter came into my room in the afternoon, dropped her books and black abaya on the floor, and rushed over to me. I was still stretched out in bed where I'd been since the night before. She burst into tears: 'The teacher was cross with me. . .' 'Never mind,' I answered. She seemed to notice my indifferent tone because she began to shake me and carried on speaking while I nodded my head pretending to show interest, until in the end I shouted irritably at her, 'I heard you! I heard you!'

Ghada ran out. I thought of going after her but stayed where I was. I thought about sending for someone to bring me a drink but then found myself phoning Suha. When she answered and I whispered 'Suha?' she slammed the phone down on me. Then I phoned Suzanne, her American friend, and asked her if she had any water melons or cakes. When she finally understood what I was saying, she made her excuses. The general hubbub throughout the house rose above the sound of the video, which mingled with the strains of Filipino music. The servants had just woken from their afternoon siesta, and I didn't take my hand off the bell until my coffee arrived. Drinking it, I thought 'What can I do for the rest of today and tonight?' I went over to Ghada whose staring eyes and audible breathing seemed to make her one with Michael Jackson's hissing dead. She was addicted to the 'Thriller' video and had watched it at least ten times, each time more avidly than the last. She reminded me of myself when I was little and used to sit alone with my Somali nanny watching Arabic and foreign films one after the other. In those days there was no video, just a screen on the wall and a projector. It was operated for us by a tailor whom my mother had had brought over from the Philippines too. These films must have aroused something in the tailor and the nanny because when I got up and wandered about the house one night, unable to sleep, I saw them on the kitchen floor. I remembered that I stood and watched them without feeling embarrassment or any other emotion. I was used to seeing kissing and men and women together on the films and in our house. A day rarely went by when I didn't hear whispering, and see two bodies clinging together in the darkness, or in daylight, behind the door, in corners of our large house: the servants with one another; my brothers with the servant girls and my girl cousins: a man and a friend of my mother's whom I could recognize from her red shoes poking out from under her abaya, as her face was veiled too. I used to be able to work out who was pregnant in our house because I'd seen if so often and knew the symptoms by heart. A woman who was pregnant would sleep most of the time, and rush to the bathroom and throw up, claiming to have a stomach upset. Then she would boil up cumin and other plants from Sudan and India, herbs and spices which had a wonderful smell, and drink these concoctions constantly. The ceiling fans would be switched off and she would cover herself with rugs and sheepskins to make herself sweat and stay in her room for two days. At this point she seemed to become more weary and sick and she would take aspirins and other medicaments. After a few days I would hear a shrieking louder than I'd ever heard on the films and would race to see the new baby. But the door was always closed. Only when Mother Kaukab came out did I go in to the room, and I would see the servant girl writhing on the bed, and no baby.

Mother Kaukab was a relation of my mother or my father, I don't know which. I became aware of her visiting us on special occasions, when a servant girl was pregnant or someone was ill, or at weddings: she was there when the bride-to-be was decorated with henna, trilling for joy at the ceremony when the girl's body hair was all removed, shouting at her to silence her if she gasped and cried out in pain, telling her, 'You have to be strong to be beautiful.' And she was there for the preparation of the special food which was buried in the sand and for the slaughter of the lambs. Even my mother used to call her Mother Kaukab, and she was the only one who dared to go into my mother's room. Then when I got my own house at the age of thirteen, Mother Kaukab moved in with me. My mother and father had promised me a house of my own when I was seventeen, but I couldn't wait and they were tired of my insistent demands. Whenever my father hugged me he would say, 'I'm building you a really special house,' and I would glow with pride and ask him, 'Like my brother Jalal's house and my brother Hamid's?'

'Of course,' he would answer. 'I don't have daughters and sons. All my children are as good as each other.' There was a vast amount of land around our house and on it my father had built a house for the male servants, a house for his mother, one for each of my brothers, and one for my sister who was married and lived in another part of the country, for her to stay in when she visited us.

Then he would add, 'You know the big date palm? Right next to it.' I don't know why, I would have liked to tell him that it was too close to their house, and that if only it were further away I could be properly alone. My mother would say, 'I'll furnish the house for you, Nur, with everything in it, just as it should be.' She was always spoiling me and her affection was at its most lavish when she was making me try on the clothes which she bought me locally or on her trips abroad; whenever she noticed the length of my hair, which reached right down to my thighs, she whispered in my ear, pointing to her stomach, 'Look what came out of there. The most beautiful girl in the world.' My mother was one of the first women to go abroad and discover life beyond the desert, and she would return bringing back with her everything which these other countries produced. I got used to her not being at home, or rather to not seeing her there, for if she wasn't abroad or visiting one of her friends, she would be asleep or talking on the telephone. From when I was small, I'd been aware of her criticizing my father for staying out late with his friends, and sometimes talking about him in a depressed sort of way and crying in front of Mother Kaukab. But when I saw them together I knew she would smile and be loving and call him 'my soul' and 'my darling'.

I remember that the glimmer of joy I felt at having a house of my own disappeared rapidly after a few days or weeks. I wearied of the red hearts which matched the bedcover, and the pillow that was shaped like a single big red heart; even the chairs were patterned with red hearts, not to mention the curtains. My father had sent for a European designer to do these red hearts everywhere. My pleasure at having her there outlasted any pleasure the hearts gave me, and I believed that she was going to live with me for ever. I remembered once when she'd been with my brother into the desert, she came back to the house as if she'd gone crazy. Distraught, she began packing her bags, crying all the time. Mother Kaukab guessed what had happened and I heard her saying to my brother, who wasn't even thirteen at the time, 'You had an old woman? But you're a young man strong as a brass pestle, God bless you!' and he answered, and he was laughing too, 'She was the one who wanted to go and see the desert at night.'

When I heard them I rushed to her, pleading with her as she picked up the receiver and asked for my parents' number. Only when she saw my tears did she give in and put it down. I wasn't thinking of the hearts on the wall which she hadn't finished yet, but of the fun I had just from her being in the house. I no longer found the Somali woman or Kaukab amusing company, and I'd stopped listening to their stories. Recently I'd begun to keep up with life outside the desert, in Cairo or Paris, and through my travels with my family or the presents my mother brought back from her own travels I learnt about the latest clothes and films and singers and songs, and the men and women who were famous in international circles. Not satisfied with just knowing about them I began to look for ways of bringing them to where I was. We would wait for occasions like family weddings and then nag the grown-ups to hire famous performers from Cairo. When they agreed to come we all rushed to arrange parties for them and give them presents. We followed them around all the time hoping for a word or a touch or a kiss, and then we discovered that the aura surrounding them grew gradually less powerful and finally disappeared altogether as they began to chase after us, or at any rate the presents we gave them. I remember the actress who borrowed some diamond ear-rings and didn't give them back. When Mother Kaukab asked her for them she pretended to look for them in fear and trembling and offered Mother Kaukab all her own jewels. But those little details didn't stand in the way of us inviting famous people we hadn't met before. Even writers and poets aroused our curiosity and I remember one writer who always hailed us with the same phrase: 'How are you? I've missed you,' and he promised all of us girls that he would write stories about us. I'd never read any of his celebrated novels although I'd seen films of them. I wasn't much good at reading. I went to school but I didn't seem capable of attending regularly. I and my Somali nanny both slept heavily perhaps because we stayed up until the early hours of the morning. The alarm clock didn't waken us and even if I managed to get up at the right time I was slow choosing what to wear and what to eat and looking for my books. It was as if I thought time ought to be subject to my will. On some occasions when I was ready in time I couldn't find the driver, and when the nanny called him he came after a while, barefooted, hurrying, rubbing the sleep from his eyes, and drove the car at breakneck speed. Then one of my mother's friends arranged for a Lebanese teacher at the school to help me after school hours so that I could catch up with my class. I was delighted with her and began to have great fun with her, because sometimes instead of teaching me she was happy to come for a bicycle ride with me – on our land of course – and she started plaiting my hair for me like in the magazines. She only stopped coming when she'd tried without success to see my mother for months on end, and on several occasions she had to wait for ages before the outside doors were opened for her.

I was pleased. In the end she'd started interfering in my affairs and giving me lectures about the shortcomings of my upbringing, and she'd let me know the meaning of the word 'frivolous'. She began to criticize the anarchy of our household and shake her head regretfully at everything, even the kitchen equipment – which she admired and said was like what you'd find in a luxury hotel: she told us we were spoiling it and ended up trying to explain to the cook and the other servants how to use it properly. She advised me to go back and live with my family and told me I didn't need a personal driver or a cook or Mother Kaukab, but my mother and father and brothers and sisters. When we didn't pay her on time she wouldn't leave the house until she had the money, saying it was a matter of principle not money. She used to make me wait with her until Mother Kaukab woke up, or until the driver had gone to my father's office to pick up some money. Once she even insisted on contacting my mother, although I'd often told her that my mother didn't like being woken from her afternoon nap. The teacher's exasperation grew when she found that my mother had unplugged the telephone and locked the door on the inside, and angrily she expostulated that my mother wouldn't know if something dreadful happened to me or my brothers and sisters. It didn't seem to occur to the teacher that we could have knocked on the door, although none of us had ever dared to do it, and she began calling my mother selfish and ignorant.

In response to my request I was sent by my father to a private girls' college in Cairo like a lot of other girls from the desert. There I discovered that the freedom which I'd thought I would gain by moving out by myself into the desert was nothing compared to my freedom in Cairo. Just walking down the street on my own two feet was freedom, so walking without an abaya was out of this world. Freedom no longer consisted of dialling a telephone number and giggling and whispering love down the line, or making the driver follow the other cars, or eyeing the shopkeepers; even kissing and sometimes other things in cars – which seldom happened anyway – weren't freedom compared to Cairo with her wide-open arms reaching out beyond the horizon.

2

I began to think about marriage after I came back from Cairo, even though I'd always said before that I wouldn't think of it until I was in my twenties. Mother Kaukab had married when she was twelve, and my own mother when she was fourteen. I wanted to have a husband and a wedding and then I would become my own mistress. Not that I wasn't that already, but I was still having to ask permission to go abroad. Then my mother would forget that she had promised to take me with her and leave when I was fast asleep in my house, or take me with a group of her friends and I would tire of being abroad for such a long time because our trip would be taken up with eating in restaurants, buying clothes and giggling. I wanted to get to know lots of the sort of people who went to parties at night, although I didn't dare to go to them without my mother and father. When I was there I became all eyes and ears and stared at the men, wondering who would suit me. When I saw Samer I knew that I had to marry him. He was three years older than me. I was seventeen. He'd heard about the motorcycle which I'd ordered and which I used to ride between my house and my parents' and my brothers'. These houses and their gardens were all surrounded by high walls over which only the tops of palm trees were visible. Samer came with my brother to see the motorbike when I decided to sell it. I was wearing a leather jacket and trousers and dark glasses. I knew by the way he rode bikes and by his wristwatch and the type of bracelet it had that he would suit me. I took it as given that he would like me, because I was beautiful: the blackness and great length of my hair and the permanent pallor of my complexion were oriental, and my clothes and everything around me were western. I found myself looking at him in a way that embarrassed him and I wanted to ask him to marry me, but I made myself wait and spoke to him and pursued him on the telephone until we'd decided to get married. He was a male Nur. He loved the latest fashions and everything conjured up by modern civilization: the newest models of cars, skiing equipment, a stainless steel model of Ali Ibn Abi Talib's sword made in Japan, an Aubusson chair, a type of honey found high in the mountains of Tibet, a handbag made of ostrich skin. He was inventive in his dress even when he was wearing a plain white robe, but he also wore blue, grey, and pistachio green, and when we travelled abroad he wore the most beautiful suits and the weirdest ties. There was always a lot going on in our house as we had friends round every night. We knew nurses, nannies, even married women, from various countries, and we danced and sang and ate and watched films until dawn and slept till the afternoon. We didn't begin our night's entertainment before eleven in the evening, then we swam or went out into the desert, and he would ride the motorcycle and try and jump obstacles on it, little natural hillocks or ones that his friend Waleed constructed for him. I was so used to Waleed being around that we seemed incomplete without him. The fame of these nights of ours spread until everybody who felt they shared our way of thinking and could entertain us or enjoy themselves with us found a friend who was coming and came along too. We soon found that the desert was crowded with people wanting to entertain and be entertained. There was a man who liked imitating famous actors, another with a guitar who pretended to be Elvis Presley, a third who acted out a pantomime of a woman giving birth, behaving conquettishly if it was a boy, and telling the other women what an awful time she'd had and how she'd passed out with the pain if it was a girl. When we were tired of these mimes, friends would bring along people they knew with mild deformities, like the man who stammered, or the simple-minded one who was funny when he was provoked. Someone brought a monkey who liked drink and we stood around it pouring whisky down its throat and watching it caper and scream in its cage.

I didn't know that Samer liked his own sex as well until in the course of one of our trips abroad he chose to stay in the hotel rather than come sightseeing with me, and when I met him for lunch Waleed wasn't with him and I sensed the tension in him. I asked him if someone from home had been in touch with him; even abroad we sought the company of show business people and night club society and we were always scared that word of our wild nights would get back to the desert. He didn't answer. I asked him where Waleed was and saw his jawbone moving as he clenched his teeth. When Waleed appeared and sat down apologizing, my husband gave him a look which was meant to be between the two of them, but I understood what it meant, as I understood the inquiries, the riddles, the jealousy which followed. He tried to hide his feelings but his face and his nerves gave him away, and gradually I realized how artificial his desire was when he slept with me as it was always connected with his fantasies and most times it subsided half-way through.

Waleed was quite attractive. I sometimes wished he would press himself against me when we were dancing together. As well as being handsome he was nice, quick-witted, with a never-ending flow of stories and information and jokes about his home country, Morocco. When I found out what was going on between him and Samer, I laughed as I thought of all the women who'd flirted with him or made approaches to him directly, or through me; I wondered if he was like my husband and liked both sexes, and planned to find out.

I wouldn't have thought of divorce if Samer hadn't sent someone to inform me that he'd already divorced me. He was on a naval training course in Belgium and Waleed was with him. Apart from the driver who gave me the certificate of divorce, nobody knew about it, and I was able to take advantage of others' ignorance by behaving for a time as if I was a married woman and my own mistress.

I was still thinking about who would come asking to marry

me, when I met Saleh's sister at a wedding. The moment I saw
her I reproached myself for letting my thoughts stray so far
from Saleh. Apart from the fact that there was an aura of
magic surrounding him because of his lifestyle and his constant travel abroad for his work, he was good-looking and an
important person in society. I'd begun to realize that I
wouldn't meet anyone else like him. Civilized young men no
longer wanted to marry young, nor on the other hand did
they abstain. They travelled abroad and went out with girls
who were very beautiful and very young, often little more
than minors, while the ones who preferred their own sex
married and had children for the sake of society, like Samer. I
found myself talking to Saleh's sister most of the time. The
happiness on her face was plain to see because I was paying
her so much attention. Like the other girls she was curious to
get to know me face to face because my flaunting of conventions was much talked about. I wore a green and red abaya,
and sometimes covered my face with a heavy black veil and
stuck a diamond pin at nose level. When the wedding was
over I stopped off at my parents' house, went straight into my
mother's room and told her that if I didn't marry Saleh I
would never marry at all. I knew how much they wanted me
to marry because they couldn't bear my impetuous behaviour
any longer, my artful adaptations of abayas, the night-time
gatherings I held, which were attended, it was rumoured, by
my brothers' friends. My mother asked me if his mother or
sister had broached the subject with me. I didn't answer. I
began phoning his sister at every opportunity just as I had
done with other girls whose brothers I wanted to get to
know, in case the brother happened to answer. Saleh never
answered and I discovered that he had a place of his own
separate from his family so, claiming to be his sister, I called
him at work in the Ministry. When I told him my name, he
gave me his private number so that I was able to talk to him
every day. Eventually we agreed to meet at the home of his
married sister; she'd been at the wedding and had looked on

discouragingly as I talked to her younger sister.

I knew that Saleh wanted to marry me. As he said to me one day, I was the bride he'd been searching for: beautiful and educated at the same time. I knew there was more that he didn't tell me: I was the daughter of a man whose millions grew every time he drew breath. Although there were many like my father, my breeding and ancestry were better established than those of many girls. As I sat opposite him his white robe and headcloth and the rosary between his fingers seemed to give off a cool breeze of freedom, not at all like the stale draught from the air-conditioners, and as it brushed my face I felt invigorated and no longer thought beyond the four walls that contained us. I felt as I watched the brown fingers that life flowed through them and that I ought to cling on to them. They were like the fingers of a giant who held the land about him in thrall. I even felt the power bursting from his car keys when he jingled them in his fingers, as if they were capable of knocking down whole walls and opening buildings up to the outside world. At the same time I began to feel a great longing to move closer to him and take his hand and bury my head against his chest, and I wondered at myself because only moments before I had thought of marriage as a way of being free and gaining access to others.

There was no question of him taking my hand. He began to talk, telling me that I had to help him. I didn't understand what he meant; he wasn't rich like my father but he was a wealthy man all the same. Rather than naming a figure, as I'd expected, he said that like me and other girls here he too lived in a state of frustration, and that the pressure exercised by the society and its traditions was great, but this was our country and we had to put up with it, despite the immense riches which allowed us to wander about the world, to go to countries where there were trees and lakes and where I could wear a low cut dress and walk freely in the street. But was it right to take wealth from one country when your eyes and heart were set on another?

I shook my head, but as if I was telling him to be quiet. I wanted him to hold me close, or to move closer to him myself. I passed a finger over my lips which had parted in anticipation of his lips touching them, but he went on talking while my urgent desire for him to hold me and kiss me distracted me and I didn't listen to what he was saying. Eventually he asked me if I was listening and I nodded my head and tried to force myself to, despite my irritation. He reached out a hand towards my neck and I rejoiced, but then he said, 'That necklace – if your father and generations of your family before him hadn't struggled against the heat and hunger of the desert you wouldn't be wearing it now.' Trying to reassure myself, I answered, 'But you travel a lot.' 'I know,' he laughed. 'I'm just trying to explain what I'm like to you, so that you can understand me and help me – when you learn to understand this country of yours and appreciate what it means to live here.'

3

The difference between Saleh and me which had drawn me to him began to annoy me and make me on edge, and I became as unyielding as stone. Since our meetings in his sister's house, before we were married, I had been aware of it, as it became clear that we were there for different reasons: I was waiting for him to take my face in his hands and kiss me and whisper words of love and admiration in my ear; while for him the purpose of our encounters was that we should understand each other's natures so that we shouldn't repeat the mistakes of our fathers and grandfathers.

His sister only agreed grudgingly to our meetings, fearful that they would cause a scandal, whether we eventually married or not. I used to phone him constantly as well, something he was unused to, and was never going to grow used to. When I asked him why he was so short on the phone he made a joke of it and said he wasn't alone in the room; and when he asked me in turn why I so much enjoyed telephone conversations I didn't know what to reply because it was true that I loved talking on the phone, and every time our conversations seemed to be tailing off I tried to inject new life into them, even inventing bits of news to reawaken his curiosity, or provoking jealousy in him by the way I talked. I remember especially when a famous Italian designer came to make my wedding dress; this man lost patience with me because I couldn't keep appointments however hard I tried, and once, pretending to make a joke of it, he remarked that perhaps the weight of the diamonds in my watch had made it stop. The version I told Saleh later was that the designer had suggested that I shouldn't wear my diamond choker in case its sparkle distracted attention from the beauty of my breasts. Instead of being jealous, Saleh upbraided me for letting the designer speak so uninhibitedly to me. When I suggested that he was reacting this way out of jealousy he denied it and said nothing more, as if he wanted the subject to be closed.

Less than a month after our wedding I began to feel restless. The happiness and the hustle and bustle seemed to vanish upon our return to the desert, and Saleh began to get up at nine in the morning and wanted me to get up with him so that we could have breakfast together. I did it once but the following day I protested that I was tired and stayed in bed. That night Saleh didn't want us to stay up after midnight but I wouldn't sleep. He reminded me of how tired I'd been that morning, and I joked that he would make me forget that I was from a family of Draculas. Despite my efforts I never managed to get up till noon or a little afterwards, when he came back from work to have lunch. He continued to insist that I must get up in the morning and when I asked him what the urgency was, he replied, 'What about the house?' and I laughed and said sarcastically, 'What about the servants?' 'What's the use of a crew if the ship has no captain?' he returned.

On one particular evening our visitors departed early because Saleh had said a pointed farewell to them even while I was begging them to stay. Boiling with rage I went back into the room: 'How can you drive them out like that?' I shouted at him. Without looking up from his book, he answered that they were spongers, a flock of sheep moving from house to house to be fed, held in submission by the videos and funny stories. 'I thought you enjoyed yourself with them,' I said challengingly. He marked his place with a bookmark and shut the book. I found myself thinking that the division between us really was vast, not because I didn't read books but because it would never occur to me to use a bookmark. Then he said in an affectionate tone, 'Nur. Come here. I want to talk to you.' Putting an arm round me he told me he loved staying up with them once or twice a week, but said that we shouldn't use them to fill up our spare time. 'How should we spend our evenings then?' I demanded. 'With one another, or are you bored with me?' Then he added, 'With one another, or with normal people.' 'With one another?' I thought to myself. 'That means him reading or watching films that I don't like, or practising tennis or training on his exercise machines. And normal people means businessmen and embassy staff and their wives.' However hard I tried, I could never think of anything to say to their wives.

Then Saleh began asking me like a school teacher if I'd read the newspapers and whether I'd liked the books he'd brought me to read. He began urging me to continue my education and enrol in a university, or even do a correspondence course. Anything rather than wasting my time sleeping or talking to friends whom he described as unfortunate because of their lack of intelligence.

I didn't show the faintest desire to listen to what he was saying, and at midnight he went to bed, while I began pleading with a servant or a guest or a relation to stay up with me into the small hours.

These differences vanished during the holidays. He no longer said my English was awful because I'd picked it up haphazardly from foreign nannies and acquaintances, or criticized me because my only interest, according to him, was a single-minded study of the goods produced by modern industry for the consumption of the rich, such as yachts and sun beds. Instead he seemed proud of me as we moved around together in our yacht or our private plane between the chalet in Switzerland, the Paris flat and the house in a London suburb. We spent the time sailing the yacht and lying on beaches which we had almost to ourselves, and in winter wore skiing clothes, although I didn't keep up with my lessons because it was always nearly sunset by the time I was ready. Still the weather and the people and their talk and laughter aroused a mood of happiness and enjoyment in me wherever we were. I quickly forgot that I'd been annoyed with him for trying to make me learn to read the compass while the white yacht ploughed through the Mediterranean; or for urging me to learn to ski and get out in the open and move at speed over the great expanses of whiteness. As soon as the holidays ended and we returned to the desert the old resentment returned too. When I asked him why we only came close to one another on holiday he answered that he liked life without work or responsibility for a while but my problem was that I wanted it to be like that all the time; of course he traced the causes back to my upbringing, as he did with all my behaviour. His continual criticism of me, even over stupid things, surprised me more and more. I remember how upset he seemed that I didn't call back as soon as I heard that someone had called me. When I blamed the servants he said it was my fault because I didn't encourage them to tell me.

One day Sally the American, the daughter of a friend of my father's, came to the desert to attend my brother's wedding. She tried to phone me more than twenty times, and as usual I knew about some of the calls and didn't pay much attention. Then Saleh happened to answer and she was on the other end apologizing because she was leaving the next day and hadn't seen me. Looking at me angrily he told her that he'd come and pick her up straightaway, and with one more furious glance at me he was off. His behaviour didn't surprise me and although I was jealous I felt relieved that he was the same as all the rest, and wanted to get to know foreign women. Sally came back with him apologizing, as if she was quite sure that I couldn't have known about her calls. I replied coldly that Mother Kaukab didn't understand English, and Sally said in some confusion that she'd asked the servants at my parents' house – where she was staying – to make the calls.

Then she turned to talk to Saleh about the time she and I had spent together in the United States when my father had left me with her and her family and they'd taken me over most of California, from Disneyland to Universal Studios. She talked enthusiastically and seemed to have captivated Saleh, as if my dress and the way my hair was done no longer mattered. Then their conversation took off beyond the table where the three of us were sitting and away from anything that I knew about or was interested in. She began to talk about her work: she was one of the people who wrote speeches for the American president; then she switched to talking about her father's club and I pricked up my ears and thought that here was my chance to make them listen to me and look in my direction since I knew most of the internationally famous clubs. But a cloud of dullness descended on the conversation once more when I heard that the club was only for men and that their activities didn't go beyond delivering speeches. Then he asked what university she'd graduated from and when she told him the name of some university he laughed and asked if she knew Candice F. She didn't, but she'd heard of her because she was president of one of the graduate societies. He hesitated a little, put his hand on mine and said, 'With Nur's permission,' then proceeded to tell us that he'd promised to marry Candice when he'd said goodbye to her after his graduation. But as soon as he'd arrived back in the desert he'd found that he couldn't begin to imagine her wandering about the house, or sitting at his side in the car or talking in sign language to the other women; the thought of her light-coloured hair, her unrestrained way of talking without regard to time or place, seemed absurd in this setting.

Sally remarked laughing that she couldn't envisage a girl like Candice here for a moment. Saleh listened to her and he pressed my hand when I tried to draw it out from under his hand; it seemed to me that his talk of Candice was to make Sally understand that his being married to me didn't mean that he was like me, or was even meant to justify his mistake. Then he began talking again in that enthusiastic voice which perhaps meant nothing when he used it to me or to people he found in our house; contradicting her, he said, 'Sally, Candice is intelligent. She could even manage to live *here*. She might have a hard time because she'd be forced to lead a double life. Take me and Nur for example: when I came back here I found that the ideas which I'd been convinced were right when I was in the States seemed ridiculous here, like the contents of my suitcase. But I made a firm decision that Saleh who wore a white robe and sandals and tore meat apart with his fingers should also be a man of the twentieth century discussing Margaret Thatcher's politics and standing to applaud dancers in a club.' Then he turned to me and said, 'Nur wears an abaya when she's here in her country but abroad she walks around in a cocktail dress. Of course she feels hard done by, but this is where she was born.'

When we took her back to my parents' house, it was the first time I'd given someone a lift to where they wanted to go; I'd always been on the receiving end of such treatment, and only contacted people when *I* needed them. Saleh got out of the car to shake her hand, then the two of them stood for a moment looking towards me. When I made do with a desultory wave, Saleh came back to the car and got in heaving a protracted sigh. He didn't speak until I asked him what was wrong with him and then he shouted at me, 'Even the Queen dismounts to say goodbye to people.' Then he muttered, 'Sorry. You're more important than the Queen.' I found myself saying that I hadn't wanted anyone from the house to see me. He stopped the car and turned to face me: 'And what would have happened if someone had seen you? Wouldn't it have been more normal to go in and visit your family? Or are they at the round table solving the world's problems?' To himself he added, 'I don't understand your family. I don't understand the stuff they're made out of. None of them are normal.' At this point I screamed at him, 'Is all this fuss because I didn't get out and shake hands with the American woman?'

Thumping his hand down on the steering wheel, he shouted back, 'How can I make you understand that it's not a question of an isolated incident? It's to do with your view of the world, your understanding of life. Is it reasonable that Sally should be with your family for a week and you don't get in touch with her? Instead you spend you time fooling about with empty-headed women and the nannies. From what I've heard, you only had to mention somewhere in the States and Sally would take you to see it. What about the telegram she sent us when we got married, and the present that would still be in its paper if I hadn't opened it? You don't only have this careless attitude towards people – you have it towards things as well. There was that orchid that was thrown to one side in the kitchen, and died still in its cellophane paper. And the plants left to wilt in their pots. Do you know the cost of orchids even before they reach the desert! Your problem is that you weren't born into one of the ruling families.'

4

When I found out that I was pregnant, and the doctor said my feelings of nausea and tiredness were normal I told him that I couldn't stand it, as if he were the one responsible for my condition. As well as feeling sluggish and sick, I began to swell up like a sponge and became convinced that I'd never go back to my old shape. Perhaps the state I was in began to bore my visitors because I no longer had people around me every minute of the day, and I grew lonely. I found that this isolation was something I didn't have the strength to endure, and one day when I was barely awake I began to scream and shout; I tore my clothes; I bit the hands reaching out to restrain me, and then I rushed out of the house; Mother Kaukab caught up with me and contacted my mother and I called Saleh at the office and told him I wanted an abortion. The main reason I could think of was that the clothes I'd had made to wear this season were such beautiful and unusual styles that they would never be fashionable again. Although he was kind and showed some understanding of what I was suffering, he tried to convince me that I would become fulfilled as a woman if I had a child and that there were maternity clothes which were as unusual as ordinary clothes. When I gave in he began pestering me to stop smoking. My reply was that the doctor had said to me that if I stopped it would make me tense, so it was better if I didn't.

When I gave birth to my daughter, jewels were showered upon me, too bright to believe in and almost too unbearably beautiful to touch; and flowers the like of which, I was told, the desert had never seen before. The day I had the baby I said I wanted to rest and wouldn't pick her up, and the same that night, but on the following day the English nurse insisted that I should hold her so that she and I could get to know each other. After a few minutes she began to cry and I pressed the bell and gave her back to the nurse. I tried the trick of feigning sleep every time I sensed the two of them in the room until the nurse gave up in despair and took her away. When one time she came in to find me talking on the phone, she told me that she was ready to collapse because she didn't sleep day or night, and our lack of concern for the child made her angry. I told her that what made me angry was her coming in without permission, and shouted at her to go away and leave me in peace. I was especially cross because I was listening, consumed with jealousy, while a friend told me about a handsome Egyptian singer who was here, and the parties they had in the evenings, and who was chasing him and who was spending a lot of time with him. As she was talking, I pictured her still in her nightdress with no pain, her breasts not swollen as mine were, in spite of my attempts to empty them of milk. Or probably her maid was putting on her make-up for her or taking it off. I could no longer stand the sight of them, when they visited me just to show off their dresses and talk to one another, not to me, indifferent to my gasps of pain.

Saleh was no help to me during this period; he began giving me words of advice, saying that I must pick my daughter up, nurse her myself instead of giving her a bottle, and not smoke when she was in the room. I was at my most annoyed with him when he woke me up every morning as soon as he heard her voice, and brought her to our bed; I don't know why but I began blaming him for everything, even for going to his office. I began to avoid talking to him and acted as if I didn't care whether he was there or not. But instead of being prompted by my coldness to make it up with me, he no longer concerned himself with me either. He began to live his life as he chose, inviting his own friends, and even though some of them came with their wives, I refused to leave my room and sat in front of the video hour after hour. Feelings of depression and resentment towards him seethed inside me and I felt like I did when my cat escaped and hid in some inaccessible place; I'd be angry to the point of tears and stamp my feet, almost choking each time I thought of the pleasure I felt when I had her in my grasp.

When he told me one morning that he was going away I didn't answer; I turned on the video and he snatched the cigarette out of my mouth and repeated, 'I'm going away.' I lit another cigarette. 'Goodbye,' I replied. His going really did make me feel more at ease, for confrontations and displays of stubbornness were no longer daily occurrences and I found myself welcoming phone calls, and if no one come to visit me I went out visiting myself. When I was asked if I had seen Saleh on the television news, I shrugged my shoulders unconcernedly. I didn't go to see his mother as I'd promised to do and when she came to my house, I left her with my child and the nanny. As soon as Saleh came home from his trip I asked him for a letter giving me permission to go abroad with my mother. But I actually travelled with Mother Kaukab.

As usual I erased the traces of the desert as soon as the plane was in the air. I went into the toilet, and from my hand luggage took out a short sleeveless dress. I bundled up my abaya, and untied my hair and let it fall loose. Feeling some embarrassment, I returned to my seat and when Mother Kaukab gasped and reproved me, I told her that my husband didn't mind. More and more I felt that marriage meant freedom, and especially material freedom. For despite the monthly allowance which I'd continued to receive from my father I'd been in debt to a lot of people; to Nahed the Egyptian woman who sold off-the-peg clothes by all the most famous designers and had threatened to complain to my father when my account was approaching a hundred thousand; to the Syrian jewel merchant, although I'd sent Mother Kaukab to him with some jewellery I no longer liked. And I knew that I was being exploited a lot: the Lebanese woman, Madame Sandra, had demanded an exorbitant amount for designing a tree with silk leaves that had a place for a bottle of perfume at the base of each leaf; and so had Jameel who designed my room for me, and Fernando with his paintings; even Ibtisam, who was from the desert herself, had sold me a fake antique claiming that it was truly old and covered with gold leaf.

I lay stretched out, wondering whether my pleasure had reached the floor under me, for the heat of it was almost burning me. In the large hotel room the rock singer was drinking water from a bottle. His face and its features appeared small, and there was nothing handsome in him; his white body was narrow and thin as he tipped his head back, and he was uncircumcised. I pictured Mother Kaukab spitting as she described the ugliness of his thin white body and said he was like an obelisk. All the same, I'd been in a state of eager excitement ever since I'd met him in a disco and he'd danced with me for hours, ignoring the woman he'd come with.

When he reached out his hand under the table to touch me I knew that he'd stay with me that night. It had been ages since I felt this happiness mixed with anticipation, even tension, and it reached a pitch when he followed me up to my room, giving me a few minutes' start so that I could lock the door leading to Mother Kaukab's room. Once I looked like staying abroad for a long time, or rather once I'd gathered up my courage and admitted to myself that my body was the main outlet for my feelings, I'd moved to an hotel, claiming to Saleh, in the course of one of our telephone conversations, that I felt car-sick every time I travelled from our house in the country into central London.

The rock singer picked up my dress from the floor and asked who the designer was. Then he put it on and looked at himself in the mirror and admired the shoulders, which were shaped like aircraft wings; I replied in a whisper, thinking that I must see him again that night. The touch of his lips, thin and unappealing as they were, made me tremble, and his chest felt broad and strong to me, even though I could see his rib cage.

I couldn't help asking him, 'Will I see you at the disco tonight?' He was fiddling with things of mine that lay about in the room, picking up a diamond ear-ring and laying it down again on the table, and he shrugged his shoulders carelessly and said, 'I don't know.'

I brought my hair close around me. He was the first man to take hold of my hair and ask if it was real. Not believing my answer, he tugged on it and said, 'Ding dong,' as if he was ringing a church bell. 'Shall I have it cut?' I asked him.

'Is this what they have instead of crisps where you come from?' he returned, holding up an old manuscript which Saleh had given me for Christies to examine, so that they could tell him if it was authentic. I asked him about my hair again, feeling a sense of loss and trying to devise a way of seeing him that night.

'Yours is the most beautiful hair I've seen in my life,' he said, turning to me. 'When I saw you dancing, I said I want that hair.'

Feeling somehow reassured, I ventured, 'Let's go to another disco tonight.'

He didn't answer and was still holding on to the manuscript which was made of torn, shrivelled vellum. 'What does it say?' he asked. He'd sat down beside me on the bed again but seemed indifferent to my body; I hadn't covered myself up and was deliberately vaunting my naked beauty because my thoughts were all channelled towards seeing him that night, and I wanted to please him at any price. I began trying to remember some of the obscure writing which Saleh had read out to me. Before I began to tell him what I knew he stretched out his hand to me, making me sit down beside him, and rested his hand on my shoulder as if we'd been friends and lovers for a long time. I noticed his amazement growing with every word that I spoke and felt happy; I was sure that it was making me figure more vividly in his thoughts, although I was astonished at his total ignorance of my country, even of its geographical location. He got up to look for a pen and could only find my black eye pencil which he stared at in disappointment and self-mockery: 'And here I was thinking you'd use kohl like Cleopatra!' He began writing letters which looked more complicated than the ones on the manuscript. He crossed them out, rewrote them, asked me to read again, then asked me more questions; I explained, and he wrote and pondered and hummed to himself.

He was so delighted to find this rare and original material for a song that he took my face in his hands and kissed my eyes and nose and lips and chin, the beauty spot on my cheek, the downy hairs on my upper lips, then my hair and my forehead. He was carried away by his enthusiasm and bent over me whispering 'I'll reward you for this,' but I just wanted to make certain of that night. When he got up he said he'd stick a red star on the country I came from, because he had a map of the world at home and he remembered countries by the women he'd met.

He left only when a smell of cardamom began to pervade the air, and Mother Kaukab tried the door. When I didn't respond she must have assumed that I was still asleep and he jumped up, hurriedly pulling on his clothes, and gathering up his papers and blowing me a kiss on the way out. I rushed to the door to ask him about the evening and he answered, 'Come to my house and I'll let you hear the song,' and told me his address. I smiled with joy at him, for my heart had sank hopelessly. When I opened the door separating me from Mother Kaukab, she asked me excitedly, 'What did you have to eat at the princess's?' I couldn't think what she meant then I remembered that I'd told her that I'd been invited to dinner with the English princess, the Queen's daughter. She sat there, asking me eager questions: 'What did you talk about? Did you have fun? What did you have to eat? What did they wear? Your dress must have been nicer than theirs! What did they say about your ear-rings?'

She wanted to know all the details so that when she went

back to the desert she could repeat it to the servants and the other women. Then she poured me a cup of coffee, remarking innocently, 'I said to myself, Nur must have switched on the radio while I was still asleep.'

When I went to his house I prepared myself for kisses, but instead, to my disappointment, he sat me down in his studio and sat at the piano, strumming and singing:

> My love is from a tribe in the heart of the desert.
> Her forefathers suffered the heat and the thirst.
> They buried alive their baby girls
> Yet took the women prisoner in battle
> Preserving them to bear men-children.
> Her blood must not be mixed with strange blood.
> And yet my love, she loves me.

5

I returned home and set off on my travels once more. This time, like a cook who can only handle a giant ladle, I spooned out for myself enormous quantities of emotion, parties often lasting most of the night, conversation and laughter. Perhaps the fact that Saleh was always travelling and showed no interest in me also pushed me further in this direction. What I was doing could quite possibly have remained a secret, but it seems that I began to frequent places where many of my fellow countrymen also spent their evenings. I was swept up into a circle of dancers, actors, musicians and men of society from the Arab world, whose fame spread because of their beauty and wit. One of them used his charm and humour to entertain professionally: sometimes he would dress up as a dancing girl and cry, 'Your donations, gentlemen, for the Prophet's sake,' and ten-pound notes would rain down on him; or he would put on a dress, tie his hair back in a scarf and imitate a housewife doing her housework, talking irritably to the saucepans and plates. When he'd done his turn one night and the applause had died down, he announced, 'I want to thank Nur, who realized that I was an artist, not just a clown, and encouraged me to turn professional.'

It was true that I'd become addicted to his wit and thought him worthy to be ranked with the great characters of comedy, and I'd offered money to the cabaret owner to let him up on the stage. This wasn't the first time such a thing had happened, as we'd already made a third-rate dancer famous by applauding wildly and opening bottles of champagne for her until she was promoted and eventually became a top dancer in the oriental clubs of London. I sank down in my seat at the sound of my name, feeling afraid, but forgot the incident by the following day as I became involved in the details of daily life once again. I never thought about the desert except when I smelt cardamom, and then when Mother Kaukab asked me one day about going back. This made me realize that it must be time, and that I'd have to do my best to keep things going here for a bit longer. I claimed appointments with doctors and urgent shopping; and Mother Kaukab commented that she was enjoying herself, although her excursions here were limited to going to the shops with the driver, and she was even happy to go in the car if it was to visit families from our country who were in London. 'They all ask if Saleh is with you,' she told me. 'I don't say no and I don't say yes. I just nod my head.'

The doorbell of the flat rang early one morning (I'd moved into my father's flat by this time). Before I could close my eyes again, Mother Kaukab came in to wake me, saying that a man from our country was asking to see me and insisting on waking me up although she'd told him that I was still asleep and that I'd gone to bed late. Many thoughts came to me but I didn't guess the reason until he showed me a piece of headed paper from Saleh's office, signed by Saleh. The letter, written in a dry official tone, said that I must leave for home that morning.

I thought immediately of contacting Saleh, but changed my mind, and wondered about my family. All of them must have heard what was going on by now. I looked at the man and said, 'But I haven't finished doing all I've got to do – I've still got an appointment at the doctor's.' 'I really don't know . . .' The man's voice tailed away and he shrugged politely.

I said nothing more, and went back into my room to pack, but I was overwhelmed by a powerful sensation that I'd only just arrived from the desert and was really unpacking. The long nights of laughter had suddenly vanished, and my heart began to pound, but I shrugged my shoulders, pretending not to mind, and told myself that I was luckier than many. My cousin had opened his eyes one morning to find himself in his house in the desert, when the last thing he remembered was going to bed in a Hong Kong hotel. The papers wrote of the fantastic amounts which he'd lost in a casino in Hong Kong, and the dud cheques he'd signed. And there was a friend of my brother's who'd been put on the first plane to the desert in handcuffs after his family had discovered that he was a drug addict.

Although the man stayed in the hall I felt as if he'd bound my hands and feet and blindfolded me. A car stood waiting at the entrance to the building and he opened the door for me and stood waiting by it while the driver and another man went up to fetch my cases and bags. I didn't feel free of the oppressive weight of his presence until I'd gone aboard Saleh's private plane. Mother Kaukab turned to me and said, 'Saleh must have missed you. Yesterday he phoned three times and I told him you were having dinner with the Queen's daughter. He said hasn't she had dinner with the Queen yet, but I told him Nur's young and she wouldn't have anything to say to old women . . .' Then she went on, 'Saleh's fame and prestige have reached London.'

In circumstances roughly similar to these I'd returned from the private school in Cairo: everyone in the plane could hear my whispering and crying the whole journey and see my blood-red eyes and my abaya flying through the air, followed by shrieks of protest. The man accompanying me on that occasion had been an employee of my father's, and although I was so young I'd promised myself that I would marry with all speed. I remember that the moment my companion went to the toilet I signalled to the foreigner beside me to order me a whisky and pour it into the glass of Pepsi Cola which I already had in front of me.

All through the flight I repeated to myself that Saleh was behind all this, that he must want to divorce me, but why hadn't he said so openly? When we landed, everything seemed normal. Saleh was waiting for me and he didn't confront me then or later. The idea of his doing so was absurd anyway, not just because men had had all the rights since the time of our fathers and grandfathers, but because there was much to be feared from a confrontation: if the sounds of our voices reached beyond the house walls, I would be removed from the family's sphere of influence and denied its protection. Saleh didn't divorce me, although he hinted to me that I could ask for a divorce if I wanted to. He was fearful for his honour and self-respect in the face of my family and society. Then shortly afterwards I found out that I'd lost my passport. It was the one thing that I guarded carefully, holding on to it as if I needed it to live, like oxygen. I'd learnt its shape and colour and number by heart. It was also the one thing which I kept hidden, wrapped in a plastic bag in a metal strong-box, while I forgot about my jewels and left them lying among the lip pencils and nail varnish and creams. It wasn't in Saleh's drawer, nor in his parents' house, not even in his office drawer. I secretly enlisted one of the people who worked for my father to help me in my search, thinking that it must be in Saleh's briefcase which he carried with him from place to place, but my emissary opened the case and didn't find it.

The only way was to make it up with Saleh and get him back. But it appeared that he'd cut me out of his life, and he no longer even visited the house since I'd tried to provoke him to argue with me. Instead he began sending for Ghada to spend a few days with him whenever he returned from abroad. Each time I asked him for my passport, he stalled and said I was still his wife and he wouldn't let me travel, but I didn't give in to him and ask for a divorce. He couldn't marry a second wife because I'd made that a condition of our marriage and the sheikh had repeated it during the formal signing of the contract which Saleh had attended with my father and the rest of the men, while I and my mother and the women had waited in another reception room: 'Nur . . . stipulates that Saleh . . . will not take another wife while he is married to her, as she fears this would result in her being wrongfully treated, and she has no defect or fault which would make living with her difficult; just as the Prophet, blessings and peace be upon him, stipulated that Ali should take no other wife besides Fatima, fearing that she would be wrongfully treated.'

I didn't want a divorce until I'd found another husband, since I was still enjoying the big house, the servants, the money to spend, and my freedom, even though I was barred from the skies and bound to the expanses of the desert. The rich needed money more than the poor, not only to preserve their standard of living but to improve it, for there were a lot of rich people and great rivalry existed between them, the men, the women and even the children. I asked Mother Kaukab and her friends to look around for a suitable husband for a friend of mine. Mother Kaukab guessed what I was up to and didn't comment. In no time she produced names and descriptions of possible suitors; among them was al-Sayrafi, an old man with two front teeth made of diamonds who swore that if I accepted him my dowry would be my weight in sheets of gold, but he was fanatical in his passions and would be jealous even of the breeze; another man wanted a second wife because his first wife had grown old, and he was blessed with plenty of money and wanted to enjoy someone younger and more beautiful. 'He follows where his heart leads,' remarked Mother Kaukab, 'and God created the heart.'

'We all act in accordance with our hearts' desires,' added another woman.

But I knew that this man lived by himself with his family all in separate houses round about him!

Mother Kaukab didn't know what had happened between me and Saleh; not even my family knew, and Mother Kaukab was convinced that he was like the rest of the men here and all that was wrong was that he neglected me and enjoyed himself when he was abroad; she assumed that I wanted someone richer or more generous and made unfavourable comparisons between our house and some of the palaces, or the houses with marble walls, and her lip curled with displeasure. Once I asked her, 'What about the private plane and the yacht?' And she answered, 'I know, but real wealth is on land, not in the skies or on the seas.' In any case she thought Saleh was mean because she'd often heard him telling the servants off for not closing the packet of tea properly, or complaining when he went into the garden to inspect the newly-planted trees and found that the water had overflowed on to the gravel and washed it away. I asked her about Fadl's son who'd been divorced for some time but she said, 'He's not good enough for you. They say there's singing coming from his house and his car night and day, and you know how the sound of drums does queer things to the brain, and you'll find the Devil behind those drums and tambourines.'

With every new day that came I realized that Suha was further from my mind; and one day I found myself thinking that this day was going to go by just like the one before, and I didn't want to spend the evening by myself. I phoned my sister-in-law and she told me that the party that evening wasn't to be missed because my brother had discovered some young man in the Turkish restaurant.

That night I set off after I'd put on a dress that sparkled, and pinned up my hair with shiny pins so that I looked as if I'd come straight from Rio de Janeiro. Perhaps the smell of my perfume was very powerful because Mother Kaukab called to me from her room, 'Wearing perfume, my precious Nur, is a kind of adultery. A man smells it and his spirit is aroused.' 'If only you were right,' I thought of saying to her. I wanted to be the most attractive woman there, as I always used to be. The other women, and their clothes and jewellery and hairstyles, had walked through my imagination, and I was especially conscious of the fact that they would still be going abroad while I was dependent on my mother's taste, and magazines, and whatever the Italian designer chose to send me.

The young Turk was at the party, answering the questions that cascaded down on him from all sides. Everybody, including me, choked with laughter at the plain straightforward way he did it, especially when he told us the story of how his father was put in prison because he loved his cow. 'The moon was rising, the breeze was fresh and cool,' said the father to the judge. 'It wasn't my fault. My heart fluttered, and my cow is beautiful . . .' After a little while I grew restless and began looking at the faces around me. Old familiar faces with nothing in them that aroused my curiosity; even when it was said that the Lebanese comic had finally been granted a visa to come to the desert, I couldn't summon up any enthusiasm. I had to have a different atmosphere, different people. I asked the driver to take me to my parents' house. My mother and father were out for the evening. I sat down on the sofa and leant my head back, and the next thing I knew was my mother shaking me by the shoulders, asking me why I hadn't come that afternoon. Then she called to her maid to fetch her the big suitcase. It was full of clothes, all punk style just like I'd asked her to get me, with the right shoes and accessories and coloured hair spray. I began to try them on and stared at my face in the mirror. Not a single spot or line marred its purity, even though my nights merged into my days and I was assailed by heat and cold and lack of sleep; though pills to put me to sleep and pills to wake me up fought each other down my throat, and my body was on display to both sexes like a shirt on the washing line, in frantic motion or quiet and still, depending on which way the wind blew.

Epilogue – Suha

I marked the sixteenth of June, the date of my departure, with lipstick on the wall calendar. I was so worked up about it I couldn't concentrate on packing my cases. Would I not regret this step when faced with the security situation in Lebanon, living temporarily with my mother, the separation from Basem and the effect of this on Umar? But my tension slipped away from me when I got into the car, and Said took me along the bumpy unmade roads and the broad asphalted streets bound by high walls. I asked myself and the monotonous desert, 'Have I ever been into those houses? Do I know that woman?' Of course. Her house passed through my mind: the brass coffee jugs and those reddish brass ashtrays which had become a trademark of all the houses here. How had I been able to put up with listening to their conversation, thought of inviting them to my house, or remembered engagements with them with some interest and enthusiasm?

One afternoon after I'd decided to leave I'd been obliged to visit Ingrid, since she'd come in person to invite me. When I came out of the house hundreds of migrating birds with blue bellies and orange wings were passing overhead through the desert air then disappearing as if consumed by fire. The grass was dying in Ingrid's garden; the new crop of sunflowers was thrusting its way upwards while the seeds of the old ones were dropping and their yellow petals fading.

Ingrid was crying; she hadn't been able to buy her mother a present for Mother's Day; the prayer times had changed with the sunset and the shops were closed. Myra was sitting sadly waiting for someone to ask her what was wrong so that she could tell them about the man who'd tried to attack her while she was hanging out the washing: '. . . he had a cap embroidered with gold and silver and coloured stones, and a patterned shawl over his shoulders; he was wearing trousers and a loose mauve cotton jacket, and on his feet he wore gold sandals that turned up at the front like the ones the genie wears in *Aladdin*.' She'd struggled with him and got him off her, then rushed in locking the door behind her. He'd tried to force it and she'd dragged sofas across and piled them up against the door. She'd sat on her own refusing to open the door for hours even though she'd been able to hear the voices of her husband and daughter outside. Ingrid interrupted her saying that she'd been hoeing her garden once when she'd caught sight of a man's feet. She'd known from his sandals that he'd come to rape her. She'd reached for the garden shears before standing up to confront him, only to find that the man was Said bringing a dish of tabbouleh from me. Maryam asked if the man who threw acid at the pretty blonde Syrian girl's dress was trying to burn it so that he could see her legs or was making a religious protest.

I was far away from them, and my heart beat with fear at the prospect of staying, when I thought of how mine and Umar's passport had been returned every time Basem had sent it to get an exit visa, because the new stamps weren't ready yet; planes bringing passengers in were making the return journey empty.

The boxes and cases were ready at the door. I went up on to the roof to make sure that Umar hadn't left anything. The pigeons' houses were empty, seed scattering the ground; the dishes of water had changed colour in the air and a thick layer of dust lay on the surface of them. I stood at the roof parapet exactly as I'd always done while Umar was riding his bike. I stretched up to look at the road and Umar said, 'You always do that,' and asked me what I could see.

At that moment as I looked down I seemed to see nothing, and I felt regret building up inside me because I'd lived here for so long. So long, and yet the passing time hadn't left many traces: a few little grey and white hairs buried in the thick mass of my dark hair, a few wrinkles round my eyes and on my forehead. I compared myself to the empty cover of a once full book of cinema tickets: the leaves torn off and handed out through the ticket-office window were the times I had wasted at tea parties and coffee mornings, or bouncing around on the back seat of the car feeling chilled by the air-conditioner, then stifled when Said turned it off and the car grew fetid like a packed and airless railway carriage on a long journey; or the years I had spent revolving in a circle of people who didn't change from one day to the next as if they'd been put in a pot with a tightly-fitting lid and drew life from the steam which rose within the confines of the pot, breathing in only their own heat, while a low fire burnt underneath them.

Umar said to me, 'Your skirt's rustling. You must have some chewing gum or chocolate.'

'If only I had, darling,' and I pulled out a lot of bits of paper with addresses written on them. I tore them up into tiny pieces and dropped them on the floor. 'Why did you tear them up, Mama?'

'We're not going to see anyone from here ever again.'

'I don't understand.'

'They're addresses.'

He asked insistently, and with some heat, 'Do you mean we won't see Sitt Wafa again, or her rooster?' 'Definitely not,' I thought, but I said, smoothing his hair, 'Her family lives in Lebanon so when we go and visit them we might see her.'

Recently Sitt Wafa had begun to take the broom with her whenever she went into the garden and beat the rooster with it so that he was knocked senseless for a few minutes while she put down the seed and water and collected the eggs. At the end of the month I'd gone to settle up with her and heard her talking about the rooster: 'It's got very mean,' she was saying to a friend of hers.

'Slaughter it,' said her friend, 'and stuff it with rice and pine nuts. Bless its heart, it's huge, it might not fit in the oven!'

'No, Sitt Wafa, you mustn't!' shouted Umar.

Sitt Wafa said calmly, 'But you like to raise rabbits and birds, Umar. Why are you so angry?' Her friend responded with a slurping noise: 'Ah, rabbits! How good they are and so tender, especially the little ones. You roast them and smother them in lemon and garlic. It's a meal you won't forget.'

I got up in the morning still tired; I hadn't slept well and hadn't been in the mood for Basem's kisses because I was in a flurry of happiness mixed with tension and apprehension about the journey. I looked down at the bed; in my imagination I saw Nur climbing over the wall of my house. As we went along in the car later I stared long and hard out at the town that I would never see after today; I knew this although I'd actually agreed with Basem that Umar and I would visit him once between his visits to us in Lebanon. As if I had just arrived I noticed the walls: every house had a different wall, made of marble, cement, natural stone like the stone you see in the mountains; tiles, factory-made stones, patterned and plain; there was a wall that took the form of a series of arches, so high that only the water storage tank was visible. New young branches were tied to one wall to give them support; electricity cables and telephone cables dangled down from another: no building, nothing in this place, was ever completely finished. The walls were high; the newer they were, the higher they seemed to be. Some were beautiful colours, as if they belonged to calm and tranquil houses. I remarked to Basem, 'Do you know what annoyed me most here?' 'Nur? Suzanne? Tamr?' 'No. The walls, constricting everybody.'

I saw a few men in the street and a single woman in black; I thought of a certain type of black beetle that makes a tapping noise with her body all day and all night when she feels the need to mate.

I sat down on a seat in the airport lounge. Umar was carrying the canary around in its cage, blithely explaining everything to it. I sighed contentedly, feeling as if I'd left all my thoughts and tensions behind outside the airport building and was a normal person again, no longer split between Suha of the desert and Suha the city dweller. I sat with one leg crossed over the other, watching the people and waiting for the flight announcement. For the first time here I was dressed as I wanted to be, in clashing colours that suited my figure and face and personality. I wore a single long earring and a blouse without a bra under it, and my hair was loose on my shoulders.

Said was the one I was going to miss. Although I'd been on edge and unsmiling that morning, he'd been his normal self, assuring Umar that he'd see him again soon. Umar asked him innocently, 'D'you want to come to Beirut? D'you know Granny's house?' Laughing and adjusting his head cloth, Said said, 'Don't worry, Umar. I'll get off at Beirut airport and sniff you out like a dog. I'll ask for the house where Umar and Madame Suha live and I'll find you.' Then he told us about the time he'd gone to Cairo and tried to find an Egyptian engineer who'd been a customer in the restaurant: 'A very important engineer. A nice man. And he lived somewhere in Cairo.' It was a long story: he'd asked a newspaper seller who'd directed him to the owner of a launderette whose son was working as a teacher in the desert. Said had gone off to the launderette and had eventually met up with the engineer who'd been delighted, unable to believe that he'd made his way through the millions of people in Cairo to find him. Proudly Said ended his tale: 'He took me to the pyramids and the zoo and to see a lady and her sisters who were belly dancers and singers.'

I don't know why I thought suddenly of Maaz's wife, Fatima, and the way she used to smile as she stood holding the coffee jug, waiting to refill her husband's cup and Suzanne's.

I craned my neck, looking down. I could see the high walls around the town protecting it from the horrors of the sand. The desert came into view, looking as it had done the first time I saw it: sand and palm trees, a way of life that revolved around human beings without possessions or skills, who had to rely on their imaginations to contrive a way of making their hearts beat faster or even to keep them at a normal pace; to search unaided for a hidden gleam of light, and to live with two seasons a year instead of four.

About the Author

Hanan al-Shaykh was born in Lebanon in 1945. She was brought up in Beirut before going to Cairo to receive her education. Upon her return to Beirut, she pursued a successful career in journalism, working for the prestigious daily *Al-Nahar*, until moving first to the Arabian Gulf, then to London, where she now lives. From a very early stage in her journalistic career, Hanan al-Shaykh started writing short stories and novels. Her previous novel to be translated into English, *The Story of Zahra*, established her as one of the most talented women writers in the Arab World. The publication of *Women of Sand and Myrrh* in Arabic has further enhanced her reputation as a writer.

About the Translator

Catherine Cobham, who teaches modern Arabic literature at the University of St. Andrews, has translated a number of contemporary Arab writers, including Yusef Idris, Nawal El-Saadawi, and Liana Badr.

Praise for
The Truth About Profiting from Social Networking

"Smart business people are using social networking to support their marketing and overall business strategies. But it is hard to do it right without understanding both social networks and the community norms you'll find there. Rutledge's book not only gives smart advice on how to navigate those waters, but does so with examples that are easy to understand and translate for use in your business."

Jason Falls, Social Media Explorer Blog

"This book could help your business make money and sales using social networking. From using MySpace and Facebook to using an internal social networking system, it covers it all."

Linda Roeder, Social Networking Weblog,
and Personal Web Pages Guide, About.com

"Social media takes community effort. As such, networking is of utmost importance on social networking sites. To become a successful contributor, you need to be a team player. Don't be afraid to reach out to anyone, big or small. Making that connection and maintaining that connection is critical; everything else will fall into place from there. Rutledge uncovers all the necessary skills to use these tools in this easy-to-understand book."

Tamar Weinberg, Techipedia

"Using online social networks for business and professional advancement requires more than just understanding the technology. Social networks are all about human interaction. This book provides numerous examples, ample advice, and easy-to-follow guidelines for those looking to navigate the previously uncharted waters of technology-enabled social networking."

Amanda G. Watlington, Ph.D., A.P.R., Owner, Searching for Profit

"With *The Truth About Profiting from Social Networking*, Rutledge provides deep insights into social networking and how to profit from its proper usage, both financially and in your career."

Allen Stern, Editor, *Center Networks*

"There is a right way and a wrong way to use social networks. Rutledge uncovers these truths and makes understanding the difference between them clear so you can achieve success and avoid failure."

Jason Bean, Blogger, b5media

THE TRUTH ABOUT

PROFITING FROM SOCIAL NETWORKING

Patrice-Anne Rutledge

© 2008 by Pearson Education, Inc.
Publishing as FT Press
Upper Saddle River, New Jersey 07458

FT Press offers excellent discounts on this book when ordered in quantity for bulk purchases or special sales. For more information, please contact U.S. Corporate and Government Sales, 1-800-382-3419, corpsales@pearsontechgroup.com. For sales outside the U.S., please contact International Sales at international@pearsoned.com.

Printed in the United States of America

First Printing: May 2008

ISBN-10: 0-78-973788-4
ISBN-13: 978-0-78-973788-5

Pearson Education LTD.
Pearson Education Australia PTY, Limited.
Pearson Education Singapore, Pte. Ltd.
Pearson Education North Asia, Ltd.
Pearson Education Canada, Ltd.
Pearson Educatión de Mexico, S.A. de C.V.
Pearson Education—Japan
Pearson Education Malaysia, Pte. Ltd.

Associate Publisher
Greg Wiegand

Acquisitions Editor
Michelle Newcomb

Development Editor
Laura Norman

Operations Manager
Gina Kanouse

Cover and Interior Designs
Stuart Jackman,
Dorling Kindersley

Managing Editor
Kristy Hart

Senior Project Editor
Lori Lyons

Publishing Coordinator
Cindy Teeters

Publicist
Lisa Jacobson Brown

Copy Editor
Karen Gill

Design Manager
Sandra Schroeder

Senior Compositor
Gloria Schurick

Proofreader
San Dee Phillips

Manufacturing Buyer
Dan Uhrig

Library of Congress Cataloging-in-Publication Data

Rutledge, Patrice-Anne.

The truth about profiting from social networking / Patrice-Anne Rutledge. -- 1st printing.

p. cm.

ISBN 0-7897-3788-4 (pbk. : alk. paper) 1. Online social networks--Economic aspects. 2. Social networks--Computer network resources. 3. Information society--Economic aspects. I. Title.

HM742.R88 2008

303.48'33--dc22

2008011517

To my mother, Phyllis L. Rutledge,
for her ongoing support and encouragement

CONTENTS

Introduction

Social networking is just one component of what's called Web 2.0, the next generation of websites and services that emphasize collaboration and connectivity. Although the experts continue to debate the exact definition of Web 2.0, one thing is certain: Social networking sites, blogs, and wikis are connecting the online world like never before. Web 2.0 has changed the way the world connects and communicates, and the evolution is continuing.

Social networking has generated a lot of buzz, media coverage, and conversation in the past few years. In spite of all this attention, however, many misconceptions remain. Social networking isn't just for the young. It now reaches a large, mainstream audience. Many popular sites report than half their visitors are over age 35. It isn't just for fun or pure socializing, either. Companies, organizations, and individuals around the world are profiting from their participation on popular social networks such as MySpace, Facebook, and LinkedIn. Social networking also isn't just for the tech-savvy. Strategy counts far more than technical skill in developing a successful social networking campaign. In this book, you learn 50 "truths" about real-world social networking and how you, too, can profit from your social networking experience.

This book is written for anyone who wants to tap the power of social networking for professional reasons. Marketers, publicists, small business owners, independent professionals, job seekers, fundraisers, and activists all can find ways to profit from strategic social networking. It's a viable business tool that opens up new ways to connect with others who can help you achieve your business goals. The goal of this book is to provide you with a solid foundation on the basics of social networking, give you some insight into future trends, and encourage you to think strategically about the best ways you can leverage the power of social networking to enhance your business, your cause, and your life.

TRUTH

Social networking is a lot more than MySpace and YouTube

Just what is social networking? Ask three people, and you'll get three different answers. Although most people have a general idea of the basic concept, social networking means different things to different people depending on their background, interests, goals, and level of computer savvy.

MySpace (www.myspace.com) and YouTube (www.youtube.com) are two of the most popular sites on the web. For many people, these two sites satisfy all their social networking needs. But the world of social networking is much larger than its two highest profile sites.

> Just what is social networking? Ask three people, and you'll get three different answers.

Business networkers could determine social networking isn't right for them after visiting MySpace and YouTube if they didn't also check out the many business-oriented sites that could offer them much greater benefits.

In other words, the world of social networking is wide and diverse. Although early adopters of social networking skew to the young, the trend has now moved into the mainstream with sites for all ages, backgrounds, and interests. There's something for everyone, but you need to know where to find it.

A quick tour of the world of social networking gives you an idea of the vast differences between these sites as well as the possibilities for how social networking could benefit you. Some of the best-known and most-visited social networking sites include

- **Bebo** (www.bebo.com)—Bebo reports more than 25 million members and is particularly popular in the UK. Bebo Bands and Bebo Authors draw musicians and writers looking to connect with their audience.

- **Ecademy** (www.ecademy.com)—A business networking site with 150,000 members, Ecademy offers numerous networking groups based on your interests. It also offers in-person networking events, primarily in the UK.

- **Facebook** (www.facebook.com)—Starting as a community for Harvard students, Facebook opened its doors to anyone with an email address in September 2006 and increased its membership by 89 percent in less than a year.

- **Friendster** (www.friendster.com)—Friendster has a member base of 50 million users worldwide and is particularly popular in the Asia Pacific region.

- **hi5** (www.hi5.com)—With more than 60 million registered members and 25 million unique visitors per month, hi5 aims for an international audience with a localized interface available in multiple languages.

- **LinkedIn** (www.linkedin.com)—The largest and most popular of the business networking sites, LinkedIn offers profiles of more than 19 million professionals and is particularly popular with recruiters...and those who want to capture their attention.

- **MySpace** (www.myspace.com)—Arguably the most popular social networking site on the web, MySpace is expanding from a youth-dominated demographic to encompass members of all ages. Although poor site design and numerous less-than-professional MySpace pages can be a detractor, MySpace is still a great networking tool for the right people (think musical artists, marketers aiming for a general audience, authors of mainstream novels, and so forth).

- **Orkut** (www.orkut.com)—Google may have founded Orkut, but that hasn't translated into worldwide popularity. Its most significant user base is in Brazil and India, where it captures a high market share.

- **Ryze** (www.ryze.com)—Another business-oriented social site, Ryze has more than 500,000 members and offers a number of special interest networks.

- **XING** (www.xing.com)—An active business-oriented social networking site that is particularly popular in Europe. XING was renamed from openBC/Open Business Club in November 2006.

- **YouTube** (www.youtube.com)—The world's most popular video-sharing site.

3

Want even more options? Niche social networking is a hot trend, with microsites sprouting up for almost every conceivable niche audience. Some examples include

- **aSmallWorld** (www.asmallworld.net)—By invitation only, for celebrities and the business elite
- **BlackPlanet.com** (www.blackplanet.com)—Emphasizing connections between African Americans
- **85 Broads** (https://secure.85broads.com)—For career women who attended a select list of leading universities
- **CafeMom** (www.cafemom.com)—A networking site for mothers
- **Dogster** (www.dogster.com)—For dog lovers everywhere
- **Gaia** (www.gaia.com/community)—For the socially conscious crowd
- **GLEE.com** (www.glee.com)—For the gay and lesbian community
- **MilitaryPlanet** (www.militaryplanet.com)—For members of the military
- **New England Venture Network** (www.venturenetwork.vc)—Social networking for venture capitalists
- **Ning** (www.ning.com)—For do-it-yourselfers who want to create their own social network
- **Shelfari** (www.shelfari.com)—A site for book lovers and authors
- **ShoutLife** (www.shoutlife.com)—A Christian social network
- **Ultrafan** (www.ultrafan.com)—For sports fans

Although these "person-to-person" sites represent the most common type of social networking, other sites also fall under the realm of the somewhat fuzzy definition of social networking.

These include

- **Photo-sharing sites**—Flickr (www.flickr.com), Zooomr (www.zooomr.com), and Photobucket (www.photobucket.com).

- **Social bookmarking sites**— Digg (www.digg.com), del.icio.us (http://del.icio.us), and StumbleUpon (www.stumbleupon.com), which enable you to share your favorite sites and news stories with other users.

- **Micro-blogging sites**—Twitter (www.twitter.com), Pownce (www.pownce.com), and Jaiku (www.jaiku.com), which merge brief blog-like text updates with social networking functionality.

- **Video-sharing sites**—Revver (www.revver.com), Veoh (www.veoh.com), and Google Video (video.google.com), as well as the frontrunner YouTube.

Savvy social networkers have found ways to promote their businesses, products, and causes—and even themselves—on the variety of social networking sites available on the web.

TRUTH

2

Forget everything you think you know about social networking

The web has revolutionized the way people network. Over the past five years, social networking sites that connect like-minded people on the web have proliferated. This new form of networking enables you to take your face-to-face network online and expand it exponentially in the process.

Around the world, hundreds of millions of people use social networking sites in a single month. Their ages range from preteens to senior citizens and include all spectrums of society—students, job seekers, recruiters, executives, small business owners, marketers, fundraisers, artists, authors, parents, hobbyists, and political activists.

The web has revolutionized the way people network.

An integral part of the Web 2.0 strategy of online collaboration, social networks are enabling people to connect with each other like never before. Web 2.0 is all about community—using social networks, blogs, podcasts, wikis, and more to create a new web experience that's connected and collaborative. The key to your success in social networking lies in your ability to embrace a new way to interact with others and make it work for you.

Mike, for example, has heard about social networking and has decided to see what this new way of networking can do for his career. A larger competitor is about to acquire his current employer, a midsized firm on the west coast, and Mike is unsure how secure his middle management position will be after the acquisition. Mike has worked for the same company for 15 years, and job search strategies were very different the last time he looked for employment. He joins a large social networking site geared toward business users and connects with a number of his current and previous colleagues. He then waits to see what happens.

Boston-based Sarah has been reading a lot about the potential of social networking. She thinks it would be a great way to promote her career as a singer/songwriter as well as generate some positive buzz about her new CD, distributed by an independent label. She joins several popular social networking sites and creates a profile on each.

To give people a taste of her music, she offers song samples and video clips. Her profiles are full of content—her bio, photos, a listing of tour dates, and blog posts about what inspires her as an artist. She develops a strategy for connecting with anyone who is likely to enjoy her style of music, and she soon has thousands of contacts in her social network.

In another corner of the world, Alberto runs a small nonprofit organization and has become inspired by the success of larger nonprofits that use social networking to reach others interested in their cause. To start, he participates on a number of social networking sites, both general interest sites and those that cater to a niche audience. By adding as much compelling content as possible—blog posts, video clips, photos, calls to action, and "tell a friend" requests—he gives his potential contacts a solid reason to accept his invitations and learn more about his cause. To get the word out even further, Alberto uploads video clips to video-sharing sites, posts photos to photo-sharing sites, and encourages a word-of-mouth campaign by asking supporters to bookmark stories about his organization on their favorite social bookmarking sites.

Which of these three will be most successful in achieving social networking success? Although it's hard to predict success in the world of social networking, it's far more likely that the approach Sarah and Alberto are taking will produce positive results. Their approach is proactive, engaging, and creative, whereas Mike's is passive and relies on what worked in the old world.

This distinction is key. With social networking, you need to forget your entrenched ideas about traditional networking and embrace a new paradigm.

But to fully embrace this new way of networking, you need to understand what it can do for you, your career, and your business. Like traditional networking, the most effective social networking centers on building relationships, engaging with others, and developing solid word-of-mouth marketing. Social networking takes person-to-person networking a step further by opening up potential contacts to the entire world of Internet users. Of course, connecting with anyone and everyone would be time-consuming and most likely

The most effective social networking is all about building relationships, engaging with others, and developing solid word-of-mouth marketing.

wouldn't generate positive results. But by using a social networking web-based platform, you can easily connect with people who would be difficult to reach using more traditional networking methods.

Although developing a larger network of contacts is the primary goal of many social networkers, online social networking enables you to do a lot more. The possibilities are endless, but here's a top 10 list of what you can achieve through social networking:

1. Create an online profile that attracts attention and opportunities.
2. Tap into the hidden job market and prepare for a killer interview.
3. Recruit qualified job candidates.
4. Launch, market, and advertise your products and services.
5. Develop an online platform that promotes your career as an expert, speaker, or consultant.
6. Develop your fan base as a musician, artist, actor, or author.
7. Publicize a cause, political campaign, or nonprofit organization.
8. Share and exchange business information with fellow contacts.
9. Conduct market research on a certain niche or demographic.
10. Find and analyze potential partners, investors, and distributors.

When you open yourself up to a new way of developing and maintaining professional relationships, social networking can offer a whole new world of opportunities for enhancing your business, your career, and your life.

TRUTH

3

The traffic stampede: numbers don't lie

Social networking sites are among the most frequently visited websites on the Internet. The traffic stampede to sites like MySpace, Facebook, Bebo, and YouTube continues to grow, now reaching the vast majority of Internet users of all ages and backgrounds.

The numbers are compelling, as these statistics indicate:

- In January 2008, MySpace had 68.6 million unique visitors worldwide; Facebook had 33.9 million. [1]

- Facebook visitors increased 51 percent between December 2006 and December 2007.[2]

- Sixty-eight percent of the MySpace user base is older than 25, as is 71 percent of the Friendster user base. MySpace's largest audience segment is between 35 and 54, comprising 40 percent of total users.[3]

- Mobile social networking is predicted to rise from 50 million to 174 million users by 2011.[4]

- In December 2007, YouTube had 77.6 million viewers who watched 3.2 billion videos. [5]

- Worldwide online social network ad spending is predicted to increase from $1.2 billion in 2007 to $2.2 billion in 2008. [6]

Mobile social networking is predicted to rise from 50 million to 174 million users by 2011.

Niche sites are growing, too. Although their niche status doesn't enable them to deliver the sheer volume of traffic that the general sites do, their growth percentages are equally impressive. Some examples include

- CafeMom, a niche social networking for mothers, increased its market share 507 percent from January to June 2007.[7]

- BlackPlanet was the fourth most popular social networking site in the U.S. in December 2007.[8]

- LinkedIn states that its site includes profiles of more than 19 million professionals, with 25 new members joining every minute of every day.

- According to Facebook, 85 percent of all college students have a profile on its site.

CafeMom, a niche social networking for mothers, increased its market share 507 percent from January to June 2007.

Social networking isn't just a U.S.-based phenomenon. During the past few years, social networking has become increasingly global. A number of sites—such as Bebo, XING, and Friendster—cite a high percentage of users outside the U.S. Global social networking statistics illustrate an equally impressive increase in both total users and percentage of market share:

- **UK**—As of August 2007, participation in social networking usage reached 24.9 million unique visitors—78 percent of the total UK online population.[9]

- **Australia**—Traffic to social networking and chat websites increased by 114 percent between July and October 2007.[10]

- **Germany**—The social networking community has reached 14.8 million users.[11]

- **Latin America**—In June 2007, more than 14 million people in Latin America visited Fox Interactive Media (home of MySpace), representing 26 percent of the online population. Argentina, Brazil, and Chile report the highest percentage of their population with online access.[12]

- **France**—More than 50 percent of France's online population participates in social networking. As of September 2007, Skyrock Network was the most popular social networking site, followed by MySpace.[13]

- **Asia**—Friendster is the top social network in the Asia Pacific region with 41 million users. [14]

Traffic statistics don't tell the whole story, however. Audience demographics also play a key role. In addition, you need to stay on top of trends to predict growth areas in the rapidly changing world of social networking. Mobile social networking (such as via cell phone) and microniches are on a growth trend, for example, and could change future traffic patterns. MySpace, Facebook, Yahoo!, and Google are focusing on the wireless future of social networking. What's critical is to determine what these numbers and statistics mean in relation to your social networking goals.

For example, MySpace may be the most-visited social networking site in the world, but if your goal is to develop a network of high-level business contacts to help you land a top-notch position in corporate management, you're much better off spending your time on LinkedIn or Ryze. On the other hand, if your goal is to promote a CD or a product with mass general appeal, a MySpace presence could be very profitable. If you want to reach the niche demographic of dog owners, a site like Dogster is the place to be.

The key is to research the statistics *and* the audience demographics and then determine the best target social networking sites for your purposes.

TRUTH

4

With social networking, change is the only constant

The year 2007 was called "the year of social networking," and for good reason. The year saw rapid growth, new site launches, and numerous announcements of strategic alliances, partnerships, and equity investments. It also was the year that one of the major players in the industry, Facebook, owned up to its mistakes and immediately changed its policies, thanks to the power of public opinion.

From its inception, social networking has been a roller-coaster ride, quickly announcing new innovations, garnering media headlines, attracting hundreds of millions of participants, and generating significant buzz—mostly positive, but occasionally negative as well. With social networking, change is the only constant.

> The year 2007 was called "the year of social networking," and for good reason.

Although 2007 may have been the year of social networking, the phenomenon actually got its start 12 years earlier. One of the first sites to use a social networking business model was Classmates. com. Launched in 1995, the website focuses on reconnecting old school friends. Classmates has been eclipsed by power players such as MySpace and Facebook, but maintains 50 million registered users and is ranked consistently in the top ten of the most popular social networking sites in the U.S.

Two years later, in 1997, SixDegrees.com was founded based on the concept that everyone is no more than six connections away from any other person in the world. SixDegrees.com no longer exists—YouthStream Media Networks purchased it in 2000—but its technology is still around. YouthStream sold the social networking patent it acquired from SixDegrees.com to social networking sites LinkedIn and Tribe in September 2003, which continue the concept of "six degrees of separation" today.

SixDegrees.com may actually have been a bit ahead of its time. Not until 2003 did social networking start to take off again with the launch of sites such as MySpace, LinkedIn, and OpenBC (now XING).

By then, the number of people online had grown exponentially, and broadband access was more widespread, opening the doors for more interest in the type of experience social networking had to offer.

In 2004 and 2005, the social web saw additional growth. Facebook was launched in the dorm room of three Harvard undergraduates, who had no idea at the time how it would change their lives. Around the same time, Google launched what was to become a major disappointment in social networking history. Despite its vast presence online, Google's social networking site Orkut never experienced worldwide popularity. It's now a niche site, focusing largely on a user base in Brazil and Asia.

But it wasn't until Rupert Murdoch's News Corporation, the parent company of Fox Interactive Media, acquired MySpace in July 2005 that people began to realize social networking was more than just an enjoyable social pastime. Its purchase price of $580 million signaled that social networking was serious business. There was money to be made, both for site owners who profited from advertising revenue and for businesses looking for a new promotional vehicle for their products and services. Social networking as a viable business tool was born.

In 2006, social networking moved into high gear. Facebook opened its registration to the public and experienced triple-digit growth. MySpace was the most searched term on the Internet. The year wasn't all good news for social networking companies, however. Xanga was forced to pay a $1 million penalty for allegedly violating the Children's Online Privacy Protection Act. This penalty delivered a clear message to the industry: There are consequences for not adhering to the guidelines that make social networking safe for all its participants.

By 2007, the social networking phenomenon was everywhere. The online buzz spread rapidly through viral, word-of-mouth campaigns. Social networking was even the topic of water cooler chatter around the world as professionals began to debate how they, too, could profit from this evolving communication platform. New sites launched with astounding frequency, including the New England Venture Network for venture capitalists, CarFolks for car lovers, and even Raxxle for people eager to find their "twin" using facial recognition technology. MilitaryPlanet, appropriately, launched on Veteran's Day to connect both active-duty and retired military personnel.

Signaling the trend toward a more open social networking environment, both Facebook and Google announced development platforms in 2007. Google launched OpenSocial, a common interface for developing social applications, supported by a long list of other industry leaders such as Bebo, Friendster, LinkedIn, MySpace, Ning, and XING. Facebook, on the other hand, announced its Facebook Platform, a development platform enabling site integration with Facebook. Not to be overlooked, MySpace announced its own development platform in February 2008, designed to extend Google's OpenSocial. Despite the challenges of having multiple platforms, the good news is that they enable developers to create social applications more easily and, as a result, deliver higher-quality, more engaging features to users.

The year 2007 also had its share of social networking controversy. When Facebook announced the Beacon service as part of its new Facebook Ads program, the public outcry was immediate. Facebook listened to its critics' complaints and privacy concerns. One month later CEO Mark Zuckerberg issued an apology and announced that users could opt out of Beacon. Facebook's quick reversal on the controversial Beacon was a clear sign of the power of the people who generate the content that's the foundation of social networking's worldwide popularity.

What's next for social networking over the next few years is anyone's guess. Sites will undoubtedly come and go. New technologies will undoubtedly improve the social networking experience that we know now. One thing, however, is certain. Social networking will continue to evolve, change, and surprise us all.

TRUTH

MySpace isn't just for teenagers

The top search term for 2006 was "MySpace." That represents a lot of searches and a lot of people looking for information on MySpace (www.myspace.com), the most popular social networking site on the web and one of the most visited sites in the world. To many people, however, MySpace is synonymous with teenagers and the collegiate crowd. Although the MySpace user base clearly consists of many people under age 30, more than half of MySpace visitors are now ages 35 or older.[1] That fact is causing marketers who seek a wide demographic audience to take notice.

One of the challenges of MySpace is that it reaches such a wide audience. Its simplicity and free access enable just about anyone to create a MySpace page. In fact, a brief visit to MySpace may initially discourage many professionals from participating. You're likely to encounter many poorly designed, unprofessional MySpace pages. To get beyond this, you need to consider MySpace as a web-based microcosm, a smaller version of the entire world where business professionals, artists, fun-seeking teens, and online predators coexist. Finding your own place in this world and targeting the right audience are initial steps to success.

> More than half of MySpace visitors are now ages 35 or older.

Bands and musical artists were among the first to discover and benefit from the power of MySpace promotion, but major corporations such as Microsoft, adidas, Wendy's, Burger King, and Honda have now recognized MySpace's potential and joined the party. The fact that Rupert Murdoch's News Corporation paid $580 million for MySpace in 2005 is a strong indication of its commercial viability.

Although creating a page on MySpace is free, major corporations pay specialized consultants $100,000 or more to launch a customized, state-of-the-art MySpace presence. With MySpace, the focus should be on brand development, viral marketing, and customer engagement rather than a direct sales pitch.

The key here is to match your content with your target audience. If you have a specific target, this isn't difficult to do. If your product reaches a wide audience of different ages and demographics, it can be more of a challenge.

A wide variety of companies and organizations have conducted successful MySpace campaigns. Aquafina (www.myspace.com/aquafina), for example, incorporates interactive games and TV ads on its MySpace page, encouraging viral marketing with "Send to a friend" links.

adidas (www.myspace.com/adidas) also uses interactivity as a marketing tool. Its MySpace site encourages visitors to create their own interactive PlayBooks, sign up for free training tips, enter contests, and download MySpace skins.

Toyota (www.myspace.com/yaris) tried a different approach with a custom MySpace presence for its Yaris vehicle. Instead of emphasizing details about the car, this site focuses more on cross-promotions with the popular Xbox game player and Prison Break TV series.

MySpace marketing isn't just for companies looking to generate sales, though. The nonprofit organization Genocide Intervention (www.myspace.com/genocideintervention) uses MySpace as a mechanism for developing awareness of the Darfur crisis and encourages viral marketing techniques to spread the word.

Successful marketing campaigns on MySpace employ elements of interactivity and engagement to build a relationship with their audience. They also employ viral marketing techniques that encourage visitors to share the site's content with friends. Don't get trapped into a "build it and they will come" mentality. The best MySpace marketing campaigns build relationships that convert visitors to advocates and evangelists.

Successful marketing campaigns on MySpace employ elements of interactivity and engagement to build a relationship with their audience.

Here are five top tips for successful MySpace marketing:

1. **Understand the MySpace community and how it works**—Many people eager to reach even a portion of the vast MySpace audience just jump in and create a MySpace page without first developing a strategy. The MySpace interface is deceptively simple. Do your research and find out what is and isn't working in your niche before creating your own presence.

2. **Be sure that MySpace is for you**—MySpace works well for people looking to reach a large general audience. For example, bands and businesses selling consumer products often do well on MySpace. If you target a highly specialized niche or focus on business-to-business markets, MySpace may not be the best option.

3. **Focus on branding rather than pure product promotion**—You need to give before you receive in the MySpace community. That means creating a site that offers meaningful content of interest to your target audience: music downloads, games, quizzes, interactivity, useful information, and so forth.

4. **Get friendly**—In the MySpace world, a friend is someone who connects with you and appears on your Friends list on your MySpace page. To increase your collection of friends, look at your competitors' friends and people who belong to MySpace groups that target your niche. A word of caution: Avoid automated tools or bots that add friends to your MySpace.

5. **Go for the wow factor**—It takes something truly unique and creative to capture the attention of a large number of people. By creating a MySpace presence that stands out and encourages viral marketing, your audience (MySpace "friends") markets for you.

TRUTH

6

LinkedIn is the place for business

LinkedIn (www.linkedin.com) is one of the top social networking sites for business, with profiles of more than 19 million professionals. Twenty-five new members join every minute of every day. The site is also extremely active with recruiters—both from recruiting firms and major companies such as Microsoft, eBay, and L'Oréal—which makes it a prime hunting ground for job seekers. Everyone from top CEOs to presidential candidate Barack Obama has a LinkedIn profile.

LinkedIn works like many other social networking sites. You create a profile and establish connections with other users—people you already know and people you want to know. What's different about LinkedIn is that its audience is almost exclusively professionals looking to achieve professional goals, such as finding a new job, recruiting employees, generating new business, or locating potential business partners.

After you create your profile, you can explore LinkedIn's other features, including special areas for job seekers or recruiters, the JobInsider toolbar that integrates with Internet Explorer or Firefox, recommendations for service providers (useful for consultants or small businesses), and LinkedIn Answers, in which you can share information with fellow members.

Because there's so much more to a successful experience on LinkedIn than simply creating a profile, several savvy networkers have established third-party sites offering best practices and advice on LinkedIn. Some examples include MyLinkWiki (www.dallasblue.com/LinkedIn/family.htm) and MyLinkedInPower Forum (tech.groups.yahoo.com/group/MyLinkedinPowerForum).

To get the most out of your LinkedIn experience, consider these tips.

Create a profile that maps to your goals

This point is critical to your success. You need to strive for a balance between providing enough information to achieve your goals and providing too much information; a profile should not be a detailed resume. Review other profiles for an idea of what works. Also, think carefully about what you want to achieve. Are you hoping to network your way to a new job, change your career, or build your business? Craft a profile that matches this goal for the best results.

In addition, ensure that your profile is complete. This doesn't mean that you need to create a lengthy profile with a lot of personal detail. It refers to LinkedIn's calculation of completeness—whether you've included all the items they feel are important to a successful profile.

Laura, for example, is an editor with 20 current connections who wants to maximize her exposure on LinkedIn. She creates what she feels is a solid profile that demonstrates her expertise in both editing and business. But LinkedIn states that her profile is only 75 percent complete. Laura's profile includes current and past positions, educational information, a photo, and one recommendation. Adding two more recommendations and a profile summary listing her specialties will enhance her already strong profile and elevate its completeness to 100 percent. According to LinkedIn, you're 40 times more likely to achieve positive results if you post a complete profile.

Not having enough recommendations is one of the common reasons your profile may not reach 100 percent. Many people just don't like asking for them. But by requesting recommendations from LinkedIn members you know—particularly former employers or other high-profile people—you can validate your qualifications in a way that your profile alone could never do by itself.

After you complete your profile, make it public. If you're concerned about privacy, create a profile that presents your most important qualifications but doesn't provide excessive personal or professional details.

According to LinkedIn, you're 40 times more likely to achieve positive results if you post a complete profile.

Expand your network beyond the people you know to the people you want to know

Using LinkedIn's search features makes it easy to find all your personal contacts who are already part of the LinkedIn network. Start with colleagues and managers, both current and former, and then expand from there. Fellow members of professional associations, former classmates, and people in your personal network are good choices. LinkedIn can review your contacts from Microsoft Outlook, Gmail, Yahoo!, or AOL to see if any of them already have LinkedIn profiles.

Expanding your network to include people you don't know is where things become trickier. Although some people like to link with anyone and everyone, in general, you'll get the most benefit from selectively linking with people you don't know. For example, if you're searching for a job, connect with recruiters or hiring managers at the companies you want to work for. To reach the most influential people, you may need to request an introduction through a mutual connection or a second-tier connection.

Participate in the LinkedIn community and beyond

Being sociable can get you far in the LinkedIn community. To start, invite others to join LinkedIn. In a few circles, almost everyone you know is on LinkedIn. But for most people, a lot of your personal contacts don't participate...yet. Send them an invitation and get them involved.

By participating in the LinkedIn Answers feature, you can elevate your visibility on the network. Providing detailed, quality answers is the best way to succeed and show your expertise. If others like your answer and it's rated as a best answer, you'll gain added visibility as an expert in your category. Remember, though, to make your answers useful. People will easily see through self-promotion disguised as an answer. Finally, promote your profile on your website or blog. LinkedIn offers copy and paste HTML code to create buttons for you to place on other sites. Doing this increases your profile as well as the number of targeted requests you receive to connect on LinkedIn.

TRUTH

7

YouTube is for profit, not just play

Although YouTube (www.youtube.com) is one of the most visited sites on the web and is the clear leader in web-based video sharing, it still has a bit of an image problem with business professionals. When most people think of YouTube, they think of funny homemade videos or video clips from favorite bands or TV shows. They don't always think of YouTube as a solid marketing platform suitable for a variety of businesses. Some even argue that YouTube isn't a true social networking site, depending on how strict their definition of the term is.

Properly used, YouTube can be a wildly successful promotional vehicle for savvy marketers who know how to use the web to build their brand and connect with their audience. YouTube's popularity is a clear sign that users love the visual impact that today's broadband access and advanced technology provide.

> Properly used, YouTube can be a wildly successful promotional vehicle for savvy marketers.

Founded in February 2005 and purchased by Google in November 2006, YouTube has become a web phenomenon and a household name in only a few years' time. As of December 2007, 77.6 million viewers watched 3.2 billion videos on YouTube, averaging 41.6 videos per viewer.[1] In just the past year, YouTube has experienced tremendous growth that demonstrates the numerous marketing opportunities that this communication medium can provide. It announced partnerships with the BBC, CBS Sports, and Apple; released localized sites in Brazil, France, Ireland, Italy, Japan, Netherlands, Poland, Spain, and the UK; and premiered its first international film competition, Project Direct, with works from filmmakers around the world.

In addition, well-known figures such as Oprah Winfrey (www.youtube.com/oprah) and the British Royal Family (www.youtube.com/theroyalchannel) have launched YouTube channels to capitalize on reaching their audience through video.

YouTube is also becoming a major player in influencing the outcome of the 2008 U.S. election with the YouTube You Choose

'08 channel (www.youtube.com/youchoose). This channel enables candidates to communicate directly with voters who can submit video-generated questions back to the candidates.

YouTube clearly has a lot to offer savvy marketers, even those who don't work for major corporations. James, for example, is an up-and-coming musician trying to gain some exposure for his new band. He's heard that some YouTube videos for popular artists and movies received over a hundred thousand views in a matter of days. James would be happy with a fraction of this type of exposure. He signs up for a musician account and creates his own channel. From there, James posts some of the band's best video clips and provides tour information and a link to purchase his band's new CD. To generate further buzz, he uses YouTube email and bulletins to spread the word, posts video responses to the videos of related artists, and joins relevant YouTube groups.

Margarita, the author of a new mystery novel, would like to use YouTube to promote her new book with a book trailer. With the help of her brother, an actor and videographer, she creates a slick three-minute video that's designed to captivate the attention of viewers and encourage them to buy her book. She posts her video to YouTube, tags it with the most appropriate keywords, and embeds the video on her blog and website. In an effort to get even broader coverage for her book, Margarita also posts her video to other video-sharing sites such as MSN Video, Google Video, and Revver.

In addition to the exposure it provides, one of the biggest advantages of YouTube marketing is that it's free. At no cost, YouTube enables you to

- Host your videos, including movie trailers, book trailers, TV video clips, music video clips, software demos, presentation clips, political statements, instructional videos, and more.

- Promote your videos to a worldwide audience of millions of potential viewers.

- View statistics on page views and links to your videos.

- Tap the power of social networking by allowing users to comment on and share your videos.

- Tag your videos with keywords that help your target audience find them.

- Create custom channels that enhance your branding.

In addition to the exposure it provides, one of the biggest advantages of YouTube marketing is that it's free.

Even if you don't have video content to post on YouTube, you can still benefit from its vast audience. YouTube also offers advertising opportunities for companies with an initial budget of at least $25,000 who want to target its demographics. YouTube advertising options include

- Display advertising, including skyscraper, leaderboard, large rectangle, and small rectangle banners.

- Custom brand channels.

- Contests that encourage involvement and interactivity.

- Video ads that appear on the YouTube home page or category or search pages.

- InVideo ads that appear within the video content of YouTube premium partners.

As of July 2007, YouTube users were 54 percent male and 46 percent female. Age ranges were spread rather evenly across all ages. What

What may come as a surprise to many: 21 percent of YouTube visitors are over the age of 55.

may come as a surprise to many: Twenty-one percent of YouTube visitors are over the age of 55. With an audience of 55 million and growing, YouTube still offers fun, free entertainment—but it means serious business as well to those who know how to tap the power of this new way of communicating on the web.

TRUTH

8

Facebook extends beyond the collegiate crowd

Facebook (www.facebook.com) has been undergoing a facelift, but instead of trying to look younger, it's focusing on a more mature image.

Facebook launched in February 2004 as a social networking site for students at Harvard. It quickly expanded to include students at other top-tier universities: Columbia, Stanford, and Yale. By the end of its first year, Facebook had nearly one million active members. The decision in September 2006 to expand from a network of students to a network that anyone, anywhere could join propelled its growth even further.

Significant venture capital funding has been integral to Facebook's expansion and success, enabling it to introduce a rapid succession of site enhancements. These enhancements include Marketplace classified ads, Facebook polls, mobile access, a multitude of third-party applications, and high-profile partnerships with Amazon.com, Forbes, Microsoft, Virgin Mobile USA, and Warner Bros. Records. Facebook membership more than quadrupled in less than a year, growing from 12 million users in December 2006 to 53 million active users in November 2007. This extremely rapid growth is one of the things that makes Facebook's story unique among the vast majority of competing social networking sites.

Although it's clear that Facebook has transitioned from its student origins to a mainstream social networking site, it still displays some of its youthfulness with features not found on more business-oriented sites (pokes, hugs, or flowers, anyone?). Regardless, business users have found a home on Facebook, for example, through the successful use of targeted profiles and groups. Facebook itself is courting the business market with its series of Business Solutions (www.facebook.com/business).

> Facebook membership more than quadrupled in less than a year, growing from 12 million users in December 2006 to 53 million active users in November 2007.

The launch of the Facebook Ads program in November 2007 was yet an additional step in solidifying Facebook's place as a mainstream social network. Businesses seeking to tap into Facebook's large audience can now establish strategic advertising and marketing campaigns on the site. There are three elements to Facebook Ads:

■ **Facebook Pages**—Facebook Pages enable businesses to develop a free Facebook presence beyond a traditional profile. Businesses, organizations, musicians, authors, and artists can use Pages to communicate with "fans" and develop a fanbase on Facebook. Pages provide special features based on the type of business you have. For example, a singer can easily post song clips, video clips, and more.

■ **Facebook Beacon**—This feature enables users to share content from participating websites via news feeds in Facebook. For example, eBay allows its sellers to include information about their current eBay listings in Facebook, increasing exposure and potential sales. Although there are benefits to Beacon, its original format had the potential to expose users' private data without their knowledge. As a result, privacy rights activists voiced their concerns loudly when Beacon was first introduced. One month later, Facebook's CEO issued an apology and announced that users could opt out of Beacon.

■ **Social Ads**—Social Ads enable businesses to advertise to targeted Facebook users based in part on the actions of their friends. You can target by age, gender, location, or interests and purchase ads by either clicks or impressions. Social Ads debuted with several big-name companies as its first participants, including Blockbuster, CBS, Chase, The Coca-Cola Company, Sony Pictures, and Verizon. A complementary program, Facebook Insight, provides valuable metrics on ad performance, demographics, and trends.

Businesses and software developers are also benefiting from new Facebook features such as Facebook Platform. With Platform, you create your own application that Facebook users can implement on their profiles, increasing your visibility on the site. To encourage the development of new applications, Facebook offers a special site (http://developers.facebook.com) with detailed information on how to create and implement a Facebook app.

With its rapid growth, recent reinvention, and frequent new developments, Facebook has generated a lot of media attention. The good news for marketers, advertisers, and developers is that there is abundant opportunity to tap into Facebook's vast and growing audience.

TRUTH

Forget the old rules of the job search

When Seth was downsized from his corporate marketing job, he knew that the tools and techniques he used to land a good position 12 years ago wouldn't work in today's world. The web was in its infancy back then, and concepts like social networking and online recruiting were far from the mainstream. Seth tapped his marketing acumen and previous experience with in-person networking to launch an online social networking job search.

He joined several business-oriented social networking sites, created profiles that emphasized his extensive experience, developed a large network of online contacts, and implemented a regular follow-up strategy. With time and perseverance, his networking strategy paid off. In three months, he started a new job at a much higher salary than his previous position offered.

The good news is that Seth's story isn't uncommon. Millions of professionals have posted profiles on social networking sites, and many of them have advanced their careers through their participation on these sites. Major companies such as Microsoft, Google, Yahoo!, CBS Television, Amazon, Toyota, American Express, and many others use social networking sites to recruit employees.

Major companies... use social networking sites to recruit employees.

Try using only the job search techniques of years past, and you'll quickly discover one thing: These techniques simply don't work in today's competitive hiring environment. If you haven't looked for a job in a while, welcome to Job Search 2.0, in which your online activities—both positive and negative—have a major impact on your future career prospects.

Job Search 2.0 refers to tapping the power of the web to find the job of your dreams. This goes beyond merely searching online job sites such as Monster (www.monster.com), HotJobs (www.hotjobs.com), or The Ladders (www.theladders.com); job search engines such as Simply Hired (www.simplyhired.com) or Indeed (www.indeed.com); or matching services like JobFox (www.jobfox.com). It encompasses developing a strategic plan that considers all that the web has to offer, including personal branding, social networking, and more. In other words, it adds a whole new dynamic to the job search process.

If you looked for a job before the web became a daily part of life, you probably remember the old rules of the job search, including creating a traditional printed resume, responding to printed job ads, mailing resumes to employers and recruiters, and attending in-person networking events.

Welcome to Job Search 2.0, in which your online activities—both positive and negative—have a major impact on your future career prospects.

All that has changed, particularly for many professional positions. While many of the old rules are still useful, you need to focus on the new rules of the job search to kick-start a solid campaign in today's market. Supplementing in-person networking with online networking is a crucial step.

Start by participating on social networking sites frequented by recruiters and hiring managers, such as LinkedIn (www.linkedin.com), Ryze (www.ryze.com), XING (www.xing.com), and Doostang (http://doostang.com). Establishing an online presence and proactively marketing yourself online are great ways to enable employers and recruiters to find you. Also, be sure to verify that your background is Google-proof. You need to be certain that recruiters won't discover anything detrimental to your job search if they search your name on Google or any other website.

Keep in mind that the web is a great tool for researching and analyzing companies, trends, recruiters, and salaries. Even 15 years ago, you had to do this the hard way, by going to libraries, sifting through magazines, and combing the phone book for far less information.

There are two approaches to making job contacts through social networking. One is to create a compelling profile and wait for jobs to come to you. If your skills and experience are in demand, you could be surprised by the number of recruiters who contact you directly, even with this passive approach. Recruiters at major companies such as Microsoft, Yahoo!, and Google are known to review profiles at sites such as LinkedIn and make direct contact with prospective employees, often for lucrative positions.

But the passive approach leaves your success primarily in the hands of others. If you're actively seeking new employment, you need a more proactive strategy. Instead of taking the "wait and see" approach after creating a profile, focus on developing your network.

If you're not an assertive networker, you need to move beyond your comfort zone and reach out to your new contacts. For the reluctant networker, this can be difficult, but many people who fit into this category find that online social networking is easier for them than in-person networking. Start small and begin with contacts you actually know, such as current and former colleagues or former classmates. Then grow your network from there. It's also easier to start with contacts who have actual job openings, such as recruiters. These people are generally eager to hear from prospective applicants with the right skills.

If you're interested in working for a company that doesn't have active openings, or you want to find an inside contact before you apply, you need another strategy. On LinkedIn, for example, you can request to connect directly with thousands of potential key contacts, such as actual hiring managers. Although most are open to hearing directly from candidates, others are not. To be sure, review potential contacts' LinkedIn contact settings where they can specify that they're interested in receiving inquiries from job candidates.

Another important thing to remember is that although the web is important in today's job search, you have to move beyond the web to be truly effective. The best job search campaign integrates online social networking with traditional networking and requires perseverance. You still need to get on the phone, have lunch with your (local) networking contacts, and transition your best online contacts to real-world contacts. Active participation and follow-up are key—whether you're networking online or off.

TRUTH

10

Throw away your traditional resume

In the era of Job Search 2.0, with its emphasis on web-based recruiting and networking, a traditional resume simply won't do. It's not that paper-based resumes are no longer used; they just aren't what will get you in the door at most companies. If you're using social networking as a job search strategy, you need a resume that's designed to work with this strategy.

Today's resumes take on multiple formats, and savvy job seekers should have versions of their resume in each format.

The first type of resume format is the printable resume created in Microsoft Word or a similar word processing program. You can also save your resume as an RTF file or convert to an Adobe PDF file to maintain formatting across platforms. This is an offshoot of the traditional resume, a resume designed to be printed, snail mailed, or emailed to recruiters who ask for resume attachments.

> In the era of Job Search 2.0, with its emphasis on web-based recruiting and networking, a traditional resume simply won't do.

Don't go overboard on formatting your print resume, however. Although it's tempting to use all the design capabilities of your word processor, it's usually a good idea to follow a simple, clean format. The selective use of bullets, bolding, and italic can enhance your resume, but try to avoid flashy design, colors, or complex formats unless you're looking for a job in a creative profession that requires you to demonstrate your creative skills.

Plaintext is another resume format that you'll need. Converting your formatted resume to plaintext is critical if you're job hunting on the web where companies and career sites ask you to post your resume in an online form. Although many allow you to create your resume on the site, it's best to have a text-based format ready. This ensures that you have a record of what you sent and that the content was spell-checked and proofread. (It's easy to generate typos when typing data directly into forms.) To create text that you can use in web-based forms, save your resume as plaintext and fix any formatting issues.

For example, you should left-justify your text, use capitalization (sparingly) to replace text that formerly was emphasized with bold or italics, and replace bullets with double dashes or asterisks.

An email resume is similar to a plaintext resume, but it often requires some extra adjustments to ensure that it displays properly when received. To avoid problems with lines that don't wrap correctly, aim for no more than 65 characters per line.

If you plan to email your resume, test your formatting first. Send a copy to your main email address as well as to any web-based email accounts you have, such as Gmail, Yahoo! Mail, or Hotmail. If you discover formatting flaws, fix them before emailing numerous resumes to recruiters or employers.

If you need some help with the technicalities of online resume formatting, refer to a good resume book published within the past few years. Some suggestions are *Resume Magic: Trade Secrets of a Professional Resume Writer*, 3rd Edition, by Susan Britton Whitcomb or *The Complete Idiot's Guide to the Perfect Resume*, 4th Edition, by Susan Ireland.

The resume format isn't the only thing that's different when conducting a web-based job search. Choosing targeted keywords to include in your resume text is critical if you want the right people to find your online resume or profile. Keywords are also important if your resume is in any kind of searchable database.

If you're seeking a position in medical sales, for example, keywords such as *sales*, *medical*, *healthcare*, and *pharmaceutical* should generate good results. If you're a PR manager, keywords such as *PR* and *public relations* are obvious, but you should also include those that pertain to any relevant specialties, industries, professional associations, or certifications. For a PR manager who specializes in food and travel, belongs to the Public Relations Society of America, and holds the APR designation,

> Choosing targeted keywords to include in your resume text is critical if you want the right people to find your online resume or profile.

additional keywords could include *food, travel, PRSA,* and *APR.* IT experts should include all software, platforms, and programming languages they know as keywords, such as *Oracle, Java, C++,* and *.NET.*

Certain job candidates may need to expand from resumes that consist only of words to multimedia resumes to truly showcase their skills. This creative approach works well for designers, photographers, writers, and artists, and it can be used on a website as an online portfolio.

Video resumes are also gaining popularity in certain niches. Before creating a video resume, be sure that it's a viable tool for the type of position you seek. These resumes work well in creative industries or for positions that require you to do a lot of public speaking, presentations, or training.

Finally, profile resumes are must-haves for most professional social networking sites, such as LinkedIn, Ryze, and XING. Although you can create a brief profile that's ready for reuse, it's usually better to create profiles based on the requirements and formats of each site, using your base resume for inspiration.

Keep in mind that your resume is just one component of a successful job search. It's a sales tool that's designed to demonstrate your qualifications and generate interest from recruiters and prospective employers. Your resume is just the starting point, however. You need to devote equal time and attention to the other aspects of the job search—online and offline networking, interviewing, and following up on leads—to achieve the full potential of a Job Search 2.0 campaign.

TRUTH

11

If you want to be hired,
go where people are hiring

If your social networking goal is to find a job, you need to participate on the sites where the hiring is happening. You need to connect with recruiters. This seems obvious, but many people lose out on good opportunities because they just aren't in the right place at the right time. It's a given that recruiters from major companies use social networking and online searches to find suitable candidates. Make their job easier and increase your chances of success by making yourself easy to find.

The idea of being in the right place at the right time isn't new. It applies equally to social networking as it does to in-person networking. The advantage of social networking, though, is that once you're in the right place (and you've created a solid profile), you don't really need to worry about the right time. Social networking sites make your profile available 24/7.

To establish an effective online presence, you need to create profiles on the social networking sites that cater to business professionals and enable you to network with recruiters and others in your field. For example, Catster (www.catster.com) may be your favorite social networking site, but if you're looking for a job as a financial analyst, it isn't the place to be.

Social networking sites make your profile available 24/7.

Here's a list of the top social networking sites for job seekers:

- **LinkedIn** (www.linkedin.com)—LinkedIn, with more than 19 million profiles, is a great place to network with hiring managers and recruiters. Nearly 100,000 recruiters have profiles on LinkedIn.

- **XING** (www.xing.com)—The dominant social networking site for professionals in Europe, XING continues to expand in other parts of the world.

- **85 Broads** (http://secure.85broads.com)—A career networking site for women who are graduates of a select number of universities around the world.

- **Yahoo! Kickstart** (http://kickstart.yahoo.com)—Career networking site for college students and recent graduates.

- **techTribe** (www.techtribe.com)—A social networking site that focuses on career opportunities for people in India that includes a recruiting referral service. Major Indian employers such as Oracle, Morgan Stanley, CoreObjects, and iGate recruit from techTribe.

- **Doostang** (http://doostang.com)—An invitation-only social networking site that began at Harvard, Stanford, and MIT and focuses on job networking. Companies including Credit Suisse, Morgan Stanley, Goldman Sachs, ABC, NBC, Disney, and Google have hired candidates from Doostang.

- **Ecademy** (www.ecademy.com)—Ecademy is a 150,000-member business networking site that offers numerous networking groups based on your interests. In-person networking events are also available, but these are held primarily in the UK.

- **Ryze** (www.ryze.com)—Another business-oriented social site, Ryze has more than 500,000 members and offers a number of special interest networks.

Although not true social networking sites, ExecuNet (www.execunet.com), NETSHARE (www.netshare.com), and TheLadders.com (www.theladders.com) are three good fee-based professional job sites that include a networking component. Also consider Spoke (www.spoke.com), an open network of 40 million professionals at 2.3 million companies, which can be a good source of finding the contacts you want.

Finding recruiters on social networking sites is usually straightforward. By taking advantage of the site's search capabilities, you can easily locate the recruiters who specialize in your profession or niche. Most are fairly open to direct contact from candidates with experience in the fields they cover. Solid search techniques can also help you hunt down key contacts at target companies, but making these connections through a common contact often yields the best results.

On LinkedIn, for example, you can use advanced search to view profiles of users whose current title is *recruiter* and who specialize in one of the more than 100 listed industries, such as civil engineering, investment banking, or human resources. Or find potential hiring managers by selecting a specific company or industry and filtering on only those who are interested in connecting with potential employees.

By developing a strong profile on the right social networking sites and ensuring that your contact information is current and accessible, you'll be on the right path to finding the recruiters and hiring managers who can make a big difference in your next career move.

TRUTH

12

Recruiters really do want to find you

A solid online presence is key to having top-notch recruiters find you, often for lucrative positions. Alexis, for example, is a recruiter for a small technology company that needs to find a new IT project manager. Although she has a database full of unsolicited resumes from prospective applicants eager to work at her company, she also wants to seek out passive job seekers for this high-profile position—people currently employed but who still might be interested in the position she has to offer.

To start, Alexis logs on to one of her favorite social networking sites that is popular with IT professionals. Alexis's ideal candidate has three to five years of IT project management experience, holds PMP (Project Management Professional) certification, and lives within an hour of San Francisco. Six Sigma certification, an MBA, and active participation in PMI (Project Management Institute) are desirable but not required.

> A solid online presence is key to having top-notch recruiters find you, often for lucrative positions.

One of the first candidates she finds is Ron. He is currently a project manager with a local company and holds both certifications that Alexis is looking for. Ron's profile includes glowing recommendations from well-respected executives in the industry. Ron looks like an excellent candidate so far. Although Ron's profile indicates that he's open to new career opportunities, he doesn't accept contact from other site members and doesn't include an external email address. It doesn't look like Ron is really that eager to hear from people, so Alexis files this for future reference. If she doesn't find a more accessible candidate, she may try contacting him directly at his current company.

Next, she pulls up Stacy's profile. Stacy is a project manager for a competitor in the same industry, which makes her a solid candidate. But her profile doesn't say much else. Alexis has no idea if Stacy has a PMP or any other certification, and her profile also doesn't provide any clue about her educational background. Other than listing her current job title and company, Stacy's profile really says nothing.

In addition, she has only a few contacts. Alexis is tempted to move on, but her industry-specific experience could make Stacy a valuable candidate, so Alexis makes a note to do more research on Stacy later.

Jason's profile is the next one that Alexis reviews. Jason has only two years of project management experience, but he appears to be a rising star in his current company. He has everything Alexis is looking for in terms of certification and education and has several good recommendations, but they appear to be from peers and not his managers. Alexis decides Jason is probably worth contacting despite having a little less experience than she would like.

She moves on to Carina, whose background looks like a great match. She has PMP and Six Sigma certification, an MBA, and solid experience. Carina also speaks fluent Chinese, which could be useful in working with offshore developers. The only problem is that, while Carina lists her current location as the San Francisco Bay Area, all of her listed jobs and schools are located in Seattle. Is Carina really a local candidate, or does she want to relocate from Seattle? Alexis doesn't have a relocation budget for this job, so she puts Carina on the "possible" list.

Alexis decides to do some additional research to find information that wasn't on the candidates' profiles on the social networking site.

First, she researches Stacy, whose profile was sparse to say the least. It looks like Stacy has given a presentation at a recent PMI industry dinner. The dinner announcement provides a bio for her that indicates she has PMP certification and an MBA. This answers two of Alexis's questions. A less diligent recruiter, however, may never have known that Stacy had these two important qualifications and never followed up with her. Alexis is impressed with the outline of Stacy's presentation and her volunteer activities with her local PMI chapter and moves her to the head of the list for now.

Next, she sets her sights on Jason, who seems to be a busy guy online. He's a member of several online groups and likes to post in online forums. This content from several years ago seems innocuous enough until Alexis discovers his page on a popular social networking site. Jason has posted several pictures of himself having a great time at several clubs and lists his hobbies as beer guzzling and partying. Alexis can't find any information about Jason's professional activities online. Although his qualifications still seem good, Alexis is concerned that Jason simply isn't mature enough for a position with this level of responsibility and moves on.

Carina appears to be active in her local PMI chapter and is involved with several local charities. These are all positive signs, but there's still one problem. All of these activities take place in Seattle, not San Francisco. Alexis still thinks Carina is a good candidate, but with relocation a concern, she keeps Carina on the possible list.

Finally, Alexis searches for Ron. He has a common first and last name, and it's difficult to find out much about him online. Several times, Alexis thinks she has found some information, but she is unsure whether she has the right person. Finally, Alexis decides to give up her online search on Ron.

Because Alexis is a proactive recruiter, she emails Carina to ask about her location and calls Ron's current company with the hope of reaching him. She soon finds out that Carina's husband accepted a job in San Francisco several weeks ago, and she is now a local resident. She also learns that Ron is interested in the position she has to offer and thought he was just avoiding spam by selecting the "no contact" option in his profile. Stacy is interested in interviewing as well. Alexis now has three quality candidates for the IT project manager role and is confident that she can make a great hire.

> # Thousands of recruiters...perform online candidate searches every day.

Thousands of recruiters like Alexis perform online candidate searches every day. If you're actively seeking a job—or even just passively seeing what other opportunities are out there—are recruiters going to find you?

TRUTH

13

It's who you know that counts...most of the time

Everyone has heard about the hidden job market—that percentage of jobs found through personal connections and not through advertisements on Internet job sites or in print publications. The actual size of the hidden job market is hard to pinpoint, but most experts estimate it between 50 and 85 percent of all positions, depending on your job level, industry, and field.

The hidden job market offers many advantages to job seekers. First, a personal referral always carries more weight than a resume from an unknown candidate. In addition, when you're vying for an unadvertised opening, your chances are much greater than if you're one of hundreds, or even thousands, who applied to an advertisement. Essentially, you're able to avoid much of your competition, which is particularly critical in a tough job market. Word of mouth is the key to accessing the hidden job market. You need to be in touch with the people who know about job openings suited to you, which requires a strong network of contacts. It's not just how many people you know, either, but the relevancy of those contacts to your job search.

> The actual size of the hidden job market is hard to pinpoint, but most experts estimate it between 50 and 85 percent of all positions, depending on your job level, industry, and field.

Although your personal contacts should be your first source for finding out about unadvertised jobs, developing an online social network can greatly expand your options and potential for success. Social networking is the ideal way to tap into the hidden job market and connect with far more people than you could ever meet in person.

Through social networking, you can reach

- Employees at your target companies, particularly those with employee referral programs that motivate them to refer quality candidates for open positions

- Hiring managers who are actively seeking job candidates for specific positions

- Recruiters with current and future job openings

- Influential people in your field or industry who have solid insight into current trends and hiring possibilities

Online social networking is particularly worthwhile if you don't have a strong in-person network. This situation is common for job seekers who are relocating, changing careers, or returning to work after an absence.

Alexa, for example, left her career as a nurse when she started her family. She now wants to return to the workforce as a sales representative in the pharmaceutical or medical field. Although she's made several contacts through local organizations, she knows she must widen her network. To do so, she creates profiles on several relevant social networking sites and begins participating in group discussions and forums related to her new profession. Soon, she starts offline conversations with several of the people she met online, two of whom have solid job leads for her to pursue.

With online social networking, who you know now becomes less important than who you're able to reach.

In addition to the obvious— contacting hiring managers directly, participating on the most relevant social networking sites, and creating a profile that attracts recruiters— here are five tips for tapping the power of social networking to access the hidden job market.

> Social networking is the ideal way to tap into the hidden job market and connect with far more people than you could ever meet in person.

> With online social networking, who you know now becomes less important than who you're able to reach.

1. Make contact with people who already work for your target employers, in addition to recruiters and hiring managers at those companies.

2. Use social networking sites as a research tool to review the profiles of candidates who have backgrounds similar to yours.

3. Take advantage of social networking opportunities with the professional associations you belong to. This pool of contacts is more relevant to your line of work, and the unadvertised jobs you could uncover are also likely to be more relevant to your career goals.

4. Don't ignore advertised jobs, but don't make them your main focus either. Focusing on sites that target your profession or using job search engines such as Indeed (www.indeed.com), Jobfox (www.jobfox.com), Jobster (www.jobster.com), or Simply Hired (www.simplyhired.com) can generate better results in less time.

Take advantage of social networking opportunities with the professional associations you belong to.

5. Get personal. If possible, meet your new online contacts in person. Some recruiters are also willing to meet with local candidates they feel are strong contenders for their current or future openings.

Remember: Who you know may definitely count, but savvy social networkers can reach almost any contact they need to tap into the hidden job market.

TRUTH

14

Following up outside your
virtual community is key

Think of visiting a social networking site as the online equivalent of attending a professional association dinner or large networking event. At the in-person event, exchanging business cards is the first step to developing an ongoing business relationship. In the online world, the request to connect is the first step.

Exchanging business cards isn't going to do you much good, however, if you never contact the people whose cards you've collected and they never contact you. The same holds true for the contacts you make online.

> In the online world, the request to connect is the first step.

The business card exchange—or online connection—is just the introduction. What you do with that introduction is up to you. Just like in real life, you may never follow up with some of the people you meet. With others, you contact them after your initial meeting and they become a part of your ongoing professional network...or even future coworkers or employers.

Even the most active social networkers don't get very far without adequate follow-up. Because developing an ongoing relationship with your online contacts is so crucial, you need to develop a solid follow-up strategy and take the necessary time to implement it.

The first step is determining the best targets for follow-up. In the world of social networking, there are three types of contacts you'll come across.

People who have a direct impact on your current job search are your most important contacts. This includes recruiters who specialize in your field, hiring managers and current employees who work at your target companies, and colleagues who share your professional background. This group represents

> Even the most active social networkers don't get very far without adequate follow-up.

your pool of key contacts—where you want to spend the majority of your time allocated to following up with your social network.

People with an interesting background but who have no impact on your current job search are another type of contact you'll come across. Although it might be easy to discount these people because they don't appear to match your current networking needs, it would be a mistake to do so. Even if you work in sales and a particular contact works in accounting, that accountant could very well have gone to school with the VP of sales at one of your target companies.

Finally, you'll meet people whom you don't want to follow up with. These are most likely individuals who initiate contact with you. Remember that you don't have to accept every request to connect. If someone's profile appears unprofessional or you just have a bad feeling about the person, don't connect. Connecting with unprofessional people can become a negative reflection on you, as others may judge you based on the people you "know"—even in the world of social networking.

The second step is the actual follow-up. For some, reaching out to virtual contacts is easier because there's no face-to-face contact. For others, this makes it even more difficult.

Here are some tips to make the follow-up process easier.

- **Create a system to keep track of your follow-up efforts and their results**—Without an adequate tracking system, you can easily forget whom you contacted, when you contacted them, and what they said. Contact management software such as ACT! (www.act.com) or Contact Plus Personal (www.contactplus.com) is the best choice for this, but you can also create a simple system in a word processor or spreadsheet.

- **Determine the right approach for each contact**—The way you would approach a recruiter with a job listing on a social networking site is very different from the way you would approach potential hiring managers or other general contacts.

- **Customize your response**—Creating a canned statement for each type of follow-up communication (one for recruiters, another for hiring managers, a third for general contacts, and so forth) can definitely save you some time. But don't send a cookie cutter message as is. Customize each one based on the unique situation and target audience for best results.

- **Get to the point**—Although you don't want to be too blunt and come across as aggressive or demanding, you also need to be clear what your request is when you contact someone you don't know. Even if you're connected via social networking, that doesn't guarantee that your contact remembers your name.

- **Remember that networking is a two-way street**—This is particularly important when you consider how you approach general contacts who aren't expecting to hear from you. Indicating a willingness to share your contacts and knowledge will get you much further than simply issuing a request.

- **Follow-up on your follow-up is crucial, too**—For example, let's say that your social networking strategy has resulted in five people requesting your resume: two recruiters, one hiring manager, and two peers who offered to pass on your resume as part of their company's employee referral program. It's been one week, and you haven't heard anything. Instead of simply sending an email asking whether your contacts received your resume, use this as an opportunity to remind recruiters and hiring managers of your unique value. With peers, don't just ask whether they passed on your resume. Ask for the name of the recruiter or hiring manager.

By implementing a solid follow-up strategy outside the world of social networking, your online contacts could soon pay off in the form of the job of your dreams.

TRUTH

15

The world of recruiting has changed forever

The Internet has forever changed the world of recruiting. Candidates for all types of jobs in a variety of industries now use the Internet as a key job search tool. And recruiters use these same means to find the best possible employees to fill their open positions. The world of e-recruitment is still evolving but, over the past decade, it has revolutionized the way large and small companies handle their staffing needs.

On the other hand, some things never change. Networking is still one of the best ways for recruiters and candidates to find each other. How that networking happens, however, has also evolved over time. Online social networking is now the tool of choice for many recruiters eager to find the candidates they simply can't reach using their own personal network. A joint survey conducted by the Human Capital Institute (HCI) and ExecuNet found that 62 percent of recruiters feel that networking is the best way to source senior-level candidates. Nearly 70 percent of managers selected networking as their top job search tool.

> The Internet has forever changed the world of recruiting.

Today's major recruiters use a variety of online tools to target and hire the best candidates. E-recruitment goes far beyond online job sites and emailed resumes. It's a way of embracing the collaborative nature of Web 2.0—tools like social networking, video, blogs, podcasts, text messaging, and more—to streamline and enhance the recruitment process.

Most recruiters understand the potential benefits of online networking as a recruitment tool. Keeping up with the latest sites, techniques, and trends, however, can be daunting, particularly for those who are time-pressed or less technically savvy. Here's a quick overview of some of the latest trends.

> Nearly 70 percent of managers selected networking as their top job search tool.

Social networking as a viable recruitment tool

Social networking is now a preferred recruitment tool. In the early days of social networking, many business professionals felt that social networking sites were the domain of the young and didn't see an initial benefit to the business world. But the world of social networking has greatly expanded to reach all demographics. Today, most recruiters understand the value that online networking can offer, and many actively participate on at least one site, such as LinkedIn or Ryze. In particular, social networking has become the optimal tool for recruiting elusive, passive candidates.

Social networking as a recruiter marketing tool

In addition to searching for potential candidates, recruiters are becoming proactive and now market themselves on social networking sites. The best recruiters develop connections with candidates even if they don't match their current search needs and use social networking as a way to demonstrate their expertise and professional reputation as a recruiter.

The growing popularity of "online Rolodex" websites

Although most of these sites lack a true social networking component, they embrace certain features of social networking, such as profiles. Sites like Jigsaw (www.jigsaw.com), Itzbig (www.itzbig.com), ZoomInfo (www.zoominfo.com), Spock (www.spock.com), Spoke (www.spoke.com), and others enable recruiters and candidates to find each other with greater ease.

The growth of software that streamlines the online recruitment process

More and more recruiters are using software that searches the Internet, including social networking sites, for potential candidates. Applications such as AIRS SourcePoint (www.airsdirectory.com) and infoGIST Platinum Recruiter (www.infogist.com) make performing a social network search even easier for busy recruiters.

Social networking as a corporate tool for employee recruitment

Corporate HR departments have also discovered the power of social networking. Many employers recognize the value of a social networking presence as a way to entice passive job candidates. The CIA and Ernst & Young, for example, both have a presence on Facebook, aiming to attract young, college-educated employees. Other companies use video as their means of communication, posting recruitment videos on sites such as YouTube. Google, the Yuma Police Department, and the CIA all use YouTube as a way to connect with potential employees.

The recruiters who profit the most from this new world of recruiting are those who are open to new ways of doing things and focus on the benefits of e-recruitment. Adapting to rapidly changing technology can be a daunting chore to some and a time-consuming passion to others, but the technology isn't what's pivotal; it's the collaboration. In essence, focusing on the increased opportunities for communication and collaboration with people you couldn't meet in the real world is what e-recruitment is all about.

Many employers recognize the value of a social networking presence as a way to entice passive job candidates.

TRUTH

16

The best candidates are often the ones who aren't looking

Recruiters love passive job candidates. Even though they may be harder to reach than the active candidates flooding recruiters' mailboxes with resumes, there is a certain cachet of recruiting top talent away from competitors.

A passive job candidate is one who is currently employed and not actively seeking employment, yet is still willing to consider other opportunities. According to a survey of more than 3,000 experienced professionals conducted by the employment website WetFeet.com, 36 percent of respondents indicated that although they were currently employed, they would be open to changing jobs in the next six months. Another 9 percent were employed and actively looking, and 2 percent were unemployed and actively looking. In essence, a recruiter's pool of possible candidates equals roughly half the potential workforce.

The Internet has lessened the challenge of reaching passive candidates over the past 10 years, and business-related social networking sites have played a substantial role in easing this access.

According to the WetFeet.com survey, passive candidates learn about potential employers in four primary ways:

The Internet has lessened the challenge of reaching passive candidates over the past 10 years.

- 73 percent through their personal networks, including online social networks

- 30 percent from employment ads

- 28 percent from general advertising, not related to employment

- 24 percent from the news media, including TV, newspaper, and online media

The hunt for passive job candidates is both direct and indirect. Direct contact, such as a recruiter contacting a potential candidate on a social networking site, is most common.

Most people who have a profile on a business-oriented social networking site are open to hearing from recruiters about potential positions. Many, in fact, join for this specific purpose. A survey of Facebook users conducted by the recruitment firm Poolia indicated that 90 percent would welcome contact from recruiters regarding relevant job openings. On LinkedIn, users can indicate in their profile whether they are open to new job opportunities. In addition to contacting viable candidates directly on social networking sites, recruiters can tap the power of referrals. Many people pass on job information to quality colleagues, which widens the pool of passive candidates.

Most people who have a profile on a business-oriented social networking site are open to hearing from recruiters.

The UK recruitment site JobTonic (www.jobtonic.com) takes the concept of the online job referral a step further. JobTonic encourages the practice of online referrals through its affiliate program. Referrers receive a cash reward any time one of their referrals accepts a position posted on JobTonic. The site offers a widget to make publicizing jobs on a website, blog, or social networking site even easier.

Many companies also promote indirectly to passive job candidates by conducting public relations campaigns that establish themselves as the employer of choice. Dylan, for example, is the recruiting manager for a Fortune 500 firm looking to fill 500 openings in the next year, primarily with recent graduates. He creates both a group and a page on Facebook that highlight the opportunities at his firm, emphasizing career growth as well as a lifestyle that's attractive to young professionals. He posts his company's lifestyle-focused recruitment video on Facebook, YouTube, and several other social video sites for maximum exposure.

Promoting employee-friendly policies such as flexible schedules, telecommuting, sabbaticals, and other perks also piques the interest of passive job seekers. Many people are lured from good jobs to achieve a better work/life balance. According to a survey conducted by *CEO Magazine* and the PR firm Hill & Knowlton, 61 percent of CEOs surveyed felt that their corporate reputation helped to attract employees.

The web has become a primary medium for reputation development and branding for many companies. Social networking sites like YouTube offer interesting options to companies looking for

The web has become a primary medium for reputation development and branding for many companies.

cutting-edge solutions. Although many companies now post recruitment videos on their websites, others are tapping the power of viral, word-of-mouth marketing that social networking can provide.

Some sample recruitment videos on YouTube include

- **American School in Japan** (www.youtube.com/watch?v=dZ6h3W97Rlc)—A video that emphasizes both the teaching experience at ASIJ as well as life in Tokyo for English-speaking expats.

- **Central Intelligence Agency** (www.youtube.com/watch?v=fg4_MuV4MpY&feature=related)—A short clip on career opportunities with the Central Intelligence Agency (CIA), aiming to attract technically savvy spies.

- **Cisco** (www.youtube.com/watch?v=MdQ9lQ-iou8)—Employees talk about their careers at technology firm Cisco with an emphasis on emerging technologies and work/life balance.

- **Google** (www.youtube.com/watch?v=JcXF1YirPrQ)—Provides profiles of Google employees and focuses on Google's unique corporate culture, including free lunches and dinners and onsite daycare.

- **Yuma, Arizona Police Department** (www.youtube.com/watch?v=PUn6Fi3_PJ4)—This video begins with a brief introduction to career opportunities with the department and ends with scenes of officers in action accompanied by background music.

By offering both direct and indirect ways to capture the attention of the elusive passive job seeker, social networking is a key tool in the arsenal of any web-savvy recruiter.

TRUTH

17

Be your own detective: finding candidates' secrets is easier than ever

Amanda is a senior recruiter for a small specialty recruiting firm focusing on senior-level marketing and sales positions. She has been a recruiter long enough to remember when "google" wasn't a verb, or, for that matter, when web search engines didn't yet exist. But the strong expertise she has developed in sourcing and researching candidates on the web keeps her one step ahead of her less technically savvy competitors.

Amanda thinks she has found the perfect candidate for her client, a Fortune 500 firm looking for an international marketing director. While searching for potential candidates on LinkedIn, she discovers Ben's profile. Ben is currently an international marketing director for a competitor, has great references, and speaks fluent Spanish and Portuguese, which is critical to the emphasis on Latin markets that this position requires. Ben also indicates in his profile that he's open to new offers. Amanda's eager to contact Ben, but before she does so, she wants to find out a little more about him.

> She has been a recruiter long enough to remember when "google" wasn't a verb, or, for that matter, when web search engines didn't yet exist.

To start, Amanda decides to google Ben to see what she can discover about him. In most cases, Amanda either finds little of interest or finds information that bolsters Ben's desirability, such as details on professional presentations or activities. But occasionally, she finds information that detracts.

Ben has an unusual last name, which makes the search process easier than if his name were Smith or Jones. This is critical to Amanda, who needs to be absolutely certain that she has the right person if she's going to make a judgment call. Her first page of hits on Google brings up Ben's LinkedIn profile and information about his presentation at an American Marketing Association meeting. So far, so good.

But Amanda digs deeper into the search results and finds a match for Ben's name on the website of an activist group. Normally, Amanda deems a candidate's personal, political, or religious beliefs irrelevant to a search, but the activities of this particular group concern her. She visits the website and sees Ben in a group photo. Amanda has viewed Ben's photo on his LinkedIn profile, so she feels confident that it's the same person. Now Amanda faces a serious dilemma. Normally, she never considers membership in a particular group as a reason to disqualify a candidate. But few people would support a group such as the one Ben belongs to, and many would be outraged at his participation. If the information became more widely known, it could prove problematic to any company that employed Ben. Amanda decides to pass on Ben and move on to other potential candidates.

Welcome to the world of digital dirt. If you're a recruiter or hiring manager, you need to know if there's anything in your favorite candidate's background that would make you not want to hire that person. Although Google might be the name of one of the world's best-known search engines, in popular English, it's become a verb that refers to the common activity of searching for information about someone online.

According to a recent survey conducted by the recruitment firm The Creative Group, at least 50 percent of employers search for information about potential candidates online. Of these, 19 percent say that they always conduct an online search, whereas 31 percent say that they do this only sometimes. Of those surveyed, 14 percent indicate that they have made the decision not to hire based on information discovered online.

Googling candidates to dig up "digital dirt" is a way of business for many recruiters and hiring managers, but not everyone agrees with the activity. A number of privacy rights activists claim that performing Internet searches on job candidates is an invasion of privacy

> According to a recent survey conducted by the recruitment firm The Creative Group, at least 50 percent of employers search for information about potential candidates online.

A study conducted by the recruitment firm Manpower indicated that 56 percent of workers surveyed felt that an Internet search on their background was unethical.

that could result in legal action if a candidate isn't selected based on the results of such searches. A study conducted by the recruitment firm Manpower indicated that 56 percent of workers surveyed felt that an Internet search on their background was unethical.

Most recruiting experts, however, feel that the benefits outweigh the risks in such cases. Employers face more legal liability having to deal with the unprofessional actions of their employees than they do from the potential of candidates suing because they weren't hired, particularly in a job market where hundreds of applicants often vie for the same position.

The moral of the story is this: Use wisely the information you uncover about candidates. By making decisions based on business judgment rather than personal opinion, you can avoid the legal liability of hiring candidates prone to inappropriate actions as well as the legal liability of not hiring candidates who claim discrimination.

TRUTH

18

LinkedIn is the recruiter's favorite social networking tool

LinkedIn (www.linkedin.com) is by far the most popular social networking site for recruiters, and for good reason. A quick look at key LinkedIn statistics shows why. LinkedIn offers more than 19 million professional profiles, including 145,000 CEO profiles. In addition, it's expanding fast: Twenty-five new members join LinkedIn every minute of every day. LinkedIn's growth for the one-year period ending October 2007 was 189 percent, higher than that of any other major social networking site. LinkedIn is fast becoming the premier business social networking site, particularly in the United States.

LinkedIn has the demographics that make it a fertile hunting ground for recruiters, both agency and in-house. Large companies can maximize the site's potential by utilizing LinkedIn's Corporate Solutions, a program that enables companies like Microsoft, eBay, T-Mobile, and L'Oréal to bundle member communications and job postings for high-volume recruitment. In April 2007, LinkedIn introduced a browser-based project management system for recruiters and a recruitment advertising program that enables companies to reach a targeted audience on LinkedIn.

LinkedIn offers more than 19 million professional profiles, including 145,000 CEO profiles.

Although LinkedIn's free features may be sufficient for the casual user, anyone wanting to tap the true potential of LinkedIn as a recruitment tool should upgrade to a paid account with more power and features. Before choosing a plan, it's important to understand common LinkedIn terminology:

- **Your Network**—Includes your direct contacts, your contacts' contacts (two degrees away), and their contacts (three degrees away).

- **LinkedIn Network**—LinkedIn members who aren't in your own network.

- **InMail**—A private message that you can send to anyone on LinkedIn regardless of whether you are currently connected. InMail is a paid feature. The number of InMails you can send per month varies based on your type of account.

- **Introduction**—A request to connect with someone who is two to three degrees away. For example, you send a request to your contact Sally asking her to forward your introduction request to one of her contacts, Rachel, whom you want to reach.

- **Invitation**—A request to connect on LinkedIn. You can send an invitation to anyone whose email address you know, whether they currently have a LinkedIn profile.

- **OpenLink Network**—A feature that enables you to contact and receive messages from other LinkedIn members at no charge. To participate, you must have a paid account, and your target contact must be open to receiving OpenLink messages. OpenLink messages are unlimited.

The ability to send InMail and more introductions are the main advantages of upgrading your LinkedIn membership. All upgraded accounts include membership in the OpenLink Network. Your number of InMails and introductions vary based on the account you choose. The options include

- **Personal Plus**—For $60 per year, you can request 10 introductions at a time.

- **Business**—For $15 per month, you can request 15 introductions at a time and contact 3 users per month directly through InMail.

- **Business Plus**—For $50 per month, you can request 25 introductions at a time and contact 10 users per month directly through InMail.

- **Pro**—For $200 per month, you can request 40 introductions at a time and contact 50 users per month directly through InMail.

To get the most out of LinkedIn as a recruitment tool, however, you need to do more than create a profile and conduct a few simple candidate searches. You need to become a power user.

Taryn, for example, is a recruiter for a large corporation that participates in LinkedIn's Corporate Solutions program. Taryn is considered the company's LinkedIn expert and advises the rest of the recruitment staff on the best ways to maximize their investment on LinkedIn.

Taryn ensures that her own LinkedIn profile is complete and up to date so that prospective candidates feel they're dealing with a person, not an impersonal company. She also participates on LinkedIn Answers, asking and answering recruiting-related questions to demonstrate her expertise. Taryn makes the most of LinkedInsight to get a complete view of her top candidates and their backgrounds as well as Reference Search to find people who may be able to provide additional information about these candidates.

Each week at recruiter staff meetings, Taryn spends ten minutes demonstrating LinkedIn power search tips, such as pinpointing the most desirable candidates using advanced search features like keywords, location, and industry.

In addition, she's a master at using LinkedIn's project management and reporting tools. She frequently trains new recruiters in how to create project folders for each search, tag candidates, enter comments, and share data with all the other recruiters on staff. Taryn also creates for her manager customized reports that demonstrate how effective LinkedIn has become as a recruitment tool. Since positioning Taryn as a LinkedIn guru, her company has maximized its use of LinkedIn and achieved a big payoff in terms of quality hires from the site.

If you recruit professionals, LinkedIn is the place to be. Taking the time to explore beyond the basics of this growing social networking site can simplify and enhance your career and open the doors to the elusive, passive candidates you want to reach.

TRUTH

19

A social networking marketing plan is not a traditional marketing plan

If your social networking goal is to market your business, launch a product, or generate awareness for your cause, you need a plan. But not just any plan will do. You need a plan tailored to the unique nature of social networking.

If you're a marketing professional or have ever been responsible for marketing or PR duties, you've probably worked with marketing plans in the past. To succeed with social networking, however, you need to do more than just tack on a few bullet points dedicated to social networking and forge ahead. You need a comprehensive plan and strategy that analyzes

- Your target audience and their preferred social networking sites

- Your goals and how to meet them

- Your competitor's presence on social networking sites

- The types of content you can include on each potential social networking site, and how this impacts your campaign on each

If your social networking goal is to market your business, launch a product, or generate awareness for your cause, you need a plan.

- Your target audience's technical skill and adoption of social networking features

- The best way to increase sales without overt selling

- A plan for converting customers into viral marketing evangelists who promote your products for you

To get an idea of this process in action, let's take a look at Monica, the product marketing manager for an eco-friendly nutrition bar that targets women. One of Monica's goals is to develop a comprehensive social networking marketing campaign to help launch this new product as the must-have nutrition bar among a sea of competitors. Her target audience is women between the ages of 20 and 50, many of whom are health-conscious, eco-conscious mothers.

To tap the largest audience, women in general between the ages of 20 and 50, Monica decides that MySpace is a good target for reaching this vast, generalized demographic, noting that more than half of MySpace visitors are now age 35 or older. Monica's social networking marketing plan includes creating a custom MySpace presence filled with engaging content that encourages viral marketing. Her MySpace plans include

- A blog with posts of interest to women who are both health-conscious and eco-conscious

- Content about and links to two partner nonprofit organizations

- Bulletins with health, fitness, and eco tips geared to women

- An interactive game that helps women discover the true nutritional value of food they eat

- Links to discount coupons for purchasing the nutrition bars at local retailers

- Short videos, also available on YouTube, that cover topics of interest to the bar's target audience

The game Monica develops, What's In What You Eat, is the focal point of her MySpace campaign. Designed to be fun and informative, the game's content is updated every month to keep it fresh and "sticky." The game provides information about the wholesome, organic ingredients found in this new nutrition bar and emphasizes its eco-friendly packaging, but it does so in a way that makes this information an inherent part of the game and not a sales pitch for the product.

> One of the powers of social networking is that its collaborative nature makes it a natural for word-of-mouth marketing.

One of the powers of social networking is that its collaborative nature makes it a natural for word-of-mouth marketing. Monica makes it easy for the bar's MySpace friends to forward information to their friends through the strategic use of "send to a friend" links, banners, and buttons.

From there, Monica develops similar plans for creating a presence on YouTube as well as on smaller, niche social networking sites that cater to women, mothers, and the eco-conscious.

Making social networking a viable marketing platform requires a solid knowledge of how social networking works, strategic thinking, and a campaign that focuses on engagement over advertising and interaction over sales. In the end, a solid, well-planned social networking marketing campaign should deliver what it's capable of—a marketing payoff that's driven by the collaborative nature of the web.

TRUTH

20

The right kind of "socializing" can lead to big profits

The huge traffic that social networking sites generate makes many marketers see equally huge dollar signs. To be sure, any site that draws in hundreds of millions of visitors on a regular basis has the potential to bring big profits to savvy marketers. The key is understanding the right way—and the wrong way—to make "socializing for profit" a viable business model.

There are two main ways to use social networking as a business development tool. First is the advertising and sponsorship model. For certain businesses, this can be a good way to generate awareness and drive traffic to their site. Advertising on the major sites can work well if the goal is to attract a large, general audience. If the target is a niche audience, such as dog owners or moms, advertising on relevant niche sites can be even more lucrative. There are some downsides to this approach, including competition, expense, and the inundation of this type of advertising that has resulted in visitors conditioning themselves to ignore website ads. The campaign must be compelling enough to stand out from the rest.

> Any site that draws in hundreds of millions of visitors on a regular basis has the potential to bring big profits to savvy marketers.

The other way to use social networking as a business development tool is the active participation model. In this model, investment is in time rather than money. By creating a solid presence on a social networking site, you can engage with potential customers and develop brand loyalty. The main downside to this approach is that it takes time to develop the kind of presence that creates a true relationship with your customers. It's an ongoing effort as well, not something that you can do once and then ignore.

When talking about a social networking marketing campaign, the second approach is what most people have in mind. Using a comparison to the traditional business world, social networking is more like public relations than direct sales. It's what creates the buzz that makes people aware of your products and want to buy them.

If your goal is to make a lot of money through direct sales on social networking sites, think again. A presence on a social networking site that comes across as a hard sell puts you at risk of alienating your audience and driving them away. On some sites, you may even violate their terms and agreements.

Emphasize a low-key, relationship-building approach when using social networking for business purposes. That doesn't mean that you can't be strategic and focus on increased sales as one of your primary goals for participation. In fact, if you don't have a solid plan, you're unlikely to succeed. It just means that you need to understand the unwritten rules of social networking and play by them to develop that special connection with your audience that makes them buy.

> Emphasize a low-key, relationship-building approach when using social networking for business purposes.

For an example of what works and what doesn't, let's look at one social networker's experience in carrying out a social networking marketing campaign to increase the sale of his products.

Andy is a fitness trainer who creates his own line of fitness DVDs. To compete with DVDs produced by larger companies with bigger budgets and better distribution, Andy decides to generate some good buzz and word-of-mouth marketing through social networking sites. To start, he creates a presence on MySpace. He uploads sample clips of his DVDs, highlights his qualifications as a fitness trainer, and reposts the heavily sales-oriented, call-to-action web copy that's focused on driving sales on his own website. He also tries to befriend as many people as possible who share his interest in fitness.

Unfortunately, he sees little impact on overall sales. He even receives a few messages from people who tell him to stop trying to sell them things. It's time for a new approach. With a revised strategy in place that emphasizes building awareness and generating buzz, Andy reworks his MySpace presence. The new page offers a custom design geared to fitness enthusiasts as well as blog posts and other useful content of real interest to his target audience. With Andy's new commitment to posting content on a more frequent basis and becoming a truly active participant, his audience begins to grow. Andy also develops an innovative contest with valuable prizes that encourages viral, word-of-mouth marketing and additional publicity. Within weeks of launching the revised site, sales are picking up.

Andy then decides to create a similar campaign on a social networking site dedicated to fitness buffs. He also posts a number of video clips on YouTube. These videos include clips from his DVDs and a series of quick video fitness tips that become popular with the YouTube community. Andy soon becomes known as "the fitness guy" on YouTube. With his combined campaign on three targeted social networking sites, Andy's sales—and his reputation as a fitness expert—continue to grow.

By focusing on the right way to use social networking, you can definitely generate a profit. But you need to clearly understand the kind of "socializing" that really works with this medium. Social networking is about relationship building. It's an online opportunity to develop a connection with your target audience, to generate the kind of buzz that makes people think of you first when they need a product like yours, and to convert casual visitors into loyal customers.

TRUTH
21

Reaching key decision makers requires trust

Trust is key to social networking relationships, even more so than personal business relationships. In the real world, you use the power of common connections and personal interaction to help you determine whom to trust.

The easiest person to trust is someone recommended by a person you already know and respect. The more you trust the common contact, the more likely you'll trust that person's referral without question. For example, which carries the most weight: a recommendation from the vice president you've reported to for four years, or a recommendation from the woman you've been taking yoga classes with the past six weeks?

When you meet someone in person for the first time and have no common connections, personal interaction is key. Most people form a first impression of someone within 30 seconds. In this short period, your personal appearance, body language, and speech pattern are critical. Developing trust requires a deeper connection. You need time to assess what that person is actually saying, and you usually want to find out what others think as well.

> Trust is key to social networking relationships, even more so than personal business relationships.

In the world of social networking, common connections and personal interactions are important, but they lack the face-to-face impression that is often very telling. In addition, the common contacts you share may be online contacts and not people that you've known and trusted for years. All this adds a layer of complexity to developing trust online.

If you're using social networking as a way to enhance your business or career, you need to be sure that your contacts are trustworthy. Most people find this an obvious step and make efforts to check out the people they meet online. But often, those hoping to land a lucrative business deal or great job through social networking forget about their own trustworthiness. Of course, you know that you're a person who can be trusted. But do others?

Trust is a two-way street. You need to verify the credentials of the people you meet through social networking sites, and you need to

Trust is a two-way street.

ensure that your own online credentials are impeccable.

To start, you need to do several things to find the kind of business contacts you can trust—and who can help you achieve your goals.

Be in the right place

If you're looking to make business connections, focus on business-oriented sites. LinkedIn (www.linkedin.com), XING (www.xing.com), 85 Broads (http://secure.85broads.com), and Doostang (http://doostang.com) are all well-known meeting grounds for success-oriented professionals. MySpace can be a lot of fun and is a useful business tool for reaching a mass audience, but it's usually not the place you look for trustworthy business contacts. The real-world equivalent: You're more likely to find reliable business contacts at a professional association luncheon than at a nightclub or basketball game.

Evaluate a potential contact's online presence

This is the online equivalent to forming that first impression when you evaluate someone's appearance and body language. A well-written, professional profile is a good sign. A few personal details are okay (such as a favorite sport or hobby), but too much can indicate that business isn't really why this person is on the site. If you're looking for a new job, which recruiter would you trust most: one who has a detailed profile listing the type of candidates she was looking for, one who has a sparse profile that said next to nothing, or one who has mixed business information with a comment that the recruiter was "single and ready to mingle?"

Check out the company they keep

On most sites, you can see who your potential contact is connected to. Are these people you would also be interested in meeting? Someone with high-profile contacts in your industry and strong recommendations from respected sources is more likely to be someone you can trust.

Get Googling

A quick Google search can ferret out a lot of information. As you're aware, people aren't always who they say they are online. For example, if someone says that he's the VP of marketing at a major company, you can probably verify this at that company's website. If someone claims to be the CEO of Unknown Corporation and you can't find that company's website or anything online about your potential contact, there's a reason to be suspicious.

Beware of the charmers

Everyone has heard stories about silver-tongued charmers who take advantage of people with whom they've gained trust—both online and off. You need to be extra careful in doing your own due diligence if a business transaction requires you to give money to someone. Qualifications can be fabricated, and even people who went to excellent schools and worked at solid companies can turn out to be unreliable. If someone offers you a deal online that seems too good to be true, it probably is.

Trust your instincts

If you don't have a good feeling about someone you meet through social networking, your subconscious is probably trying to tell you something. Trust your gut instinct and move on.

On the other hand, if you're the one trying to gain trust, you need another approach. Here are three steps to take:

1. **Create a profile that earns trust**—Keep it professional. Links to your company website and any professional publications or appearances are helpful in earning trust.

2. **Get recommendations**—Recommendations from trustworthy people make you more trustworthy. Use tools on sites such as LinkedIn to get recommendations from coworkers, clients, vendors, and so on.

3. **Clean up your digital dirt**—Taking steps to ensure that everything on the Internet indicates you're a quality, reliable person elevates your online trust quotient. Most digital dirt you can delete yourself, but you may have to request a site owner to delete some items.

TRUTH

The $2.2 billion tip: advertising where the crowds gather pays off

Advertisers like to go where the crowds are and, on the web, social networking sites are definitely gathering those crowds. MySpace, YouTube, and Facebook are routinely among the most popular sites on the web, reaching millions of people on a daily basis. Even niche sites such as Black Planet, LinkedIn, and Gaia are demonstrating big increases in both traffic and market share. Not only are the masses visiting these sites on a regular basis, but they stick around for quite a while when they do log on. In December 2007, for example, visitors to MySpace and Bebo stayed for an average of 30 minutes on each visit.[1]

An added bonus is that all this traffic is paying off in converting social networkers to shoppers. Between March and September 2006, for example, MySpace was responsible for an 83 percent increase in traffic to shopping websites—in just six months.[2] The traffic surge doesn't show any signs of stopping in the near future either.

All of this is great news to advertisers, who are increasing their social network advertising budgets to tap the huge potential that this form of advertising offers. In just one year, worldwide online social network ad spending is predicted to increase from $1.2 billion in 2007 to $2.2 billion in 2008.[3] The key, however, is understanding what makes a social network advertising campaign successful.

In many ways, advertising on social networking sites is similar to advertising in print media. You still need to understand audience demographics, analyze readership, and create a compelling campaign that resonates with your target customers. But there are also big differences. Social network advertising requires that you make the most of your traditional advertising expertise, while at the same time be willing to think out of the box and, in many cases, take a risk on untested campaigns. To get a better idea of what the opportunities—and challenges—are, let's take a tour of the advertising

In just one year, worldwide online social network ad spending is predicted to increase from $1.2 billion in 2007 to $2.2 billion in 2008.

possibilities with some of the top social networking sites: YouTube, LinkedIn, and Facebook.

YouTube (www.youtube.com/advertise) offers five distinct advertising options. These include traditional online advertising such as skyscraper, leaderboard, large rectangle, and small rectangle banners; video ads that appear on the YouTube home page, category pages, or search pages; and InVideo ads that appear within the video content of YouTube premium partners. You can target YouTube ads by age, gender, location, and time of day. YouTube also offers less traditional advertising options that provide the opportunity to engage with customers. These include custom brand channels and contests encouraging customer involvement and interactivity.

LinkedIn (www.linkedin.com/static?key=advertising_info) offers four different types of ad placements on its site: text links as well as three types of banner ads using either static images or rich media. Like most other sites, LinkedIn enables you to target ads based on profile data. Because of the business orientation of the site, however, LinkedIn states that its profiles are ten times more accurate than many other sites' registration data. In other words, people who create a LinkedIn profile to connect with their work colleagues—or boss— are less likely to be deceptive in their profile data. Although there is nothing particularly innovative about LinkedIn's rather traditional advertising options, the site's solid demographics make it a desirable option for anyone looking to reach the professional and executive market.

Facebook (www.facebook.com/ads) launched its new advertising program in November 2007 with three main offerings. Social Ads enable you to create targeted ads by age, gender, location, or interests, purchasing through either a cost-per-click (CPC) or cost-per-thousand impressions (CPM) model. Facebook Pages represents the relationship-style advertising that's become popular in the social networking world. A Facebook page gives businesses, nonprofits, politicians, bands, authors, and more the opportunity to create a more customized presence than a traditional user profile offers. The third component, Facebook Beacon, gives businesses the power to enable customers to share their purchases and other online activities with their social networking contacts. The launch of Beacon, however, caused an uproar within the privacy rights community. One month after its release, Facebook executives issued an apology and announced that users could now opt out of Beacon entirely.

When creating your own social network advertising strategy, there are several things you can do to increase your opportunity for success. Two of the most important are thinking long-term and thinking outside the box.

Making social networking a long-term, strategic investment is crucial. People who visit social networking sites do so because of the social interaction. Customers aren't looking to be marketed to; they're looking for genuine communication—a conversation. It takes time to build up this kind of presence, and the only way to do that is with a long-term campaign that builds over time.

In addition, don't be afraid to mix it up a bit. Combining traditional display advertising with newer forms of advertising is key. Branded content, sponsorships, and contests work well in a social networking environment because of the noted fact that social networkers crave connectivity. Even though banner and text ads continue to be the most popular form of online advertising today, many users have become conditioned to ignore them or only recognize them subconsciously. Remember that social network advertising is still in its infancy. Avoid focusing on old paradigms, and instead create a new way of advertising to and connecting with your customers.

> Avoid focusing on old paradigms, and instead create a new way of advertising to and connecting with your customers.

TRUTH

23

If you don't "get" social networking, your campaign won't work

To create a social networking campaign that really generates results, you have to understand what makes social networking work in terms of human interaction and motivation. Too many people focus on—or are scared away by—the technology that's behind social networking. Or they maintain the erroneous perception that social networking and Web 2.0 are fads, targeting only the young or tech-savvy. Perpetuating misconceptions like these can hurt your bottom line.

Social networking and the collaborative web are moving mainstream at a fast pace. With nearly half the U.S. adult population predicted to participate in some form of social networking within the next three years, its popularity appears to be on a continual growth spurt for the foreseeable future. Understanding what makes sites such as MySpace, Facebook, and YouTube among the most visited on the web will help you better learn how to use this phenomenon to your business advantage. Gaining some experience as a social networking user is also an important first step before starting your own marketing campaign emphasizing social media.

To create a social networking marketing campaign that really generates results, you have to understand what makes social networking work in terms of human interaction and motivation.

The growing popularity of user-generated content (UGC), also known as consumer-generated media (CGM), is the foundation of social networking today. Social networking sites are built on a business model that emphasizes user-generated content. In other words, you don't visit MySpace or YouTube to see what staffers of these companies have to say, or to read the words of professional writers. You visit these sites to connect with other people, collaborate on ideas, and view the words, images, and videos of likeminded individuals.

Noticing this trend, *Time Magazine* named an unusual Person of the Year in 2006: you. Using the tagline "You control the Information Age," *Time* emphasized the power of user-generated content not only to control the digital world, but also to impact real-world change through online community and collaboration. Although not every social networker has such lofty goals, it's important to keep in perspective the possibilities that social networking does offer. For now, we've only scratched the surface of what's possible to achieve through this medium of communication.

The importance of understanding the impact of "you" and the reach of user-generated content in your own social networking campaigns is clear. Following are three tips for ensuring that you "get" social networking and devise a campaign that works in a social networking environment.

Personalize your customers' experience

Personalizing your customers' experience is one of the best ways to get them interested in your product, service, or cause. Customer involvement is crucial in the world of social networking. Merge your marketing message with interactivity. Engage in storytelling. Make your customers part of your marketing campaign. Solicit feedback. Involve your customers, emotionally and literally. It's no secret that contests, quizzes, videos, and personal testimonials are often more successful than traditional advertising on social networking sites. Static display advertising still has its place, particularly to reinforce your personalized message, but the best campaigns are the ones that reach out to people and convert casual viewers to loyal customers. The bottom line is that if you want your campaign to succeed, make it revolve around human interaction.

If you want your campaign to succeed, make it revolve around human interaction.

Plan for the worst

No one likes to think of things going wrong with a campaign, but every savvy marketer knows that it's better to be prepared for problems than let them take you by surprise. User-generated content clearly offers a lot of advantages. But there is one big disadvantage: You can't control what these users are saying, and it isn't always positive. Anticipating negative user content, commentary, and buzz and having a plan for dealing with it is essential.

Negativity doesn't have to come from a true flaw in your product either, such as the recent backlash about toxic toys, contaminated food, and lead-tainted lipsticks. Sometimes your campaign starts the controversy: an ad that's too overtly disguised as pure content or a video that offends certain people. Some marketers actually strive for campaigns that generate controversy, however, using the old "there's no such thing as bad publicity" philosophy. This may generate buzz, but you have to ask yourself whether the benefits are worth the possible damage to your company's reputation.

Inspire evangelism

Customer-evangelists can be your greatest assets. The trick is to inspire your customers to become such huge fans that they willingly spread the good word about your products and services to their friends, colleagues, and acquaintances—for free. First, you need to have something worth raving about. Then you need to create a campaign that engages your customers to the point that they're eager to start spreading the word. Finally, make it easy for them to do so with viral videos, widgets, send-to-a-friend links, and more tools readily available for them to use. It sounds simple enough, but it takes solid strategy and execution to make it work. Converting viewers to buyers to loyal customers to customer-evangelists should be the ultimate goal of your social networking campaign—the effort is well worth the ultimate payoff.

TRUTH

24

Marketing to the MySpace generation is different

You'll often hear that marketing to the "MySpace generation" is different. Today's Generation Y, encompassing individuals born between 1980 and 1995, represents an era of teens and young adults who grew up with technology and are among the most avid users of social networking. Although young, this large segment of the population, alternatively referred to as Echo Boomers or Millennials, has huge spending power: $200 billion per year.

The fact that Generation Y represents a distinct category of consumers is clear. Industry analysts publish frequent reports on how best to reach this target demographic, and entire research firms are devoted to helping their customers access this coveted market. But it's important to put things into perspective before creating a special campaign dedicated to a single target audience based solely on age.

The popular term "MySpace generation" is a major misconception. It's actually a misnomer. More than half of MySpace's audience is now over 35; two-thirds is over 25.[1] Thinking that social networking revolves only around those under 35 or 25 would be a huge marketing mistake. But Generation Y does use social networking differently than older users. Typical Gen Yers, particularly those from a background that's middle class or above, tend to run their lives online. MySpace or Facebook are more than just a place to visit on occasion. They're where they live their online lives.

> The popular term "MySpace generation" is a major misconception.

This is in stark contrast to older users, who tend to focus on tasks when visiting social networking sites. Although they, too, may enjoy the social aspects of social networking, often their primary goal is to complete a task such as find a job, promote a cause, find an answer to a question, or market their business.

That said, there are several "truths" about the Generation Y market that can help ensure your campaigns targeted to them are as successful as possible. Because today's youth audience uses social networking in a different way, the way you market to them online also needs to differ.

Generation Y represents a wide, diverse audience

With Gen Y, you're dealing with a wide age range and a generation of diversity. Although certain trends transcend this entire generation, there are also many niche segments based on sex, geographic location, ethnicity, personal interests, and further age segmentation. There is a big difference between the tastes and preferences of a 13-year-old girl in suburban Kansas and a 27-year-old Tokyo hipster. Although there are a lot of commonalities, Gen Y marketing is clearly not aimed at a one-size-fits-all audience. For example, if your target audience is under 18, you need to take into consideration certain legal requirements that aren't an issue with an older Gen Y audience.

Because today's youth audience uses social networking in a different way, the way you market to them online also needs to differ.

Young adults are technology-driven

Growing up in a web-based world has made Gen Y more technically sophisticated than their predecessors. This is the generation that uses computers, digital cameras, iPods, text messaging, cell phones, instant messaging, and more as an integral part of daily life—and does so with ease. It's no wonder that Gen Y recently named technology firm Apple its most trusted brand.[2] With technology so inherently a part of who they are, they "get" social networking, and so should you if you want to market to them successfully.

Young adults like multimedia

Most young adults today don't remember when the Internet was a text-based medium. They grew up with the web. Interactive, multimedia content such as audio and video is how they've always defined their web experience, and they're among the most frequent creators and consumers of multimedia online. To attract the youth market, you need to engage—and entertain—them with interactivity.

Generation Y is socially conscious

Gen Yers are big fans of cause marketing. Nearly 70 percent consider the social and environmental track record of a company when making shopping decisions. And almost 90 percent are likely or very likely to switch brands if a new brand is associated with a good cause.[3] A social networking campaign that merges marketing message with social responsibility is clearly one more likely to resonate with a young audience.

Young adults are flocking to virtual worlds

Virtual worlds, such as Second Life and There.com, which merge social networking with video gaming, are the latest trend among the young. By 2011, it's predicted that 20 million U.S. teens will actively participate on virtual world sites. [4]

TRUTH

25

Making them hungry makes them buy

A favorite marketing technique among supermarkets is to make shoppers hungry. Hungry shoppers, supposedly, buy more food. Smart online marketers know this as well, which has led to the creation of numerous food-related campaigns on social networking sites such as MySpace and YouTube. Although these campaigns reach all ages groups, their focus most often targets young consumers.

Social networking enables you to create a multimedia campaign that attracts the senses. No, you can't smell or taste food online, but you can certainly see it, and the right mixture of verbal and visual messaging along with strong product placement can make people hungry. That's why social networking campaigns for food products have become so popular. If you can make people hungry, you can make them buy.

Wendy's, for example, is making the most of YouTube. The company posted a short video titled "Molly Grows Up," which received hundreds of thousands of views in a short time. The video details the story of a young teen ordering her first 99-cent Junior Bacon Cheeseburger and Frosty and includes a link to an external website that contains a Wendy's menu. Burger King, on the other hand, created a MySpace campaign with a branded Have It Your Way page offering free downloadable episodes of the popular TV series *24*.

> If you can make people hungry, you can make them buy.

Food marketers are flocking to social networking sites such as MySpace, Facebook, and YouTube because they meet their target demographics, deliver an audience of millions, and facilitate the type of loyalty marketing that these companies crave.

Although all this buzz generation sounds great if you're a food marketer, there is a darker side to marketing food products on social networking sites: criticism from health professionals, scrutiny from government regulators, and even potential backlash from consumers. The Wendy's YouTube video, for example, was a big hit in terms of viewer popularity, but it received a lot of negative criticism for being a thinly veiled advertisement for Wendy's. Other campaigns have

experienced backlash for manufacturing "characters" who pose as
"friends" online. Hundreds of thousands of unsuspecting youngsters
befriend these characters who tell them how great the food is at the
company sponsoring them.

In April 2006, the Federal Trade Commission (FTC) and the
Department of Health and Human Services (HHS) released a
report (www.ftc.gov/os/2006/05/index.shtm) focused on how
food marketers can help the widespread problem of childhood
obesity through ethical, responsible marketing practices.[1] Along
with numerous other recommendations, the report urged food
marketers to self-regulate the extent to which they used paid product
placements on websites such as MySpace, YouTube, and similar
sites. The theme of the report was simple: When your goal is to
encourage young consumers to buy—or ask their parents to buy—
less than healthful foods, there must be some amount of corporate
responsibility.

Shortly afterward, in November 2006, the Children's Food and
Beverage Advertising Initiative announced a voluntary self-regulation
program supported by 13 companies, including Burger King, Kraft
Foods, McDonald's, the Hershey Company, The Coca-Cola Company,
PepsiCo, and others. Each company issued a pledge stating how it
would modify its advertising to comply with the initiative. Burger
King, for example, pledged to modify its national Internet advertising
to focus on meals that meet nutritional standards and to promote
healthy lifestyle messaging.

In spite of these initial efforts, the scrutiny continues. In May
2007, the Center for Digital Democracy and the American University
released a joint report detailing how food marketers' use of the latest
Web 2.0 technologies such as social networking, instant messaging,
and mobile phones is still increasing youth obesity and poor
nutrition.[2] The report, titled "Interactive Food & Beverage Marketing:
Targeting Children and Youth in the Digital Age" (www.digitalads.
org/home.php), documents the online marketing techniques that
firms like Burger King, Wendy's, McDonald's, and others have used
to increase sales and the health consequences of these successful
campaigns.

The report authors forwarded their finding to the FTC and HHS to provide additional support to those organizations' joint research into the impact of food marketing on childhood obesity, which will undoubtedly prompt further repercussions, recommendations, and regulations, not to mention a flurry of publicity.

The message to take home from all this? Practice responsible marketing and advertising—online and off. Even if you aren't a marketer of fast foods or snacks, there is a lesson to be learned. It's clear that the right social networking campaign can yield a powerful and persuasive message, one that encourages viral marketing and generates product demand—and sales. But what defines the distinction between advertising and entertainment? Or between product placement and pure content? To some, it's quite clear; to others, it's still a bit fuzzy.

> What defines the distinction between advertising and entertainment? Or between product placement and pure content?

This bottom line is corporate responsibility. Be genuine with your customers. Be creative, but don't be deceptive. Customers want to do business with a company that they can trust. By practicing socially and ethically responsible online marketing, that company can be yours.

TRUTH

26

Viral videos are for business, not just fun

Viral videos sell airline tickets, athletic wear, software, food, DVDs, and a whole lot more. Incorporating video into your social networking campaign can generate the kind of media buzz, not to mention website traffic, that catapults your campaign and greatly increases your profits—if you do it the right way.

In November 2007, 75 percent of U.S. Internet users viewed an online video, with 2.9 billion video views just on YouTube.[1] That audience alone makes YouTube a viable marketing tool for those who know how to take advantage of what it has to offer. Savvy marketers are making millions from viral YouTube campaigns.

Southwest Airlines, a low-cost airline based in Dallas, Texas, is just one example of a major corporation that designed and implemented a successful YouTube marketing campaign. In late 2006, Southwest launched a YouTube contest called Wanna Get Away in which it invited customers and employees to submit 20-second videos emphasizing the theme "Wanna Get Away." Southwest further engaged its customers by enabling public voting both on its website and on YouTube. The winning entry was aired on national TV, and travel prizes were awarded to the top three entrants, further encouraging participation. Although the contest is over, you can still view the winning videos at the contest site (www.southwestwannagetaway.com).

> Savvy marketers are making millions from viral YouTube campaigns.

The Southwest campaign wasn't the most innovative viral marketing campaign ever created, but it succeeded in several ways. It engaged its target audience, generated buzz through word-of-mouth marketing, offered enticing incentives, and delivered an enjoyable end product (the videos themselves). On top of that, it kept costs low by incorporating user-generated content.

Southwest is one of many companies turning to YouTube to market their products or generate positive publicity for their company. Oprah Winfrey, Cingular Wireless, the National Hockey League, and the British Royal Family, for example, all employ YouTube viral video campaigns for marketing and publicity.

When considering the idea of a viral marketing campaign on YouTube or related social video sites, note that you can do several things to increase your chances of success.

Start with a killer concept

It all starts with a concept, preferably one that will have the whole world talking about your video and rushing to buy your products. You can run contests such as Southwest did, become a YouTube content partner, or—if your budget is tight—simply create your own YouTube channel for free. The key is to spend as much time creating your concept as you do implementing it. With the number of videos on YouTube growing every day, you need a way to leap over your competition and demand attention. The right video, promoted in the right way, can do that.

Think outside the box, but not too far outside the box

Whether you're running a contest on YouTube or simply creating a YouTube channel to promote your brand, you need to stand out from the crowd. There is no one best way to do this. A lot depends on the risks you're willing to take and the willingness of your target audience to embrace risky videos. Sure, outrageous, bizarre, and truly off-the-wall videos will always draw attention. When it comes to online video, being controversial is more likely to generate buzz and media coverage, but you need to be aware of the potential backlash. It's great to garner numerous media headlines and have thousands of people around the world sending links of your videos to their friends, but make sure that all this buzz is consistent with your company image. The old saying, "There's no such thing as bad publicity" no longer rings true, if it ever did.

> When it comes to online video, being controversial is more likely to generate buzz and media coverage, but you need to be aware of the potential backlash.

Remember the bottom line

To be successful, you need to think big picture and bottom line. Creativity is great and is a necessary component of any viral video campaign, but getting people to watch your videos or enter your video contest isn't enough. You need a strategic plan that ties your campaign to bottom line results. In other words, you need more than just a fun video or contest. You need something that translates into sales, converting video viewers into buyers. Your videos need a call to action; you need to ask viewers to visit your site or buy from you, but in a way that doesn't overshadow the entertainment or informational value of your video.

Engage your customers

Engaging your customers is critical if you want a winning campaign. Whether you engage them through the content of your videos or through their own participation, you need to connect with your audience if you want them to take the desired action: presumably to buy your product or service. Remember that online video isn't just a way to communicate to your customers; it's a way to communicate with them. In essence, it's a dialogue with your customers. Involving them in the process is an even stronger way to encourage participation. The idea of user-generated content isn't new, but combining it with an enticing contest doubles the benefits. Your customer engagement increases while your costs decrease.

Get viral

For a campaign to truly succeed, you need to go beyond YouTube. Yes, it generates billions of video views, but still, not everyone in your target audience is going to search YouTube. You need to pursue them, not just wait for them to find you. Fortunately, there are several easy ways to encourage word-of-mouth marketing. Promote your videos or YouTube campaign on your own website and blog, during podcasts, in your e-zine, in press releases, and so on. Also, post or link to your videos on other sites such as MySpace, Facebook, Twitter, and others. Encourage the people who do see your videos to become evangelists for you by sending links to their friends and submitting your videos to their favorite bookmarking sites. Buzz builds buzz, and soon your viral campaign will take on a life of its own, but only if you get it started.

TRUTH

Corporate social networking
has arrived

The era of Enterprise 2.0 and the collaborative corporation is here. Today's connected world and the demands that go along with it are driving corporate interest in social networking, wikis, blogs, and other collaborative tools. And for good reason. Corporate social networks fulfill a myriad of business requirements—creating a collaborative work environment for teams around the globe, engaging directly with customers, improving employee morale, and much more.

A viable social network, however, requires a lot more than just moving the functionality of a site such as LinkedIn or Facebook to your corporate intranet. It's all about community—among your employees, customers, and partners. Corporate social networking offers several distinct benefits.

The era of Enterprise 2.0 and the collaborative corporation is here.

Improved knowledge management and sharing

Knowledge is key in today's corporate environment. The distribution of the workforce across the globe, however, makes it hard for teammates to share information. Gone are the days when all the employees participating on the same project worked side-by-side in the same building. Today, a work team could be composed of staff in San Francisco, London, and Bangalore, with little, if any, work time overlapping. A corporate social networking solution helps make sharing information and ideas across the globe easier, faster, and more reliable.

Enhanced employee communication and retention

Social networks link employees, fostering greater camaraderie. In addition, social networking enables senior management to communicate and connect with employees, keeping them up to date on what's going on. Lack of communication from senior management is a common employee complaint, and even if corporate executives can't meet everyone in person, their use of social networking can personalize their message far more than a static email.

Increased business development

Corporate social networking doesn't just reach employees; it also reaches out to customers. More and more, today's customers want to feel a connection with the companies they buy from. You no longer can just sell to your customers; you need to engage them.

It's all about community— among your employees, customers, and partners.

You might assume that younger companies less rooted in traditional technologies would adopt corporate social networking more readily than established corporations, but corporations such as IBM, Oracle, JPMorgan, Dow, and Deloitte are among some of the early adopters.

Although corporate social networking is still in its infancy, both IT and business professionals are warming to the concept. Gartner Research rated social software as one of the top ten strategic technologies for 2008.[1] According to Gartner, companies will increasingly turn to social software solutions to augment their existing collaboration tools, bringing about innovation, consolidation, and competition within the industry. In fact, it estimates that social software will be the biggest workplace technology success story of the coming decade, as more than 30 percent of corporations will create MySpace-style social networking to foster collaboration among employees, partners, and customers.[2]

Anticipating this coming trend, many companies have introduced or are developing software for the collaborative corporation. Interesting offerings include

- **IBM Lotus Connections** (www-306.ibm.com/software/lotus/products/connections)—Social software that enables your staff to create profiles, communities, blogs, bookmarks (called dogears) and group activities, integrated with IBM's already popular Lotus Notes and Lotus Sametime email and instant messaging applications.

- **Neighborhood America** (www.neighborhoodamerica.com)—
Companies using Neighborhood America solutions include
Reebok, adidas, CBS News, Comcast, HGTV, and Kodak. HGTV
selected Neighborhood America to create an enterprise social
network for design enthusiasts called Rate My Space (http://
ratemyspace.hgtv.com). Within 15 weeks, the community had over
20,000 members, received millions of page views, and generated
a profit in little more than three months.

- **SelectMinds** (www.selectminds.com)—With clients such as
Dow, Lockheed Martin, and JPMorgan, SelectMinds offers a suite
of niche social networking solutions including AlumniConnect,
EmployeeConnect, NewHireConnect, and InternConnect.

- **Socialcast** (www.socialcast.com)—Combines traditional
employee intranet functionality with social networking features
such as profiles, comments, and collaboration in a highly
customizable solution.

- **Visible Path** (https://www.visiblepath.com)—Offers internal
corporate social networking solutions for large to mid-sized
companies as well as a partner solution that enables you to
integrate social networking into your own sites, services, and
software.

Obviously, there are a lot of options to choose from, with more on the
way. But the key to successful corporate social networking is strategy,
not technology. There are many questions to ask yourself before
making the strategic decision to implement a social network. Why do
you want to implement this social network? What can it achieve that
your existing systems cannot? How will it affect your bottom line?
Have you considered all security and legal issues to avoid the leaking
of proprietary information? What impact will it have on customer
relationship management and business development? With solid
answers to these questions and others, you'll have the
foundation for a successful corporate social networking
implementation.

TRUTH

28

You need to embrace the virtual water cooler

It's commonly known that you can often get the best information from your informal networks. "Water cooler gossip" is more than just a cliché. Most people get a lot of good information through those informal chats with teammates in the kitchen or hallways, exchanging ideas about current projects, sharing news across departments, and just experiencing camaraderie among colleagues. This informal connection to others can be crucial to your success at your company, both strategically and politically.

But the organizational structures at most companies today don't always revolve around a team of employees working in the same office. Many work teams are now composed primarily of people who may have never met face to face. For geographically dispersed work teams like these, web-based collaboration tools such as social networking are quickly becoming the new water cooler.

Kate, Ravi, Nadine, and Donovan, for example, are all product managers recently assigned to create business requirements for a new global compensation product that their company, a large software firm, plans to introduce to the market during their next release. Kate and Donovan met briefly at a conference a few years ago, but neither has met Ravi or Nadine, and none of them have worked together before.

> For geographically dispersed work teams like these, web-based collaboration tools such as social networking are quickly becoming the new water cooler.

Fortunately, their company just implemented a new internal social network to supplement the basic collaborative features available on its existing intranet. The new system takes its current collaboration tools a step further, offering employees the ability to create detailed profiles and blogs, provide commentary on each other's work and ideas, share bookmarks of useful web content, collaborate using common work areas, and integrate their new environment with their existing email and instant messaging tools.

Kate, located at the company headquarters in Seattle, knows the IT project manager responsible for implementing the new social network and thinks this tool will greatly facilitate her work with Bangalore-based Ravi, Nadine in Paris, and Sydneysider Donovan. They're scheduled to have a kick-off conference call at 11 PM Pacific time the following week, but doing all their collaboration during ill-timed conference calls will soon take a toll, Kate feels, particularly with a project estimated to last several months. She sends an email to her new colleagues to suggest using the new social network as their primary collaboration tool. All respond favorably by the next day, so Kate sets up a secure project area for them to store common work documents, as well as a blog for them to post ideas about the project and provide commentary.

Donovan is eager to use the social network to make it easier to work with his new global team. He starts by reviewing the profiles of his fellow product managers. He hates to admit it, but he doesn't remember Kate from that conference in Boston several years ago. But when he looks at her profile photo, he suddenly recalls the American woman with the long, dark hair whom he met at a customer presentation. With the detailed background data the profiles provide, Donovan feels like he's beginning to get to know his new team. He adds some posts to the blog about the brainstorming sessions they held locally in Sydney and awaits his colleagues' replies.

Ravi is new to the company and is eager to develop rapport with his teammates. As the youngest and least experienced member of the team, he's also eager to validate his contributions. He replies to Donavon's blog posts with commentary of his own and shares some of his favorite articles and content on the latest trends in global compensation through shared bookmarks and uploaded content. He also starts a side conversation with Donovan, an industry veteran with more than 20 years of experience, who mentors Ravi on how the industry works and the best ways to succeed.

As their work progresses, the team discovers that they need information from their peers in other countries, as well as other compensation experts throughout the company. Previously, they would have handled this the old-fashioned way: calling varied contacts until they finally found the people who had the answers they needed. But with the detailed profiles that the new social networking system offers, Nadine is able to do a search for the key contacts who have the knowledge they're looking for. In addition to obvious resources, such as people who are currently involved with compensation at the company, she finds employees who have relevant previous experience that wouldn't be obvious based on their current positions. Some of these contacts turn out to have the most useful information, and Nadine invites several to participate in their online community, further benefiting from the wider pool of resources that the new internal social network offers. The team is soon making much faster progress than they ever imagined.

Scenarios like these are frequent occurrences in companies that offer their staffers internal social networking tools. If your company has an internal social network, the key to making the most of this tool is quite simple—use it. As with any social network, it's easy to set up a profile and then do nothing. Instead, take the time to learn about the features that your company's network has to offer, and think out of the box in terms of how it can make your life easier and more productive. In today's increasingly global workplace, extending your network beyond your local colleagues isn't just a good idea; it can be a critical factor in your future success.

The key to making the most of this tool is quite simple—use it.

TRUTH

29

You can get something for nothing: free, open-source social networks

Tony and Emma are colleagues at a large company in Colorado who yearn to start their own small business focusing on their true passion: skiing. Emma, a senior product manager, is the visionary of the two and came up with the idea of a social networking site for skiers. Not only could they create a fun, friendly community for fellow skiers, they also could profit from the venture by selling ski-related products, travel packages, sponsorships, and advertising. There's only one problem: They don't have much money to spend on their venture.

Tony works as a Java developer and is eager to use open-source software such as Ruby on Rails, Joomla, Drupal, or PHPizabi to develop their social network. Open-source software, which is freely distributed, is a viable option for those with great ideas but limited capital. By providing a free alternative to custom social networking development, open-source software is leveling the social networking playing field.

Tony and Emma also consider free hosted alternatives such as Ning, but they eventually decide that Ruby on Rails (www.rubyonrails.org) is the best choice for the custom network they want to create. It also offers them room to grow, up to millions of users—if their online ski haven becomes a big hit.

> Open-source software is leveling the social networking playing field.

An ambitious duo, Tony and Emma hope to eventually attract venture capital funding as soon as their site is stable and they have a solid number of users. The fact that a number of Rails-developed niche social networking sites have had good success in raising venture capital funding is a good sign to them.

While Tony focuses on learning the Rails development environment, Emma does some market research. Looking for inspiration, she checks out some other niche social networking sites built with Ruby on Rails that have successfully merged personal passion with profits:

- **YFly** (www.yfly.com), an entertainment-oriented social networking site for Generation Y (people born between 1980 and 1995). Features include user and celebrity profiles, video and music sharing, personalized media players, and SmackTalk, an innovative feature that offers the ability to morph your own photo into a talking web-based character with messages you can send to friends.

- **Curbly** (www.curbly.com), a design community for do-it-yourself designers. Users can share photos of their own design projects, interact with other do-it-yourselfers, and get information and inspiration for additional home design projects.

- **GHive** (www.ghive.com), social networking for surfers. Surfers mingle with other surfers, create their own customizable sites, share photos and videos (including integration with YouTube), view the location of local events through an integration with Google Maps, and more.

- **WineQ** (www.wineq.com), an online wine club. Wine lovers can meet online, share their wine experiences, and shop for—what else—wine.

Inspired by what she sees, Emma starts on the must-haves for their site: skier profiles, friending functionality, a forum, member blogging, groups, photo sharing, and product recommendations. She would also love to include video sharing, mapping, and other sophisticated multimedia features, but Tony advises her to consider those as enhancements for the future. Emma knows that multimedia-enhanced niche social networks are the wave of the future and is eager for the time when they can add those desired features.

As Tony develops their site based on Emma's specifications—as well as his own input—Emma creates a marketing plan. Because they have little cash to devote to a splashy launch or much paid advertising, Emma feels it's fitting to create a social networking campaign to promote their new site. As soon as

> Multimedia-enhanced niche social networks are the wave of the future.

their site launches, both Emma and Tony get busy on carrying out their marketing plan.

Tony creates a presence on MySpace and Facebook that includes both solid content as well as information about their new niche social network. Emma puts together a fun video from the footage shot during her last ski trip that she posts on YouTube and other video-sharing sites. A blog commenting campaign on ski-related blogs generates an additional flow of traffic. Their only expense: distribution of a social media press release that Emma writes.

Their launch is a success, thanks to Tony's programming expertise and Emma's marketing acumen. With traffic steadily on the rise and income increasing from ski-related product sales, they decide it's time to open the door to advertisers. Emma strongly recommends that they outsource their advertising. Neither she nor Tony has any experience in advertising sales and, with all the other demands of the site, this is one area she feels they should leave to an expert, at least for now.

While Emma is talking to various online ad agencies, Tony begins to investigate funding options. They would love to grow their social network from a niche site with 5,000 members to the web's premier ski community. Venture capital funding is the obvious solution to their current lack of funds, but this is another area in which neither has any experience. Tony attends a virtual seminar on venture capital basics sponsored by a small business social network and starts to make some contacts.

Tony and Emma feel confident that their growing site will expand greatly over the next few years, generating a solid income focusing on what they love—skiing. The most incredible aspect of their success is that they started it all with practically no budget, tapping the power of the collaborative social web for both product development and marketing.

TRUTH

Social networking is changing the world of online fundraising

Social networking sites are a magnet to millions, and this vast audience represents a huge pool of potential donors for charities around the world, both large and small.

No matter what the cause—children's health, global warming, the arts, or endangered species—savvy fundraisers have discovered that connecting with likeminded individuals and businesses is a powerful, low-cost way to raise funds. The numbers speak for themselves: Online donations increased more than 50 percent from 2003 to 2004, with more than 8.6 million households donating more than $3 billion online.[1]

Traditional charities aren't the only ones to benefit from online fundraising. Political candidates have also found the web to be a great place to raise funds. The top six candidates for the 2008 presidential race—Hillary Clinton, John Edwards, Rudy Giuliani, John McCain, Barack Obama, and Mitt Romney—raised a combined $42 million online during the first six months of 2007.

> Social networking sites are a magnet to millions, and this vast audience represents a huge pool of potential donors for charities around the world.

Here's a quick survey of how the most popular social networking sites are networking for good and helping charities raise funds.

- **Causes on Facebook** (http://apps.facebook.com/causes/about) helps Facebook users to raise funds for any U.S. or Canadian registered charity. Partner nonprofits include the American Heart Association, Habitat for Humanity, World Literacy of Canada, and Teach for America.

- **LinkedIn for Good** (www.linkedin.com/static?key=groups_ giving) enables LinkedIn's millions of business users to post badges for their favorite charities on their profile page. Other users can then click a badge to find out more about the charity or make a donation. Some of the participating organizations include the American Red Cross, Doctors Without Borders, Women for Women International, and the World Wildlife Fund.

- **MySpace Impact** (http://www.myspace.com/index. cfm?fuseaction=impact) is a special MySpace channel for charities and politicians wanting to connect with likeminded people in the MySpace community. Impact offers news, polls, and video as well as opportunities to donate. Featured participants include Planet Aid, New Orleans Musicians' Relief Fund, Invisible Children, and all major U.S. presidential candidates. Impact also provides channels in other countries such as the UK (www.myspace.com/impactuk) and Canada (www.myspace.com/canada).

- **The YouTube Nonprofit Program** (www.youtube.com/nonprofits) offers nonprofits with 501(c)(3) tax status their own YouTube channel where they can broadcast their cause to YouTube's huge audience of video viewers. Features include branding, an increased upload capacity, rotation of videos on the site's Promoted Videos areas, and the ability to raise funds using Google Checkout donation buttons. Participating partners include Friends of the Earth, International Rescue Committee, The Asia Society, and Youth Noise.

Several of these programs tap the power of viral fundraising, in which supporters not only make donations themselves but encourage others to do so as well by posting charity badges on their website, blog, or social networking sites. Another good choice for those looking to help raise funds is Network for Good (www.networkforgood.org/pca/ pcalandingpage.aspx), which enables individual fundraisers to quickly create a badge for one of many possible charities, integrate it into their site, and then, hopefully, watch the donations pour in.

In addition, online payment services such as PayPal and Google Checkout are making it easier than ever for supporters to contribute to a favorite cause online. PayPal has teamed up with MySpace (www.myspace.com/paypal) to

> Several of these programs tap the power of viral fundraising, in which supporters not only make donations themselves but encourage others to do so as well.

provide select charities and political campaigns the ability to raise funds through their supporters' MySpace pages. MySpace users can select from the available causes—from presidential campaigns to relief funds—post a badge on their MySpace page, and have PayPal process and distribute the funds they collect. PayPal also offers the PayPal Developer Donation Kit (www.paypal-promo.com/developer_ donations), which teaches nonprofits how to utilize PayPal for online donations. Google Checkout for Non-Profits (http://checkout.google. com/seller/npo) offers free donation processing through 2009 for recognized charities that are IRS Certified 501(c)(3). Using any of these payment services, nonprofits can collect donations on a website, blog, or social networking site.

One of the main benefits to online fundraising is that it enables smaller groups to compete with large, well-funded nonprofits for donations. In today's connected world, people care most about finding a charity that resonates with what's important to them. Because of the ease and low cost of a social networking campaign, a lot more charities are able to capture the attention of potential supporters, business partners, and contributors. This trend has also encouraged more individuals to help raise funds for their favorite charity or even establish their own nonprofit foundation for a cause close to their heart.

TRUTH

31

Networking for good makes good sense

In addition to raising funds, nonprofits are finding that social networking pays off in terms of advocacy. Social networking sites reach a worldwide audience of millions on a daily basis. Through the right mix of strategic content (news, inspirational stories, video, and photos) and engagement (participatory activities and viral marketing), charities can create powerful campaigns on a limited budget that speak to the hearts of their supporters. Social networking for good is a win-win situation.

A quick tour of some of the many charities that are raising awareness through social networking clearly illustrates that there's more than one way to use social networking as a viral marketing tool.

Social networking for good is a win-win situation.

- **OurPlanet** (www.myspace.com/ourplanet) has designed a compelling MySpace presence with more than 150,000 friends dedicated to stopping global warming. The site includes news, numerous videos, and informational tips, as well as content from other related nonprofits.

- **Friends of the Earth** (www.youtube.com/friendsoftheearth) hosted an international green film competition on YouTube to raise awareness of worldwide environmental problems.

- **Presidential candidate Joe Biden** (www.joebiden.com) highlights his social networking connections in a Get Connected box that appears on every page on his website, linking to his pages on MySpace, Facebook, YouTube, and Flickr.

- **24 Hours for Darfur** (www.youtube.com/24hoursfordarfur) developed a grassroots video advocacy campaign on YouTube. Ordinary citizens and celebrities created and posted their own short videos speaking out against genocide in Darfur. In addition to the YouTube exposure, the campaign emailed the videos to politicians and played them at a UN rally.

- **WildAid** (www.myspace.com/wildaidsf) offers an extensive MySpace presence filled with blog entries, viral marketing banners, celebrity endorsements, slide shows, shopping and donation opportunities, shareable fundraising widgets, a newsletter, pledges, and petitions. This busy site offers something for everyone and encourages participation on many levels.

- **Save the Children** (www.savethechildren.org and www. savethechildren.org.uk) uses social networking extensively as both an advocacy and fundraising tool. It maintains a presence on all the main sites (MySpace, Facebook, and YouTube) and has an innovative campaign on Second Life (www.secondlife. com). Save the Children created The Yak Shack on Second Life, where people can buy a virtual yak (yaks are critical to families in places such as Tibet) and actually donate the amount to Save the Children.

It's obvious that a social networking campaign is a must for any charity hoping to raise awareness and funds online. But there's more to success than just creating a page on MySpace or Facebook and waiting for supporters to join your cause—and for the money to roll in. You need to be strategic to succeed.

Mallory, for example, is the executive director of a small nonprofit institute dedicated to protecting marine wildlife. Although she has achieved a lot of publicity in the coastal town in which the organization is based, she would like to spread the word and receive support from people around the world. She is already an active user of MySpace, Facebook, and YouTube and feels that a social networking campaign is the best choice for reaching out to likeminded people.

Mallory has done some research into what makes a social networking campaign successful and has decided that her campaign must break away from the cookie-cutter mold of all the competing animal and environmental organizations. She also knows that inspirational stories help your supporters get up close and personal with your cause. Developing a strong emotional connection with potential supporters is a key part of Mallory's strategy.

Inspirational stories help your supporters get up close and personal with your cause.

Because she has extensive experience with videography, Mallory decides to make video a major component in the institute's social networking presence. Her first video emphasizes the plight of dolphins and combines a fact-filled voice-over narration with captivating video images of the dolphins. Mallory feels that this is just the type of video that could spread thanks to viral, word-of-mouth marketing.

To start her campaign, Mallory posts the video on YouTube and other video-sharing sites with links back to the institute's main website. She also creates a presence on MySpace and Facebook as well as other relevant niche social networks, keeping in mind to match the institute's profile with the personality of each site. To further emphasize the visual component of her campaign, Mallory posts still images of her close-up photos of dolphins and other marine mammals on all her social networking profiles as well as on Flickr. By joining numerous groups of likeminded people and encouraging tell-a-friend links, Mallory's social networking campaign starts generating strong buzz as well as media coverage.

But her goal isn't just to spread the word. Mallory also wants to raise more funds for the institute. To do so, she adds fundraising badges to each social networking profile and encourages the institute's growing number of supporters to do the same on their own sites. Within several months, Mallory's well-executed campaign is paying off. Site traffic and fund donations have tripled, all thanks to Mallory's emotional imagery shared with the world through social networking.

TRUTH

32

Get social, get elected

The power of social networking plays a pivotal role in who will win future elections, both in the United States and around the world. Today, the Internet has become as critical a medium as TV and newspapers have been in the past in reaching out to voters and forming public opinion. Welcome to Politics 2.0, a world where social networking, blogging, podcasting, text messaging, grassroots email campaigns, video-sharing, and a persuasive web presence are must-haves for any serious political candidate.

Netroots campaigns, grassroots political campaigns that take place on the Internet, aren't really new to this election. From their inception, savvy political activists have utilized social networking sites, blogs, and more as a way to spread the word. But now it's reached the mainstream. All demographic groups—young and old, liberal and conservative, urban and rural—use the web as a means of information and communication. Netroots campaigns reach beyond the United States as well. The web played a strong role in influencing recent elections in Australia, France, and other countries.

> The power of social networking plays a pivotal role in who will win future elections, both in the United States and around the world.

A 2006 study conducted by the E-Voter Institute revealed the significance of the web on political communication and campaigning. More than 70 percent of political consultants feel that the Internet is effective in getting supporter email addresses, taking surveys, motivating supporters, and raising funds. In addition, the percentage of consultants spending more than 20 percent of their campaign budget on the Internet will more than double between 2006 and 2008.

Social networking sites are becoming active in the political process as well, knowing that political content will continue to drive traffic—and profits. YouTube, for example, launched the YouTube You Choose '08 channel (www.youtube.com/youchoose), providing nonpartisan video content about the candidates and relevant issues, as well as the opportunity for site visitors to comment and submit their own videos.

ABC is providing the Facebook audience with election news, blog content, and photos, while allowing Facebook users to influence its election news coverage.

MTV and MySpace partnered to present presidential debates featuring real-time interaction between the candidates and the public, who can submit questions via MySpaceIM, mobile devices, and email.

It's clear that, to get elected, a candidate needs a strong web presence. Savvy politicians know this and are developing web-based campaigns to reach out to this vast pool of potential supporters.

Barack Obama, for example, earned nonpartisan praise for his campaign's savvy use of social networking as a means to engage voters. In February 2007, he launched his own social network (http://my.barackobama.com/). The site received positive comments from the social networking community for its design and stability and quickly became popular with voters, too.

The Obama team members weren't content with just having their own network, though. They also created a compelling presence on almost all the other prominent social networking sites, including MySpace, LinkedIn, YouTube, Facebook, PartyBuilder, Gather, MyGrito, Twitter, and iTunes. Each presence is targeted to the demographics of the site's particular audience, which helps potential voters connect with him as a candidate. For example, Obama held a question and answer series on LinkedIn that focused on start-ups and small business, key issues to this site's audience.

Although mock elections and the number of social networking contacts that a candidate has may not be the final deciding factor in who wins an election, it's impossible to ignore the widespread impact of this new means of connecting with voters. The benefits to candidates are many. Social networking campaigns

> MTV and MySpace partnered to present presidential debates featuring real-time interaction between the candidates and the public.

are relatively inexpensive, reach millions of people, and provide a more personal view of the candidates, their platform, and their personality. This impact is so great that a number of websites are now exclusively dedicated to tracking the influence of social media on the election, such as techPresident (techpresident.com).

Social networking fame isn't always good, however. Although Hillary Clinton's official Facebook profile had more than 118,000 supporters as of February 2008, the Facebook group Stop Hillary Clinton: (One Million Strong AGAINST Hillary) had more than 850,000 members. In addition, the media immediately brought it to the public's attention that Rudy Giuliani's teenage daughter indicated that she supported Barack Obama on her Facebook profile. After the uproar, the younger Giuliani withdrew from the Facebook Obama group.

It's clear that the power of the web can influence the outcome of an election. But to do so, candidates need more than a static website. They need to engage with the public on a personal level. Only by truly connecting with potential voters can candidates reach the full potential of the Internet and social networking.

TRUTH

33

Online networking is still networking

Online social networking is still a fairly new phenomenon and is in its infancy. It's only in the past few years that social networking has reached the masses and, to many, its concepts and jargon are still quite new. It's important to remember, though, that social networking is still about networking, a tradition that dates back more than a thousand years to the first time that one person's connection to another made a difference in their business success.

The platform may be different but, in many ways, social networking is still similar to in-person networking. Building relationships is at the heart of networking, whether you're connecting with someone across town or someone halfway around the world you've never met.

Online social networking may have its truths, but networking itself also carries its own set of truths that are as relevant today as they were 20 years ago, before the concept of online social networking was even born.

> Social networking is still about networking, a tradition that dates back more than a thousand years.

Let's go back in time to remember what networking was like before the web. It's 1988 and Dave, a local realtor and master networker, is busy making new contacts at a Chamber of Commerce mixer. Although Dave is sure to spend time with his current circle of friends, he always devotes part of the mixers to seek out new members. Dave knows that networking with the people he doesn't know is often more beneficial than networking with the people he does know. Dave likes to forget the old saying, "Don't talk to strangers." The right "strangers" are often the best networking contacts he could ever make. This meeting is no exception. By introducing himself to a handful of new members, he's already found a potential prospect and a lead to another, the brother-in-law of a new business owner.

Later that evening, Dave talks to a current acquaintance, Betty, about her plans to invest in rental property. She isn't ready to invest yet, but she would like to get some advice from Dave. Although he knows that she's unlikely to buy for several months, he makes a lunch appointment with Betty and her husband for later that week.

As a master networker, Dave is aware that the hour he spends with Betty and her husband, who are both influential in the community, is bound to pay back even bigger dividends in the future.

Dave is a firm believer in making his own luck and feels that luck by pure chance is often overrated.

Networking with the people you don't know is often more beneficial than networking with the people you do know.

He knows that he needs to be in the right place at the right time and make the effort to connect with others. His favorite filmmaker, Woody Allen, once said that "ninety percent of success is showing up." The mere fact that Dave regularly attends numerous networking events within his community clearly increases his chances of positive results.

Although most people who know Dave think that he's a born networker, that wasn't always the case. Dave has always had an outgoing, gregarious personality, but fear of rejection held him back initially. He's an independent guy and doesn't like having to ask for anything, even sales leads. Over time, however, he's learned to focus more on making solid connections and less on hard sales tactics. As people get to know and trust him, his referrals continue to flow naturally.

Twenty years later, Dave's son Dustin uses many of the same networking techniques his father taught him. The only difference is that Dustin does most of his networking online. He's a member of several business-oriented social networking sites and credits his active participation with helping him grow his career as a financial consultant. Dustin makes it a point to connect with new people each

Filmmaker Woody Allen once said that "ninety percent of success is showing up."

week, searching for new members that match his target client profile and reviewing his own contacts' new connections. Dustin doesn't just focus on local prospects, however. Networking online helps him find good clients throughout the country. By continually networking, Dustin maintains a full pipeline of potential clients.

Dustin also gives advice freely online, a tip he picked up from his dad. He participates on group discussion boards and forums related to financial planning, answering questions and offering his expertise. Dustin knows not to give away too much information, but he's also aware that his active participation helps to cement his online reputation as an expert in his field, not to mention his reputation as a reputable person whom others want to do business with.

Although Dustin has had good luck with social networking, he's aware that he's made a lot of his own luck just by being diligent in keeping up his participation. Dustin has a hectic schedule, but by scheduling time for online networking in his calendar, he knows that he'll always make time to keep up with this important business development tool.

Like his dad, Dustin isn't a born networker. He isn't a big fan of contacting people he doesn't know and, for that reason, feels more comfortable networking online and at in-person events where he knows at least some of the members. Despite his reticence, Dustin's business is thriving because he's willing to move out of his comfort zone. Every week he reaches out to one high-level contact he would like to make. These contacts are much easier to find now thanks to the numerous successful people who have profiles on social networking sites. Not all of them respond, but a few have become clients, showing Dustin that risking rejection can lead to great rewards.

Social networking may primarily be a twenty-first century phenomenon, but the basic principles behind connecting with other people for mutual gain were established many years ago. By blending the old traditions with the new, you can create your own perfect networking environment for today's world.

TRUTH

34

Quality counts:
more isn't always merrier

When you first catch social networking fever, you're likely to become enamored with what this collaborative tool can do for your career, your business, and your life. But remember, with social networking, quality counts more than quantity. In other words, don't sign up at every social networking site you find. Be strategic. Find the one—or two or three—that meets your goals, and focus your efforts there.

Hundreds of social networking sites exist, and more are launched every day. Whether you're looking for a general site that attracts millions per day or a niche site that focuses on a target audience, you're likely to find a social networking site that's just right for you and meets your exact needs.

Keep in mind that the type of social networking that pays off in positive results takes time. That's why it's important not to let social networking fever compel you to sign up at every site you come across. You have to invest in establishing your presence and nurturing your network on your chosen sites. Large organizations may have a staff dedicated to developing an online presence, but most busy individuals just don't have the time to devote that many hours a week to social networking.

As you research and plan your social networking strategy, you should identify no more than three top sites to focus on. If you're really pressed for time, focus on the single top site. Avoid the temptation to feel that you must establish a presence on each of the largest

> Keep in mind that the type of social networking that pays off in positive results takes time.

social networking sites. If they don't suit your needs, you'll waste your time—even on a site that draws millions a day. If you're looking for dog lovers, a million cat lovers a day won't do you any good.

By focusing on quality rather than quantity, you're far more likely to stick with your social networking campaign and see it pay off in the results you want to achieve. Efficient time management is key, even with a manageable number of sites to focus on. Here are five tips to help you make the best use of the time you devote to social networking:

■ **Focus on strategic objectives**—One hour of strategic time spent on social networking can be worth far more than ten hours of aimless surfing on social networking sites. Based on your strategic plan, focus on the areas where you're going to see the biggest payoff. This may be obvious right from the beginning, or it may take time to see where you're getting the

> Avoid the temptation to feel that you must establish a presence on each of the largest social networking sites.

best results. But once you notice a success pattern, keep up your efforts in that area. In addition, if something doesn't pay off after a while, stop wasting valuable time pursuing it and invest your time in another direction.

■ **Have a schedule**—Carve out a special time and day to devote to social networking. This could be 15 minutes every morning or a single hour on Friday afternoon. Social networking success doesn't come with a one-time effort. If you're committed to success, you must participate on a regular basis, whether it's daily, weekly, or monthly. Make your participation in social networking part of your regular calendar, just like any other business task you need to accomplish.

■ **Be realistic**—As wonderful as social networking is, it's unlikely to be the top priority in anyone's life. If you know that you're already working 70 hours a week, scheduling 10 hours a week on social networking isn't realistic. Focus on a more realistic schedule. Alternatively, if you want to make a big PR splash on several sites, a few hours a month won't generate much buzz. Be realistic in

> One hour of strategic time spent on social networking can be worth far more than ten hours of aimless surfing on social networking sites.

matching your schedule to your goals or make some adjustments to one or the other if there's a mismatch. In addition, even though a set schedule is bound to increase your chances of success, know that there will be times you'll have to deviate from it.

- **Get help**—If social networking is a priority for you or your business, but time is an issue, consider outsourcing some of the routine tasks. An assistant or intern can often handle the day-to-day activities while you focus on strategy. Or if your goal is generating buzz rather than developing a personal network, consider handing off an entire social networking campaign to a consultant. Numerous companies and individuals offer comprehensive programs that will get you up and running in no time. If you do choose to outsource, be sure to clearly articulate your goals and expectations. Remember that even if you're not doing the work, it's your name, or your company's name, that appears on these sites, and you're ultimately responsible for your own positive image online.

TRUTH

35

Online branding:
your profile is how the
world sees you

Online, image is everything. Most of the people who encounter you on the web don't know you and haven't met you, so they don't have the opportunity to form an opinion about you in the traditional sense. They don't know what your qualifications are, whether people they respect recommend you, whether you have a good sense of humor, what's most important to you in life, or anything else for that matter. Their entire opinion is based on the information they view online—on your website, your blog, or your social networking profile.

By now, you're well aware of the importance your profile carries in the world of social networking. But your individual profiles on social networking sites are also part of a bigger picture—your online brand.

Online, image is everything.

Your online brand is what drives your reputation and your success; it's how the online world sees you. Do it right, and you could achieve stellar results. Do it wrong, and your results could be minimal, or worse, you could end up with a negative reputation.

A strong, strategic online profile should answer three important questions.

- **Who are you?** People want to know the basics—name, location, profession, qualifications, contact information.

- **What do you look like?** Yes, appearance shouldn't count, but it does—both online and off. People want to know what you look like to make up for the lack of visual cues that an in-person meeting would provide.

- **What are you like as a person?** You need to be more than a static image and list of qualifications. Your profile must make you come to life and seem real.

Here are five tips for developing your own personal brand online:

Match your profile to your goals—A business profile needs to be professional, yet still show some personality. Trust is also key in business, so you should make the effort to convey that you're worthy of trust through your profile contents. Links to articles you've written, presentations you've delivered, and so forth help convey trust, as do recommendations from key people in your industry.

On the other hand, a band aiming for exposure on targeted social networking sites would strive for a totally different kind of profile. For example, Jeff is a jazz guitarist with a new CD, and his profile on MySpace, Facebook, and Bebo is cool and edgy. He doesn't want to get lost in the crowd and feels he can afford to take a few risks with a cutting-edge image to get noticed.

Make the words in your profile come to life—Your words comprise the first, and often final, impression people make of you online. You need to make these words count. This goes beyond ensuring your text is free of grammatical errors and typos. Your profile needs to answer the question of who you are and what you do, give some indication of what you're like as a person, instill trust in those who are reading it, make these readers take the action you desire, and do it in a way that doesn't come off as a promotional piece or sales pitch. If you're not a wordsmith, find someone who is to help you polish your prose. Another helpful tactic is to review your colleagues' profiles. Which ones generate a positive reaction and why?

Get visual—Today's web relies heavily on images. Static text alone is no longer compelling, if it ever was. You need visuals, and the most critical visual is a photo of yourself—even if you hate having your picture taken. Everyone has heard the expression "a picture paints a thousand words.

A successful visual image often has little to do with age, gender, or even attractiveness. People just want to see who they're dealing with. In many cases, not having a photo indicates, right or wrong, that you have something to hide or that you aren't who you say you are. Anita, for example, is a happiness coach who originally didn't post

> Make the words in your profile come to life.

a photo on her website or social networking profiles. Later, she posted a photo, but it portrayed a rather formal professional image taken during her days as a corporate manager. Anita eventually replaced that photo with a series of informal snapshots taken at her seminars. In these images, Anita appears relaxed and happy, yet still professional. Not surprisingly, her business increased with the posting of the "happy" images, which helped to further brand her as a happiness coach. Anita's online visual image finally matched the image portrayed in her text.

Show some personality, but not too much—The key here is balance. You have to humanize yourself so that people get a true feeling of who you really are. This can be a touchy area and, again, what's appropriate for one site may not be for another. When discussing your opinions and personal interests, keep your target audience in mind. Yes, freedom of speech is important, but sometimes self-editing is more important when your social networking goals relate to business and not personal enjoyment.

You have to humanize yourself so that people get a true feeling of who you really are.

Get interactive—Your online brand on social networking sites extends beyond your own profile. It also includes your interactions on other areas of the site. Get interactive, and join in the conversation on site forums, groups, question boards, and on others' profiles. Be sure, however, that your words enforce your brand and don't detract from it. The right collaboration on social networking sites can lead to a big payoff in enhancing your online reputation and in achieving your social networking goals.

TRUTH

36

Learning from the masters can make you a master social networker

In almost any new endeavor, you can get up to speed faster and easier with the guidance of an experienced pro. Social networking is no different. It's both art and science. Yes, there are certain standards and conventions to follow, and you need to understand how social networking sites work, but it is rather straightforward once you learn the basics. Making the most of your online network, however, is an art.

Many technically savvy people participate in social networking, but their level of technical skill doesn't always translate to the level of their success. To win at social networking, you need to find the right balance of technical know-how, marketing savvy, networking mastery, and street smarts.

If you're new to social networking or your social networking campaign isn't generating the desired results, turn to a master social networker for advice. There are three main ways to benefit from a master social networker: Tap the expertise of your own network, learn by observation, or hire a consultant.

Tapping the expertise of your own network is an easy, inexpensive way to master social networking. If you can find a master social networker to take you under his wing, you'll also enjoy the benefit of hands-on assistance, whether your mentor is a personal contact who lives around the corner or an online associate across the country. Duncan followed this method when his new online contact, PR executive Kyle, offered to barter his PR savvy. As an independent green building consultant and first-time author, Duncan knows a lot about green building, but he is rather "green" when it comes to PR skills and the world of social networking. His collegiate daughter, a fan of MySpace and Facebook, convinced her dad that social networking could help him promote his book and business, but neither had any experience in developing a solid online campaign.

> To win at social networking, you need to find the right balance of technical know-how, marketing savvy, networking mastery, and street smarts.

As the head of his own PR firm, Kyle has many years of expertise in developing solid PR campaigns. When the popularity of social networking began to grow several years ago, Kyle invested significant time in mastering the world of social networking and social media. He's since added online campaigns to his publicity arsenal, with great results.

Using the collaborative power of the web, Portland-based Duncan and Atlanta-based Kyle met and formed an alliance that benefited both. Duncan needed a buzz-worthy social networking campaign for his new book on green remodeling. In exchange, he gave Kyle some free advice on how he and his family could make their home more eco-friendly. Thanks to this alliance, Duncan was able to learn social networking from a master, and he was able to do it in his own network at no cost to him.

Learning by observation is another inexpensive option. If you don't personally know a master social networker, you can still learn from the masters. Spend an hour or two on your favorite social networking sites reading the profiles of others. You'll soon find the people who stand out as the leaders in their community.

> If you don't personally know a master social networker, you can still learn from the masters.

Sara tried this approach when her initial foray into social networking didn't work out as planned. Sara's goal was to locate a more lucrative business analyst position with a larger company. She joined several business-oriented social networking sites, created profiles, and waited for good things to happen. They didn't. Discouraged, Sara was about ready to give up on her social networking job search campaign. She had heard so many good things, but it obviously wasn't working for her, and she didn't know anyone who had much more expertise than she did on the topic.

But before giving up, Sara decided to take a look at what others were doing to see if their approach was different from hers. After reviewing more than a dozen profiles of other business analysts, Sara began to see a trend. Some profiles matched hers—rather basic and utilitarian. Others seemed to take a different approach. Their profile really "sold" their expertise and qualifications—without an obvious sales pitch. In particular, Sara found three profiles created by other analysts around the country that she really admired.

She decided to give her social networking job search campaign a complete overhaul. She revised her profile on each of her target social networking sites, asked key colleagues for recommendations, included links to presentations and volunteer work she performed for her professional association, and participated in forums and other community areas to showcase her expertise. Soon, recruiters started contacting Sara for the opportunities she was seeking, and her revised social networking campaign was on its way to positive results.

If your social networking goals relate to your business, you may be in the position to hire a social networking consultant. The main benefit of consultants is that they will be dedicated to your success because it's their responsibility to do so. It's hard to pressure an unpaid mentor to spend more time with you, answer your questions, or give you extensive help.

Larry is the VP of marketing at a small sporting goods manufacturer. He and his marketing team need to vie for consumer attention against their more well-known competitors and have decided an online campaign that incorporates social networking would be a great marketing tool. The only problem is that no one on Larry's staff has expertise in this area, and they can't hire any new staff members. They do have a consulting budget, however. Larry decides to spend it on hiring a top consulting firm to develop a killer campaign on MySpace and some niche sports-related social networking sites. The consulting firm also trained Larry and his staff so that they can continue the campaign after the consulting period ends. Although this option required a monetary investment, it was money well spent for Larry's company, which introduced its innovative, original campaign within six weeks of hiring the consultants.

TRUTH

37

Six degrees of separation is more than just the name of a movie

When you see the term "six degrees of separation," the first thing that comes to mind may be the 1993 film of the same name based on the play by John Guare and starring Will Smith, Donald Sutherland, and Stockard Channing. The film is credited with coining the popular term, but the concept originated in 1929 by Hungarian author Frigyes Karinthy in his short story "Chains." This story centers on the theory that the impact of modern life is increasing the connectedness of people around the globe. The characters in the story felt that any one person could be connected to any other person in the world through no more than five people and created a game to prove their point.

Almost 40 years later, in 1967, Harvard University researcher Stanley Milgram conducted a real-world experiment based on the concepts theorized in Karinthy's fictional story. In his research, Milgram asked 160 people in Nebraska to try to reach a man in Massachusetts using the fewest number of intermediaries. Each participant started by sending a package to the personal contact most likely to know the target recipient with instructions to continue forwarding the package until it reached its destination.

This small-world theory, however, wasn't just the domain of intellectuals and academics. In 1994, it took on a pop culture spin. One year after the popular film version of Six Degrees of Separation appeared, three students at Albright College in Reading, Pennsylvania, invented a game called Six Degrees of Kevin Bacon (who, coincidentally, was not in the film). The game's goal, using the six degrees of separation concept, was to link any other actor to Kevin Bacon through no more than six connections using common films as the connector. Reportedly, Bacon originally indicated his dislike for the game, but he later warmed to it as it became a pop culture phenomenon.

Today's social networking, conducted on the web, is rooted in the same concepts first discussed almost 80 years ago.

Interesting, you might say, but what does all this have to do with online social networking, and what it can do for you? Today's social networking, conducted on the web, is rooted in the same concepts first discussed almost 80 years ago. One of the earliest social networking sites was called SixDegrees.com, founded in 1997 and based on the idea of six degrees of separation.

The popularity of online social networking sites has encouraged others to reinvestigate—and reinvent—the six degrees of separation theory on the web, reaching the worlds of academia, entertainment, and nonprofits.

In 2001, Columbia University professor Duncan Watts updated Stanley Milgram's 1967 experiment for the twenty-first century using email as the delivery and contact method. Called the Small World Project, more than 60,000 people tried to reach 18 target recipients in 13 countries using only email connections (no Googling allowed). The results? The emails reached their targets in a median of five to seven steps.

In 2006, the UK gaming company Mind Candy launched the website Find Satoshi (www.findsatoshi.com) with a puzzle to solve using the six degrees of separation concept. The only clue: a photo of a man named Satoshi taken in the Alsatian town of Kaysersberg, France. The puzzle prompted participants to ask themselves the question, "Is it possible to locate a man given only his photograph and a first name?"

And in January 2007, Kevin Bacon founded Six Degrees (www.sixdegrees.org) capitalizing on his surprising fame in the "six degrees" world to help nonprofits around the world raise funds. Six Degrees focuses on social networking for social good. Partnering with the nonprofit social networking site Network for Good (www.networkforgood.org), Six Degrees

> The popularity of online social networking sites has encouraged others to reinvestigate—and reinvent—the six degrees of separation theory on the web.

enables people to create a fundraising badge for their charity of choice, post it online, and raise money. Although the goal of Six Degrees is to involve the general public, Bacon's celebrity cachet has spurred the participation of other celebrities as varied as Tony Bennett, Jon Bon Jovi, Hilary Duff, Ellen DeGeneres, Nicole Kidman, and Kanye West. In a little over a year, the Six Degrees program has raised well over a million dollars for a multitude of worthy causes.

When strategizing about the best way to tap the power of social networking today, it's helpful to think of its origins. The concept of six degrees of separation may have its intellectual roots, but they're roots that apply readily to all our relationships, whether personal or professional. It is a small world after all, and we're all linked more closely than we may believe. Social networking sites are far more than fancy, online address books or random lists of people. Used wisely and correctly, social networking is your link to the rest of the world.

> Used wisely and correctly, social networking is your link to the rest of the world.

38

Social networking doesn't happen in a vacuum

Social networking isn't an activity for the lone wolf. Yes, your experience with social networking may take place in a small room with just you and your computer, but its reach is far greater than that. Social networking doesn't happen in a vacuum. It happens in the world of Web 2.0, a world all about collaboration and interaction.

To succeed in social networking, you have to open yourself up to this world. Using the six degrees of separation concept, you know that you're approximately six degrees away from anyone else on this planet. That's a lot of "friends of friends." Obviously, you don't want to connect with billions of people, but there are those you do want to reach. Social networking is the technology that enables you to reach anyone you want (well, almost anyone). You just need to open your eyes and believe in the power of human connections.

> Social networking doesn't happen in a vacuum. It happens in the world of Web 2.0, a world all about collaboration and interaction.

Josh, a college student in California, wants to contact a famous marine biologist at a research institute in Australia whose name is Decker. Josh is interested in a career in marine biology, admires Decker's research, and would like to ask him for an internship. Of course, Josh could easily look up Decker's email address on the website of the research institute that he is affiliated with, but Josh decides that connecting with Decker through a common contact might yield better results than sending him an unsolicited request. Can his social network on Facebook really lead him to the man he wants to reach?

Josh's Facebook network doesn't include anyone in Australia, nor does it include his former marine biology professor who once worked with Decker. But Josh's contacts do include someone who has been to Australia, his high school classmate Natasha.

He contacts Natasha via Facebook, asking for help in his quest. Natasha doesn't know Decker or anyone else in Australia involved in marine biology, but she is still in touch with the daughter of the host family she stayed with in Perth. Natasha puts Josh in touch with Amy. At least he's on the right continent now.

Josh hopes that Amy may be able to lead him closer to Decker, but she is thousands of miles away from Decker's research center. To top it off, Amy is a fashion design student and has no contacts even remotely related to the world of marine biology. Suddenly, she remembers a friend in Paris whose father is a marine biologist. She puts Josh in touch with Sophie and is pleased she was of some assistance.

Josh reviews Sophie's Facebook profile and wonders how a French fashion design student is going to lead him to his target, Decker. He's not even on the right continent anymore. He contacts Sophie, hopeful that she will be the intermediary who leads him back on the right track again. Sophie responds quickly, but Josh is dismayed to learn that her father Pierre is a molecular biologist, not marine biologist. Sophie goes through all her existing contacts trying to find someone who would be a better match for Josh, but the Paris fashion diva's contacts are all in the wrong countries and wrong industries. She decides that her father may still be the best bet and connects the two.

Pierre isn't a Facebook member, but he does have a profile on LinkedIn. Josh joins LinkedIn and connects with Pierre. Despite the fact that Amy was incorrect about Pierre's scientific specialty, he still may be of some assistance to Josh. Pierre used to be a professor at a local university, and one of his former students, Lucas, is now a marine biologist on the island of Dominica. Pierre introduces Josh to Lucas via LinkedIn.

Josh is beginning to have fears that his six degrees experiment isn't going to work out as he moves on to yet another country. Would the French marine biologist have any good contacts? More than a week passes by without a response from Lucas, and Josh's concern increases. Lucas, however, was just away on an expedition without email access. Josh learns that Lucas met Decker at a summer program in Australia several years ago and is happy to provide an introduction. Lucas is also full of useful information and offers to stay in touch with Josh.

Josh has finally reached his ultimate target—Decker. Decker accepts Josh's LinkedIn introduction through Lucas, and the two begin to communicate. Decker is impressed with Josh's academic background and creativity and offers him an internship the following summer. Mission accomplished.

Your attempts to reach a particular individual may not be as complicated as those of Josh trying to reach Decker, but the moral of the story is that reaching the people you want may not take on a linear path; there may be detours along that path. But detours aren't always a negative. Josh not only got his internship at Decker's research institute, he also made another important professional connection with Lucas, and he met two interesting women in France and Australia along the way.

Be open to the adventure that social networking takes you on.

The person you meet on the path to your ultimate goal could be the best contact you'll ever make.

Although it's important to focus on your social networking goals, also be aware of the opportunities you find along the way. The person you meet on the path to your ultimate goal could be the best contact you'll ever make.

TRUTH

39

Connect and reconnect: develop a network that works for you

If you're new to social networking, the thought of developing a solid pool of key contacts can be a bit overwhelming. Downright daunting, in fact, for those who place any form of networking—online or off—way down on their list of favorite things to do. Relax. In many ways, developing your online network is easier than an in-person network.

Your existing contacts are critical to social networking success. Without them, you have no network. If you've explored many social networking sites, you've undoubtedly come across people with only one or two contacts—or worse, no contacts. On every site, there are people who never do anything beyond signing up, or who accept an invitation from a colleague and never return to the site. If you want your social networking experience to be a powerful one, however, you need to connect with enough people to make it worthwhile.

In many ways, developing your online network is easier than an in-person network.

But before you start sending connection requests to anyone and everyone, you need to focus on *why* before you think about *who* and *how*. Essentially, you need a plan. Asking yourself the following questions will simplify the process of developing your network and ensure that you connect with the people who can help you meet your goals.

- **Why do you want to participate in social networking?** Articulating a goal makes it easier to develop a strategic social network.

- **What sites are you using to develop your contacts?** Every social networking site is a little different, and the techniques you use to develop your network on each vary.

- **Who are your ideal contacts?** Are you looking for recruiters, corporate executives, potential supporters for your cause or political campaign, or music lovers who might want to buy your new CD?

Most social networkers fall into one of two categories: those, such as job seekers, who are trying to develop a business network of specific, targeted contacts; and those who want to reach a wide, general audience potentially interested in their product, service, or cause.

Aubrey, for example, is ready to transition from full-time student to full-time employee. She already has a network of contacts on Facebook from her college days, but she knows that she needs a new approach to find a job in the competitive New York advertising world. She must expand her existing collegiate network into a targeted group of contacts that can help her land her dream job in advertising.

To start, Aubrey joins several other social networking sites popular with professionals. To build her contact pool, she initially focuses on the people she already knows: classmates she wasn't already connected with on Facebook, colleagues she worked with during several internships, and people she met at local professional association meetings. Not surprisingly, many of these individuals already participate on her target social networks, so it's easy for Aubrey to connect with them.

To take it a step further, Aubrey views the profiles of people her contacts know and sends an invitation to connect to anyone with a background relevant to her job search. Next on the list: members of local professional associations she hasn't yet met in person and former graduates of her university who work in advertising. Because these people already have something in common with Aubrey, they are more likely to respond positively to her connection requests. Soon Aubrey has a pool of more than 200 contacts, and a plan for using her network to land her first job in advertising.

On the other hand, if your goal is to make contact primarily with people you don't know, you need a slightly different approach than the one Aubrey took. In this case, you're really creating a publicity campaign through social networking rather than developing a select network of contacts. To succeed with this strategy, consider the following suggestions:

■ **Focus on your presence on the site**—A solid presence with lots of interesting content is going to make people more likely to befriend you.

- **Start with likeminded people**—Search the site for others who share your interests and match the target audience you're trying to reach. If your goal is to befriend jazz fans, for example, search for others who share this interest and contact them. Your success rate will likely be higher.

- **See who has befriended your competitors**—These are people who may also be interested in what you have to offer.

- **Be selective**—Yes, you want to reach as many people as possible, but you still need to weed out anyone whom you really don't want to associate with. Before blindly accepting every friend request or sending a request to someone you don't know, verify that this person is really worth making a contact with. This takes some time, but it helps you avoid associating yourself with the small percentage of problem people in the social networking world.

- **Be patient**—You need to avoid the temptation of trying to connect to thousands overnight. By doing so, you run the risk of developing a poor network or losing your network altogether. If you misuse one of the tools that automatically adds MySpace friends, for example, you run the risk of MySpace deleting your account.

Be strategic about connecting and reconnecting on social networking sites, and your chances of reaping rewards should more than double.

TRUTH

40

You can never have too
many friends...
or can you?

You can never have too much of a good thing. Or so the saying goes. But does this really hold true with social networking? Although the "more the merrier" approach can bring solid results to some social networkers, in many cases, less really is more.

How many connections—also referred to as contacts or friends on certain social networking sites—are optimal for success? The answer is...it depends. There are two schools of thought when it comes to making connections in the world of social networking. The first dictates that social networking is a numbers game; therefore, the more connections you have, the better your chances are for success. The networkers who follow this approach are the people wanting to connect with as many people as possible, hoping that this huge number of connections will pay off in solid results. There are two strategies for handling this approach:

> You can never have too much of a good thing. But does this really hold true with social networking?

- **Semiselective strategy**—Using a semiselective strategy, you narrow your requirements somewhat, but you still aim for the largest pool of contacts possible that meet these basis requirements. For example, you could attempt to connect with everyone you can in a particular industry, all R&B music fans, or all sports enthusiasts. This could amount to several thousand people. You'll never make direct contact with all of them, but they at least fit your basic criteria.

- **Anyone and everyone strategy**—With this strategy, you aren't selective at all and deem anyone who's a member of the same social networking site as a potential contact. This tactic isn't for everyone, but if you decide it is for you, be sure to avoid using software tools such as automated friend finders, which amass thousands of contacts in a brief period. These are frowned on by many in the industry.

Whether this "more the merrier" approach is a viable plan depends on your social networking goals. For example, an independent musical artist who develops a solid MySpace presence might benefit from trying to befriend anyone on MySpace who indicates the slightest interest in her kind of music. A high-tech recruiter with a profile on LinkedIn could also benefit from connecting with as many people in the technology industry as possible. Having a lot of contacts could boost a political candidate's profile as well.

Beyond business benefits, there are other less obvious reasons that people try to amass a huge collection of contacts. For some, adding connections becomes a game or even a mild addiction, with the goal of being the person with the most connections. For others, it's a case of self-worth. These networkers equate their professional value with having a large number of professional connections. Their thought is that having so many connections is a demonstration of their professional standing and competence. If this sounds like you, keep in mind that unless your social networking goals warrant this approach, you may not see much business benefit for your efforts, other than to be able to say that you have more contacts than anyone else on your favorite social networking site.

Keep in mind that having too many contacts could also backfire as a professional strategy to social networking. If you're indiscriminate in choosing your contacts, you could end up connecting with people whose profile is less than professional. A jobseeker or specialized consultant, for example, could actually achieve better results with more selective tactics. If you're seeking a high-level position or high-level business contacts, being connected to some people could be viewed as a negative. For example, if your social networking goal is to boost your business and elevate your professional standing, you don't want to have a pool of contacts that includes individuals whose profiles indicate that they're hawking pyramid schemes, looking for dates, or engaging in spam tactics. But if you connect with others without even reviewing their profile (quite likely if you aim to have many thousands of contacts), you could easily end up with such "friends."

Too many contacts could actually backfire as a professional strategy to social networking.

The second school of thought regarding social networking connections emphasizes the "less is more" approach. This tactic focuses on developing a smaller pool of contacts whom you actually have a professional relationship with, either online or offline. These contacts don't need to be close friends, but they should at least be people who recognize your name. If you have 20,000 contacts, it would be impossible for you to know them all or even remember that you were connected to them if they ever did meet you in person. Networkers whose goal is finding a new job or developing solid business contacts often benefit from a more selective approach. Having 150 solid contacts can often be worth far more than connecting with 20,000 people who have no idea who you are.

To implement this second approach, start with your known associates, both current and former. From there, get more strategic. Based on your goals, whom do you want to connect with? If you're looking for a high-level sales job, focus on recruiters who specialize in this area. If you want to change careers, create a profile suited to your new industry and try to connect with others already working in that field. If you're a marketing consultant looking for consulting assignments at major corporations, your target contacts could be marketing VPs at Fortune 500 companies.

The bottom line is that there is no one right answer regarding the optimal number of social networking contacts you should have or how you should go about finding them. But by matching your approach to your goals and avoiding any questionable or unethical tactics, you have the best chance of social networking success.

TRUTH

41

You *can* connect with the rich and famous

One of the biggest benefits of professional social networking is the ability to reach people whom you couldn't reach in your day-to-day life. Whether the barriers are geographic, professional, or economic, some people may be beyond your grasp for in-person networking.

Online social networking, however, opens up a whole new world of opportunity. Social networking reaches a wide demographic audience, skewing toward the middle class and above. CEOs, industry leaders, top politicians, bestselling authors, and numerous celebrities participate in social networking, including many people you would probably like to contact.

> Online social networking, however, opens up a whole new world of opportunity.

Consider the following facts:

- Approximately 145,000 CEOs have profiles on LinkedIn.

- Hundreds of celebrities from the world of film, TV, and music have profiles on MySpace.

- Social networking has its own site for the rich and famous, aSmallWorld (www.asmallworld.net), but you need an invitation to join.

Before you start sending invitations to connect with the world's elite, however, you need to think strategically. Why do you want to connect with these people? What, if anything, is the value to them? In addition, you need to verify that the profile actually does belong to the well-known person in question. On MySpace, for example, a number of the celebrity sites aren't really connected to the actual celebrity. In general, you'll have better luck catching the attention of successful people with moderate fame than you will connecting with the truly world famous.

To get some inspiration on how you can reach the movers and shakers in your industry through social networking, let's look at the experiences of two diverse social networkers.

Bianca is the author of a new novel to be published early next year. She knows that her own marketing efforts are critical to the success of her book, but she doesn't consider herself very marketing-savvy and, as a stay-at-home mom, she doesn't have a lot of professional connections. Her publisher has now asked for Bianca's help in finding testimonials for her book. Although she's eager to get involved, as a new author she doesn't know anyone even remotely famous who could provide a testimonial. She had already decided to implement a social networking campaign to publicize her new book when it's published. Now, in addition to connecting with potential readers, she hopes to network with some key players in her industry who could potentially provide a testimonial for her.

To start, Bianca joins four social networking sites:

- A social networking site for authors (and the readers who enjoy their books)

- A general-interest site that includes numerous author participants

- A site for dog lovers (a family pet figures prominently in her novel)

- A site for moms (her main character is a stay-at-home mom, like Bianca was for five years)

Although one of Bianca's ultimate social networking goals is to connect with potential readers who might buy her book, she knows that her book won't be available for another six months. So for now, her focus is on connecting with other authors. First, she creates a presence on each site that clearly indicates she is an author whose book will be published later that year by a well-respected publisher.

Next, she sends connection requests to authors in her genre whose work she admires. She personalizes her requests so that they know Bianca is familiar with their work and is serious about her writing career. Bianca also decides to contact a well-known author of pet care books and the head of several organizations devoted to animals, parenting, and the stay-at-home mom lifestyle. Although not everyone is interested in engaging in a conversation with Bianca, several are.

From her initial contacts, Bianca has formed a few online and one in-person friendship. Soon, she has three great testimonials—two from successful authors whose readers may also enjoy her book, and one from someone very active in the stay-at-home mom community, which is also a target readership. Bianca's social networking strategy has paid off both in finding solid testimonial contacts as well as in laying the groundwork for a social networking marketing campaign once her book is released.

Jason is a speech coach whose business focuses on helping professionals excel at public speaking. Jason has strong credentials and has developed a solid clientele in his local area, but he would like to expand his business to celebrity clients. There's only one problem: He doesn't know any celebrities.

Thinking that networking is the solution to his problem, Jason decides to supplement his in-person networking efforts with online social networking. He's already a member of one professional social network, but he would like to join another site that focuses on an even more exclusive clientele. However, he needs to receive an invitation from an existing member to join.

Rather than trying to connect with celebrities directly, Jason's strategy is to connect with the people whom they already work with, hoping to receive a referral. He starts by sending connection invitations to individuals in the sports marketing and entertainment PR fields. Insightful comments about public speaking posted on the networking site's discussion forum further enhance his professional reputation online.

He begins conversations with two good networking contacts, a sports marketing executive whose celebrity athlete client is hoping to transition to a lucrative speaking career, and an entertainment publicist who is a member of the elite network he would like to join. These connections soon pay off for Jason. He receives an invitation from the publicist to join the elite networking site and an offer to coach the well-known athlete, who becomes Jason's first celebrity client.

TRUTH

42

You've got mail...
but you shouldn't always
answer it

In business, sometimes you have to say no. The same advice holds true in the world of social networking. If your goal is to develop a top-notch online network, not every person is going to be a valuable contact. Being selective in your response to invitations to connect can make a big difference in the quality of your network and in how others perceive you. You may have mail, but you shouldn't always answer it.

After you join a social networking site, you'll invariably start to receive connection requests from people you don't know. Many of these people may be good contacts; others may not. Knowing whom to respond to—as well as how to respond—can make a big difference in how successful you are in meeting your social networking goals.

Let's look at two IT managers, both of whom joined a social networking site with the goal of finding new, more lucrative employment opportunities. They both created quality profiles and proceeded to develop a network of contacts. Jessica's strategy was to amass the largest collection of contacts she could find, hoping to break the site's "more than 500 contacts" threshold. Her reasoning was that if she had that many contacts, recruiters and employers would deem her successful and employable. Jessica accepted all requests to connect without hesitation. She rarely reviewed the profile of the sender; she just clicked the Accept button and happily added another contact. By following this strategy, however, she ended up with a large number of contacts in totally unrelated professions who could have little impact on her job search. In other words, she connected with a lot of other "name collectors."

> In business, sometimes you have to say no. The same advice holds true in the world of social networking.

Bart took a totally different strategy. His "less is more" approach made him review every connection request individually. If the request came from someone whose profile was professional, and ideally in his own industry, he would accept. He would answer the requests from the most viable contacts with a personalized response, with the goal of making a true business contact and not just adding another name to his collection. Bart's professional, but friendly response to these selected requests helped his new contacts remember him favorably.

In the end, Bart's strategy paid off even though his total number of contacts was just 127. One of the people who received Bart's personalized response knew of an unadvertised opening for an IT director at his company. He referred Bart to the hiring manager, and Bart was selected for the position. Because Jessica was focused more on collecting names than on developing relationships, she never made direct contact with the person who led Bart to his new position.

Sometimes the problem isn't selecting which invitations to accept, but how to handle requests from your existing contacts. Although most people keep their requests reasonable and professional, you're bound to encounter one or two that make you cringe. For example, your social networking contacts could

- **Ask you for special favors in finding a job**—If someone you don't really know asks you for a personal recommendation, think twice. You're not just helping an online contact, you're putting your own reputation on the line. It's one thing to pass on basic information to a little-known contact, such as the name of a recruiter or a link to a job posting that could suit him. It's another to vouch for the credentials of someone you don't really know, even if that person appears to have a solid background based on his profile.

> Sometimes the problem isn't selecting which invitations to accept, but how to handle requests from your existing contacts.

- **Ask for free advice or services**—Online contacts often ask each other for advice about their area of expertise, and most people answer routine requests in the spirit of cooperation and collaboration. But some people take this too far, asking others to review detailed documents, provide extensive professional or legal advice, or offer consulting services—for free. Also be wary of contacts who ask for comprehensive proposals requiring you to reveal the details of what you would do and how you would do it—if they were to "hire" you. Many proposal requests are legitimate, but some are veiled solicitations for free advice.

- **Ask for money**—How to handle this type of request is pretty obvious. Unless it's a legitimate investment opportunity (very rare), most money-related requests are scams. And unfortunately, most people involved in social networking for any length of time receive a request or two of this nature.

- **Make a personal request, such as asking personal questions or asking for a date**—Yes, it's obvious what to do with these requests and yes, it's unfortunate that they do happen, even on professional, business-oriented social networking sites. Remember that it's in the social networking site's best interest to provide a professional environment for its members. Most offer a way to report unprofessional or abusive behavior and often ban offenders. Be sure to report this type of activity.

Keep in mind that the email you receive on social networking sites is a lot like your regular email. There's the good, the bad, and the ugly. Although common sense dictates the best way to respond—or not—to most mail, you also need to be strategic in a social networking setting. Finding the right balance between acting in the spirit of online cooperation and doing what's best for you professionally is the key to making the most of your email communications through social networking.

TRUTH

43

Social networking makes your past an open book

Digital dirt. By now, you know that this term refers to negative information about you that's found on the Internet, including social networking sites. You may even have some of your own digital dirt to contend with, such as

- Profiles on social networking sites that contain unprofessional content

- Unprofessional website and blog content, both content on your own sites as well as comments you leave on other sites

- Inappropriate photos or videos

- Contradictory information (what you tell an employer doesn't match your LinkedIn profile, for example)

- Negative news stories about you or your company

- Critical comments others make about you online

- Comments or reviews you post online, such as on blogs or sites like Amazon.com

Social networking and other forms of participation on the web make your past an open book. Some of the information about you is positive and can benefit you, such as news about your professional achievements, articles you've written, and so forth. Other information is neutral, such as most content that relates to hobbies and personal interests. And then there's the digital dirt.

> Social networking and other forms of participation on the web make your past an open book.

If there's dirt about you online, it's obvious that you need to clean it up before it becomes an issue during a job search or other professional situation. The same goes for anything that doesn't really fall under the digital dirt category but is something you would rather not have others read about you online.

Run your own Google check on your name to see what's out there. Review your profile on every social networking site you've ever used. If there's something you don't like, remove it. But, of course, it isn't always that simple. For example, it's unlikely that you can delete a news story that mentions you unless the information is clearly false. You might also have trouble deleting content or commentary on sites that you don't control. Usually a polite request to the site owner results in the deletion of the content in question, but not always. In these cases, honesty is the best policy. If a prospective employer or client brings up this information, be prepared with a response that puts the situation in the best light possible. Another potential situation is having the same name as someone whose reputation isn't as stellar as yours. To differentiate yourself from this person, consider using a middle initial or some other variation of your name.

Also keep in mind that, although about half of all employers do search the Internet for information about prospective employees, the other half do not. The same most likely holds true for people interested in doing business with you. It doesn't pay to stress about something that you can't change. Instead, focus on adding more positive content about you online that appears higher in your search engine rankings.

Just because you know that there are no questionable photos or unflattering content about you on the Internet right now doesn't mean that you can take it easy, however. Even if you don't post anything yourself, new content about you could pop up online at any time, particularly if you're active in your profession or community. To keep track of what's being said about you or your business on the web, sign up for an alert service. Both Google Alerts (www.google.com/alerts) and Yahoo! Alerts (www.yahoo.com/alerts) will send you an email notification any time a new mention of your name appears on the web—on a website or blog, on a publicly available social networking site page, or in a news story. You can be notified on a daily basis or get regular roundups at a specific interval. If you're monitoring the online reputation of a larger company, however, you may be better off signing up with one of the many online reputation management services now available.

> New content about you could pop up online at any time, particularly if you're active in your profession or community.

Sometimes it's the lesser dirt, or content you don't even think of as unflattering, that can cause problems. The issue is perspective. In other words, not everyone agrees on what constitutes "negative" information online. Sure, most people feel that uncovering provocative photos or stories about your arrest record would be a cause for concern in the business world, but other areas are more nebulous. What about information concerning your political opinions, lifestyle choices, religious beliefs, health conditions, volunteer activities, or even hobbies? Could certain individuals also construe this information as "negative?" For example

- A recruiter finds information about your handmade jewelry business on MySpace and thinks you may be too busy with your sideline vocation to take on the top job you're interviewing for.

- A hiring manager who's an atheist is dismayed to find out that you're active on a Christian social networking site.

- A business partner comes across a fundraising badge on your Facebook page and is outraged that you support this cause.

- Your new boss reads your profile on the Mothers of Many social networking site and fears that, as a mother of six children, you might not be the right choice for the upcoming promotion at work.

Most people are able to remain objective in a business setting, but biases do creep into professional decisions from time to time. The question you need to ask is this: How much do you want to censor yourself online? It's one thing to clean up truly unflattering or unprofessional information, but do you really want to hide everything that could possibly irritate even one person? Where do you draw the line?

Other than the small amount of online information about you that you can't delete or change, for the most part, you're in control of what you reveal about yourself online. Developing and protecting your online image is something that every social networker needs to consider. In the end, how much of an "open book" you want to be online is up to you.

TRUTH

44

You never know who is reading your profile

Your social networking profile introduces you to the world. Not everyone is going to read your profile, and most who do won't take action. The few communications that you do receive are generally positive or innocuous, such as job or business inquiries, greetings from old friends, introductions from likeminded people, or even connection requests from "name collectors" who just want to add you to their massive collection of online contacts.

But the truth is, you never really know who is reading your profile. Keeping this in mind, knowing that you're prepared for the worst will help you make the most of your social networking experience. Most

> Your social networking profile introduces you to the world.

people run into relatively few problems during their time spent on social networking sites, particularly if they use common sense in what they post online.

But occasionally even a straightforward, professional profile can draw unwanted attention from a predator, scammer, spammer, or overeager "fan." These problems span all demographics but, in general, children under 18, younger adult women, and very active social networkers (who encounter a higher volume of people) tend to be more prone to run into an occasional unpleasant situation.

If you're a parent with children who participate on popular sites such as MySpace, you're probably well aware of the potential dangers online and do what you can to

> The truth is, you never really know who is reading your profile.

protect your offspring from the online predators who've made headlines in recent years. But kids aren't the only ones at risk, and online predators shouldn't be your only concern.

As an adult social networker whose social networking goals are business- or career-related, you do have several distinct advantages in preparing yourself against unpleasant situations online: Your experience gives you the "street smarts" that kids haven't developed yet, you're probably networking on professional sites that have a lower incidence of problems, and you may be less likely to fit the target profile of a predator. On the downside, you may very well fit the target profile of a scammer looking for online profits.

In general, it's fairly easy to avoid obvious predators and scammers. But sometimes what starts off as an innocuous situation catches you off guard and takes a turn in a different direction. Consider the following scenarios:

- A recruiter contacts you through a social networking site and says that you're nearly a perfect match for a job he's trying to fill. The job and its high salary sound great to you, and you quickly dash off a copy of your latest resume. When the recruiter receives it, he emails you right away to say that his client loves your background and feels you're a top contender for this lucrative job. The recruiter just needs your social security number to complete the client's required paperwork and then will set up a formal interview for you.

- You're an author with a popular MySpace presence and encourage contact from readers to further develop your audience and increase sales. One particular reader starts sending you fan mail on a regular basis. At first, his communications seem innocent enough, but soon he begins to send you romantic poetry, asks you for detailed personal information, and indicates his desire to fly across the country to meet you in person because you're the woman of his dreams.

- You're eager to hear from potential employers, so you include your email address in all your social networking profiles. Because you network primarily on business-oriented sites, you assume that your contact information is safe and won't be shared with others. However, you soon start receiving an email newsletter that you didn't sign up for. In addition, your volume of spam has greatly increased.

- You receive a request to connect from a recent college graduate who would like to work at your company. Her academic credentials look good, so you accept her request and exchange a few emails in which you tell her she would be a great fit for a new position opening up. She sends you her resume and asks you to forward it to the appropriate hiring manager, which you do. Two weeks later, she sends you an angry email stating that she didn't get the job she applied for and wants to know why. She then starts calling you at your office on a daily basis over the next few weeks.

No social networker wants to deal with an initially pleasant interaction that takes a decidedly unpleasant turn. In these cases, avoidance is the best practice. Follow your instincts in your interactions with the people you meet online. Treat your new online contacts just as you would any other strangers you meet, approaching with the restraint and caution that the situation requires. Few people are likely to scam or stalk you, but you should still trust your intuition if something just doesn't seem right with an online contact, and stop communication before things move in the wrong direction.

Be aware, but don't let unfounded fears of danger lurking behind every email make you lose out on all there is to gain from social networking.

Keep danger in perspective. Like the world itself, social networking sites are generally a safe place for those who make efforts to avoid bad situations. Be aware, but don't let unfounded fears of danger lurking behind every email make you lose out on all there is to gain from social networking.

TRUTH

45

Knowledge is the key to safeguarding your privacy online

One of the best ways to avoid problems online and protect your privacy is to understand the privacy policies of all the sites that you create a profile on. Knowing how a site uses the information you post and what efforts it makes to protect your personal information is a key step in safeguarding your privacy online.

Some things are obvious when it comes to avoiding privacy breaches online—not sharing personal information, protecting your computer from intrusion, and so forth. But if you're not current with the latest online privacy strategies, you may think that you're more protected than you are. Surprisingly, most people never read the privacy policies of their favorite social networking sites. Educating yourself helps bridge the gap between online savvy and common sense.

The first place to start is to actually read and understand the privacy policies of the social networking sites that you participate on. These policies explain how the

Most people never read the privacy policies of their favorite social networking sites.

site plans to use the information you provide. Here are links to the privacy policies of some of the most popular social networking sites on the web:

- Facebook (www.facebook.com/policy.php)

- LinkedIn (www.linkedin.com/static?key=privacy_policy)

- MySpace (www.myspace.com/index.cfm?fuseaction=misc. privacy)

- XING (www.xing.com/app/user?op=tandc;what=dp)

Privacy policies are rarely easy reading, so it's also a good idea to review the site to see its privacy controls in action. On most sites, you can choose what information to display and to whom. Unfortunately, many people simply don't take the time to adjust these settings and then are surprised when the world can see information they thought was private, including email addresses, physical addresses, and phone numbers.

Adhering to privacy policies is serious business for social networking sites, as the penalties for lack of compliance can be severe. In 2006, the social networking site Xanga (www.xanga.com.) was fined $1 million for violating COPPA, the Children's Online Privacy Protection Act of 1998 (www.cdt.org/legislation/105th/privacy/coppa.html). Xanga allowed children under the age of 13 to sign up on its site without parental permission, an activity that clearly violated COPPA. The $1 million fine was the largest ever imposed for violating online privacy rights.

Social networkers are a vocal group. If they don't like a site's privacy policy, they speak up. When Facebook introduced its new Beacon advertising program in November 2007, privacy activists were outraged that Beacon shared information on Facebook users' private web transactions with others without their permission. These activist groups began a heavy campaign to force the social networking leader to change its Beacon program. Within a month of Beacon's introduction, Facebook caved in to the complaints. CEO Mark Zuckerberg issued a public apology for the way Beacon was implemented and announced that users could now opt out of the program entirely.

In addition to understanding your favorite sites' privacy policies and implementing the right privacy controls on each site, there are other things you can do to safeguard your privacy.

If you're concerned about people misusing your personal or company email address, don't reveal it. Use a free email service such as Gmail (http://mail.google.com), Hotmail (www.hotmail.com), or Yahoo! Mail (http://mail.yahoo.com) instead of your regular email address.

Don't feel you need to complete all fields in your profile. Some social networking sites include fields for providing all sorts of personal information you might rather not share. Just because there is a field for home phone number doesn't mean that you need to enter something there! You have the right to create the profile with which you're comfortable.

Keep your personal information off the Internet. This can often be easier said than done, however. It's simple enough to control the information you provide on your own, but people who search sites such as ZabaSearch (www.zabasearch.com), Intelius (www.intelius.com), and PeopleFinders (www.peoplefinders.com) can list your address, home phone, and age for all to see, even if you have an unlisted number. This information doesn't appear in a Google search, so unless you go to the site directly, you wouldn't know it contains your personal information. Fortunately, most people search sites will remove your data if you request it.

Have a plan for dealing with spam. Any online activity, including social networking, increases your chances of receiving spam. Learn about your email provider's spam tools and implement a strategy that works for you. This is particularly important if your social networking goals relate to your own business and it makes sense to include your business website and email address in your social networking profiles.

Install comprehensive security software with antivirus, antispyware, and firewall features such as Norton Internet Security (www.norton.com) or McAfee Internet Security Suite (www.mcafee.com/us/). Be sure to download updates on a regular basis and ensure that your software is activated at all times.

Speak up. If you receive inappropriate communications through a social networking site, report it to the site. Social networking companies take privacy rights seriously; they face sanctions and a barrage of negative publicity if they don't. Most sites will investigate your complaints and take action against the offending party if necessary.

By educating yourself on privacy rights and tactics—and using good common sense—you'll greatly reduce your likelihood of encountering social networking's dark side and instead be able to focus on reaping the rewards of interacting with the world online.

TRUTH

46

Social networking will expand exponentially in the next decade

The fact that social networking is one of the big trends of the past few years is a given. It's a phenomenon that has affected not just technology, but also business, entertainment, and humanity in general. But what about the future?

Industry analysts rarely agree on everything, but one thing is clear: Social networking is predicted to continue its growth trend, reaching out to a wider, more diverse population that spans multiple age groups, ethnicities, and geographic locations.

Beyond more universal adoption, where is social networking headed? Without the proverbial crystal ball, it's hard to paint a precise picture of how social networking will fit into the world of the web and daily digital life in the distant future. Will today's top sites still remain at the top of the list in ten years? Possibly, but not probably. Will many niche sites come and go? Definitely. Will the world of social networking look different than is does today? Another definite yes.

Social networking is predicted to continue its growth trend.

Although it's hard to predict with exact certainty what the world of social networking will look like in five years, let alone ten years, one thing is certain: The type of social interaction and community that social networking sites provide is something that humans crave based on our nature, and it's not something that's going away. Favored sites may come and go, consolidation may occur, and someone will undoubtedly come up with the next "big idea" of the collaborative web, but collaboration is here to stay.

Niche sites will become the social networking trend of the future

Niche sites are becoming increasingly popular and will continue to do so. People like to spend time with people who think like they do. They like to view content that's relevant to their world. They even like to learn about new products and services that target their interests and lifestyle. As a result, social networking sites for every possible segment of society have launched over the past few years with no end in site. Sites for moms, soccer fans, wine lovers, the eco-conscious, nurses, gamers, fashionistas, dog owners, design divas, and more are now up and running, with more in the development stage.

The key to the success of niche sites, however, will be their ability to connect with their audience in a way that creates a genuine community. An established, engaging community combined with a viable business model is the recipe for a niche social networking site that generates buzz, staying power, and profits.

Social network advertising budgets will increase

Social network advertising is a billion dollar business, with predicted expenditures at $2.2 billion for 2008 alone.[1] Social network advertising is clearly on a growth trend, but the advertising must be relevant to pay off. Look for advertising to shift from reliance on traditional display advertising to a model that combines tradition with innovation. Sponsorships, branded content, contests, and more will create a whole new dynamic to online advertising. Also look for new advertising paradigms to evolve over the next few years as creative marketers start to tap the potential of this new advertising medium.

Open standards for sharing data across the social web will emerge

The opening of the social web was big news throughout 2007 and into early 2008, with numerous announcements about enabling social networking and other sites to exchange data with each other. Facebook announced its Facebook Platform, a development environment enabling participating companies such as Amazon, Newsweek, Twitter, Digg, and others to develop applications that interface directly with Facebook and its user data. Then, Google announced its OpenSocial platform, supported by industry leaders such as MySpace, Friendster, LinkedIn, Ning, Plaxo, Video, XING, and others.

> Social network advertising is a billion dollar business, with predicted expenditures at $2.2 billion for 2008 alone.

Although Facebook is the one major player not part of OpenSocial, it joined with Google in supporting the DataPortability Workgroup, another group focusing on the common goal of sharing data across the social web. These announcements are just the beginning, however. The next few years should show the results of these new standards and partnerships and the benefits they offer the average social networker. What does this mean for the future of social networking? For one, profiles and widgets will become more portable. You won't have to enter profile data and upload images on each site you join. You'll have the control to say when and how you share and reuse your data. And that's just the beginning.

Social networking's exponential growth will drop

This doesn't sound like a positive sign, but it is. And there's a good reason why. As with any new technology or trend, adoption of social networking will eventually reach a plateau. For example, the number of people who own computers or have access to the Internet in the United States won't likely increase by huge numbers in the next few years, because the market is already near saturation. Double-digit or triple-digit growth happens at the beginning of a new trend, not at the end. Social networking is rapidly expanding from its initial early adopters to society as a whole. All ages, sexes, ethnicities, and nationalities are now part of the social web. The expansion will continue over the next few years until it reaches a point at which exponential growth will no longer be possible.

This means that social networking will finally reach the masses. Its audience will be even larger than it is today, its adoption will be widespread, and all the opportunities that this vast audience provides today will be even greater.

TRUTH

47

Social networking is going mobile

Mobile social networking is a major growth area in the fast-changing world of social networking. Mobile accessibility is becoming an increasingly important component of everyday digital life. As more and more people are on the go and away from their computers for lengthy periods, the more critical it becomes for them to connect to the online world from their mobile devices.

Many mobile phone users already check email and send text messages. Adding social networking functionality is a natural extension of that. Today's mobile society wants the freedom that their mobile lifestyle brings, yet they still crave the connectivity that their social networks provide, both personally and professionally.

The future impact and potential of mobile social networking solidifies its place as a growth area. Mobile user-generated content revenues from social networking and related content services are predicted to increase to nearly $6 billion by 2012. In addition, active mobile social networkers will increase from 14 million in 2007 to nearly 600 million by 2012.[1]

Statistics like these are driving the leading social networking sites to offer mobile components, as well as encouraging numerous start-ups to develop their own mobile social applications.

Facebook, for example, offers three options for mobile Facebook devotees. Facebook Mobile Web provides an alternate version of Facebook for use on mobile phones. Facebook Mobile Uploads enables you to upload photos and notes directly to Facebook. And Facebook Mobile Texts lets you connect with Facebook friends, view profiles, and use text messaging. Facebook's mobile services work with a variety of carriers in the United States, Canada, and the UK, as well as with a variety of phones. The iPhone, in particular, works well with Facebook's mobile functionality.

> Today's mobile society wants the freedom that their mobile lifestyle brings, yet they still crave the connectivity that their social networks provide, both personally and professionally.

In addition, Facebook Platform for Mobile enables Facebook developers to make their Facebook applications work with mobile phones. A Facebook application for Blackberry Smartphones also exists for users of that mobile device.

MySpace offers its MySpace Mobile service in the United States for customers using Helio (www.helio.com/myspace) and AT&T (www.wireless.att.com/source/uconnect/myspace.aspx). Europe offers mobile access through a partnership with Vodafone. Using these services, MySpace users can edit profiles, add friends, send messages, and post photos.

Active mobile social networkers will increase from 14 million in 2007 to nearly 600 million by 2012.

UK-based Bebo provides mobile services in several countries, including the UK and Ireland, with features including free text alerts, access to a special version of Bebo through their mobile phones, and posting via text message.

Although popular social networking services such as MySpace and Facebook generate the most mobile social networking activity, niche players are gaining ground as well. Some focus on the purely social aspects of mobile social networking. Others offer useful tools for day-to-day living. Here's a quick survey of this rapidly changing market.

The friend finders

Want to know where your friends are? Consider Dodgeball (www.dodgeball.com), recently purchased by Google. This service is now available in 22 cities across the United States and helps users connect with friends, friends of friends, and nearby soon-to-be friends by alerting them of other Dodgeball members' locations within a certain radius.

Loopt (www.loopt.com) is a new entrant into the mobile social space, with a launch in January 2008. Its social mobile mapping application alerts you when friends are near you, shares your location with approved contacts, and lets you know about places that your friends recommend.

The communities

Some mobile social networking services are actually communities, whether in the real world or in an alternate reality.

Mig33 (www.mig33.com) is a worldwide mobile community that offers its users profile capabilities, photo sharing, chatrooms, VoIP calling, and integration with instant messaging services such as AIM, Yahoo!, and Google Talk.

With LimeJuice (http://limejuice.hyphen-8.com), mobile social networking meets multiplayer gaming. The system enables people to interact with others in a social setting such as a bar, nightclub, or café using profile-based avatars, text messaging, and location-based technology on the mobile web.

Mobile goes global

European mobile innovators appear to be at the forefront of the mobile revolution as Europeans are adopting mobile social networking at a more rapid pace than their U.S. counterparts. As a result, several European start-ups have introduced innovative new mobile applications and services.

Copenhagen-based Imity (www.imity.com) uses Bluetooth technology to sense when your friends, and interesting strangers, are nearby. It integrates with other social networking sites, allowing you to know when another LinkedIn user is nearby, for example, and enables you to set up online afterparties following conferences and events.

Aka Aki (www.aka-aki.com) is a mobile social network based in Berlin, Germany, that also uses Bluetooth technology to locate your connections and let you know where they are.

Mobile social networking is not without its challenges, however. Among them is the issue of privacy. Do you really want to be notified when an interesting stranger is around the corner? Ensuring that users understand and properly configure privacy controls is key to future success.

Although the introduction of new mobile services shows no slowdown in the near future, some consolidation will naturally occur. It may be hard to predict who the main players will be in five years, but one thing is certain: Mobile social networking will be part of the digital life experience of hundreds of millions of people worldwide.

TRUTH

48

Not all social networking occurs on social networking sites

When you think about social networking, what first comes to mind is usually a traditional social networking site such as MySpace or Facebook—sites that receive near-daily media coverage and draw an audience of millions. Fans of niche social networking sites, on the other hand, may think of their own personal favorite. Or your first thought could be of the internal social network that you use on your job every day.

Although these are the types of sites that traditionally define social networking, there is another type of social networking that's gaining ground. And it's not on any social networking site. It's the social networking component that appears on media sites, shopping sites, corporate branding sites, and many other sites that proliferate on the web.

Creating a social networking component on a traditional website is an idea that's growing in popularity. Companies such as Reebok, adidas, CBS News, Comcast, HGTV, and Kodak have created social communities as a means of enhancing customer experience, increasing interaction and interactivity, conducting market research, and driving traffic, not to mention generating profits. When HGTV launched a social site for design enthusiasts called Rate My Space (http://ratemyspace.hgtv.com), it created a profitable community of more than 20,000 participants within months.

Smart marketers who foresee this trend are developing innovative ideas that extend their own brand and site functionality with the social component that customers crave.

Jasmine, for example, is the online marketing director for a new, niche women's fashion shopping site. Her goal is to increase sales by boosting traffic, generating buzz, and creating the type of social shopping experience that she knows their target audience will love. Their site is only three months old, however, and it shows. Although it's well designed

> When HGTV launched a social site for design enthusiasts called Rate My Space, it created a profitable community of more than 20,000 participants within months.

and offers the type of clothes that their market research indicates is what their customers want to buy, it's a bit impersonal. The newness hasn't quite worn off, and this is obvious to site visitors.

To begin the process of creating a personalized experience for its customers, Jasmine focuses phase one on the foundation of the site's new social component. Encouraging other fashionistas to create a profile on its site, network with likeminded women, comment on fashion trends, and review its products is the first step. The company plans a media campaign emphasizing word-of-mouth, buzz marketing to generate interest in its site and encourage women in its target demographic to create a profile. As an incentive for signing up, Jasmine suggests offering special discounts and bonuses to its "customer-members."

To engage customers further, Jasmine plans phase two to give them a say in what they can purchase on the site. The "be a fashion scout" feature will enable customers to recommend what products to sell. Customers who sign up as scouts will receive their own blogging space where other members can comment on the scouts' suggestions. The most popular items will then become available for sale on the site, assuming Jasmine and her colleagues can arrange with the manufacturers to sell their clothing.

Phase three will emphasize further interactivity with the added excitement of a contest. Customers with profiles will be encouraged to upload photos of themselves wearing the clothes they bought at the site as part of the "be our spokesmodel" contest. The company's president, Jasmine's boss and a former fashion model, will choose the new company spokesmodel from among the entrants. Jasmine feels confident that when it finishes its three-step approach to creating a social shopping community, its sales should triple.

Chad, the editor of an outdoor travel magazine, is looking to create a similar sense of community among a very different target audience. Sales and advertising revenue for the glossy print version of the magazine are static, and website traffic hasn't picked up despite the extensive—and expensive—site redesign six months ago. Chad knows it's time for something new and decides to add social networking to the magazine's website. His vision is clear: make the magazine's site the go-to destination on the web for its niche audience of outdoor travel enthusiasts. His goals: generate a stronger sense of community among its readers, increase site traffic (and tangentially print readership), and attract the high-profile advertisers that the magazine needs to boost profits.

Chad's plan is based on supplementing the magazine's professionally written content with user-generated content in the form of reader travelogues. Readers who sign up will have the opportunity to create a profile that connects them to likeminded travelers and to use the site's sophisticated tools to design their own custom travelogues with audio, video, and images. Fellow readers can comment on the travelogues and vote for their favorites, leading to exciting travel prizes for the winners. Chad feels comfortable that this format will widen readership and site traffic, while still maintaining the integrity of the magazine's professional travel content. As a professional writer himself, he knows it's particularly important not to antagonize the high-caliber writers and photographers who contribute to his publication.

The future of social networking will see computer users enjoying the benefits of the social web without ever visiting a site such as MySpace or Facebook.

These are just two examples of how strategic marketers can incorporate the power and potential of social networking into their own brands. The future of social networking will see computer users enjoying the benefits of the social web without ever visiting a site such as MySpace or Facebook.

TRUTH

49

Creating your own social network is easier than you think

You want to create your own social network, but you don't have venture capital funding or the financial backing of a solid company behind you. You may be a solopreneur, a small business owner, a hobbyist, or an activist with a cause to promote. Your goal could be to retire on what you earn from your social networking venture, or you could be striving for a reward that's not financial. Can you create your own social networking site without breaking the bank? The answer is a definite yes.

Let's say you're an avid spelunker, and you want to create a community for other cave explorers worldwide. So far, no one else has created a social networking site targeting your favorite activity. You don't understand why and think that you're just the person to do it. You're already envisioning a site where fellow spelunkers could connect with each other, share tips and adventures, and shop for their favorite items. Your big question is this: Where do you start?

> Can you create your own social networking site without breaking the bank? The answer is a definite yes.

The good news is that there are dozens of options for creating your own social network. The bad news is that it takes time to learn what's available and determine what works best for your goals. After you weed out solutions designed for larger businesses, there's still a rather lengthy list of options for do-it-yourselfers, both those who have web development skills and those who need a true end-user solution. Two good options that require little technical skill are Ning and CollectiveX.

Ning (www.ning.com) enables you to quickly create your own network with its easy-to-use tools that require no programming knowledge. You can brand your network with your own logo and select from a long list of possible features such as profiles, photo sharing, video sharing, music, podcasts, groups, discussion forums, blogs, and much more. If you are technically inclined, you can join Ning's developer program to make advanced customizations.

Although there's no charge to create a basic social network (Ning profits from ads placed on your site), you can choose to upgrade to premium features for a fee. These extras include the ability to run your own ads rather than Ning's ads, use your own domain name, and increase your storage and bandwidth. One of the few downsides to Ning is that your users are pooled with the common Ning user base, rather than one specific only to your site.

CollectiveX (www.collectivex.com) also makes creating a social network easy. Free, advertising-supported CollectiveX groupsites offer a long list of features, including member profiles, email blasts, photo galleries, calendars, discussion forums, and more. Fee-based, premium features give you the option to remove advertising, enhance member privacy and security, map to another domain, make advanced customizations, and more. Although CollectiveX doesn't enable you to profit from your own ads yet, that feature is planned for the future.

Looking for even more options? If you're a fan of open-source software, consider PHPizabi (www.phpizabi.net). KickApps (www.kickapps.com) is also a viable option if you're eager to customize and you have some web development skills. Others solutions to consider among the dozens available include CrowdVine (www.crowdvine.com), ONEsite (www.onesite.com), and PeopleAggregator (www.broadbandmechanics.com).

Creating a successful social networking site comes from solid knowledge. Here's a short list of things you should know before you start to implement your own site.

Know what's possible

Your first step is to do some research. Do you want a solution that's easy to set up and is hosted on another company's servers? Is it important that you brand your network to your own specifications using what's known as a "white label" application? Do you want to host your network on your own servers? What features are critical to have? Often, your initial answer to these questions will be "I don't know."

By doing some research into the types of solutions available and what each offers, you'll get a better feeling for what is currently possible in terms of creating your own social network. This is a rapidly evolving field, with new software and solutions announced on a frequent basis. In addition to the previous options mentioned, search for "create your own social network" on your favorite search engine to discover even more possibilities.

Understand the cost of free solutions

As the saying goes, you get what you pay for. Know that if you want to create a social networking site on a shoestring budget, you'll have to make concessions. You may have to live with the hosting company's ads on your site (they get the revenue, not you) as well as the lack of a domain name and other branding options. True "white label" applications that you can completely rebrand to your own specifications usually charge a fee.

Be sure that a do-it-yourself social networking platform is what you want to use. A free, easy-to-use system is a big plus, but not if it doesn't offer the features you want. If your plans are ambitious, you may be better off purchasing a more-robust, customizable solution.

Know your level of technical skill

If your don't know the difference between PHP and API, choose a solution that's designed for do-it-yourself end users or be prepared to spend the money to hire someone who does. Knowing what you don't know, or can't learn quickly, is critical. Technical skill isn't required to set up a social networking site, but you'll have to live with certain limitations. If you want a slick, customized solution and don't have the right skills, factor that need into your budget from the beginning.

Know the business model you want to pursue

A clear business model is critical to success. Do you plan to create a site that generates profit from advertising revenue, sales of your own products, or affiliate sales? Will your network be a fee-based membership site? Is your goal to generate publicity and awareness for your business or a social cause? Or are you creating a site that brings together a group of likeminded people with no profit motivation?

The time you spend on assessing your goals, options, and skills will be time well spent and lead you to success in your social networking adventure.

TRUTH

50

You don't have to follow the trends just because they're there

By now, it should be clear that the popularity of social networking is a trend that's here to stay. In the near future, it's predicted that more than half the world's population online will participate in some form of social networking. In certain demographics, that number is much higher. With an estimated 1.5 billion people online by 2011, that's a lot of social networkers. [1]

The challenge is that the world of social networking is evolving rapidly. The basic tenets of successful networking may have developed slowly over time, but the impact of fast-changing Web 2.0—and soon, Web 3.0—technology keeps social networking in a rapid state of evolution and reinvention.

On a daily basis, something new is announced that changes the face of social networking. Some announcements are minor and affect only a few; others are widespread and change the direction of the industry as a whole. On any given day, you can read news about social networking site launches, new site features, partnership agreements, advertising and marketing innovations, new technologies and platforms, and even retractions and apologies.

If your social networking goals are personal, such as networking to find a new job, most news won't affect you. You care most about changes on the specific sites that you currently use, the launch of new sites that might further your career ambitions, or perhaps, ways that others are using social networking to achieve similar goals. But if you want to use social networking as a true business or promotional tool, you need a much broader understanding of the dynamics of this collaborative medium.

Here are my top three rules for making the most of following—or not following—social networking trends.

Follow the trends as they relate to you

Keeping up with all the changes in the world of social networking is a

> The impact of fast-changing Web 2.0—and soon, Web 3.0—technology keeps social networking in a rapid state of evolution and reinvention.

daunting task, particularly if you need to be in the know on a broad range of topics. To avoid information overload, you should focus first on the big picture and then drill down to the details that affect your world. Social networking is all about connection and community, about matching up people who think alike, share common goals, and support common causes. When scanning the volume of headlines related to social networking, you need to personalize this data as it relates to your needs and ask yourself these questions:

- Where is the industry headed, and how does this impact me?

- What announcements or news stories are generating the most buzz and why?

- What new technologies are on their way, and how can they support my social networking goals?

- What are my competitors doing, and how should I respond?

Fortunately, several blogs already have done some of the basic research for you. Check out Mashable (www.mashable.com), Social Networking Watch (www.socialnetworkingwatch.com), and the blog companion to this book (www.patricerutledge.com/socialnetworking) for summaries of some of the latest news. If you want comprehensive coverage, set up a Google Alert or Yahoo! Alert for the specific topics you want to track in the general media.

Don't be afraid *not* to follow the trends

Insight into the latest trends shouldn't force you to be a slave to those trends. Just because "everyone else is doing it" doesn't mean that a particular social networking trend is right for you. Knowing what works best based on your specific goals, budget, and target audience may make pulling away from the herd mentality a critical success step.

It's often said that luck comes about when you're in the right place at the right time. If you run a business-to-business consulting firm, for example, the fact that MySpace is the most-visited social networking site in the world with millions of daily visitors isn't particularly relevant to you. Even if some of those millions might be suitable clients, they probably aren't on MySpace looking for your type of business. You'd be much better off on a site that has less traffic but is more focused to your needs, such as LinkedIn. On the other hand, the opposite may be true if you're promoting an alternative rock band through social networking.

Yes, you need to be aware of what's going on in the world of social networking if you want to make it a successful component of your business life. But you still need to match current trends to your specific goals. A solid knowledge of your own brand and how it resonates with your customers should tell you when to follow the trends...and when to break free.

Start your own trend

In the ever-evolving world of social networking, where constant change is the only rule, you can often win big by ignoring the existing trends and starting your own. A winning social network marketing campaign requires out-of-the-box thinking and innovation. Breaking the rules may just be the best way to win the game. For example, who would have thought that a Christian humanitarian organization like World Vision would create a successful social networking campaign on the edgy, youth-dominated Second Life? Or that the British Royal Family would employ YouTube as a publicity platform?

Instead of chasing trends, focus on creating your own innovations that meet your customers' needs. What do your customers want that no one else is offering? Often the best ideas come from your customers. Pay attention to what they're asking for. Find out where they're currently spending their time online. Determine how they're responding to current campaigns. And then come up with something better.

If you're an individual using social networking for professional reasons, there are still opportunities for innovation. What can you do that other people who share your goals aren't doing?

A winning social network marketing campaign requires out-of-the-box thinking and innovation.

Innovation is the first key to success; solid execution is the second. Be different. Be bold. Be first. And profit from the unlimited potential of a social phenomenon that links you with more than a billion people around the world.

REFERENCES

Truth 3

1 "comScore Media Metrix Releases Top 50 Web Rankings for January." comScore Media Metrix (February 18, 2008). http://www.comscore.com/press/release.asp?press=2067

2 "MySpace Received 76 Percent of U.S Social Networking Visits in 2007." Hitwise (January 16, 2008). http://www.hitwise.com/press-center/hitwiseHS2004/social-networking-visits-in-2007.php

3 "More than Half of MySpace Visitors Are Now Age 35 or Older, As the Site's Demographic Composition Continues to Shift." comScore Media Metrix (October 5, 2006). http://www.comscore.com/press/release.asp?press=1019

4 "Mobile Social Communities: Understanding a New Way of Social Networking." ABI Research Brief (December 2006). http://www.abiresearch.com/abiprdisplay.jsp?pressid=780

5 "U.S. Internet Users Viewed 10 Billion Videos Online in Record-Breaking Month of December, According to comScore Video Metrix." comScore Video Metrix (February 8, 2008). http://www.comscore.com/press/release.asp?press=2051

6 Aho Williamson, Debra. "Social Network Marketing: Ad Spending and Usage." eMarketer (December 2007). http://www.emarketer.com/Reports/All/Emarketer_2000478.aspx?src=report3_home

7 Prescott, LeeAnn. "Social Networking for Moms, Retirees, and the Ill." Hitwise Intelligence (July 3, 2007). http://weblogs.hitwise.com/leeann-prescott/2007/07/social_networking_for_moms_ret.html

8 "MySpace Received 76 Percent of U.S Social Networking Visits in 2007." Hitwise (January 16, 2008). http://www.hitwise.com/press-center/hitwiseHS2004/social-networking-visits-in-2007.php

9 "U.K. Social Networking Site Usage Highest in Europe." comScore World Metrix (October 10, 2007). http://www.comscore.com/press/release.asp?press=1801

10 "Hitwise Australia Social Networking Update October 2007."
Hitwise (October 18, 2007).
http://www.hitwise.com.au/press-center/hitwiseHS2004/
au-socnetwork-10182007.php

11 "German Social Networking Community Reaches 14.8 Million."
ComScore World Metrix (September 19, 2007).
http://www.comscore.com/press/release.asp?press=1737

12 "comScore Publishes First Review of Latin American Internet
Usage." comScore World Metrix (July 25, 2007).
http://www.comscore.com/press/release.asp?press=1531

13 "Skyrock Network the Dominant French Social Networking Site."
comScore World Metrix (September 19, 2007).
http://www.comscore.com/press/release.asp?press=1735

14 Hanchard, Sandra. "Friendster Still Dominates in Singapore."
Hitwise Intelligence (July 18, 2006).
http://weblogs.hitwise.com/sandra-hanchard/2006/07/
friendster_still_dominates_in_1.html

Truth 7

1 "U.S. Internet Users Viewed 10 Billion Videos Online in Record-
Breaking Month of December, According to comScore Video Metrix."
comScore Video Metrix (February 8, 2008).
http://www.comscore.com/press/release.asp?press=2051

Truth 22

1 "MySpace Received 76 Percent of U.S. Social Networking Visits in
2007." Hitwise (January 16, 2008).
http://www.hitwise.com/press-center/hitwiseHS2004/
social-networking-visits-in-2007.php

2 "Hitwise Releases U.S. Consumer Generated Media Report:
MySpace Responsible for 83 Percent Increase in Traffic to Shopping
Websites." Hitwise (November 8, 2006).
http://www.hitwise.com/press-center/hitwiseHS2004/
us-08112006cgm.php

3 Aho Williamson, Debra. "Social Network Marketing: Ad Spending
and Usage." eMarketer (December 2007).
http://www.emarketer.com/Reports/All/Emarketer_2000478.
aspx?src=report3_home

Truth 24

1 "More than Half of MySpace Visitors Are Now Age 35 or Older, As the Site's Demographic Composition Continues to Shift." comScore Media Metrix (October 5, 2006).
http://www.comscore.com/press/release.asp?press=1019

2 "2007 Trusted Brands Index." Outlaw Consulting (May 2007).
http://www.outlawconsulting.com/pdf/TrustedBrandsrls_final.doc

3 "Civic-Minded Millennials Prepared to Reward or Punish Companies Based on Commitment to Social Causes." Cone, Inc. (October 24, 2006).
http://www.coneinc.com/Pages/pr_45.html

4 Aho Williamson, Debra. "Kids and Teens Online: Virtual Worlds Open New Universe." eMarketer (September 2007)
http://www.emarketer.com/Article.aspx?id=1005405

Truth 25

1 "Perspectives On Marketing, Self-Regulation, & Childhood Obesity: A Report on a Joint Workshop of the Federal Trade Commission and the Department of Health and Human Services." FTC/HHS (April 2006).
http://www.ftc.gov/os/2006/05/index.shtm

2 "Interactive Food & Beverage Marketing: Targeting Children and Youth in the Digital Age." Center for Digital Democracy and the American University (May 2007).
http://www.digitalads.org/index.php

Truth 26

1 "Google Sites' Share of Online Video Market Expands to 31 Percent in November 2007, According to comScore Video Metrix." comScore Video Metrix (January 17, 2008).
http://www.comscore.com/press/release.asp?press=2002

Truth 27

1 "Gartner Identifies the Top 10 Strategic Technologies for 2008." Gartner (October 9, 2007).
http://www.gartner.com/it/page.jsp?id=530109

2 Predicts 2007—Big Changes Ahead in the High Performance Workplace." Gartner (December 5, 2006). http://www.gartner.com/DisplayDocument?doc_cd=144476

Truth 30

1 "Donors Increasingly Going Online Before Giving." Association of Fundraising Professionals (June 27, 2005). http://www.afpnet.org/ka/ka-3.cfm?content_item_id=21190&folder_id=2345

Truth 46

1 Aho Williamson, Debra. "Social Network Marketing: Ad Spending and Usage." eMarketer (December 2007). http://www.emarketer.com/Reports/All/Emarketer_2000478.aspx?src=report3_home

Truth 47

1 "Mobile User-Generated Content Revenues to Rise Tenfold by 2012." Juniper Research (August 13, 2007). http://www.juniperresearch.com/shop/viewpressrelease.php?pr=54

Truth 50

1 "JupiterResearch Reports Over One Fifth of the World's Population Will Be Online By 2011." JupiterResearch (July 23, 2007). http://www.jupiterresearch.com/bin/item.pl/press:press_release/2007/id=07.07.23-world-online-population.html/

Acknowledgments

Special thanks to Michelle Newcomb, Laura Norman, Karen Gill, and Lori Lyons for their feedback, suggestions, and attention to detail, all of which made this an even better book.

About the Author

Patrice-Anne Rutledge is a social media consultant, bestselling author, and Certified eMarketer (CeM). She specializes in teaching others to maximize the power of new technologies, such as social networking, blogging, podcasting, and social media, to promote their business, career, or social cause.

Patrice is the author of 25 books on technology, business, and communications for leading publishers including Pearson, Macmillan, Prentice Hall, Random House, and Ziff-Davis Press. Her most recent books include *Special Edition Using Microsoft Office PowerPoint 2007* and *The Web-Savvy Writer: Book Promotion with a High-Tech Twist*. Her books have received strong reviews and endorsements, several awards, and have been translated into 11 languages. Patrice has also contributed hundreds of articles to magazines, newspapers, and websites around the world including *Interactive, Business Strategies, Microsoft Office Solutions, Dot-Com Builder, Small Business, Career Woman, InformIT,* and *ZDNet.* In the corporate world, she has held senior communications management positions at leading technology firms including Oracle and PeopleSoft, where she led a team of 60 professional communicators around the world.

Patrice is a member of the eMarketing Association and Public Relations Society of America (PRSA). She is active on several social networks—including LinkedIn, Facebook, XING, and Ning—which she credits with further developing her own career as well as increasing sales for her many books. She can be reached through her website at www.patricerutledge.com.